NEWSPAPER CURTAINS

Now you've peeked through the curtains…
dare you read on?

NEWSPAPER
CURTAINS:

Who Really Knows
What Lies Behind?

MIKE LEAVER

The Book Guild Ltd

First published in Great Britain in 2023 by
The Book Guild Ltd
Unit E2 Airfield Business Park,
Harrison Road, Market Harborough,
Leicestershire. LE16 7UL
Tel: 0116 2792299
www.bookguild.co.uk
Email: info@bookguild.co.uk
Twitter: @bookguild

This work is entirely fictitious and bears no resemblance to any persons living or dead.

Typeset in 12pt Minion Pro

Printed and bound in the UK by TJ Books LTD, Padstow, Cornwall

ISBN 978 1915603 173

British Library Cataloguing in Publication Data.
A catalogue record for this book is available from the British Library.

To Samantha, whose epic teenage temper tantrum inspired this grown-up tale of loss, liberty, and love…

CHAPTER ONE

The night nurse stood outside the open doorway to Matron's office. Nervously, she gave a slight cough. "There's a visitor," she said, "refuses to leave."

Matron glanced at the official wall clock. Its highly polished walnut case surrounded a face with Roman numerals, giving the impression it held great authority over the affairs of men. In any event, it governed all ward procedures with military precision. "8.59," she said crossly. "You waited fifty-nine minutes to tell me?"

The nurse took a defensive step backwards. "It's difficult," she said. Then, lowering her voice to a submissive whisper, "Mrs Smith in Side Room Three… you know."

Matron found great displeasure in doing anything which resulted from an observation made by a junior nurse. Accordingly, she stood with her coat draped over her arm, as if about to go home.

Clunk-click, said the clock, as it counted precisely two seconds.

Matron, as if acting on her own initiative, then placed

the coat neatly over the back of her chair. "Tut-tut," she said to register her annoyance, as she emerged from her den to walk briskly along the corridor towards Room Three.

The night nurse knew the terrifying matron would not need any help evicting after-hours visitors, whoever they might be. So, finding herself surplus to requirements, she turned her attention to the clock in the now-abandoned office. According to legend, it had occupied the same dominant position on the wall since the hospital had been built in 1860. For the past 102 years it had faithfully counted every second that passed: some uneventful; others the moment a human life came to an end. But to the clock, both seconds were the same.

On hearing Matron's returning footsteps, the nurse looked back to the corridor.

"The patient will not survive the night," said Matron, "and her daughter refuses to leave. So you have not told me. I know nothing. Understood?"

The nurse blinked in astonishment. Previously, Matron had always given the impression that she enjoyed gladiatorial combat with a visitor. Never before had she backed away from an opportunity to enhance her battle-hardened image.

Matron ignored her stare. She recovered her coat and, knowing she had sixteen minutes to catch the bus that would take her home, hurried away. She also knew those same sixteen minutes would likely take the patient in Room Three to her death.

The side room was just able to accommodate a narrow bed, together with one hard wooden chair which could be wiped with disinfectant in accordance with hospital procedures. Given the limited space, and the need for a sterile environment, personal trinkets were not allowed.

Mrs Smith lay on her back, unaware of anything that might be happening in the world of the living. Janet, her daughter, just turned twelve, was remembering her mother's words, spoken three days before.

"Promise me," she had whispered, "that you will take your O levels… somehow." Then the cancer had taken control of her throat, causing a desperate gasp for breath, and her mother had not spoken since.

The feeding tube in Mrs Smith's nose had provided just a further three days of fragile life. But this, and other medical equipment, made the room very cluttered, so Janet put the chair in the corridor and returned to sit on the bed. She clenched her mother's right hand. It felt cold and appeared to be lacking a pulse. Gently, she trailed the fingers of her other hand a little way above her mother's wrist, the bones clearly visible beneath the stretched skin.

"Yes, Mother," she said, "I promise to take my O levels." And then, instinctively, she knew her mother was gone. She looked towards the ceiling. "Yes, Mother," she repeated, "I promise to take my O levels… somehow."

Even as she said it, Janet knew the word 'somehow' had been added as a dark cloak to hide the word 'impossible'. *Like the Devil*, she thought. *He wraps himself in a dark cloak of deceit as he sneaks around the world, to hide beneath the beds of naughty girls, so as to carry them away, the moment they fall asleep.* Okay, that was how a teacher at her infant school had described it. But things like that stick in the mind. Indeed, at the age of five, Janet had believed the

Devil lived in the cloakroom down the school corridor; a place she refused to go. To begin with, her father had aided her in this by spending all the family money down the pub so, as a little girl, she never owned a coat. Then, one very icy winter's morning, a teacher had seen her hurrying to school wrapped in a blanket. The following day the teacher had presented her with a coat, into which she was 'expected to grow'. That is to say, it had once belonged to a girl who had left for big school. Anyway, it was so ragged that her father would never be able to take it to the pawnbroker's. And so it was that, at the age of seven, Janet was forced to face her fears in the dark cloakroom.

Five years later, sitting on her mother's deathbed, she thought about the last word her mother had whispered: 'somehow'. Had it been carefully chosen to hide the truth of what she was leaving behind: a desperate and hopeless situation? Then Janet thought about her mother – who was now watching over her from above, filling the room with light, driving away the Devil – and, in that moment, she realised the battle between good and evil made the promise to complete her O levels unchangeable and yet impossible to keep.

Later, at home, Janet gave further consideration to the word 'impossible'. It was, she decided, most often used by grown-ups to describe things they did not wish to believe. Once she had even heard a woman use it regarding a lot of lumps that had 'magically' appeared in a saucepan of custard. Other times it might apply to a gas meter cutting off the supply a mere two hours after it had been fed a shilling. *Grown-ups*, she thought, *have such an unusual view of the world*

4

– half the time they talk complete nonsense. This caused her to think about Miss Kent, the headmistress of her old junior school. Now that woman really was 'impossible'. Yet she existed! During the dinner break, you could often see her flapping about the school playground, waving her arms as she pretended to be a butterfly. This, apparently, really upset the Devil, who preferred the company of slithering serpents. Because Miss Kent was short-sighted, children frequently had to leap out of her way to avoid getting a slap around the face.

And so it was that Janet realised the word 'impossible' was merely a sliding scale of highly unlikely events. This made her feel much better about things. Never again would she think about the awful word which, she realised, led to despair.

So, she reasoned, her current challenge came down to the simple fact that all the other children hated her for being a 'smarty-pants'. This meant they liked making her life a misery. And it was not even her fault! Her misfortune mostly originated from an idea conceived by Miss Kent, who had entered her for the eleven-plus examination a year early. Janet had tried to explain that she was only ten and three-quarters, but the dotty woman had refused to listen. Eventually, Janet had become more forceful and told Miss Kent that numbers, even fractions, had to remain in their correct order. It was like leaving the house at just gone eleven and arriving back home fifteen minutes earlier – it could not be done. And what did the batty woman do? Only go and make an announcement during the following morning's assembly that: "All children should do their sums nicely, like Janet Smith, aged ten and three-quarters."

After two months of relentless bullying, Janet left the eleven-plus examination hall to be confronted by Miss Kent.

"So clever," she wailed, "I bet you answered all the questions correctly."

Not wishing to cause any distress, Janet told her the exam had been easy.

"Oh," Miss Kent had squeaked eagerly, "you are going to a most wonderful place called a grammar school, near the countryside. You will see trees, turtle doves, and all the children are so well behaved…"

In the real world, what actually happened after the summer holiday was that Janet found herself deported to a place she had never been, nor had any particular wish to go. It was so far from her 'own country' that she was given a weekly allowance of foreign-looking plastic bus tokens to get there. Because she was short – four feet while standing on tiptoe – the girls at her new school also hated her, asking occasionally if she was looking forward to her ninth birthday. Soon their teasing focused on her coat, which still trailed along the floor; then the fact that she came from inner-city slums. And not just ordinary slums, but the pre-Victorian dwellings originally built to provide the first batch of migrating country peasants with basic shelter. They had allowed their first tenants to work in the factories of the early Industrial Revolution. Now, for one reason or another, they housed those who preferred to pay an unusually low rent of ten shillings and sixpence a week.

Janet considered the houses fronting the street to be similar to the fortified castle walls of olden days. They were built on a ridge of slightly higher ground, making them appear taller. The consequence of this was that their doorsteps could be scrubbed, allowing their residents to announce to all that they possessed a level of cleanliness which lifted them closer to God. While at infant school, Janet had written a story about this. It included the words 'The doorstep made the house taller, so it was easier for God to look through the bedroom windows to make certain all the children were saying their prayers nicely.' The English teacher had given her a gold star, and then Miss Kent had spoiled everything by reading out the story during the next morning's assembly. So, even before the other children had hated her for doing her sums nicely, she had been known as a goodie-goodie who they needed to hit at regular intervals.

While the houses fronting the street had a continuous upper storey, the lower level was occasionally cut through by tunnels which gave access to the yards behind. (These pedestrian walkways were more correctly called entries, but, as they were both narrow and gloomy, Janet always thought of them as tunnels.) Down these dark tunnels, a great, sprawling mass of humanity existed, generally on lower land, the earth having been excavated to make the street houses taller. "Down in the dumps," Janet called it. In any event, the area was sufficiently sunken to keep her yard hidden from the rest of the world.

Given all this, the five-year-old Janet had realised the only biblical figure likely to visit her home was the Devil. He liked bedroom windows to be close to the ground so he could use his pointed tail to *tap-tap* on the glass. The thought had made her hide beneath her blankets, pretending to be a pillow. This was quite sensible because, whenever the Devil came to visit, the wind blew through gaps in the ill-fitting window frame, filling her room with swirling cold air.

Associated with her childhood ideas about the Devil was a belief that the tunnel connecting her yard to the street was where the bogeyman lived. He was a dark figure who might leap out to get her at any moment. However, by the age of ten, she had managed to make some sense of the dark forces which surrounded her. If she met a gloomy figure lurking in the tunnel, she knew it must be a drunk or a vagabond seeking shelter. Thankfully, her mother's warning about the bogeyman had given her the basic instinct to avoid danger. She could run fast, dodge quickly, or wait until a grown-up she trusted could escort her from the street to the safety of her house.

The houses fronting the street had a rent of nineteen shillings a week, so were unsuited to families headed by a father who only worshipped the God of Alcohol. Janet knew her mother worked really hard, but her pay was half that of a man doing the same job, so their rent also needed to be approximately half.

At the centre of Janet's yard was a communal toilet shed. Once it had been covered by a slate roof, but now many sections had nothing but rotting timber rafters, to which a few surviving slates managed to cling, often at odd angles. Throughout the summer, the building gave the yard a characteristic smell to which the residents had become accustomed. But on cold winter nights, all water became ice, so the sewage remained frozen in the toilet bowls. Hence, the residents tended to use a bucket in their own living room, which was at least heated by a coal fire. However, if they were 'posh', or simply insane, they took their bucket to a bedroom, where they could gaze at ice-clad walls while they did their business in private. But wherever they went, the end result was the same: the bucket had to be taken to the toilet shed to be emptied, the contents frequently overflowing onto the brick floor and oozing slowly into the ground beneath.

According to folklore, the yard where Janet lived had once been inhabited by the local muck-men. It had been their job to shovel the sewage from all the toilet sheds into wheelbarrows and, from there, take it through the tunnels to horse-drawn carts parked in the street. From here, it was taken to the countryside, where the cargo became high-value fertiliser. Apparently, the men leading the slowly plodding horses were so smelly they were only allowed to stop at one particular place on the route: a pub that no one else dared enter. How true this was, Janet had no idea, but it was generally understood the muck-men had formed their own communities, isolated from the rest of society. In any event, Janet's yard was now universally known as 'Stink Alley' – the formal name of Wellington Place, cut into the capping stone of the entrance tunnel, being ignored.

Not that her accommodation worried Janet, because she had never lived anywhere else. Indeed, before passing the exam to get into grammar school, she had not been aware that modern council estates existed. No, her problem was her father. As far back as she could remember, he had been addicted to alcohol, making family life a struggle from one week to the next. After learning of her mother's cancer, his drunkenness had become continuous. He had never visited the hospital to see his wife. Even aged twelve,

Janet had worked out that he could not face the truth that her mother had been the breadwinner of the household, so now the cupboard would remain bare. Then one day, Janet had returned from the hospital to find all of the furniture gone. From the living room she walked into the kitchen to discover it had become an empty space: a single tiny window sending its meagre light to the bare, whitewashed walls. Even the ancient sink, large enough to bath a child, had vanished. And because water was collected from a standpipe in the yard, there was no tap to indicate a sink had ever existed. Next she looked to where the gas stove had been. It crossed her mind that its loss meant cooking would now go back to how it was when the house was first built: the residents using the fire in the living room.

Eventually, she turned and opened the door to the coal-hole beneath the stairs. Empty – even the shovel had gone. Instinctively, she knew that her father was never coming back. Good!

More unfortunate was something her mother had said after being transferred to the hospital, a month or so before the end. "I have saved some money. It's to get whatever you need to take your O levels, because I know you are going to get a Grade A in everything. It's in a bag, taped under my sideboard smalls drawer. It's the only place I could think of where your father would never find it… for his drink."

By the time her mother told her this, all the furniture had vanished, but Janet did not let on about that. On returning home she asked around the yard, until she found someone who remembered that it was the rag-and-bone man who had done the house clearance. Well, that explained the missing blanket which had previously covered the window as a makeshift curtain. As a rag it was probably worth a penny. Bones were worth more, because they were used to make glue. In any event, this was how the rag-and-bone man had first made his money, which he had since invested in a yard, allowing him to begin a sideline in furniture and, it seemed, coal.

Janet realised she needed to demonstrate that she was now a proper grown-up who did not mess about with crooks and lowlifes. After walking a mile to the scrapyard, she looked between the gates into an area where a timber frame supported a canvas awning. Here, the sideboard was on sale for four pounds. She then went to a garden shed in which a man was slouched in an old armchair. Hearing her footsteps, he looked up, then hurriedly sat on the magazine he had been reading. Janet told him she wanted to buy the sideboard, whereupon the price went up to five pounds, to include delivery.

"I don't want it delivered," she said. "Shake on the deal."

"How can a kid not have it delivered?" the man questioned. "I hardly think you can carry it on your back like a horse."

Why he thought this funny, she had no idea. In response to his rough laughter, she looked at him long and hard. Her survival required her to no longer be a kid.

"Shake on it," she said.

The man took her hand and held it for rather a long time, while talking about giving her a discount for… But she paid no attention and pulled her hand free before he could explain further. Then she went to the sideboard, removed the drawer, and looked underneath. The bag was there. With lightning speed – the sort only a child can manage when stealing a sweet – she grabbed it. Then, remembering her mother telling her how important it was to always be honest, she reached inside to recover four pound notes, which she gave to him.

"Keep the stupid sideboard," she said. Then, before the crook knew what was happening, she ran. Grown-ups, she realised, were quite easy to outwit – if they believed they were only talking to a stupid kid.

After leaving the yard, she hurried to an undertaker's. Again she used her childhood vulnerability to get a deal which she genuinely believed to be below the list price for their most basic cremation service. If the rag-and-bone man wanted the money back now, tough! All that remained in the envelope was ten pounds and, because it meant the difference between eating and not eating, there was no way he was going to get it.

Walking home from the undertaker's, she passed a Second World War bomb site, whose scattered debris included many useful things which could be scavenged. From the rubble she selected an armful of bricks which, strangely, kept getting heavier as she walked the final quarter-mile to her house. She made two further journeys to the bomb site, on these occasions returning with just five bricks per visit. However, there were enough of them to build a little seat in her living room. For a table she used an old, upturned tea chest. This done, she said, "Just so." She liked using grown-up phrases, and Kipling's *Just So Stories* suited her very well indeed.

After her mother died, the undertakers sorted everything out. She did not follow the coffin into the crematorium, where she would no doubt hear a vicar, or somebody like that, going "Blah, blah, blah." That would make no difference to anything. Anyway, with the discount she had obtained, it would probably be just one 'blah'. Instead, she stood outside the building to gaze up at the chimney on top of the dome. When a puff of smoke came out, she watched it float away on the breeze.

"Yes, mother," she said, "I will get my O levels… five A grades. Okay, six, you say? Done."

After returning home from the crematorium, Janet sat on her neatly stacked pile of bricks and tipped the contents of her cash bag onto the tea-chest table. She now had four pounds, plus a few coins. The rent was ten shillings and sixpence a week, and was due to be paid. As far as the outside world was concerned, her father was still living here. If social services got to hear otherwise, she would be sent to an orphanage or, as she preferred to think about it, be kidnapped with evil intent. Avoiding this disaster was another implied promise she had made to her mother. To get her O levels, she had to stay at the grammar school and keep her home life private. That afternoon she collected some old newspapers from a nearby bin and, with a little flour paste, made a new set of window curtains to keep out prying eyes.

She knew her plans would pose a challenge. In her area, children generally drifted away from school to start work around the age of fourteen. However, given her promise to her mother, this was not an option for her. She had to reach the higher school-leaving age of fifteen – and even this would only be possible because she had entered grammar school a little early.

Two days after the funeral, Janet returned home from school and made herself a marmalade sandwich – marmalade being cheaper than jam. However, her money was still set to run out after two more rent payments. Everything in her life seemed to be heading towards a dreadful end. Then she heard a knock on the door. Fearing 'the social', she peeped between the partly glued sheets of newspaper which covered the kitchen window. Why was the rag-and-bone man here? After a second knock, he walked into the house. Locking doors was something grown-ups did. Janet registered her mistake, then went to the gloomy living room to confront the towering figure. There was just sufficient light sneaking through the papered windows for her to detect his smile.

"I was thinking about things," he said, "and your visit worried me."

"I spent the money on my mother's funeral."

He nodded. Then, without being invited, stepped across to the tea chest, on which he placed a large bar of chocolate. "Thought you might be hungry," he said. "Even though you did con me."

I am a grown-up, thought Janet. *Don't mess with me.* "You bought the sideboard," she said sharply, "not what had been left inside it. But thank you – had my father known the money was there, it would have gone on drink by now."

The man did not seem surprised. "I got the impression your old man was selling up to go," he said, "because he even sold me the coal. And I see your hearth is cold. The candle on the mantel shelf tells me the electric has already been cut off." He reached over to try the light switch.

Nothing happened. He then took a box of matches from his pocket and walked over to light the candle.

"No," she cried, "it's the only one I have."

He ignored her and, in the flickering light, she saw him place the box of matches beside the candle. "A box of matches is threepence," he said. "A fair swap. And I can't be doing things in the dark."

Janet could not argue with this, if only because the local shop refused to sell matches to anyone who looked under the age of thirteen. However, she still felt very cross with the man, because the candle had only about an hour of burn time left.

"So," he continued, "I thought you might like the chocolate."

Why he might be buying her chocolate, she had no idea. "Thank you," she said. "I'm sorry about the drawer."

"I sold the sideboard for five pounds the following day," he said casually. "So I thought you might also like this."

Janet looked incredulously at a pound note which he placed beside the chocolate. Chips were nine pennies a bag, so that was twenty-six hot meals. "Thank you," she said, submissively. Anyone who wanted to feed her was surely a friend. Perhaps he wanted her to work in his yard – on Saturdays, maybe. Then she could buy some more candles.

"That's twice you've said thank you," he said. "Perhaps a hug to show how much you really mean it?"

"Or I could say thank you for a third time, would that do?"

"Depends how you say it," he said.

"*Dane schuss*," she said playfully. "I am doing German at school; I'm going to take it at O level."

"So you are... er...?"

15

"Grammar school, yes."

"Oh, hoity-toity."

"With bells and whistles. I reckon I will be doing my O levels when I'm fifteen."

The man frowned; then he smiled. "You look older," he said. "I can see now that you have breasts; in fact, I reckon you are sixteen already."

Janet shook her head. She did not like talking about breasts, because hers had not really developed. The older girls in her class often teased her about this. But, truthfully, the main difference was they had started wearing bras at the earliest opportunity, while her father would never have thought about such details. A bra likely cost as much as a night down the pub.

"Show me," said the man.

Instinct made her retreat.

At the same time the man went to stand by the door, which he bolted. "Show me," he repeated.

As he towered above her, she saw the candlelight flickering yellow in his eyes. His smell entered her nostrils, as if to say, *I am the Devil, awakened from my pit of sulphur. Your life now belongs to me.*

Within five minutes the conversation turned into an argument in which the man let another pound note fall to the floor, claiming that she drove a hard bargain. Then, suddenly, his mood changed. Hard now, and lacking any trace of kindness. "I know your father's done a runner," he said, "and your mother's snuffed it. No brothers or sisters, so you are here on your own. Bet you haven't told the council, because if you had, the social would have come to take you away by now."

"He will be back, my father," she said, "and he gets very violent from the drink."

The man shook his head calmly. "You're a lying bitch," he said, "but your secret's safe with me. And with two pounds, my little visits might keep a roof over your head. Now, are you going to show me your tits, or do I go from here to telephone the council? Your choice!"

Even though Janet did not understand what was about to happen, she knew the Devil now controlled her life – at least if she wanted to take her O levels, as she had promised her mother.

And in a distant hospital, a clock with a highly polished walnut case carefully counted down each second until the blood of a stolen childhood soaked into the flattened sheets of cardboard that Janet used as a bed. Then, a short while after the Devil had left, the candle went out, and she rolled over to face the wall, like a wounded animal who knew the surrounding darkness represented the cloak of death.

CHAPTER TWO

Janet soon learned how the world of grown-ups was supposed to work. It meant she had to do unpleasant things – but for children, this had always been the case. In one history lesson the teacher had told the class about the coal-mining communities of the early 1800s. Apparently, in those days children started work at the age of eight, to do fifteen-hour shifts below ground. Most were employed to push trucks through tunnels that were too low to take a pit pony. By these standards, Janet considered herself to be slightly privileged.

Then, as the winter of 1965 approached, fifteen-year-old Janet began to see her examinations as something real; a light at the end of her own personal 'tunnel' which she would reach in a few months' time.

"There," she would say to the spirit of her mother, "nothing is impossible."

The most important thing about understanding the grown-up world, she now realised, was the phrase 'supposed to work'. In truth, it was necessary to remember that half the time they got it wrong, which meant knowing how to correct their mistakes. Her motto was to be sensible at all times. This philosophy was helped by the fact that all the other children avoided her, leading her to spend dinner times in the school library. Here she would root out the most difficult books she could find. The clue, she discovered, was to go for the ones in pristine condition, indicating they had never been read. This led her to the uncertainty principle of quantum mechanics, which she particularly liked because it implied impossibility did not exist. Slowly her confidence grew until she felt able to ask questions about it in physics class. The teacher responded by saying it was beyond the scope of the syllabus. His thinly disguised panic attack reminded Janet of the biology teacher who, during her time in the second form, had also been confronted by a difficult question and had answered in the same way. When 'rude biology' had finally arrived in the fifth form, the perspiring teacher had done a lot of mumbling while pointing to indistinct line drawings clipped to the blackboard. But why the physics teacher should be embarrassed by quantum mechanics, she had no idea. Well, she would soon put a stop to such silliness.

"I accept Planck's constant is a very small number," she said firmly during one lesson, "but that is not the same as saying it is zero. So surely it is fundamental to this theorem that impossibility cannot exist within a universe governed by the coefficient of proportionality?"

It was only when the teacher told her to "Shut up and behave" that she realised it would be necessary to approach this subject by private study. But on her next visit to the library, she discovered the advanced physics book had mysteriously disappeared. Grown-ups clearly believed there were certain things children should not know. But she had written down the various formulae, so was able to work out that quantum physics could even explain how lumps might appear magically in custard, without warning or explanation.

Anyway, given all her sensibilities, Janet came to be sitting at her usual desk in the back corner of the classroom; effectively a grown-up in the world of children. Meanwhile, the English teacher, Mr Edwards, being an actual grown-up, had got it wrong again, his understanding of time being somewhat approximate. Or maybe he was just a little deaf, so had failed to hear the school bell telling pupils the dinner break was over. The absence of Mr Edwards created a power vacuum which, governed by the laws of youthful female rebellion, needed to be filled. It seemed to Janet that all the dominant girls spontaneously coalesced to form a single military unit, which advanced on the other back corner of the room. Their target was a boy who had no time to escape, even if that had been his wish.

The victim, known colloquially as 'Freaky Fred', possessed the sort of weirdness that fascinated girls. They seemed unable to believe such a strange boy could exist, so, to check he was not a hallucination, they frequently poked him in the ribs. But he was real; a fact proved beyond doubt when, back in first form, the girl sitting behind him had attacked his bottom with a knitting needle. Fred had leapt up, then turned around to squirt all the ink from his fountain pen at his attacker. But she had ducked, so he had merely sprayed the wall behind. Because the knitting-needle part of the incident had taken place beneath the desk, the teacher had only witnessed Fred's response. Consequently, he was given a detention which involved cleaning the wall and then writing five hundred lines stating, 'I must not be horrible to girls, because they are really nice.'

So, by the age of eleven, the boy had obtained the honorary title of 'Freaky'. By the second form, the girls' increasing academic ability meant they understood that 'Freaky' lacked poetic resonance with his true Christian name of Michael, and also that the laws of poetic licence allowed them to correct this inconvenient detail. By the third form, whatever he had once been called had been lost in the mists of time. A more serious consequence of the knitting-needle incident was that Fred had come to insist upon always sitting in the back corner, where his bottom would be safe from attack. However, this was a terrible military tactic because it meant he could never retreat, making it far easier for the girls to trap him.

Clearly, Freaky Fred's name prevented any girl from becoming his friend. But Janet noticed a girl named Leonie often chose to occupy the desk in front of his. And sometimes, very, very secretly, she glanced behind to observe him. Janet thought that, had it not been for Fred's freaky image, Leonie might even have admitted to liking him, regardless of the ridicule it would bring. At least, that had been a possibility until Fred had brought in his collection of matchbox labels to show them. That was like stamp collecting, only a hundred times worse. Oh, and the eyebrow pencil he now used on the 'bumfluff' beneath his nose. Fifteen-year-old boys should proclaim their maturity by moaning about how often they had to shave, not by engineering a pretend moustache. It did not look right, given that he still wore short trousers and obviously took his socks from their storage space at random. Today his left sock was green wool, while the other one, in red, looked a bit like those worn by footballers.

Janet realised the rules that had produced the name 'Freaky Fred' also applied to herself. Those who merely disliked her called her 'Scraggy', while those who hated her added a second, more derogatory name. Anyway, the end result was the same: no girl could admit to being her friend, so she sat alone in the opposite corner to Fred.

Presently, Janet cast her mind back to the time Fred had been called up on stage during morning assembly. Here, the headmaster had proclaimed him to be a weird child, whose sloppy dress and odd socks brought the school's otherwise good name into disrepute. Fred had responded by sticking a finger in his ear and twisting it, as if to have a good think. He had then replied that the school's uniform policy said nothing about socks, which made the audience of children laugh. Predictably, the headmaster had then taken the cane to the back of Fred's legs, which Janet had considered legally dubious because the boy was technically correct about the socks. His other characteristic of being weird was not actually illegal either.

Now she turned to Fred's current difficulties. The girls had formed a circle of chairs, both to rest their legs and to construct a physical barrier over which he could not easily escape. The encircling army of terror were talking about virginity – or, more precisely, the process of losing it. A truly terrifying girl named Priscilla was accusing Carol of being sixteen. Carol was arguing back by saying the same about Priscilla. Fred interrupted, remarking that he was fifteen.

"Oh, it doesn't matter for you," said Carol sharply.

Fred looked about his audience for clues. In response the girls looked at him with blank faces. He hated not knowing what they were talking about.

"He doesn't know," said Priscilla.

"Yes I do," he protested.

"Of course he knows you can't do it until you are sixteen," said Leonie.

Janet could not decide if this statement was brave or stupid. The key to success was to remain part of the in-crowd and not draw attention to yourself – in Leonie's case, by coming to Fred's rescue. As if to demonstrate this, the other girls looked at her as if she had let out some vital secret.

"I was only saying," muttered Leonie, pulling her jumper halfway up her face to peep over the top.

But the others would not let her escape that easily.

"Admit it," said Carol, "you've told us all you really fancy him."

"I do not!" exclaimed Leonie.

"And you are over sixteen," said Priscilla.

"I am most definitely not," said Leonie. She removed the jumper from her face. "And besides," she added, "it's you who fancies him."

There followed an argument about who fancied Fred the most. For his part, Fred thought about all the ways the girls tried to attract his attention – one had even speared his bottom with a knitting needle. Had she really been saying, *I fancy you*? And now the truth was out! Having no particular wish to have a jumper knitted, he decided he liked Priscilla the best.

"Right," interrupted Sharon, "to settle it, I think we should play True Dare, Double Dare, Kiss or Promise."

This made Janet feel sorry for Fred because no boy could ever understand the rules of that game. In fact, given her grown-up sensibilities, she had no understanding of the rules either. She could only suppose it was a bit like the Masons secret society: you had to be formally initiated to understand its rituals.

Across the classroom, Sharon gave the audience a few seconds to adjust to the increase in hostilities. "Fred," she said, "I dare you to put your hand on Carol's knee."

Carol glared at Fred, and then at Sharon. "He didn't say dare," she said.

"But he was trying to look at your legs," responded Sharon.

"What's that got to do with anything?" said Carol.

Fred looked between the two girls, trying to work out which of them he feared the most.

Suddenly Carol grabbed his wrist and brushed the backs of his fingers across her knee.

"There," she said, "he's done it. Now, Fred, I dare you to put your hand up Sharon's shirt. She's wearing one of those bras to make her tits look bigger, so don't be too disappointed when you grab a load of tissue-paper packing."

"No," said Sharon. "The rule is, we go around in a circle."

Fred felt a bead of perspiration drip from his chin. Then he realised Carol was trying to work out what to do next. He hoped it would be feeling her knee again, because it had made his fingers go all tingly.

"Just us two playing?" asked Carol eventually. "Unless Priscilla wants to join?"

"I can see this ending up with Fred losing his virginity," said Priscilla. "But okay. Fred, I also dare you to put your hand up Sharon's shirt. That'll teach the stupid cow to pretend she's got tits as big as mine."

Sharon gasped in horror. And now the normal boys in the class had all turned to spectate, probably trying to assess the girls' relative breast sizes.

"You're the lying cow," said Sharon to Priscilla – and to anyone else who cared to understand the injustice of the statement.

Fred put up his hand, then waved it about to indicate his excitement. "Cows can't tell lies," he said. "All they can say is moo – which is why, when they are eating grass, they are called lawn moo-ers."

For a moment, the girls united in groans and lowering their faces into their hands. Then Priscilla looked up with a confident smile.

"You're backing out," she said, "because to continue he has to do the dare on Carol… or is it Sharon? I've kind of lost the plot. Tell you what, Fred: do it to them both, then you can tell me who uses the most tissue paper. I win!"

Priscilla knew she always won at everything. It gave her a particular satisfaction to realise Sharon was trying to control her rage by breathing in and out through her nose. Suddenly, Sharon reached out, grabbed Fred's hand and pushed it up her shirt. Fred reacted as if he had received an electric shock. Janet thought this implied Priscilla was indeed telling lies about the size of Sharon's breasts. Certainly the look on Fred's face suggested there was no tissue paper involved.

In the round that followed, Carol sat on Fred's lap,

Sharon agreed to go out with him, and Fred had absolutely no idea of what was going on.

"Right," Carol screamed, "Fred, I want you to take Priscilla into the stock cupboard and give her the biggest snogging she's ever had."

"That's got to be a double dare," said Priscilla.

"He said double dare," said Carol.

"He didn't say anything," said Priscilla.

"Yes he did, inside his head. Now go on, Fred – you know how to snog, don't you?"

Of all the girls he fancied, Fred had now returned to liking Priscilla the best. For the first time in his life, this made him the same as every other boy in the school. But he had never kissed a girl, so his eyes merely registered terror. Seeing this, Priscilla realised no harm could come from grabbing his hair and dragging him into the stock cupboard at the back of the room. After the door had banged shut, both Sharon and Carol understood this increase in hostility was beyond them. Priscilla had won again, as she did with everything – cow!

Suddenly a scream came from the stock cupboard. Carol rushed across and dropped to her knees to look through the keyhole. "Oh my God," she announced, "he's got his hand up her shirt."

At that moment, Janet realised that Mr Edwards had stepped into the room. She quickly performed a risk assessment of the situation. Her main concern was Mr Edwards' relative youth. She suspected this was his first year as a proper teacher, so while he might understand basic classroom politics, she doubted if his apprenticeship had covered situations like this. In fact, the panic on his face suggested his natural instinct was to take flight. However, perhaps foolishly, he raced down the centre aisle to pull Carol back from the keyhole, then swung open the cupboard door.

"He tried to rape me," wailed Priscilla.

Janet knew the cupboard was so small, either Fred or Priscilla would have been forced against the door, so the only thing Carol could have seen through the keyhole was a bottom. What Fred might have done was therefore a mystery, though Janet expected it would have occurred through a mixture of confusion, panic, and uncontrolled hormones. But that was not important: the sole purpose of Carol's announcement about Fred feeling Priscilla's breasts was her need for revenge. For weeks to come, the main gossip of the fifth form would be that Priscilla had let Freaky Fred feel her tits. But Priscilla knew how to manipulate people, particularly grown-ups. This was a case for playing the victim. Janet doubted their teacher would understand this.

Mr Edwards stepped back from Priscilla, who was now screaming hysterically that Freaky Fred needed to die. Her arms waved about so frantically that she appeared to be conducting a dramatic Beethoven symphony at fifty times its proper speed. To any rational observer, she was obviously going to combust at any moment. In addition, she was jumping around like a kangaroo with a firework up its bottom, so there was no telling where she might land next. Janet, remembering this was supposed to be an English class, thought of the phrase, *Exit Mr Edwards, pursued by a screaming kangaroo*. But he seemed paralysed with fear, so adopted a survival strategy of pretending to be a statue.

"He tried to rape me," screamed Priscilla. "The headmaster needs to be told." Then, as if by magic, she fainted, sprawling across the floor.

For Mr Edwards, escape would now mean stepping over her apparently lifeless body. The headmaster would certainly expel Fred, if only because Priscilla's father was a high-profile businessman of considerable wealth. Often he brought her to the school entrance in his Jaguar; otherwise she arrived in the housekeeper's car or a taxi. Arguing with Priscilla's father would have far-reaching consequences. Anyway, in this situation, Mr Edwards knew there was only one course of action he could take. A girl had alleged rape, so he would have to take Fred to the headmaster. Then his thoughts were distracted by a quiet, calm voice coming from the corner of the room.

"It was just a children's game," it said.

Mr Edwards quickly attributed the voice to Janet. Then, miraculously, Priscilla leapt up, apparently completely cured of whatever had caused her to faint, and stomped over to Janet.

"I am not a child," she screamed.

Janet did not flinch. "Yes, you are," she said, "and you were playing a child's game that got out of hand... maybe."

"You tramp," yelled Priscilla. "You're just the Scraggy Prostitute who does it behind the picture house with any boy who asks. Scum."

Janet looked at Mr Edwards. "It was Priscilla who dragged Fred into the cupboard," she said, "though perhaps events leading up to his kidnap got him a little confused as to what was happening."

"He was feeling my private parts," protested Priscilla.

"So you want everyone to know Freaky Fred has been inside your knickers?" asked Janet.

Priscilla rushed towards the door, but Janet leapt over her desk and was there first to block the way.

"If you go to the head," she said, "I'll tell him about what you did in the woods with those bikers on the field course last year. You know, the time you lost your knickers in the undergrowth. Don't reckon your father's going to be very impressed by that."

Priscilla stared at the scraggy girl blocking her way. Her hollow cheeks could have belonged to a child on a poster for a famine relief charity. Even worse, her face was without a trace of colour – not even lipstick to accentuate her exceptionally thin lips. How could any boy find that attractive? But more horrible was her stunted growth. She needed a pair of four-inch heels to stop her looking like a twelve-year-old. Even worse than her height was the way her thin body was squashed into a school uniform from maybe two years ago. You could not even make out the shape of her breasts – if she had any. Indeed, her whole image was seemingly designed to make her look like an annoying little child. As for her mousy hair, that was just a frazzle, possibly cut using a pair of garden shears.

Priscilla knew herself to be so unlike the scraggy girl. For one thing, her own school uniform was replaced every six months. This was essential to display the shape of her perfect breasts, modified by a well-designed bra to project far above her flat tummy. Her waist-length hair was blonde and made silky smooth by frequent visits to the best hairdresser in the city. As for her height, she remembered how her clever daddy had got her a special exemption from wearing flat, regulation school shoes due to the unusual arrangement of the bones in her feet, which made it a medical matter. The subsequent deal was quite sensible: Daddy had made a donation of a hundred pounds to the school's gym equipment fund, and she was allowed to wear two-inch heels. And now this scraggy-monkey prostitute was getting in her way, almost as if the creature believed she was the same species as herself. How dare she!

Mr Edwards watched helplessly as Janet slowly took control of the situation. Priscilla was again jumping up and down in such a tantrum that her legs appeared to be imitating the pistons beneath a steam train: whizzing around so fast no human eye could follow their frantic movement. However, it was reasonable to conclude the locomotive was hopelessly unstable and likely to come off the rails at any moment. Instinctively, Mr Edwards retreated to the safe side of his desk, hands over his ears to reduce the pain of all the shrieking. From here he looked at Janet, marvelling at her bravery.

Janet watched Priscilla with detached interest. Compared to seeing her mother die, or the things she had to do with dirty old men to keep her O level pledge, it was all rather trivial. If this was how children played games, she was glad to have become a grown-up before reaching her teenage years.

Mr Edwards realised Janet was arguing Fred's case so effectively that getting him expelled now seemed the wrong thing to do. But how could he not report this situation to the headmaster? Then he looked around the classroom to discover the mood among the pupils was changing in favour of Fred. Priscilla, meanwhile, fell to the floor in another faint.

"She's only pretending," said Janet, "in the hope you get the nurse."

"I am not," shouted Priscilla.

"Bet you are really," responded Janet.

Priscilla realised the class were laughing – at her! How dare they?! They all needed to die! But, after taking a moment to calm down, she began to consider how her daddy might react to this situation – or the time she had returned from the field course, minus three pairs of knickers. She stood up, then looked aggressively at Janet.

"You fancy Freaky Fred," she said. "You're a stinking prostitute, so why not just shag him and save anyone else the bother? I believe half a crown is what you charge."

"Thanks for the free advert," said Janet calmly.

Again, the class laughed. Priscilla had been on this planet for fifteen years, and this was the first time she had been humiliated. Fred too had been on the planet for fifteen years and now, for the first time, knew himself to be helplessly in love… with Janet. Mr Edwards realised he could make no useful contribution to this debate, so sat down in the hope of becoming less prominent. Janet, the girl without friends, had rescued the situation. Priscilla stomped out of the room.

"Remember the missing knickers," Janet called after her. "And I know all the shops your father owns. I am quite able to do a leaflet campaign."

But Priscilla knew she had a far greater problem than the Scraggy Prostitute or Freaky Fred. She had a hopeless crush on Mr Edwards, who she reckoned was very sexy. How could she ever face him again?

It was only when Mr Richard Edwards got home that evening that he felt able to put the afternoon's events into some sort of order – no, 'order' was the wrong word. A better description would be rearranging the chaos. But as he sipped his coffee, he knew he had been right.

On reflection, he realised that yet again he had used a wrong word, at least when applied to himself. It was Janet who had been right. The situation had been resolved without his intervention. He now felt certain Priscilla would not tell her father, or the headmaster, about what had happened. Her revenge would be something she organised herself. But Fred would not be expelled, and that was the important thing.

Richard's next worry was Janet. When Priscilla had accused her of doing bad things behind the picture house, she had made no attempt to defend herself. But surely gentle Janet, who sat in the corner of the classroom, could not be... He disliked using the word Priscilla had said, at least regarding his pupils. Then he relaxed further. Priscilla was just a silly girl from a privileged upbringing. She was famous for this, while Janet was equally famous for coming from the slums. Obviously they were destined to hate each other... except that Janet appeared to tolerate Priscilla well enough. Girls, he decided, were impossible to understand.

By the following morning, his problems had become a dilemma. He really needed to speak to Janet about what had happened the previous day. But how and where? Could he ask her to stay back after lessons for a proper talk about what he now assumed to be a common albeit false rumour? That really ought to be done by a lady teacher, who would be above suspicion when dealing with such personal matters.

Had he been older he might have got away with it, but at twenty-two, the head would be looking out for any display of weakness concerning the more mature female pupils.

During the lunch break, Richard wandered casually into the secretary's office. He wanted to ask if there was anything he needed to know about Janet Smith – obviously not regarding Priscilla's fantasy, but about the death of her mother, or why her father never came to parents' night. Finding the office empty, he did something extremely reckless. He opened a filing cabinet and quickly found the folder for Janet. 'Address: 1 Wellington Place.' That sounded rather posh; further proof that Priscilla and, to a lesser extent, her friends were accomplished liars. He hurried from the office feeling somewhat better about the situation. Okay, Janet probably lived in a house that did not have a very big garden, and perhaps the bathroom did not have a proper shower cubicle. Then his gloomy thoughts returned. Sometimes, when Janet got close, her smell made him wonder why she did not always take a shower in the morning. Perhaps the shower and the lavatory were in the same room, and her father took a long time to do his morning ablutions. Though the housing situation was probably a false fear. His own house had a conventional bathroom upstairs, a separate lavatory downstairs, and his bedroom was en suite. He could not believe houses with only one bathroom still existed.

As the afternoon lesson progressed, he realised that he had blown the whole Janet situation out of all proportion. As for Priscilla, who had bullied her way to the front desk, he noticed that she often stared at him in a way that was all wrong. She had no need to get so close to announce she was there. Her perfume made the whole classroom stink.

After school finished for the day, Richard made his way to the staff car park – or at least that was his intention, until he saw Janet walking down the driveway. She was quite easy to identify because she was the only girl who carried her books in an old hessian sack, like the ones used to store corn. A strange idea, he thought, but he found teenage fashion impossible to understand.

On reaching the school gates, Janet turned left. Richard frowned. To catch a bus to the city, she needed to turn right. Forgetting his car, he diverted to the gates, from where he followed Janet with his gaze. Then he closed his eyes in shock. She was heading towards the cinema. Opening his eyes, he saw two boys standing near the rear of the building, sharing a cigarette and trying to look cool. After taking a moment to compose himself, he followed at a discreet distance until he came to the main crossroads, beyond which the picture house towered above the adjacent shops. Then Janet disappeared from view, quickly followed by the boys.

Richard hurried to the cinema... but now what? He was no longer on school property, so his authority was lacking. Indeed, his grand titles of 'sir' and 'Mr Edwards' ended at the school gates. Now he was just Richard, a citizen of no great importance. But what he had just seen, or imagined was about to happen, needed something to be done. But what? However, he decided that before committing himself to any decisive course of action, he needed time to think. To his later regret, he walked away, back to his car. After all, the awful deed he imagined was taking place off school premises. His authority behind the cinema was zero.

After the boys had gone, Janet smoothed down her clothes, then waited a minute or so. Leaving at exactly the same time as them was unwise, given her increasing notoriety. Then her eyes opened just a little wider. Before her stood Freaky Fred.

"You are the last boy I expected to see," she said.

He stared down at his shoes, then turned to walk away, before changing his mind and stopping. "I really like you," he mumbled.

"That's a very brave thing to say," she said. "I really like you too."

Fred turned, a great big smile contorting his whole face in an expression which suggested he believed in magic. "I was wondering…" he began. Then he appeared to experience a surge of courage. "Would you go tree-climbing with me?" he asked.

Later, Janet was to reflect this was the first time she had laughed since the death of her mother. But, as she stood in the dead-end alley, her initial thought was one of surprise. "Okay…" she said presently. "Not about the tree-climbing, but…" *But what?* Finding herself alone in an alley with Freaky Fred had confused her sensibilities. "Okay," she repeated, "I need you to explain how you think, so I can understand what you are saying."

"Tree-climbing really good," he responded.

"So talking about tree-climbing was not just a way of building up the courage to ask for what's really on your mind?"

The boy looked confused.

"Tell you what," she said. "Begin by telling me your name. I have a vague memory you were called something other than Fred in the first form."

The boy shuffled his feet nervously.

"Ah, go on," she said. "Tell us, then it can be our extra-special big secret. What do your parents call you?"

"Michael," he mumbled.

"Freaky Michael," she said, "completely lacks poetic resonance. In fact, it merely emphasises the Freaky, as in 'Help, he's going to attack me.' Fred dilutes the Freaky to something... well... more like you. And there is nothing wrong with being strange but harmless. So it's best to stick with Fred for now. Then, when you meet a girl you really like, Michael can be your special secret – like having a pet name."

Then Janet felt the hunger pains in her tummy. The previous boys had given her a total of five shillings, so she could afford chips and a chocolate bar. But really she needed to put the money aside for the rent. "Tell you what," she said, "you buy me a bag of chips and I'll watch you climb trees."

Fred nodded, his face a picture of happiness. Though, as it turned out, it was not quite such a good deal because he only had the money for one bag, which Janet then felt obliged to share. Also, when walking along the pavement, sharing proved quite difficult because he seemed unable to maintain a straight line. She gave him the bag, then took a step back. Again, she laughed, quite loudly this time. He was avoiding treading on any cracked paving slabs. She hurried ahead and stood on the only good slab, with two cracked ones on either side. Fred stopped before her, which allowed her to grab the last four chips. Then, blocking his way, she asked why he would not step on cracked slabs. He replied that it made bad things happen. At least now she understood why the other girls teased him. He was an obvious target. She strongly suspected that boys used fists, while girls, as far as she knew, stuck to words. Telling him to stay where he was, she stepped back, then went for a circular walk, making certain to step only on cracked slabs. She reflected that, strangely, this activity meant she was effectively playing a back-to-front version of his game.

"There," she said. "Nothing bad happened to me at all."

"But you're a girl," he said.

Okay, she thought, *now I* fully *understand why the other girls think you're weird.* But thankfully they were only a few yards from the gravel path that went around the reservoir, where he would no doubt want to give her a tree-climbing demonstration. However, she had other ideas. She would sit him on a log or something, and tell him all the things which made the girls tease him. Well, there were quite a lot of those, but for today she would concentrate on paving stones, his short trousers, and the odd socks.

CHAPTER THREE

Richard fell backwards onto his sofa, exhausted, then closed his eyes to pretend the outside world did not exist. He had hardly slept since seeing Janet go behind the cinema with those boys. There *was* a prostitute in his class! His teacher-training course had not even mentioned such a difficulty might arise, and now he had no idea what to do about it. Slowly, his mind was turning towards a decision that, deep down, he knew to be unwise: he must go to see Janet's father, to investigate the situation, because now an even darker thought occurred to him. Did her father know about her behaviour, and if so, was he…? Richard could not bring himself to follow the thought to its awful, but possible, conclusion. If things were that bad, he would need to contact social services. They would take Janet into care, where she would be safe. But if social services got involved they would contact the school, and the head would expel Janet for being a prostitute. Though, had she gone to a normal school, she would by now have left to start work anyway. As far as Richard could see, he had no choice but to make some preliminary observations before hitting what could only be considered a nuclear panic button and placing a telephone call to social services.

The following morning, Richard realised the weekend would be a good time to visit Janet's father at home. If he worked on Saturdays, he would speak to Janet directly. Either way, he would gain a better understanding of what was going on. But a home visit, without telling anybody? That was questionable. Visiting a prostitute's house was even worse. Finally, he stumbled upon a rather brilliant idea. He would buy Janet a proper satchel, which he could say somebody had given to him. "And because I was just passing," he would add, "I thought you might like it… for coming top of the class…" The exact details he would work out later. Then he lost confidence in the plan, at least until he imagined how the head would react to finding out there was a prostitute in the school. Their reputation was at stake, so the satchel plan would have to proceed. Then at least Janet could stop coming to school clutching an old hessian sack.

After driving to the general area where Janet lived, Richard parked his car on the fringes of what was undeniably a rough neighbourhood. (Certainly not the sort of place where a nearly new Jaguar could be left unattended.) Nervously, he continued on foot, constantly looking down to navigate an obstacle course of litter, broken glass, and dog poo. Then he was forced to stop due to a fat old woman kneeling on the pavement, scrubbing her doorstep furiously. After a few moments she looked up.

"Bugger, ain't it?" she said. "Weren't like this till Hitler dropped all his bombs. He thought we could see his aeroplanes, you know, because we all ate carrots."

Richard took great care never to say 'err' because it communicated indecision, but on this occasion he was struggling. "It's a very clean doorstep," he said weakly.

"When I were a kid they were all like this," she replied. "They 'ad proper hangings back then. Queen Victoria saw to that. It was Churchill who invented radar, you know. The carrots was just a decoy."

Awkwardly, Richard stepped into the road to circumnavigate the woman, but after two paces he stopped in horror. The way she was kneeling meant he could see the soles of her shoes – or, more accurately, where the soles had once been. Now, through the matching holes in her thick woolly socks, he could see the soles of her feet instead. He looked at his own shoes: highly polished, with good heels and nearly new leather soles. Without rationalising what he was doing, he took his wallet from his jacket pocket, removed a pound note, then continued his circumnavigation to place the money on the pavement by the woman's side.

He was about to scurry away when she shouted, "Oi!"

He hesitated, and a moment later she stood before him, her fists clenched, as if ready for a fight.

"I ain't no pauper," she rasped. "Give your God-money to the corner shop. They've a poor box behind the counter for kids with empty bellies."

But Richard was so terrified by the encounter that he fled before she had time to return the cash.

After a few hundred yards, he came to a road running from left to right. The street ahead could be ignored because most of its windows were boarded up, and from the terrible dilapidation of the houses it was obvious nobody lived there. Then, thinking sensibly, he went into the shop on the far corner, first to make a donation and then to get directions to Wellington Place. Initially, the man behind the counter stared goggle-eyed at the five-pound note Richard offered, then shrugged as he put it into a wooden till. Richard had seen one of these in operation in the old-fashioned gentlemen's tailor shop his father used, so knew the transaction needed to be written on a roll of paper which ran beneath a little window in the top. However, the man made no effort to do so.

"I wonder," said Richard, "if you could tell me where I might find Wellington Place?"

"Too poncy for these parts," the shopkeeper replied, "but I'll ask me kid, 'cause 'e does a penny-errand service for two miles around." He then turned towards an open door behind the counter. "Nipper, come 'ere," he shouted.

A moment later, a scruffy boy came through the doorway. Richard found it difficult to judge his age because he was trying to push a sandwich into his mouth, the bread of which was almost as large as his face. Possibly he was eight, which excluded him from any sort of work. But the man still asked him about Wellington Place.

"Stink Alley?" said the boy, spraying bread and jam across the counter. Quickly he ran his hand across the dirty wooden surface and, having recovered the jam, sucked his fingers.

"Ah," said the man, pointing towards the wall at the back of the shop. "Stink Alley's that way, four entries after the foundry."

Richard thought it likely that the boy would soon collapse with food poisoning, and, not wishing to get involved further, hurried from the shop. Against his better judgement, he then headed up the street in the direction the man had pointed – and where it was obvious that nobody lived. On reaching the foundry, he looked up to discover the building towered above the houses like a great cathedral, its chimney acting as a spire. Then, looking down, and between the great wooden doors that opened directly onto the pavement, he saw many furnaces breathing out fumes and spewing molten metal. He thought it ironic that such a cathedral-like building could portray so accurately an image of Hell. Well, he was an English teacher, so was always looking for poetic connections between apparently contradictory ideas. But what had the woman scrubbing the doorstep meant when she had talked about God-money? Of course – he had now entered the world of the damned, and had needed to make an offering to God before doing so. In addition to English, he had studied a little history, so knew that when factories like this had been built, they had generally operated reduced hours through the winter because working by candlelight was difficult. Only after gas lighting came to the area in the 1880s could this image of Hell have become a twenty-four-hour operation – a place even God decided to abandon.

Excited by all this poetic resonance, Richard continued, counting the entries until he stopped at the fourth. Looking up, he saw a capping stone above an archway. Chipped into its surface was the name Wellington Place, together with a date: 1822. Okay, he had to accept Janet lived in one of the city's first slums. Then he lowered his gaze to inspect the entry beneath the capping stone, and suddenly had a terrible flashback to an essay Janet had written the previous year. In this she had used the phrase 'walking down a tunnel', and he had corrected her because it implied the character was descending below ground.

"The phrase you want," he had noted, "is 'walking through an entry', because your character remains above ground."

But now he understood that Janet had been correct, and what he had assumed to be a work of fiction had, at least in part, been based upon her own experience. He shuddered, then walked down the tunnel to find himself gazing across a yard of cracked blue brick, much of which had subsided into pools of water. If he wanted his socks to remain dry, walking further would require navigational skills. To think people had once lived here made him gasp in horror. Thankfully, the area had obviously been abandoned long ago... though this idea contradicted his other observation; namely some washing hanging out to dry on a rope stretched between opposing houses. Also, there were a couple of rats scampering around, which suggested there was a food source nearby. Or perhaps they just used the houses for shelter, and commuted to one of the nearby factories when they wanted to eat, presumably picking up crumbs scattered about the canteen floor.

Eventually, Richard turned his attention to a dilapidated shed-like building in the middle of the yard. It took him a few moments to realise that it had once been a lavatory block. This explained why the row of grey-planked doors only occupied the middle of the frame: to allow ventilation from bottom to top. Beneath one door he could see a pair of boots with trousers wrapped around the ankles. It looked a bit funny, but the noise coming from within told him something quite disgusting was taking place. Well, that accounted for the smell: those who wandered down the entry to do their emergency ablutions were unlikely to clean the lavatories, if they had already been messed up by a previous visitor. Looking around the yard, he was astonished to see a woman emerge from one of the doorways. She was carrying a bucket, and walked casually across to a tap fixed to the side of the toilet shed. After filling the bucket, she returned to her doorway, uttering a very rude word when some of the water slopped over her legs. Richard realised he had walked through a time tunnel which had taken him back 150 years to a different world, when Charles Dickens was still a boy. His writings now took on a new, more real existence.

Presently, Richard remembered why he was here. He looked to a door with a number '1' painted on it. The window to the side was plastered with newspaper to slightly above head height, presumably to allow some light to enter whatever gloomy rooms lay behind. But of course nobody would be living there now, which came as a great relief. When he had looked up Janet's address, his hurry had clearly led him to make a mistake. Perhaps she lived at Number 11? But this did not really help. The mistake needed to be Wellington Place itself. Anyway, he could hardly go around knocking on random doors, so, for want of anything better to do, he went to tap on Number 1. Then he would go home, and perhaps see Janet at school on Monday...

Hearing the knock on the door, Janet went to the kitchen window and discreetly parted the newspaper. There was a man clutching a satchel! Was he completely mad? Around these parts, he was certain to be beaten up for being a poof. And why was he knocking on her door?

Then the man stepped back. Mr Edwards! What on earth was he doing here? Oh – he had recently learned about what she did, and now wanted to… Still, while doing it with Mr Edwards would be embarrassing, it would pay the rent.

Richard had only vaguely heard the lavatory flush, so was surprised to discover a man standing by his side – an awful man, with three crooked, tobacco-stained teeth in an otherwise cavernous mouth. Perhaps he was around fifty, but his ragged appearance made him look older, and quite frightening. Richard realised the man was looking at him with equal curiosity – and with particular interest in the satchel. He decided he needed to explain. "I was hoping to see a girl called Janet," he said, "but I seem to have the wrong house."

"Men in poncy clothes have to knock three times," said the man, "otherwise she'll be thinking you're from the social."

"Janet? Here… there?"

"Bang on – best shag I've ever had, well worth a quid—"

It will never be known if the man had intended to elaborate further, because Richard's uncontrolled anger sent a powerful fist smashing into his jaw. This reflex action sent the man falling backwards, cracking his skull upon the bricks and staining them with blood. His neck looked to be at a funny angle and his eyes showed no trace of consciousness. Because Richard had put no premeditated thought into the punch, he could not at first understand why there was a body lying on the ground. Then he remembered the man's words: *well worth a quid*. Instinctively, he knew the man would never speak again. In panic, he ran back up to the street, then towards a telephone box on the corner. From there he called an ambulance, then raced back to his car, where he relaxed just a little. This could only be one of those nightmares in which you keep running away from some unimaginable terror. Soon, he was certain to wake up in his nice, warm bed...

Plonker, thought Janet. Not for hitting Old Farty-pants, as she liked to call him, because that was what he kept on doing as he forced himself inside her. No, she was referring to the way Mr Edwards had drawn attention to himself by running. One should always walk away from a fight when the loser is... well, in this case, obviously dead. However, an even greater sin was dropping the satchel, which would have his fingerprints all over it.

Quickly, she raced out of the door and recovered the satchel, throwing it into a bucket of water. How much rubbing she would have to do with a bar of carbolic soap, she had no idea. Perhaps five minutes passed before she was happy no fingerprints could remain. Then she lifted the newspaper a fraction to look outside. A crowd had gathered, mostly enjoying the entertainment, though some looked towards her door. She could imagine the headline in the local newspaper: 'Man found dead outside prostitute's house'. Her existence here was soon to be made known to the authorities. Social services would not let this one go. Quickly, she threw all her belongings into her sack and put the soggy satchel on top. But when she looked beneath the newspaper again, she saw two policemen standing a discreet distance from the crime scene, no doubt waiting for backup, given the nature of the crowd.

Plonker, she thought again. Not the policemen, but Mr Edwards for bringing all these problems into her life.

Then Farty-Pants' wife pushed her way through the crowd. She was okay, and often thanked Janet for keeping her "old man" occupied. According to her, he had stopped bothering with her "down below" altogether. Apparently, their physical contact had dwindled to the odd punch, which she had learned to live with. Indeed, she was so grateful to Janet that she passed on her rent money to the collector when she was at school. Occasionally, if she was a shilling short, the woman would make up the difference herself, just to say thank you. And now she was looking at her husband, apparently quite happy that he lay dead upon the ground. She squatted over his face, and slowly a puddle of urine mingled with the blood.

"You pissed on me all these years," she announced. "Now it's my turn to piss on you."

A policeman rushed to pull her off. She looked up and smiled at him. Her ill-fitting false teeth pushed her lips forwards, as if she were expecting a kiss.

"Now I'm free to have a proper shag," she said, "and you know I'm not wearing any knickers. Which of you wants to be first?"

The residents of the yard thought this good entertainment, but the policeman leapt back in an effort to escape. The distraction was just enough to let Janet slip out of her door unnoticed. On reaching the street, she walked away, knowing that she had escaped social services. She also realised that the police were certain to contact her school. She was effectively expelled already.

"Plonker," she said out loud, now thinking about Mr Edwards in a less kindly way.

Richard reached the safety of his house without incident, but his primeval instincts refused to allow his legs to remain still. He paced about his lounge, unable to sit, presumably because it was easier to escape from a standing position. As his feet pounded the carpet, his mind raced through the facts of his situation. Had anyone seen him punch the man? No, and he had soon fled the crime scene to telephone the ambulance, even though he had known him to be beyond help. Had he left any fingerprints? No, he had used his knuckles to knock on Janet's door. Then he remembered the satchel...

By the afternoon Richard had managed to get the facts into some sort of order. He had visited a prostitute (who happened to be his fifteen-year-old pupil) and killed a man – one of her customers. That would not look good, if it ever came to court, but there was hope, because there was a lot of talk in Parliament about the death penalty being abolished. In fact, it seemed likely to happen before the end of the year. All he had to do was remain a free man for maybe six months. Life imprisonment? No, he would try to find the courage to take his own life before that happened. Or perhaps they would catch him immediately, and he would take the long walk to the gallows, screaming in fear.

Okay, he thought, *the police are bound to visit the school.* But would they take the fingerprints of the teachers?

Probably not. Chances were he would get away with it. The important thing was to attend school on Monday and behave as if nothing had happened. On the way he would buy a local newspaper. If it said anything about the police wanting to question a teacher, he would simply drive away to somewhere new.

Janet walked around the reservoir to where, a few days earlier, she had tried to give Fred lessons on how to become a normal boy. She hoped he would keep doing the 'homework' she had set, at least to the point of summoning the courage to step on whichever paving slab happened to be the most convenient. Then Leonie might admit to liking him, so long as he kept their friendship a secret.

Eventually Janet turned her mind to more serious problems. Obviously, she could never return to Wellington Place, but around the reservoir were a few acres of land the council liked to call a nature reserve. More truthfully, it was a place where young boys could get their first taste of cider, older boys their first experience of fumbling sex, and a few criminals escape the law. (Any policeman sufficiently stupid to attempt a solo visit was likely end up in the water.) However, to the various animals who lived in the trees or undergrowth, it was indeed a nature reserve, conveniently situated near the city streets, where they could scavenge for food.

After walking a little further along the reservoir path, Janet dodged between a few trees, then searched the bushes for a suitable place to sleep. Eventually she found a space beneath a tangle of branches, with sufficient leaf cover to protect her from a passing shower. So her accommodation was sorted. Indeed, not having to find the rent every week would make things a lot easier.

A far greater misfortune was her O levels. No longer able to take them at school, she would have to sit them at college. She knew enough to get top grades in all her subjects, but colleges charged students, presumably on the grounds they would be working while studying. She had already made vague enquiries about taking A levels at night school, though only in the way of playing out a magical fantasy in which her mother was watching her from above. Now she had to think about the real world, and what it would cost to sit her O levels at college. Probably fifty times more than she had in her bag.

During her first afternoon in the bushes, Janet knew she must remain alert to what might be happening in the world beyond. She did not think the authorities had a park keeper, but had a vague notion a motorcycle gang used the area as their headquarters. The odd kid racing along the path on a moped did not worry her. Chances were, the boy would be as illegal as Janet herself, so unlikely to make a fuss if she pushed him into the reservoir.

As darkness crept into the undergrowth, she felt able to relax. People would no longer push their way through the bushes to take a secret pee. Though she hoped drunken men would not urinate into the reservoir instead, given that it was now her drinking water. Once completely safe within the pitch-black night, Janet began to think seriously about how she might fund her O levels at college. Slowly she came to accept an awful truth. She would have to return to the place of terror she had last visited aged thirteen…

It was just after her periods had stopped, but because

they had only recently begun, she had thought little of it. In fact, back then, she had had very little idea about grown-up stuff, except for what men liked to do, at which she had become rather expert. Anyway, eventually she had found the courage to visit the district where the professional prostitutes worked. She got two offers of casual employment, but that was not why she was there. Eventually she had found a woman who looked relatively kind.

"You're just a kid," she had said. "Go away."

By the standards of the street, that was quite friendly. Eventually Janet had worn the woman down, even to the extent she took an hour off work to explain how these things worked. She then introduced Janet to the man who controlled the territory. She never saw any of the money for her work but, true to his word, the pimp took her to a street somewhere – in the back of a van, so as to keep the address secret. Once inside the house, the wartime blackout curtains seemed to take her into a world of nightmares. Then the 'medical practitioner' had told her to lie on the kitchen table.

"Are you sure you want to go through with this?" she asked. "Because, though the procedure is quite routine at two months, given your age, and you being so far gone, it might have unpredictable consequences…"

"I have no choice," Janet whispered.

The practitioner had nodded, then mumbled something about God. But Janet had thought only of her mother, who would now be closing her eyes in horror…

On returning home, Janet had haemorrhaged. Perhaps she had nearly died alone in her living room but, for her, hospital was not an option, and within ten days she was able to earn a little money to buy some food. She had then gone back to work the street, just enough to pay to get a coil fitted by the same practitioner. It was just in time, because the summer holidays were over and the following week she would be back in school to begin her O level courses. That was the last time she had bought a school uniform. Being self-employed was far less profitable than working for a pimp, who always carried a truncheon to protect 'his property', and let it be known he had access to a gun.

That summer spent working professionally had been the darkest days of her life. The district was a place to which she had vowed never to return, but now, aged fifteen, she had two weeks to earn some serious money to pay for her O level exams. Yet again, she had no choice.

CHAPTER FOUR

The Monday morning after the 'incident', Richard stopped his car at the school gates, and peered through the windscreen. A passing shower required his wipers to swish occasionally, thereby allowing him a brief but clear view to the top of the driveway. A police car was parked neatly in a space near the entrance to the building. However, this was to be expected, and it was not as if there were any vehicles with flashing blue lights parked hastily at crazy angles, and armed officers waiting to throw him into the back of a riot van. He drove on and, to demonstrate his false confidence, parked next to the police car. Seeing it was unattended, he walked casually into the building, ready to run at the first sight of handcuffs.

During his first lesson, a prefect entered the room to hand him a note. That was to be expected, as was its content: the headmaster was holding an emergency staff meeting during the lunch break. Also, as Richard had anticipated, Janet was absent from his class.

At the meeting, the head vented his anger by stamping around the room, speaking in Latin. He always did this in situations he found distasteful, believing the ancient tongue protected common folk from the moral corruption undisguised knowledge would mete out upon their less able minds. Though truthfully, it also protected half of the staff, who only pretended to understand. Fortunately for Richard, his various Latin masters had assumed their pupils were training to undertake high public office, preferably in positions that required Victorian discipline and morals. This now gave him a considerable advantage: as far as the head was concerned, anyone who knew Latin was one of the elite and should be running the country. Additionally, he refused to believe 'his own kind' were capable of doing anything illegal, even committing a parking offence. Richard felt this put him beyond suspicion of murder.

"*Sino meretriĉem ad putrescant in platea gutter,*" ranted the head at full volume.

Richard thought 'Let the prostitute rot in the gutter' to be a little extreme, but responded with an appropriate Latin speech of his own – taking comfort in the fact that the ideas expressed within were meaningless in the modern age.

The head gave a respectful nod, then, having dealt with the issue of prostitution, drifted back into English. "And," he whispered, "she has now fled the scene, because one of her clients has been murdered right outside her front door."

Even the masters who had no idea of what was going on cried out in horror, this being the expected response. Though, because they only took *The Times*, they would remain forever in blissful ignorance of the situation, unless they happened to glance at the front page of the local newspaper, and make a connection to the head's bumbling rant.

Richard had guessed it would be like this but, as the meeting progressed, it became apparent the police were only trying to locate Janet. There was no mention of staff being required to provide fingerprints. The teachers, it seemed, were not part of the police enquiries. Of course, there was the satchel, which implied an educational connection, so maybe they would get around to the fingerprints later on? Feeling safe, at least for the time being, Richard turned his mind to Janet. Where was she? Then, with horror, he realised that it was his actions which had brought the police to her house, and so forced her to run. Once they discovered how she had been living, social services were certain to take her into care. At fifteen, she would then be expected to find a job, without any consideration being given to her completing her O levels. In any event, the school would never take her back. As far as the head was concerned, she was already employed, servicing the needs of men.

After school had finished for the day, the teachers hurried home, mostly in cars, but a few pedalling furiously on bicycles. Only when they felt safe within domestic environments could they better contemplate the traumatic experience of the staff meeting.

The biology teacher realised that, as he had once struggled to explain to the fifth form how babies were made, there had been a prostitute among them. Had she been looking at him and thinking, *I will give you a personal demonstration for a fiver*? He had a five-pound note in his wallet now! The idea the crisp paper, with its portrait of the Queen serenely contemplating important matters of state, could be exchanged for… He shook his head to keep the thought from developing further, but this only made it bounce about inside his mind. With no control over his actions, he walked through to the sitting room to ask his wife if he might visit her bedroom at ten o'clock that evening. She replied it would not be convenient. Well, that put the world back into good order... until his mind returned to the prostitute who, only a few days earlier, had sat in his laboratory. She clearly did not fit into an institution whose pupils generally came from middle-class families, or at least diligently attended elocution lessons to hide their origins.

Meanwhile, the physics teacher was even more traumatised. He had always known that girls, with their frivolous brains, were unsuited to understanding the great works of Isaac Newton. That was why his current fifth form only had one female pupil taking the subject at O level... no it wasn't! The tramp was only taking physics to surround herself with boys. *Oh, look at me,* she was essentially saying, while disrupting his lessons with all her fancy talk of Schrödinger's wave equation. In reality, she was promoting her services. Slowly, he looked at the shelf where the university-level physics book he had removed from the school library now lay abandoned. In the first week after the confiscation, just looking at all those squiggly equations had almost driven him insane. And now he was free. He jumped up, grabbed the book and threw it into the fire. The tramp was no longer in his class, so he no longer needed to learn impossible mathematics.

"Poppycock!" he shouted at the burning book. Einstein's ridiculous ideas contradicted all common sense. Like the tramp, they did not belong in the physics teacher's world of predictable outcomes.

And then there was Richard, tossing and turning in his bed, unable to sleep as the details of the staff meeting circled around his mind. Above all, he knew it was he who had brought all this misfortune into Janet's life.

Two days later, Richard realised that he had to find Janet so as to put things right. How he would achieve this, he had no idea, but common sense dictated it would include helping her to sit her O levels at college. This would require a respectable adult to be involved, because such an institution would never accept a girl who lived… nowhere… and lacked financial resources… No, she had money, because she had a job which involved doing unspeakable things with old men. What had changed was where she did it.

Like most people in the county, Richard knew where the local prostitutes plied their trade. Even the police turned a blind eye to the activity, so long as 'their kind' did not contaminate respectable streets. Anyway, Richard had a vague idea that prostitution itself was not actually illegal, just the organisation of it – when they worked in groups, supervised by pimps. Not that he had studied the finer legal details, but he felt certain his interpretation was a good approximation. Though a more common understanding could be expressed as 'Out of sight, out of mind', or, as the head might say, 'Let them rot in the gutter.'

The 'red-light district', as it was generally known, covered about a square mile. Most of it lay behind the gasworks, but it also extended to a number of dead-end lanes that ran down to the canal, or 'cut', as it was known locally. It was not a place he had ever been, so decided to drive to the nearest respectable street, then walk to the area where he might find Janet working. His car was, after all, a Jaguar, and two years old – not the sort of vehicle one would use for what might be termed cruising; no, kerb-crawling. Where had all these horrible words come from? Eight days ago, he had given the topic of prostitution very little thought. Now, under cover of darkness, he was proposing to visit their place of work.

After parking on the respectable side of the gasworks, he walked to the red-light district. The term intrigued him, because the area was lit by Victorian gas lamps, which only cast dull circles of yellowish light onto the pavement surrounding them. Idly, he wondered if there was a pipe running directly from the gasworks to the lamps. If so, he liked the poetic imagery:

Great, towering gasometers,
Gently hissing lamps,
Beneath the cobbled streets
Be thin threads of friendship,
Holding back the night.

It reminded him that he was an English teacher, and not here for pleasure. Indeed, it was the sort of obscure poem only an English teacher could understand.

Eventually he found himself standing before a high fence surrounding a shunting yard where coal trains unloaded their cargo. This was yet another scene that had not changed since Victorian times, with powerful locomotives pulling half-mile chains of open coal trucks at twenty miles per hour. You needed a lot of coal to produce so much gas. Deep down, he knew all these teacher-like thoughts were a defence mechanism to protect him from the nightmare in which he was trapped. Tonight he was here for one thing: to find Janet and take her away to… well, he did not really have a plan to deal with whatever came next.

"Need any help?" came a voice from the shadows.

Richard replied that he did not and walked on, eventually refusing five offers of 'company'. Then he passed the first woman for the third time. She was leaning against a lamp post, smoking a cigarette.

"This your first time, luv?" she asked.

"No." He meant that he had not come for sex, though had not considered it also implied that he came here often.

The woman dropped her cigarette on the pavement and squashed it with her shoe. "It's okay," she said. "A lot of fine gentlemen find it difficult to ask for company."

"I'm looking for a girl," he said.

"Kind of gathered that."

"No, I mean a particular girl, called Janet."

"I'm called Janet."

"The one I'm looking for is still at school."

"Understood. Give us a fiver and I'll sort it."

"You know her?"

"Janet the schoolgirl? Yes. You got the fiver?"

With great relief, Richard took his wallet from his jacket pocket and handed over a fiver. As instructed, he then followed the woman to a nearby mid-terrace house. Entering a narrow hallway, he found his way partially blocked by what, in a respectable setting, might have been a telephone table. However, the dominant feature of this obstruction was the man sitting behind it. His muscular arms could easily have wrestled a grizzly bear to the floor. Just so human adversaries might understand the danger of upsetting him, his over-sized biceps were covered with tattooed images of death. Lower down, his legs projected forwards, making it seem as if the table was resting on his lap. What particularly frightened Richard was the great pair of boots resting on the wooden floorboards, their leather worn away to reveal steel toecaps beneath. Richard thought his female guide was very brave to approach such a beastly man. However, she casually placed two pound notes on the table.

"Three," said the man.

Richard naturally assumed three pound notes were required, but the woman squeezed past the table and gestured for him to follow. A few terrifying moments later, he found himself looking at a number 3 painted on a door. The lady opened this to reveal an ill-decorated room, furnished with a settee against one wall, a bed against the other. The woman sat on this.

"I'm Janet," she said. "Pleased to meet you; take a seat."

"I'm Richard," he responded. "The Janet I am looking for is in my class."

The woman rolled her eyes like a teenager. "Yes, sir," she said, "how can I help? Oh, gosh, the bulge in your trousers – what is it, exactly?"

"Stop!"

"Sorry. Do you want to look at my fanny, then? Next you can… well, you're the sir; give me a clue."

"Janet's fifteen, works the streets. I want to speak with her."

"Understood." The woman stood up and wriggled a bit of material, which might just have met the skinniest definition of knickers, down her legs.

"Hello," she said, "I'm Janet. My daddy can't afford to buy me any knickers, so I have to walk about without them—"

Richard, furious at her slanderous remarks about Janet, rushed at her in a fit of rage. He had no idea what he would do, only that it would require his fists. The woman stepped efficiently to one side, then pushed his back as he dived onto the bed. He turned around just in time to see her push a button on the wall. A few seconds later, the door crashed open and two men rushed in, the first kicking his legs and the second swinging a fist into his face.

"He's just a paedo," said the woman. "He was going to hit me because he wanted a real schoolgirl."

One of the men spat in Richard's face, the phlegm oozed into his mouth. "Paedos disgust me," he shouted.

"Yeah," said the woman, "but he's got a bulging wallet in his jacket pocket – perhaps we could overlook it this time?"

Richard felt his wallet being removed, then heard the man give a whistle.

"Sixty quid," he said. "We can get you a real schoolgirl for that, but you have to do it properly. Come back tomorrow with another sixty, and I'll take you to a mate who can sort it." He handed the prostitute four five-pound notes before putting the remainder of the cash into his own pocket. He then warned Richard that, if he tried to hit one of his girls again, he would end up in the 'cut' with a knife in his back.

After Richard was thrown from the front door, he

hobbled back to his car, then made his way home. Finding Janet was proving to be impossible! For now he had to focus on getting to school tomorrow and behaving normally, though he would probably have to claim to have fallen down the stairs. But as the hours passed, he realised just how important finding Janet had become to him. Some primeval instinct meant he needed to get her to a place of safety. But where was she? For all he knew, she could have fled the city. The way he had left a dead body outside her door might have caused her to panic and jump onto the nearest coach going anywhere but here.

The following evening, Richard was driving home from work with his mind on other things when, about a mile from the school gates, something appeared in the road ahead. Instinctively, he braked hard, but managed to stop without skidding. The next moment, Janet was banging on the rear door. Astonished, he unlocked it and allowed her to jump in. She lay down on the back seat, out of sight.

"Drive," she said. "We can't be seen together. Take the first right, the second left, then keep going until I tell you to stop."

Richard knew he was the teacher who should be giving the instructions, but was too confused to argue. After two miles, Janet told him to stop, adding that it would be quite safe here. Then she sat up. "You complete plonker," she said. "What on earth did you think you were doing? I heard you wanted me – bit late for that. You should have told me while I was still at school, before all this madness happened."

"I... I... I..."

"Oh, shut up. I'm only here to warn you off. What our pimp said about you ending up in the 'cut' was no idle threat. It happens, especially to men who try to hit one of his girls. As for walking the streets with a packed wallet – just carry enough money to do the business. For a schoolgirl, there are procedures that need to be followed. For one thing, how would my manager know you're not the fuzz? I'm under contract for the next week, so no more 'Janet this' or 'Janet that'! Now, my shift starts in forty-five minutes, but I can catch a bus from the bottom of the lane. Just try to keep yourself out of trouble, okay?"

"I will not allow it, for you to go back to—"

"So who's going to pay for my O level exams at college?"

"Me."

"Right, and what about food?"

"Me."

"I can't eat you. I need two quid a week for living expenses. And what about my bus fare to college?"

"Me."

Janet looked confused. "That's three 'me's," she said. "Interesting. But I'm under contract, and my manager uses his truncheon on girls who run off early. That's a truncheon as in a lump of wood, not the one he keeps in his trousers, understand? And I have no intention of joining you in the cut."

In truth, Richard understood very little of what she was saying. His response was to continue saying 'me' without thinking of the consequences. He ended up offering her a place to stay, the only condition being that she never again went within a mile of the gasworks.

Janet indicated she was thinking by rubbing her

forehead. "Okay," she said eventually, "take me to the reservoir. I'm living in some bushes there and I keep my stuff in a plastic bag." She felt guilty about selling the satchel to a second-hand shop to buy food. Oh well, she wouldn't tell him about that. Anyway, getting back to the reservoir would give her time to think. If she needed to do a runner, he would never catch her, and from there she could still be at her proper job on time.

When the car stopped, Janet raised herself from the seat. When Mr Edwards turned around, she discovered his face was white with shock. She had no idea why – he had recently risked his life trying to buy her body and, now she had agreed to service him, he no longer had any need to be nervous. Though, for herself, it would still seem really odd doing it with Mr Edwards. But she had been with a lot worse and, if he was going to pay for her exams, well, that was her main purpose in life.

Richard watched Janet walk along the reservoir path. Subconsciously, he copied one of her recent gestures by rubbing his forehead as he thought. Where was he going to take her? To keep her safe, there was only one place he could think of. *Oh my word...* He was going to be sharing his house with a former pupil, who was still only fifteen. If anyone found out, he would be instantly dismissed and never allowed into a school again. But his house was a few miles beyond the city boundary, and his gardens, front and back, were well protected by high hedges. He could get away with it – probably.

Janet returned, threw a hessian sack into the car, then lay on the back seat. She had never been in such a posh car before; not even her manager owned one like this. As Mr

Edwards drove away, there were no clunky gear changes, just a smooth ride to wherever she was going. Well, she decided, wherever she slept tonight, it would be better than the bushes – probably.

When the car stopped again, she sat up to discover Mr Edwards had parked on a driveway, with a massive lawn to her left and a high hedge to her right. She watched him get out and walk to a garage door. Well, actually there were three garage doors, but he only opened the one in the middle. Above the garages was some sort of house, or perhaps even a hotel? In any event, this upper storey extended to the left of the garages, where it was supported by a lower house-like building. This had a front door, and a huge window overlooking the lawn. She decided the building was definitely too big to be a house.

When Mr Edwards returned, he drove into the garage, then pushed a button on the wall to close the door behind them. Confused, Janet got out and followed him to a side door, which led directly into a sort of cloakroom. Then another door took them into a massive kitchen, with a lot of stuff she did not recognise.

"Get yourself cleaned up," he said. "Use the bathroom upstairs, second door on the right."

That made no sense whatsoever. Why did he have a bathroom, and what was it doing upstairs? Believing herself to be a great explorer, she found some stairs… with carpet on them? This place was seriously weird! Houses in Wellington Place had bare floorboards in the living area and a slate floor in the kitchen. Only in front of the fireplace did a few of the posher residents have a peggy rug made by bodging worn strips of old clothing into sackcloth. Carpet on the stairs just did not make sense – all you did was walk on it to get from one place to another.

The bathroom turned out to be even stranger. The toilet lacked a cistern, or any sort of hanging chain by which it might be flushed. Not wishing to be caught out in an emergency, she looked around to locate the bucket of water that would serve the same purpose. This made her aware that the room was similar in size to her old living room back at Wellington Place. And yet, no bucket? She could do no more than shrug her shoulders and hope for the best.

After a few seconds of confused thought, she walked to a glass door in the wall. This took her to a secondary room, which proved to be similar in size to her old kitchen. The floor at one end had a sloping tiled floor, with a drainage hole at its lowest point. The ceiling above had four shower heads, presumably so the person beneath could take a little walk around while getting clean. More confusingly, the three enclosing walls also had shower heads pointing sideways. Oh well, at least now she understood what was happening. She was to get undressed, stand somewhere within the shower area, then act surprised as Mr Edwards came into the room. For his part, he would also feign surprise at seeing her all soapy and naked. Well, she had done a lot more gruesome things in her life.

But Mr Edwards did not arrive. After ages of being blasted with hot water, she took an enormous towel from a hot rail to dry herself. *Okay*, she thought, *this entire house is from another, quite fluffy planet that sort of floats like a spaceship above the garages.*

After walking downstairs to the kitchen, she found Mr Edwards preparing a meal.

"Good shower?" he asked. "You took a long time."

"Yeah, well…"

And then he fed her! She imagined it was the sort of food posh people ate in hotels, except in this case there were no other guests. For want of anything better to say, she began to tell him of her recent diet – mainly bread and marmalade. He looked horrified, which was strange, because it tasted quite nice. She then explained it tasted better when she had the money to buy lard to coat the bread instead of eating it dry. To change the subject, she then confessed to something which had been troubling her for the past couple of years. According to the girls at school, cleaning their teeth was an essential part of their morning routine. But in Stink Alley nobody had heard of such a thing. The residents generally lost all their teeth during their twenties, so it seemed pointless to keep cleaning them. As she told Mr Edwards this, she noticed tears running down his cheeks.

"I was only saying," she whispered.

"And a diet of bread and marmalade!" he exclaimed.

"Sir," she replied, "don't upset yourself. I mainly eat marmalade because it's half the price of jam."

He frowned. "I want you to call me Richard," he sniffed.

Janet had never considered teachers might have a first name. Surely when they came out of university, all males were called 'sir'?

She watched sir… Mr Edwards… Richard stand from his chair. He then asked her to follow him upstairs. She entered a room containing a double bed with only one pillow in the middle – if this was his room, it suggested he had a fear of turning over in his sleep and falling onto the floor. But not tonight, it seemed. He had brought her here to do it – and all because she had told him that her teeth would soon fall out.

From the bedroom, she followed him through a side door into yet another bathroom. He opened a wall cupboard. Inside she saw maybe a dozen strange brushes, and a neat pile of boxes called toothpaste.

"I change my toothbrush every week," he said, "and throw the old one in the bin. And you had nothing." He took six brushes and three tubes of toothpaste from the cupboard and handed them to her. "Take them to your room," he said. "There's a number '6' on the door."

She had seen that door; it was next to the bathroom she had used earlier. What confused her was the phrase 'your room'. It was like he expected her to stay... here? *Oh my word*, she thought, *I am like one of those high-class escorts I've heard about. Me!* But getting her head around Mr Edwards wanting to do it with her was still really weird. Briefly, she fantasised about telling Priscilla about this. The girl would die of envy. But what happened between Janet and her customers was always top secret.

Then Richard broke into her thoughts. "And no more talk about teeth falling out," he said. "Tomorrow I will take you to see my private dentist. At your age, any damage can be corrected."

Janet did not actually know how escorts worked, but was surprised to discover it included a visit to the dentist. And she was further pleasantly surprised when Richard did not immediately follow her into her bedroom. It would give her time to get accustomed to the soft, clean-smelling sheets. Inquisitively, she lowered herself onto the edge of the mattress. *Aargh* – she was sinking! At Wellington Place, her bed of cardboard had merely squashed down to vaguely match the shape of her body. She also had a vague memory of the bed her father had sold to the rag-and-bone man. It had had a rusty iron frame, and the flattened mattress meant she had kept rolling into the middle. Generally, it had offered the same degree of comfort as cardboard – except new cardboard smelt rather nice, whereas her previous mattress had been soaked with a hundred years of toilet-related fluids. And now, as she looked at the great soft thing in the middle of her bedroom, she wondered how she would sleep on something which made her float, and whether she should climb into such luxury while wearing her old clothes, which, she realised after her shower, were a bit smelly. Was it possible to sleep without them? Back in Wellington Place, everybody wore their day clothes in bed to keep warm… unless they were doing it, she supposed.

Eventually, feeling very guilty, she undressed and got into bed, desperately hoping Richard would not get any man-urges in the middle of the night. Just for now she wanted to experience luxury and think about tomorrow, when he would fulfil his part of the contract and take her to college to sort out her examinations. She gave up trying to work out why he was doing this, because everything seemed to be heading in the right direction – except for her not knowing how to flush the toilet!

The following morning, Janet became even more confused when Richard telephoned the school to say he was sick. Not only because it was a lie, but because he had a telephone in his house!

After breakfast, he took her clothes shopping, then to buy a pair of shoes. The assistant actually screamed in horror at the sight of her existing footwear, for the soles were mostly holes, their remnants smeared with blood from walking along the gravel path by the reservoir. Then he took her to the hairdresser's, where the stylist also screamed. Janet did not understand why, because until that day she had always cut her own hair with a pair of borrowed scissors, and had never once felt the need to scream about it. Okay, she could not see the back of her head, so that part of the operation involved some guesswork. She watched curiously as the stylist staggered back to sit in the waiting area. Puzzled, Janet looked around the room for clues, until she happened to see the price list. Just to keep things constant, she also screamed. Having her hair cut was going to cost the same as her food bill for the entire preceding year! Then came an even greater mystery: her haircut took two hours and involved three stylists all fussing about, stopping only to wring their hands anxiously. When she had cut her own hair, it had taken less than five minutes. The next visit was to the dentist, which she liked less. Two injections and three fillings sort of stopped her talking. But the most surprising event of the day was when Richard called in at a hardware store to get a spare key cut for his front door. He just gave it to her on a fob, as if…

I can just walk into your house?! she would have exclaimed, had her jaw not been paralysed. Instead, she just made a distorted sequence of indistinct sounds.

"I'm back at work next week," he replied, "so I'll not always be there to let you in. If the neighbours say anything, just say you are my niece."

And that was it. She was living with Mr Edwards, who she was now expected to call Richard. Her Uncle Richard! Weird or what?!

CHAPTER FIVE

Janet's first two weeks at Richard's house were something of a learning curve. On day three, or thereabouts, she discovered that you could not use an electric kettle to boil milk. In her defence, she explained to Richard that Wellington Place only had electric for lighting, so to her, fancy plug-in gadgets were a complete mystery. He had not believed her, which she found most annoying – had she decided to tell lies, she would have chosen a subject rather more interesting than plug sockets. However, given that she had redecorated the kitchen ceiling with plaster-of-milk, she let the matter pass, for now.

At the hardware store the following day, she launched her counteroffensive. As Richard was selecting a new kettle, she went to the counter to distract the sales assistant with idle talk about the weather. When Richard approached, carrying a kettle, she took control of the situation.

"Do you have a light-bulb plug?" she asked the assistant.

The assistant reached beneath the counter to produce something that Richard thought should not exist. It looked like the push-in part of a light bulb, but without the actual bulb.

"So," said Janet to the assistant, "if I put a wire into this plug, I can push it into a light socket to power one of those fancy electrical kettles?"

"No," said the assistant, "they are only recommended for low-amp devices. I know some people use them to plug in an iron, but it's not advised—"

"To do their ironing in the dark?!" exclaimed Janet. "I can see that would be very dangerous."

"Certainly," said the assistant. "To power an iron you would have to push silver paper into the main fuse board. I know this is common practice, but it's hardly fire safe. We recommend only using the lighting circuit for things like a record player—"

"So," interrupted Janet, "it is possible to live in an older house that does not have fancy plug sockets and listen to music in the dark?"

Richard shuffled his feet. He could see where this conversation was heading, and knew himself to be on the losing side.

After they had left the shop, Richard immediately said sorry. Janet responded firmly by saying she always told the truth, unless… She held out her hand, indicating that he should complete the sentence. But he looked really miserable, though whether it was because he felt guilty or because it had taken them an hour to clean the kitchen the previous night, she could not say.

"It's okay to tell a lie," she continued, "if the truth would hurt others, or if your survival is at stake. I am also happy to tell a little fib if it makes people laugh. But only a compulsive liar, a horrible person, would tell lies about plug sockets."

The fact Janet had given so much thought to the nature of honesty restored Richard's good humour… until he got home and discovered the refrigerator had broken down – or, as it transpired, been turned off! Again, Janet defended herself.

"You can't just go out and leave all that electricity burning away," she said firmly. "My mother often told me that, if I left a room, even for a few seconds, I had to turn off the light."

Richard shook his head in despair. The following day he returned home with a book called *Good Housekeeping*.

Towards the end of the second week, Janet thought she was starting to get the hang of living in a spaceship – with buttons on the wall to flush the loo! While she considered all the fancy gadgets to be unnecessary, she let the matter pass. Okay, she rolled her eyes occasionally, because that was what teenagers were supposed to do when grown-ups behaved strangely. But otherwise their lifestyle seemed relatively straightforward. In the evenings Richard taught her to play chess, or they worked through the A level English syllabus. According to him, she could expect to get 130 per cent in all her O level subjects. When she told him that mathematical progressions sometimes had limits – in this case one hundred per cent – he replied the extra thirty per cent meant she was already part way through her A levels.

What Janet liked best about her new life was her visits to the upmarket tennis club. They had an entry standard, but overlooked her haphazard play as she was

Richard's guest – assuming the adjacent courts were unused. However, though the trajectory of her tennis balls remained somewhat unpredictable, after four weeks she mostly knew how to fit in with what she now understood to be upper-class society.

Given her early move to grammar school, Janet began her O level examinations at the age of fifteen. She considered the physics paper childlike and the mathematics one very basic. After her English exam she left the college building and looked to the sky.

"130 per cent!" she exclaimed.

Then, responded her mother, *I am at peace.*

After her final exam, Janet arrived home to find Richard preparing a celebratory meal. Obviously, there was no alcohol involved – she had seen what it had done to her father, so had no intention of ever touching the stuff. What she liked instead was coffee, made with beans taken directly from the electric grinder on the wall. Also, bubbly milk – from a saucepan that was not liable to explode. Cappuccino, Richard called it. Anyway, she imagined it was much nicer than getting drunk – as she supposed her former classmates would be doing on finishing their final exam.

After the meal, Richard looked at her across the table. "Happy?" he asked.

"Seven Grade As for certain," she replied. "You bet."

Richard noticed she was starting to talk more like a normal teenager. Occasionally, she even rolled her eyes to communicate her sentiments. But now he needed to have a serious talk about something which had been worrying him for the past month.

"My parents," he said, "are coming back from the Bahamas next week, and… er…"

"You don't want them to know you are living with an ex-pupil?" she finished.

He nodded.

"So you want me to go away?"

"Absolutely not, but my father is a bit of a control freak and has an awful lot of power. He believes I should never make friends with any lady who is not destined to inherit a stately home. Okay, if she's related to royalty he might downgrade his expectations to a multimillionaire heiress, but neither of those appeals to me. Truth is, I hate grand balls and have no interest in shouting 'Tally-ho!' as I chase some poor fox."

Janet was struggling to cope with what he had just said. He had used the word 'friend', not… well… something else. As for being called a 'lady', that was a million times better than being called a prostitute.

Then Richard interrupted her thoughts with a discreet cough. "Have you never wondered how I came to own such a house on a teacher's salary?" he asked.

"Grown-up stuff," said Janet. "I just know what I see. To me, you are already living in a stately home."

"Hardly that, but I don't actually own it. My father gave it to me when I left university – but only sort of, because he still holds the deeds. It's mine for life, so long as I don't upset him by making friends with ladies who are not rich. So I think it best if we go away for a summer holiday."

"I've never been on holiday," said Janet, "but I imagine they are rather expensive, so I'm sure I can hide instead."

Richard looked embarrassed. "My father drives a Rolls-

Royce," he said, "so if you see that in the driveway, then perhaps… err…"

"It's okay to say the word 'hide'," said Janet. "Honestly, I don't mind at all, though maybe I will stock my wardrobe with chocolate, a torch and a book. After all, you did tell me it was called a walk-in wardrobe."

Richard looked rather cross about the image this created. "But as soon as term ends," he said forcefully, "we *will* disappear somewhere nice for six weeks."

It was only that night, as Janet lay in bed, that her thoughts became confused. Richard had been talking as if he expected her to remain here for… well, she did not know how long. Then she tried to imagine a holiday. Where she came from, this might mean a day in the local countryside after taking the Number 66 bus that went… oh, she did not know where exactly, but beyond the city limits. But this notion did not fit well with hiding from Richard's father for six weeks. Oh well, she would just have to take each day as it came.

The awful thought lurking at the back of her mind was that the holiday would be the time Richard would want to start doing it. In her mind this idea had become increasingly awkward, but she fully understood it would be his long-term plan, because, however wonderful he might be, he was still a man. Suddenly, it became clear why they had not done it earlier: her sixteenth birthday had been too far in the future. Perhaps it was a little like the police not prosecuting a driver for travelling three miles an hour over the speed limit. Given Richard's sense of middle-class propriety, he had clearly decided to wait until doing it became approximately legal. And, in addition to reaching the legal age on the 2nd July, her planned move to college to do her A levels meant she was no longer his pupil… She closed her eyes in recognition of these facts. She would go on the forthcoming holiday of her own free will. Doing it would obey all the social conventions.

This was confirmed the following morning, when Richard said he was going to give her a big, wonderful surprise.

No, she thought, *I know what is going to happen when we are on holiday, because it is what all people do. And yes, I will remember to call it big and wonderful when I see it for the first time. Because, yet again, I have no choice.*

CHAPTER SIX

The holiday began very much as Janet had expected – that is to say, after loading the car with luggage, she settled into a comfortable passenger seat to experience a chauffeur-driven ride which made her feel like a member of the royal family. Where they were going was still part of Richard's big secret. In her imagination, their destination might be Buckingham Palace, to receive a military salute as they swished through the gates using a special pass.

After half an hour of travel, curiosity about the big secret made Janet take a second discreet glance at the milometer. They had been averaging thirty-five miles per hour. She particularly liked the way Richard showed no desire to kill her in a car accident. Always so thoughtful, yet practical. In three hours they would be… 105 miles away? Looking out of her passenger window, she noticed the morning sun flitting between the trees that edged the roadside verge. So, she reasoned, they were heading west. If they kept travelling in a reasonably straight line, it seemed inevitable that, sooner or later, they would run out of land

and arrive at the seaside. Obviously, she had no interest in sandcastles, but thought it would be nice to see what an ocean looked like, and perhaps learn to swim.

Around midday, Janet was surprised when Richard parked near an ordinary-looking village shop. She got out of the car, stood on tiptoe, and performed a 360-degree turn as if to say, *Where is the seaside?* But he failed to pick up on the gesture, so she made it more obvious by folding her hands around an imaginary telescope. "I see no ships," she said.

Richard ignored her light-hearted banter, explaining this was where his parents had stopped on their way to a holiday when he was about five.

Oh my God, she thought, *he really is going to buy a bucket and spade to relive his childhood.* Except the seaside was nowhere to be seen. Curious.

Richard's second surprise was to lead her into the shop, where he bought her a bottle of pop and a bar of chocolate. Well, she could live with that! After leaving the shop, he strode purposefully along the pavement to the side of the premises, where there was an insignificant lane, into which he disappeared. Then, thinking more logically, Janet realised a man could not actually disappear; nor could a lane be insignificant to any person who cared to use it. *Curious*, she thought as she gave chase.

It soon became apparent that Richard was deliberately giving her no clue as to what might happen next. One moment she was walking down a narrow lane; the next following him through the overgrown vegetation of a much-neglected footpath. Somewhere along the route they even walked through a field that had no obvious right of way, just a lot of bullocks who regarded them cautiously. Janet thought it odd that Richard could just ignore them. But he seemed lost in his own private world, seeing with tunnel vision and throwing his normal caution to the wind.

Suddenly, she remembered his mysterious 'big, wonderful surprise'. She had assumed it would relate to a hotel bedroom because she had just turned sixteen, but, given the nature of this trail, they were obviously going to a *very* secret place where another kind of big, wonderful surprise might await her. Though, given how long it was taking them to reach it, she would have settled for a simple ice-cream van.

After Janet had become totally disorientated by wandering through wild countryside, she stopped abruptly to watch Richard climb over a gate – the sort that was obviously not meant to be climbed.

"Don't tell me," she said, "you came this way when you were five."

He looked back and smiled sheepishly, but said nothing.

"And you climbed this gate, like naughty schoolboys are prone to do?"

Janet thought the image of Richard wearing short trousers was rather cute. More embarrassingly, she realised his excitement about their mysterious destination was starting to affect her own sensibilities. She climbed over the gate, then walked along a dirt track. Soon Richard stopped and pointed between two trees. Looking through the gap, she saw a railway cutting. Clearly he did not want her to look at that, so what had she missed? A rare plant, or perhaps a great, hollow oak tree in which some mythical king had once supposedly hidden?

Not wishing to appear thick, she covered all options by exclaiming, "Wow!"

"I know," said Richard. "It's all the work of Robert Stephenson himself. Built in 1850, using hardly anything but wheelbarrows and shovels."

She knew he had a thing about railways. However, she could not see what possible relevance this might have to her own life. She tried to think of something funny to say, like, *Not my fault he only had a wheelbarrow*, but he looked rather serious, so she kept quiet. After Richard had finished giving her a rather long railway-themed lecture, she followed him back along the dirt track and, after climbing the gate, onwards to stand beneath a massive stone-built viaduct. Looking ahead, she saw a great high bridge going to a place unknown. Was this Richard's mythical kingdom; the place where his big surprise would be revealed?

"This is the Menai Strait," he said. "The bridge was built to extend the railway line from the Welsh mainland to the island of Anglesey."

"Built by Robert Louis Stevenson," she interrupted, "using only a wheelbarrow. Wow!"

Richard failed to register her mock astonishment. Instead, he expressed only horror that she had confused the great Stephenson with the man who wrote *Treasure Island*.

"He might have written the book so passengers had something to read on the train he had just invented," she said. "Or possibly he wrote the book first, then invented the train second, so people had somewhere to read it. Chicken and egg."

Richard finally understood the teenage gesture of rolling your eyes. It meant, *You are completely daft, but I sort of like you.* Then he smiled. This was Janet venturing into a new world of idle chatter – because she was on holiday, as his friend. And it was nice that she had chosen the important 'railway section' of the adventure to discover her inner happiness. Then he decided to take control of the conversation by saying they were now going to walk across the bridge.

Janet wondered how he had managed to say it so casually. Exploring railways on land, where you could hop over a fence if a train approached, was one thing. Doing so on a bridge was likely to involve clinging to some girder or other. Was his big, wonderful surprise that he liked doing extreme dares? The sort which, if miscalculated, meant you could die – or at least get very wet as you dived into the Menai Strait hundreds of feet below? Then he broke into her thoughts by saying they needed to follow a cart track uphill to reach the road that had recently been built on top of the original railway bridge. This made her laugh.

"But it was a great engineering triumph!" he exclaimed. "And all using the original Stephenson pillars."

"That's as maybe," she said, "but until you mentioned the addition, I had a vision of us running like crazy before a great, thundering train."

Having crossed to the island of Anglesey, Richard turned right, then took a path down a wooded hillside. Here he led Janet along the water's edge to stand beneath the bridge, where he pointed upwards.

"Was walking across that thing actually legal?" she asked.

"No. But I did it when I was five, and old habits die hard."

What Janet heard most clearly was the word 'die'. But before she could think about it further, he remarked, rather strangely, that he had checked the tide tables, so knew it was possible to walk along the shore to the equally famous Thomas Telford bridge. According to Richard, the circular walk crossing the two bridges was the best thing he had ever done on holiday.

As they plodded along the shore, zigzagging between the muddy bits strewn with seaweed-covered rocks, she had to admit that, for a five-year-old boy, it would have been absolute Heaven. As they walked, she kept up her frivolous chatter, wondering if Richard would pick up on its simplicity. Well, half her brain was preoccupied with what was going to happen tonight, in the bedroom, so anything complicated was too difficult for the remaining half to process. Of course, she accepted that he had acted as the most amazing boyfriend ever. He had cared for her both emotionally and financially. He had even waited until she was sixteen before bringing her away for a night of passion. The only problem was that she did not want a boyfriend, however perfect he might be. But how could she deny him what all men wanted, and some simply took, either in return for cash or with threats of violence?

After a mile or so, they crossed a causeway to reach a small, low island. At its centre stood a solitary building that could easily have passed for an ancient cottage, had the rest of the land not been cluttered with gravestones. Janet wandered between these, occasionally peering down in the hope of reading an inscription, but they were all engraved in a language she did not understand. She wished her mother's life was marked with a stone monument, regardless of the language used upon it. As it was, a hundred years from now, her existence would be completely forgotten.

Sad now, Janet walked towards Richard, who was standing near the building, gazing down the Strait towards the railway bridge. To distract him, she stood in front of him.

"I'm guessing some religious guy lived there," she said. "Who else would want to be surrounded by constant reminders of death?"

"Don't let the local people hear you talking like that," he said. "This is an ancient, almost mythical place. A hermit monk lived here in the sixth century. He would have stood where I am now standing. This church was built to provide a place of worship for the pilgrims who came later."

Janet noticed how skilfully the boulders had been stacked to build the walls. A little to her left, the stonework had a narrow gap. Richard, presumably noticing her interest in this, broke into her thoughts.

"In medieval times," he said, "glass windows were far too expensive for ordinary people. Hence, windows were just small gaps with shutters to keep out night-time draughts."

This knowledge made Janet remember her gloomy living room behind the newspaper curtains, before Richard had come to rescue her. "And to keep out the Devil," she said, "because he mostly crawls into houses after dark. When I lived in Stink Alley he was always tapping my bedroom window with his tail."

She walked around the church until she came to an entrance, where she stood before a child-sized door of rough-sawn timber planks.

"I've never had to bend to get into any entrance before," she said. "It's almost like the rabbit hole in *Alice in Wonderland*."

"When this was built," said Richard, "peasants were half starved, so their survival was helped by being small."

Janet was conditioned to look upwards when talking to an adult of average height, so found the 'small peasant' concept hard to grasp. "In olden times I would have made a good peasant," she said.

"But you always had enough to eat," he replied, "and natural selection has since made everybody taller. You would have been considered a giant when this church was built."

I can never remember having enough to eat until you came into my life, she thought. It made her very ashamed that she was so reluctant to meet his sexual needs.

After leaving the island, a promenade allowed them to continue their walk in a civilised fashion. After a short distance, Richard became increasingly excited about another bridge which, Janet had to agree, did appear to be floating in the sky. He told her that in the 1820s it was by far the longest suspension bridge in the world. They climbed a steep hill and approached the bridge, then walked along a pavement bolted to its side, apparently as an afterthought. This returned them to the Welsh mainland.

"You surprised?" asked Richard.

She replied, truthfully, that it was nothing like she had been expecting and, yeah, it was okay, in a countrified sort of way. Then, thinking of all the crabs they had seen in the rock pools, she visualised the five-year-old Richard playing there. Realising he had been revealing his childhood, she added the words 'pleasant' and 'thank you' to her assessment.

After the bridge, they set off to complete the circular walk along an ordinary road. Glancing sideways, Janet realised Richard now looked rather sad.

"Back there," she said, "on the bridge, you seemed to be on a real high. I thought it was because of the hundred-foot drop to the water, but now sense it was more of an emotional thing?"

Richard looked awkward. "I told a fib earlier," he said, "about doing this walk with my parents. But only because I did not want to spoil anything by thinking about bad things."

So he would have time to explain everything before they arrived back at the car, she slowed her pace.

"Truth is," he continued, "my parents considered me to be an extreme inconvenience. A lot of it was grown-up stuff I did not understand at the time. But now I am certain my mother only had me to trap my father into marriage. The moment my umbilical cord was cut, she had no further use for me. My father tried to avoid me and, given the size of his mansion, this was quite easy to achieve. I was mostly brought up by a nanny, though sometimes the chauffeur or the housekeeper would watch over me. And by that, I mean if I ever went outside the estate's boundary wall, they watched me all the time. My father was paranoid that I might come across a working-class person. He told me they would put me in their cooking pots—"

"Knowing things want to eat you," interrupted Janet, "is the key to survival. Our brains are programmed to believe cooking-pot stories. It's a good way to stop children running off."

Richard nodded. "Later," he continued, "I was told the working classes kidnapped children and sold them to ruthless gangmasters in Australia, to build the railways."

"And to be eaten by kangaroos, presumably," she replied.

"Cannibals."

"Wrong continent."

"I had a home tutor until the age of eleven," he said. "Let's just say my early history and geography lessons were somewhat selective. Back then I knew only two things for certain: that beyond the estate wall, working-class criminals roamed wild, all waiting to kidnap me; and that my parents thought me a nuisance. Me being eaten by something would have suited them very well, because it would save them the inconvenience of attending my funeral. Anyway, when we came on holiday to this place, they went off to do grown-up things. It was the chauffeur and the nanny who took me on this walk – or, more precisely, it was the chauffeur, because he had a thing about bridges. The nanny became slightly irrational about various things along the way, mainly the mud. After it was over, she tried to get the chauffeur sacked for doing dangerous activities with children. Actually, I think she was successful, because after we returned home, I never saw him again. Anyway, I am sorry I told the fib earlier; it was only because I wanted today to be really special, with you as a friend."

"Now I know all this," said Janet, "it was a special day for me too, so thank you again for bringing me." She sensed he had not finished his story, but the car was now in sight, so they walked on in silence.

After driving away from the parking place, Richard headed towards what he told her was a pre-booked hotel.

She had been expecting a bed and breakfast, but supposed the hotel was where he had stayed as a five-year-old with his rich parents. On entering, she was astonished to discover the cost of a room was similar to a year's rent in Stink Alley. And he was proposing to use two of them – or perhaps buy them, given what the receptionist was expecting him to pay.

"One room's fine," Janet interrupted.

The receptionist raised his eyebrows. Richard pacified him by saying two rooms would be better. Janet then became rather cross about all the money he was wasting.

"It's not like I haven't seen you in your pyjamas before," she said.

"But—" said Richard.

The receptionist looked between them.

"One room," said Janet.

"Twin," said Richard.

Janet had no idea what that meant, but she had other things to worry about. Another man had appeared and stolen their luggage, which he was now carrying up an enormous grand staircase. The receptionist gave Richard a key and asked whether they would like dinner. Janet felt very much out of her depth in this situation, so decided to look and learn.

She was resigned to the fact that tonight was going to be the time she and Richard did it. This was what happened in hotel bedrooms. *Or*, she thought, *just for tonight, I could claim to be really tired after my exciting day of surprises.*

Dinner was really posh, with waiters, and men walking around in penguin suits. But thankfully, Richard had now given up wine to be teetotal like her, which meant there was one less waiter to disturb their conversation, which, strangely, was about Thomas Telford and his wrought-iron suspension bridge. No, cast iron; wrought iron was the other one. Richard was very specific about such details.

"Earlier in the day," said Janet, mostly to change the subject from bridges, "did you notice how I became a little quiet when you showed me the wonderful railway line?"

"Because when I talk about such things, it's impossible to shut me up," he said. "I know, I've been told already. Sorry."

Janet shook her head. "It's a bit more complicated than that," she said. "I have a very bad memory of a railway line near my childhood home. It's where I used to pick up the coal that had fallen from the locomotives. The best place was the start of the incline, because ascending that required the engineer to do a lot of frantic shovelling, and much of the coal obviously missed the firebox. Sometimes I could fill a shopping bag, and delight my mother when I returned home. Then, one day, a gang of boys thought it funny to throw stone chippings at me. Usually when that happened I could dodge them, but on this occasion I tripped, fell, and banged my head on the rail. The next thing I remember is the rail starting to rattle. Opening my eyes, I saw a locomotive thundering towards me. I suppose the driver thought we were playing chicken so did not want to apply the brakes at the bottom of the hill. At the time I thought I had only a second before the wheels chopped my head in half, but in reality it was probably longer. I only really know the locomotive looked very big and angry, and hissed a lot of steam. Anyway, after I managed to roll clear, I looked up to see the engine whooshing by. The driver shouted at me, but the locomotive was making too much noise for me to hear what he said. But I really believed a man was going to leap from the footplate to clip me around the ear. Well, I was only six, so had no idea of just how hard it is for a driver to stop a train or, indeed, leap from it—"

"Six?!"

"I was a lot younger than the boys, who I think went to big school. Anyway, I collected half a bag of coal…"

She stopped talking because Richard had run to the toilets. When he returned, she could see he had been crying.

"Sorry," she said. "But perhaps you now understand why I have no great affection for railway lines. Anyway, enough about me. I sense there was something you wanted to say when we were walking towards the car earlier."

Richard nodded, then gave a heavy sigh as he gazed into the candle flames which cast their flickering light onto Janet's face. "Have you ever wondered," he said eventually, "why I decided to defend Freaky Fred in class? I mean, given that he was accused of rape, I should have passed the matter to the head."

"Because you are a wonderful man who likes doing the right thing," she said. "Also, I imagine you were terrified by Priscilla, so an extremely brave man to boot."

"I hid behind my desk."

"Okay then, a very *sensible* man. But this ties in with something you mentioned on our way back to the car. You said you were homeschooled, which implies that before you became a teacher, you had little previous experience of mixing with children. And Priscilla can be terrifying when she wants to be."

"I suppose. As for homeschooling, that came to a sudden end when I was eleven and sent away to a boys-only boarding school."

"So, having no childhood social skills, you were the equivalent of Freaky Fred?"

"Sort of, but the bullying was more physical than emotional. During my first week, I was beaten up half a dozen times."

"Makes sense – so you learned how to fight back."

"I learned the benefit of getting in the first punch. By the age of fourteen, I was ranked number five in the school boxing ring, and that was sufficient to stop the bullying. Not that anyone wanted to be my friend, because I never did dares and worked hard on my studies. So, you see, I understood how Fred felt, and I admired you for protecting him."

"I also understood how Freaky Fred felt, alone and without friends. If you remember, I was called the Scraggy Prostitute."

On hearing this, Richard fell silent, and bowed his head to avoid eye contact.

"You are the first friend I have ever had," he said. "That's what made today so special."

"Likewise," said Janet.

After dinner they headed towards the stairs – the receptionist pretending not to notice, except for coughing, raising his eyebrows, and saying, "Huh!" On second thoughts, Janet decided he was *pretending to pretend not to notice.* Indeed, she was surprised he had not asked to see a marriage certificate, or at least a birth certificate to prove she was sixteen. But now it was all legal, if only by a few days. Still, she hated the idea of what was to come. It did not seem right – with other men, she had just pretended to enjoy it while waiting for it to be over. Richard, she suspected, would want something more genuine. This proved to be the case because after entering their room, he sat on the bed, and asked her to sit on the other, facing him. He then reached inside his jacket pocket to recover an envelope, which he held out for her to take.

"I was going to give you this to your sixteenth birthday," he said, "because I wanted it to be special, but things kept getting in the way—"

"I don't want money," she interrupted, now genuinely horrified.

"Think of it more as a document to confirm your adulthood," he said. "I know you reached this stage many years ago, but now it's official."

He stood up, placed the envelope on her pillow, then headed directly to the bathroom. *To make certain he is hygienically clean*, she thought crossly. *And all because his pompous ideas mean he wants all the legal paperwork to be in good order. This is going to be so horrible, I wonder if I could pretend to have a headache.* Then she opened the envelope to discover...

For some seconds her mind struggled to understand what she was seeing. An official grown-up passport! It even had her photograph on the inside page. *Oh*, she thought, *he told a fib. He had said he needed that so he could get me a replacement birth certificate. And all the time he had been planning this... situation, whatever it is.* Then she felt terribly guilty for her recent horrible thoughts. As she heard the water splashing over his naked body she decided if he came out of the shower wanting to 'do it', she would let him, without protest.

But in the event, he emerged wearing his pyjamas and headed directly to one of the single beds. "Thank you for a wonderful day," he said.

A little later, when she too came out of the shower, he was asleep.

CHAPTER SEVEN

The morning after the Menai Bridge walk, Richard led Janet down to the hotel dining room for breakfast. This was a world he understood. Janet looked at the wide variety of food displayed on the various trays. To her, it made no sense whatsoever.

"I was hoping for boiled egg and soldiers," she said.

"This is a four-star hotel," he replied.

"And that makes proper food illegal?" she asked.

Richard doubted if the hotel staff would know what 'boiled egg and soldiers' meant – unless, in their youth, they had a really naughty nanny who served forbidden foods behind her employer's back. However, he decided not to get involved in such a ridiculous argument. "What you want is off," he said.

"Off where?" she asked. "They aren't real soldiers who can run away to avoid being eaten."

To Richard's embarrassment, he instinctively rolled his eyes. A waiter, seeing this, stepped across to ask if everything was to their liking.

"Most acceptable," said Richard.

"And the lady?" asked the waiter.

Janet looked around to see who he might be talking to. There being no obvious candidate, she turned back to the waiter, a questioning look on her face. When she pointed to herself, he responded with a smile. Janet thought playing the naughty schoolgirl would be inappropriate, given the circumstances. Being considered a lady, though ridiculous, was sufficient to make her behave – even though what she really wanted was boiled egg and soldiers.

After breakfast, they packed their suitcases, then walked down to the reception desk to announce their departure. It was then Janet got the final shock of their stay: the room Richard had 'bought' did not include food! She did a quick calculation in her head. That single night had cost more than her entire living expenses for her final year in Wellington Place.

As soon as they got outside, she turned to Richard. "Right," she said, "I'm choosing what we do today. It will be a girly thing, so I don't want any arguments about it being illogical."

Richard liked the way she had become so self-confident. No more submissive postures, or accidentally calling men 'sir'. In fact, he realised, she had even won the argument over them sharing a bedroom. Not that the money worried him, because his father still paid him a substantial 'student allowance'. Theoretically, this would come to an end when he was twenty-five, though he was under no illusion his father did it to maintain control over his life, so was likely to keep the payments going. But if he ever discovered his son was spending the money on a sixteen-year-old girl from a non-aristocratic background, he would be disinherited. Janet must remain a secret. That would not be too difficult because his parents spent mid-winter in Australia, but the preceding ten weeks would require a great deal of discretion… and possibly a Plan B, like turning a wardrobe into a proper hiding place.

Richard was distracted from his thoughts when Janet said they needed to drive into Bangor to do some shopping. He had never understood females and their wardrobe, so thought it best to remain quiet. Perhaps he could wander about the High Street to see if they had any books about the railway line? Thinking this to be the best plan, on reaching the city centre, he gave Janet some money and said he would meet her back at the car park in an hour. What she planned to do later, he had no idea, but he expected it would be sensible. Perhaps her shopping trip would include buying a swimming costume and a towel, so they could go to the seaside.

Richard returned to the car before Janet, so he sat in the driving seat to read his new book about Telford's epic battle to build the A5 to Holyhead. He discovered that, before this route was completed in 1826, the only sensible way to reach Holyhead from England had been by boat. The Snowdon area was then called the Welsh Alps, and crossing them was such a major challenge all but hardened mountaineers took a long detour to go around them.

Eventually Richard was distracted from his exciting discoveries by a gentle tapping on the window. Looking up, he saw Janet standing outside with so much shopping that she had needed to buy a massive rucksack to carry it all. Spending so much money was unlike her, but he supposed it was her first holiday, so why not go a little mad? Though perhaps the rucksack was a bit extravagant: had she asked, he could have collected everything in the car and she could have avoided loading herself up like a mule! He reached behind his seat to open the rear door. This was when he noticed a second rucksack. Whatever was happening here appeared to be a bit more complicated than clothes.

"What on earth…?" he gasped.

"A tent," she said. "There is no way I am letting you waste all that money on a hotel again."

"But I've never stayed in a tent," he said.

"Neither have I. It will be fun."

"Yes, you have; at the reservoir. Remember, I took you back there to collect your possessions."

"That was just the bushes, I told you. But now I am considered a lady, so want some luxury. I have bought sleeping bags, airbeds, a torch – everything we need. But we'll have to visit a garage to get paraffin for the stove, and go to the grocery store for food – I simply did not have enough arms to carry it all. Whoops – sorry, past tense, and with you being an English teacher and everything. However, I am pleased to announce that I had the same number of arms then as I do now."

"The words I noticed most," he said, "were 'English teacher', because English teachers do not sleep in tents."

Janet then noticed his mood become more serious as he started to ask questions about her life in the bushes. She answered honestly, yet without any apparent concern. Or, at least, this is what she wanted him to believe; in truth, she did not tell him that she had sold his lovely satchel to buy food. It made her shiver to recall that the man at the second-hand shop had only given her two shillings for it. Replacing it had cost Richard… it was too awful to even think about. But at the time, selling it had saved her from starvation, and in return she was determined that for the rest of their holiday they would stay in the tent, so this sort of paid him back.

Richard was so horrified to learn about Janet's life in the bushes that he decided to try to survive one night in the tent. He watched her load up the back seat, then opened the passenger door for her.

"The assistant in the outdoor shop told me the best place to stay," she said. "Go straight ahead, and I'll tell you when to turn right."

Well, thought Richard, *'the best place' sounds a bit more positive.* He expected the campsite would have showers and a restaurant – a stove that worked on paraffin was clearly impractical unless you were in the army or something.

After stopping for paraffin and food, Richard followed all of Janet's instructions until she told him to pull into a lay-by.

"Here we are," she said.

He looked around. There was no campsite to be seen, so why had she got out of the car and hauled a rucksack onto her back?

"We are in the middle of nowhere," he said.

"Your rucksack is on the back seat," she replied.

Her response confused him. It had no obvious connection to his own entirely sensible statement. Then he realised she was pointing to a great, wild forest on the far side of the lane. Picking up a shopping bag, she walked towards this, then disappeared between two bushes. Richard remained by the car, waiting for her to return. She would be embarrassed about attempting something so insane. He tried to think of something to say which might make her feel better as she came to terms with her inevitable defeat. In the end, he came up with 'Dr Livingstone, I presume?' But Janet did not return.

Janet was sitting on a fallen tree, her feet dangling idly a few inches above the ground. While waiting for Richard to catch her up, she amused herself by watching various animals going about their daily business, apparently paying her little regard. She realised her preference for grey clothes meant animals (including people) often failed to notice her, which made life far more agreeable. This was a world she understood, so unlike the silly hotel, which did not even offer boiled egg and soldiers for breakfast.

Janet's interest in the natural world had begun while living in the bushes near the reservoir. Back then, her ability to identify different species had been very limited, so she had come to think of each animal as an individual with its own distinct personality. Anything with whiskers and a long tail, she had called Mickey, after the famous mouse. Spiders were always called Stephen. She particularly remembered a fine, hairy specimen who had made his home near the entrance to her den. The way he had constructed his web demonstrated he had a good understanding of geometry, with a particular interest in parallelograms. So he had quite a large brain, which made her wonder how he viewed her, as she sat in her den. Well, she reasoned, he must be thinking something, because he often passed a whole afternoon in idle contemplation while waiting for supper to entangle itself in his web.

Later, when she was living in Richard's house, she had purchased a book on birdwatching, then busied herself by putting up numerous nest boxes in his back garden. This aspect of her personality had impressed Richard, unlike the time she had thrown a piece of cake to a mouse scampering bravely across his lawn.

"It's from my lunch," she had said defensively.

"The neighbours," he had whispered.

"I did not realise the man who lives in the big house half a mile away was hungry," she had responded. "Whereas I am sure Mickey did not have a proper breakfast this morning."

Now, on her first ever holiday, she turned her attention to a group of rabbits hopping around the clearing without any apparent sense of purpose. She decided that, given their preference for digging simple burrows, they were less intelligent than Stephen and, because they failed to notice her, probably short-sighted. Really they needed spectacles – though how they could be balanced on their noses and hooked over their ears, she had no idea. Presently, she was distracted from her rabbit-watching by a caterpillar struggling heroically along the rough bark of the tree trunk towards her legs. She classified all of these animals as Mr Munchkins. *Poor thing*, she thought, *this tree is quite dead, and without leaf.* Gently, she picked up Mr Munchkins and took him to a nearby bush. *Dinner is served.*

How long passed before Richard came into the clearing, she could not say; only that he looked troubled about something. Awkwardly, he explained that he had never carried a rucksack before, and it had slowed him down when he had needed to crawl under low branches. She could not remember any such obstacles, but he was a foot taller than her, so she let the matter pass. It would soon be dark, and they were still only a hundred yards from the lane.

After walking a little further, Janet realised that, yet again, Richard was nowhere to be seen. *How? A man cannot just disappear!* Then she remembered the embarrassed way he spoke about 'lavatory situations' and gave a little giggle – he had obviously needed to sneak into the bushes for what he sometimes called a 'comfort break'. She hoped it was not a 'number two', because there was only so much waiting around a lady could do.

When he finally reappeared, she asked if he felt better, to which he replied, "Not really."

Oh well, she thought, *nature will get the better of you in the end.*

After this second break, she slowed her pace so Richard could keep up, which, given he had longer legs, she thought an odd arrangement. Then her mind returned to something which had happened at the beginning of the day, when he had led her to the hotel breakfast room. Because she had not known how to behave in that situation, she had descended the stairs at a slower pace than necessary. Then he had led her into a frightening world in which boiled eggs and soldiers did not exist. Well, now it was time for her to lead him, and to take great care to avoid encountering another disaster at the end of it.

Having trekked uphill for another mile or so, they entered a glade with just enough sunlight breaking through the upper branches to allow wild flowers to survive at its centre. Avoiding these, Janet dropped her rucksack onto a patch of grass nearer the trees. Perfect!

Richard thought it strange that his leader was unpacking in the middle of nowhere. However, eventually he managed to gather himself sufficiently to point out the absence of a shower.

"It might rain," she replied casually, "and if not, there's a stream over there." *Ah*, she thought, *the shower is just a euphemism for a bathroom, which is a euphemism for something else.* How many euphemisms it would take to get down to Stink Alley language, she could not imagine. But she had a tent to put up, so did not have half an hour to waste on such trivialities. She resolved the problem by taking a garden trowel and a toilet roll from her rucksack and placing them on the ground where Richard could see them. "Like I said," she concluded, "I've thought of everything."

And so it was that Richard found himself in a wild wood, with darkness fast approaching, trying to deal with things of which he had no understanding. Added to this, in their recent conversations Janet had frequently used the word 'posh', which he thought odd when combined with the word 'tent'. He was still trying to understand this strange new world of anti-logic when Janet, holding the trowel and the toilet roll, disappeared between the trees. A few minutes later she re-emerged.

"Toilet," she said, pointing behind her. "Like I said, it's a girly thing – all very posh, so no peeing in the stream because tomorrow it's going to provide us with drinking water. Happy now?"

The truthful answer to this was no, but he pretended otherwise. *I can do this*, he thought, *for one night. After all, she survived in the bushes, and so will I.*

The next disaster was the Primus stove. Janet had failed

to read the instructions, so had not bought the methylated spirit needed to prime it. But at least that made Richard laugh.

"The clue," he said, "is in the name Primus." *And*, he thought, *it means we can walk back to the car and find a hotel.* He hoped Janet would not be too embarrassed by her mistake. Then his optimism faded, because she simply took some toilet roll, splashed paraffin over it, and used it to set light to a collection of sticks. Half an hour later they were squatting around the fire drinking coffee, the remaining boiled water having been used to make soup from dry powder.

"Like I said," said Janet, "I'm no good with all this posh stuff, but I expect I'll get the hang of it in a week or so."

Richard did not like her use of the word 'week', but quickly realised she must be joking. And this was something he liked about her: the way she kept trying to make him laugh. A little later, he was surprised to discover that he quite liked her version of dinner. The soup that should have been inedible actually tasted okay when dunked with bread. As for all the claustrophobic bushes that surrounded him, he decided it was necessary to tell Janet something really embarrassing.

"Remember what I told you earlier," he said, "about my childhood?"

"A cruel childhood," she said, "without friends."

"Not really – we had a chef to cook us a proper dinner every evening."

"What, with napkins and lessons in etiquette?"

Janet realised from his expression that she had correctly described his childhood.

"Child torture," she said. "As for me, you will remember I told you about those kids throwing stones at me when I was picking up coal from the railway line. What I remember most about that day is the evening, when my mother made a point of using her marriage certificate, mixed with old newspaper, to light the fire. She said it was to signify the man who had spent our coal money down the pub was no longer part of our life. 'From now on,' she said, 'it's me and you, girl.' Then she used one of those long-handled forks to make toast before the flames. Just the two of us sitting there, munching, with my mother telling me how well I had done to collect so much coal. Now that is what I call a proper childhood tea."

Richard thought about the dinner they had eaten the night before and decided he liked this better: just sitting and gazing into the flames while eating bread and soup.

"Okay," he said presently, "now it's time for another confession. When I was around eight, we took a motoring holiday in France. Forty miles south of Paris is the ancient forest of Fontainebleau. It's like those which covered much of England in medieval times. The few roads cut through it go on for miles, with trees towering on both sides. To stop me wandering off, the new chauffeur and my nanny told me the forest was where witches lived, and that they would want me for their cooking pot. That was, if the wolves and bears didn't eat me first. I was terrified, so hid in the car. And this fear stayed with me – in fact, over the years, it grew. That stuff back there about struggling with the rucksack was rubbish. I was just terrified to enter a forest for the first time."

"With your first ever, true best friend," she said. "Had

you told me earlier, I would have got behind you to give you a push. But how are you feeling now?"

Richard looked at the surrounding bushes. "It takes time to recover from childhood trauma," he said, "but I am glad you didn't laugh at me."

"Once it was your job to protect me. Now it's my job to protect you, and I kind of like that. I will never laugh at your cruel upbringing."

Richard felt reassured, and hence his thoughts moved to the question of the tent. It seemed quite small, meaning they would have to sleep side by side. Nervously, he peeped inside. What he saw represented a gross corruption of the English language. For one thing, sleeping bags were only suitable for Egyptian mummies, who had no need to move their arms because, technically, they were dead as opposed to sleeping. Airbeds looked nothing like real beds, since they lacked both legs and springs. Then came the real panic – he had forgotten to bring his pyjamas from his luggage in the car! Embarrassed, he told her bedtime would be impossible because of this.

"You know how I hate that word," she said crossly. "It should be taken out of the dictionary. Just undress to whatever you think comfortable."

Richard was astonished to discover it was actually possible to sleep in a tent while wearing only his underpants. Indeed, the following morning he sat up in his mummy bag and gave a good stretch – at least as far as the tent canvas allowed. Then he turned his attention to Janet squatting just outside before an open fire. The smell of woodsmoke told him she had been collecting sticks again in order to make coffee. What a brilliant start to the day. He was slightly puzzled when she presented him with a tin plate. In the middle, what he assumed to be a boiled egg was held upright by three stones. To the side were a number of 'soldiers': narrow slices of toast and margarine.

"A proper breakfast," she said. "Enjoy!"

And, to his surprise, it did taste better than their breakfast at the hotel. It all made him wish his father had employed a naughty nanny who liked to amuse children.

After breakfast, Janet decided they would leave the tent where it was to create a 'base camp'. Then, with less to carry, they could go to explore the surrounding area in comfort.

To Richard's amazement, their first woodland camp lasted three days, after which, they moved further up the hillside. Not that the tent was a particularly important part of their days; more a place they used as a bed and breakfast. Eventually they found a little cafe in an idyllic village, and so frequently returned 'home' after a normal tourist adventure. The one exception was the time they boarded a ship to spend the day in Dublin. They missed their ferry back, and the night sailing saw them stranded in Holyhead, with Richard saying he was too exhausted to drive safely, let alone walk half-way up a mountain to reach their tent.

"Okay," she replied, "just for tonight we will stay at that hotel we passed, a mile out of town."

"Unless it's a five-star establishment," he protested, "their reception desk will be unattended at this hour."

"That's the one," she replied casually, "now stop moaning, and start walking."

Richard thought it odd that Janet had agreed to stay in a five-star hotel. Then he reasoned that, like himself, she was exhausted. Tonight, it seemed, he was going to be sleeping beneath a duvet, so why question Janet's thinking at all. Anyway, she was already walking away, so he hurried after her until, just beyond the outskirts, the street lights came to an end, leaving their way lit only by a slight moon. Then his leader deviated into a lay-by, the other side of which he could just make out a barn, part-filled with hay.

Janet had known Richard would have made a fuss about her sensible solution to the problem of their accommodation. Also, that by the time he reluctantly reached the barn, she would be comfortably settled on a nice soft bed of hay.

"We can't sleep here," said a voice from the darkness.

"Oh," she responded, "I can put up with all the luxury for just one night."

Richard stood in the open, nervously shuffling his feet. Walking back to the car on his own was impossible! Dragging Janet from the hay was equally impossible! The whole situation was madness!

Finding no solution to all his exclamatory thoughts, Richard looked up at the stars, their light effectively weakened by the moon. Next he turned back to Janet, and realised his statement 'we can't sleep here' was fundamentally incorrect, due to the fact she was obviously already lost within the world of dreams.

After a little while, he sat on a bale, using a higher one behind as a backrest. The freshly mown hay smelt nice, and soon he too fell asleep, more from exhaustion than comfort. Then, in the morning, he awoke to something gently stoking his face. Opening his eyes, he realised Janet was brushing his skin with a sprig of hay.

"Oh, you're such a sleepy-head," she said. "Don't get too

accustomed to all this five-star malarkey, because tonight it's back to our tent."

Richard watched Janet walk to a road-side bush, where she began to feed herself on fresh blackberries. She seemed to believe all of this was entirely normal behaviour. As he joined her for 'breakfast', he glanced back at the barn, vaguely astonished to realise he had become 'a gentleman of the road', a vagabond, who cared nothing for the laws of civilisation.

As the holiday progressed, they kept clean by going to the public baths, where Janet finally learned to swim. They also located a tennis court, where she advanced her game to a stage that she could join the club back home on her own merit, as opposed to simply being tolerated as Richard's companion.

When the last day of the holiday arrived, their camping gear was loaded into the car for the final time. Next came their last meal in their special cafe. Richard could not work out why he felt so sad. Then, as they sat at the table, he instinctively reached across to put his hands over Janet's. At least until he saw his knuckles – which had been used to commit murder. He quickly withdrew. How could he have put his dirty fingerprints onto such gentle hands? Then he realised why he was so unhappy. He might have got away with murder, but if the police ever had cause to take his fingerprints, he would spend the rest of his life in jail. For him a close emotional relationship with a woman would be impossible, and certainly one with a lady so perfect as Janet.

Janet looked at her hands from which Richard had

retreated in horror. Yes, she was disgusting. She could still smell the body fluids that had been pumped into her by dirty old men. It was everywhere: in her anus, on her hands… how could she have let Richard touch her filth? At least now she understood why he did not want sex with her, and she was glad, because the thought of doing it with him filled her with shame. By the age of fifteen, she had done it many thousands of times, and now that part of her life was over forever… Except for one thing. The coil the abortionist had fitted was still in place, stuck in her uterus with all of its filth and disease. It needed to be gone – but how? She did not know how to find the house where the woman who had fitted it lived and, in any event, she had no intention of ever going back to face that awful, dirty kitchen table. According to the abortionist, coils needed to be replaced every three years – or, in her new circumstances, removed altogether. A hospital was also out of the question – the contraceptive pill had been legalised four years earlier, but only for married women. The ways streetwalkers solved the problem were probably still illegal.

It seemed she had no choice but to tell Richard about her darkest secret. He had a private doctor – a quiet word, perhaps; something the government did not need to know about. But now she saw he was looking at his own hands in horror. She had nothing to lose by telling him what he knew already: that she was a disgusting slut. But she would not tell him today, and so spoil their perfect holiday.

CHAPTER EIGHT

There had been many times during the holiday when Richard had thought about his distant bed. He had even come up with the slightly biblical phrase '*Sleep, my child, for thou art covered by a heavenly duvet.*' So why, on returning home, did his first night pass without sleep? Only in the morning did he face the truth. He had liked listening to Janet's gentle breathing as she lay beside him in the tent. A few days into the holiday, he had not so much fallen asleep as drifted gently into happy dreams to the sounds of an angelic lullaby. But, being a logical man, he knew this made no sense whatsoever. Hence, there must be something he had overlooked; a mysterious factor that explained why six weeks of living in a tent had brought him a degree of happiness he had never previously imagined possible. What about the cold, damp nights? Or sitting in the launderette while their clothes tumbled about in a dryer? He could only conclude that he had wandered into a strange new universe in which everything was back to front, and he was permanently confused.

In addition to his own concerns, Richard noticed Janet was also having gloomy moods. But when he asked her what was wrong, she merely smiled and said everything was fine. Gradually he came to understand she too was sad because their perfect holiday was over, so did not question her further.

With the exception of his general tiredness, everything in Richard's life was remarkably well organised. He got Janet enrolled in college to do her A levels without difficulty. Also, as expected, the tennis they had played on holiday meant that, when they returned to his private club, her skill was noticed by the elite. They were even invited to play doubles against quite worthy opponents. This reflected both the improvement in Janet's game and her ability to fit in with respectable society. But deep down, Richard knew why they attracted so much attention. It was because their pairing generated curiosity. He supposed the idea of a romantic relationship with a sixteen-year-old did not generate outrage, but it certainly raised a few eyebrows. And, in truth, he liked the way men regarded him with envy for having captured such an amazing girl.

Priscilla stared out of a window at the tennis clubhouse, her mouth open wide in shock. She moved her face closer to the glass, not because it improved her vision, but to show any man who might be watching just how horrified she was. Mr Edwards was playing a game of doubles – and the Scraggy Prostitute was his partner! She then realised the true situation was even more horrendous: the couple they were playing against seemed to accept the prostitute as one of their own class! Fuming at the injustice of it, Priscilla remembered all the times she had gazed at Mr Edwards in class, using her best dreamy expression.

Whenever possible, she had brushed against him, saying how wonderful his voice sounded when he spoke about poetry. And now he was playing tennis with the whore whose profession she had told him about. She had indeed advertised Janet's services! How unfair could life be?

Then, thankfully, two men came to stand next to her – one either side; so close she believed they would eventually put comforting arms around her shoulders. The one on her left was quite hunky, and she knew the other drove a Daimler. Her look of horror had attracted them, but who should she choose? Then one of the men gave a deep sigh of longing. Priscilla responded by fluttering her eyelashes, thereby giving him permission to ask her out to dinner.

"Just look at that forehand smash," said the man to his friend. "Janet's so amazing."

"Yes," said the other, in a refined English accent. "Richard is so lucky to have captured such a lovely girl."

"I actually spoke to her over coffee last week," the first remarked.

"So you have said," replied the second, "many times."

Priscilla knew there was only one possible conclusion to this conversation. She gave one man a kick on the shins, the other a slap across the face. Then she fled to the foyer. "I hate her!" she screamed. This situation was like what had happened in the classroom, only a million times worse. Of course, she must tell the headmaster as soon as possible. But on reflection, she thought, *Tell him what?* Janet was now of legal age, and no longer Mr Edwards' pupil. And what information did she actually have – except for the fact they were playing a game of tennis together?

When Priscilla had joined the upmarket club she had

expected to meet lots of proper boys who had cars and things. Her daddy had got her in, but only sort of, because she was only allowed on court when taking lessons from a professional coach. Daddy did not understand how stupid the game of tennis was, because he was only interested in golf... Suddenly, a brilliant idea came to her. Daddy had once mentioned that he knew Mr Edwards' father because he attended the same golf club. She now hurried to a telephone to call for a taxi. She would never return to this stupid club again, for the boys were only interested in playing tennis and were, most probably, all homosexual.

Back at home, she made her way to her daddy's study, where she found him sitting at his desk. She explained that she was curious about golf, and would very much like to try it. Given his enthusiastic response, she realised that she was destined to meet Mr Edwards Senior. Then she would put the world to rights!

Richard had three problems. First, he was unable to sleep properly. Second, his feelings for Janet had become more complicated than they had been at the beginning. And third, he was a murderer, who could never become romantically involved with anyone in case he was destined to spend the rest of his life in jail. Oh! And a fourth problem: Janet was unhappy that their perfect holiday was over. Well, at least this was an easy one to sort out. The next time she looked unhappy, he told her everything was fine and promised her another holiday.

"How about we take the ferry to Africa for Christmas?" he said. "It's going to be warm there, and I'm off for two weeks."

And finally, Janet found the courage to tell him about the coil. She was astonished when he showed no revulsion on learning the reminder of her past life was still festering away inside her. Then, deciding to have no secrets from him – her protector – she told him everything, including the way she rubbed herself down with a disinfectant-soaked flannel to try to get rid of the smell of men which, she was convinced, still lingered on her flesh. His response was immediate. He went to the kitchen, collected all the disinfectant and locked it in his safe. On his return he seemed unusually cross.

"You don't need it," he said, "and I am sure it will damage your perfect skin!"

She thought this an odd thing to say, but supposed he was just trying to make her feel better, as usual.

The following day, Richard went to visit his private doctor. Initially, the man expressed professional outrage at the suggestion he might consider becoming involved with such a sordid procedure on an unmarried woman. But, after fifteen minutes of indignation, he presumably remembered the woman in question was now associated with someone with a large bank balance. He rummaged about in a desk drawer, while glancing at the wall clock. (Under practice rules, visits were always rounded up to the next quarter-hour.) As the big hand dropped to sixteen minutes, he miraculously located a small card, on which was printed a telephone number.

"This," he said, passing it across the desk, "might prove useful."

The number was for a clinic in Holland. That afternoon, Richard telephoned the operator and booked an international call to Amsterdam. This was scheduled for eight o'clock the following morning. After another sleepless night, he telephoned the school to say he was sick, then waited to be connected to Holland. At the appointed time, he was put through to a lady who clearly had English as a second language. Without any great concern, she told him to just turn up whenever it was convenient. Well, at least this temporarily solved the problem of how he was going to keep Janet a secret from his father. Going to Holland was a lot safer than hiding her in a wardrobe.

A few minutes after the telephone call, Janet hurried down the stairs, saying she would be late for college. Richard told her to stop.

"I'll grab something to eat on the way," she said. "Stop being such a fuss-pot."

"But we're leaving for Holland – within the hour," he responded.

The fact they were leaving England at all surprised her. The notion of doing so within the hour left her slightly confused. "What about college?"

Richard answered that she was so intelligent taking a week off would not affect her A level results.

A week? thought Janet. *And no mention at all of his need to go to work?*

Though Richard was trying to convey confidence, deep down he was seriously concerned about the criminal act he was about to commit. Not the medical procedure, because in Holland it was sort of legal, or at least ignored by the authorities. However, as part of the post-war recovery plan, British holidaymakers were limited to taking no more than five pounds in cash out of the country. If he was caught at customs carrying more, they might take his fingerprints, which could later be matched to the satchel. So he needed to hide fifty pounds somewhere in the car, without telling Janet. Given her reaction to the cost of the hotel, she must never know what this procedure was going to cost. Then he managed to put things into perspective. He had committed murder – compared to this, a little currency smuggling was hardly significant.

Before leaving, he pushed ten five-pound notes down the back of the rear seat. 'Oh,' he would exclaim, if the customs found it, 'how did that get there?' They would not believe his innocence, but would be unlikely to take his fingerprints?

The sailing to Holland passed without incident, which made Richard think life as a low-level criminal was rather exciting. *And tonight*, he thought, *I will sleep next to Janet, which will help emphasise the role I am playing in her life: keeping her safe from all those who want to do her harm.*

The following day they were walking along an ordinary street in Amsterdam when he noticed the nature of the shops beginning to change. Then his gaze fell on a large window in which a lady was sitting on a stool in a most unusual pose. She was wearing hardly any clothes, and waving in a manner which suggested she knew them. Then she pointed to an adjacent door. Janet returned the friendly wave as they walked by. Ten yards further along the pavement, they looked back to discover the lady in the window had already forgotten about them.

A few minutes later, they came to another shop with a lady sitting in the window. It seemed in this part of town they were a compulsory decoration. So, having become accustomed to this, Richard looked at the number above the door: it matched that on his card, so he entered and gestured for Janet to follow.

Inside, a receptionist said something neither of them understood.

"We are English," responded Richard.

The woman smiled. "Welcome country... our," she said.

"Mr Edwards," said Richard.

"Ah," said the lady. "And Mrs Edwards."

Richard liked the sound of that. The receptionist pushed a button on her counter, which brought another lady from a back room. After a brief conversation in Dutch, the second lady beckoned Janet to follow her through a side door.

"Anything... other services?" the receptionist asked Richard.

He shook his head.

"Your wife be pleased, us thinks. You good man." She smiled at him. "The money," she added.

Richard handed her three five-pound notes, then stood to one side to study his feet awkwardly. Truthfully his mind was fully occupied by the fact that, in this less conventional society, people just assumed he and Janet were an item. Or perhaps in this country, as in England, only married women were allowed to use contraception, and they were just covering the medical procedure from a legal point of view.

After Janet returned from the back room, they hurried into the street. Instinctively she stepped away from Richard. She was still disgusting inside, as proved by the lady, who had given her a bottle of penicillin "to make sure – better". Giving Richard space would keep him safe from her germs.

After escaping from the bad area, they headed to a respectable part of town, where Richard took her into a coffee shop. When settled at a table with two cups of cappuccino between them, Janet looked away to avoid his concerned gaze.

"It was fine," she said, "but I don't want to talk about it, or my past life, ever again."

He nodded. He was too busy thinking about how the lady in the shop had presumed them to be a married couple to worry about the past. His father would go berserk at the very idea. He was always going on about lower-class women who captured men for their money. Janet was not like that, but his father would never believe it. If he discovered what was really happening in his son's life, he would throw them both from the house. That was why he held the deeds: to control the situation. In truth, had Richard been offered the chance to move to a bedsit with Janet as his wife, he would have left his father's house without a second thought. But this conversation would have to wait until she was ready to hear it.

"Well," he said, "now it's your turn to help me."

She nodded.

"But you don't know what I am going to ask yet," he said. "I'm afraid you will think it silly."

"Probably, but when you took me on a hundred-mile journey to see a railway line, I neither laughed nor cried. I'm a tough cookie when I need to be."

"I want to visit the forest of Fontainebleau," he gasped. "To be cured of… you know."

"That's not silly," she said. "Until recently, forests were dangerous places. Forest phobia is a primeval survival instinct. It's why, in children's stories, it's where witches live, or maybe highwaymen with their pistols. I imagine the word 'ambush' comes from bad things hiding behind a bush. Anyway, those who carry the fear into adulthood solve the problem by simply not going into forests where carnivorous animals or deadly snakes might be encountered."

"Aargh – too much information."

"How are you with blood-sucking bats?"

"Stop!"

"Just helping you to face your fears. Because I fully intend to take you into the darkest bit of forest I can find."

Richard thought back to the chauffeur, the nanny, and all the frightening stories embedded deep within his mind. Even though he had since read about the forest of Fontainebleau, he did not quite believe the claim that the last recorded sighting of a wolf there had been in the 1860s. How did anybody know for certain? Wolves were quite likely to eat those who saw them.

Two days later, Richard found himself in a tent, isolated from the rest of the world. He knew they were hopelessly lost, because they had trekked many hours to reach this clearing and, to him, all trees looked the same. But what did Janet do? Inexplicably start talking about punctuation.

In truth, Janet was trying to distract him from their present situation by making him think about... well, something other than being lost in a forest. She thought it quite possible they would come across a footpath in a day or two, so there was no real need to panic... though she had no idea where they might be, and to her, all trees looked the same.

"Punctuation," she continued, "should be like road

markings which warn drivers about what lies ahead. So, a full stop signifies a place where you stop; a bit like those solid white lines before a crossroads. Sometimes it might be a totally unexpected plot development, like an escaped bull charging down the carriageway."

"We could be lost in this forest for weeks," responded Richard, "and all you talk about is animals with horns."

Janet pressed on regardless. "As for hyphens, those are like the dotted white lines in the middle of the road. For instance, 'plaster of Paris' is not hyphenated because it is a commonly used noun. But you remember the time I redecorated your kitchen ceiling? Well, for that, 'plaster-of-milk' *is* hyphenated because only those with fancy electric kettles would understand what the writer is trying to say."

Richard managed a weak smile. Such happy times, when Janet had first moved into his house. And now, sitting in the tent, he enjoyed listening to her analogy between punctuation and road markings. Suddenly he saw himself in a schoolroom, excitedly telling children about punctuation using Janet's brilliant metaphor. He was, after all, an English teacher.

Later, after darkness should have engulfed the tent, somehow the canvas started to glow. Janet opened the flap to investigate. "Wow!" she exclaimed.

Richard looked out upon a wonderland of magical, swirling light. Who needed a torch when swarms of dancing fireflies were displaying their stunning photo-fluorescence? Presently, he lay back on his airbed to gaze up at the glowing canvas. He wanted to be lost in this forest forever. And a little later, he fell asleep to the gentle lullaby of Janet's breathing. He was safe, his childhood fears gone.

CHAPTER NINE

The Royal St Mark's Golf Club took great pride in catering for the most refined gentlemen in the land. Ladies were reluctantly tolerated, if they knew their place and did not make a fuss about the gentlemen-only bar.

Then Priscilla arrived. She knew her brilliant understanding of the world allowed her to think about complicated stuff in ways stupid people found confusing. And so it was on her first visit to the club she was able to step sophisticatedly from the taxi and immediately place all relevant facts in their correct order. Parked near the main building were three Rolls-Royce, one Bentley and two Daimler, all owned by rich old men. (The cars were a simple observation; the rich old men, her insight.) A short distance from this hub of wealth was a lesser building surrounded by lower-range cars. This area was obviously inhabited by boys with rich parents.

Priscilla grasped these details within a few seconds. She then dismissed the taxi driver by giving him a pound note and telling him to keep the change. He replied the fare was twenty-five shillings. She said that was fine, and he could still keep the change. She ignored his further attempt to make conversation and hurried away, swinging the golf club she had taken from her daddy's study. *Silly Daddy*, she thought. *Fancy wanting to come with me so he might introduce me to the secretary. Why would I want to dictate a letter to someone I have never met?* Fortunately Daddy had developed influenza, so in the end it had been a simple matter to come without telling him.

A little later she was standing in a stupid sandpit, into which both her high heels and a golf ball kept trying to sink. When a man announced his presence with a slight cough, she turned around to discover he was carrying a huge bag of funny-shaped clubs. She thanked him, then removed one in the hope it might better send the ball where it needed to go. But the man snatched the club back. To her astonishment, he said his master wished her to leave the course after the first hole because her ten over par was causing a queue. She thought this a good score, because her daddy had told her you only had to get a twelve over par when playing all eighteen holes to become a full member. Then, wishing to distract herself from the stupidest game ever, she looked to the edge of the pit where another grumpy old man was standing. To her further amazement, he was wearing fancy dress. She decided he must have got out of bed that morning believing he was going on a grouse shoot, then forgotten Queen Victoria was no longer on the throne. In any event, his muddled mind could not tell the difference between a Scottish moor and a golf course. Given the presence of the two fuddy-duddies, both of whom she already hated, it crossed her mind to have a temper tantrum… but in a sandpit? She imagined herself becoming engulfed in a dust cloud that would mess up her hair. If she walked to the grass first, her performance would lose all spontaneity, and in any event, these things worked better in a closed space where observers could not simply run away in panic. On reflection, she therefore allowed herself to be escorted to a practice green.

"This," explained the man carrying all the clubs, "allows ladies to better develop their putting skills."

Because there was less walking involved, she agreed. In addition, from the practice green she could see both car parks, so it was easier to identify all the rich boys who would want to take her out to dinner. So long as they owned a top-of-the-range Jaguar like Mr Edwards, it would probably be fine.

It took her two more visits to identify Mr Edwards Senior. Then she overheard one of his companions call him Reginald; a name she would keep in reserve, just in case something interesting happened – which, at a golf club, she thought unlikely. But that was not important. The central purpose of her life now was to release some of the hate which boiled away inside her. Every time she saw Mr Edwards Junior in class, she felt sick. Knowing that he was doing it with the Scraggy Prostitute was more than her pride could bear. Really they both needed to die, but she would worry about that later. For now, all she needed to do was keep returning to the putting green, from where she could scan the surrounding area for Mr Edwards Senior.

She got her chance when she saw him walking towards a Rolls-Royce parked just outside the VIP clubhouse. Throwing aside her club, she raced across to reach the car at the same moment.

"Mr Edwards Senior," she gasped, gazing up to flutter her eyelashes. "What a delight."

The man looked at her, frowned, then turned towards his car as if she was of no importance.

"I know your son," she said. "He's a most brilliant teacher with all the complicated stuff he understands, and he says I am certain to get top grades in my A levels."

Mr Edwards gave a disinterested nod, then opened the car door, but she slipped into the driving seat and sat with her legs outside the vehicle. Unless he sat on her lap, this would prevent him from getting in the car.

"And his girlfriend," she said, "such a lovely girl, who is so lucky to have captured his heart."

"My son does not have a girlfriend," he responded. "Now please remove yourself; I have places to go."

"Oh, I expect he is saving her for a surprise, though of course they met when she was taking her O levels."

"If Richard had a girlfriend, I would know," he responded.

Priscilla noted Mr Edwards Junior's Christian name. Then she increased her attack. "Janet," she said, "was in our class at school, and please don't worry; I happen to know she gave up prostitution shortly after… whoops. But now she plays really good tennis, and they always seem to be at the club together."

Without a word, Mr Edwards Senior pulled her from the car, then got in and drove away at a frightening speed. He knew! He believed her! Mission accomplished!

Then Priscilla realised something rather interesting. Now Janet was history, Richard was certain to fancy her. All she had to do was stand close to him in class and wait for his legs to start trembling with passionate desire. Not that she would go with him after he had been doing it with the Scraggy Prostitute, but it would be nice to tease him. And if he took her to dinner, maybe the word 'never' could be renegotiated in the bedroom of some posh hotel.

One November evening, Janet was sitting at a small fireside table in the spacious living room of what she now considered her house. Richard sat opposite. The chessboard between them demanded all her concentration. She knew if she moved a pawn to queen six, she could use a 'fork' manoeuvre to capture a castle three moves ahead. But would Richard see it, or was his entire focus on a checkmate he could get four moves ahead? She could block that with a bishop if need be, but it would mess up her fork?

Without warning, they heard the front door crash open. Before the shock of the unexpected noise subsided, the living-room door swung back and smashed against the wall. In the doorway stood a man who looked ready to explode with rage.

"A prostitute," he yelled, "in my house?!"

Janet decided the only realistic explanation for the man's extraordinary arrival was that he had a key to the house, so was likely to be Richard's father. Quickly she stood up and did a little curtsy. "Mr Edwards," she said, "how very nice to meet you."

Mr Edwards ignored her, instead looking directly at Richard. "I want the prostitute to leave my house now," he shouted. "Before she gets her dirty hands even further inside your wallet."

Janet knew her hands were dirty, so let the wallet

falsehood pass. She walked across to stand before him. "Mr Edwards," she said, in an extreme fit of optimism, "maybe you could help me with my next move. I was thinking about pawn to queen six."

But the words did not soften his attitude. He pulled a cheque from his jacket pocket and waved it in front of her. "I have paid the prostitute to leave you alone," he said. "Forever. Never to return."

Janet took the cheque, tore it in two, and watched the pieces drift to the floor.

Mr Edwards ignored the gesture. "You do know," he shouted, looking directly at Richard, "that the prostitute is only after your money? And now she wants more! What will it cost to make the prostitute leave you alone?"

Janet thought him very ill-mannered. Then she glanced back and saw the horrified look on Richard's face. She retreated to stand by his side, forming a single unit, ready to take on the world if necessary. Also, by this simple action she ensured Mr Edwards could not avoid looking at her without also ignoring Richard.

"Your son is a really nice gentleman," she said, "and the most amazing English teacher."

"Shagging a prostitute in your class," said Mr Edwards. "I don't call that nice! Do you realise how much this is going to cost me? She just tore up a cheque for a thousand because she wants more."

So as not to dominate the situation, Janet bent her knees slightly. "It's okay," she said to Richard, "your father is only trying to protect you. But I shall win him over yet."

"There is no way I would ever shag a prostitute," said Mr Edwards.

Bet you do, thought Janet. *You seem to know an awful lot about the money aspect.*

Mr Edwards walked over to the main table, where he quickly wrote another cheque. "Two thousand," he said, "but I want lawyers involved – a signed contract stipulating that the prostitute will never see you again. All you will see of her is her fat arse as she runs away with the cash."

Janet decided to change tactics and hopefully force Mr Edwards to take a defensive position. "You should not be looking at my bottom," she said. "But, as it happens, only if Richard asks me to leave will you see it moving away."

"Never!" shouted Richard. Then, having made the initial attack, he found the strength to continue. "That is something I will never ask Janet to do," he added.

"Oh," said Mr Edwards sarcastically, "the prostitute really has you hooked like a wriggling fish sucking on a maggot. But this is my house and, if the creature has not gone by the end of the week, I shall have the bailiffs secure the doors. The prostitute can go back to working the street, and you will come to live with me, where I can keep an eye on you until I find you an acceptable lady."

"Janet is the girl I intend to marry," said Richard.

Both Janet and Mr Edwards stared at him in astonishment. Then Mr Edwards backed away.

"Get the prostitute out of your life by the end of the week," he shouted, "or you will be homeless, while she goes off to her next customer with two thousand in her handbag. Naturally, I will take that from your student allowance, so your hobby of being a teacher – a pauper, bringing shame upon the family name – will come to an end. You might even need to get yourself a proper occupation." Then he marched away, slamming the door behind him.

Janet was very impressed by Richard's understanding of dramatic theatre. The marriage proposal had been a perfect way to disorientate his father and force him to take flight. But, sadly, her too, because she could never allow Richard to become homeless, and…

Her sensible thinking came to a sudden halt. What Reginald had just said implied the 'student allowance' was so massive it made Richard's teacher's salary inconsequential. She had never given any thought to his finances, but now realised the allowance was akin to having a magic money tree in the garden. Then she remembered their holiday, when Richard had expected to spend six weeks in a hotel – until she had intervened with a tent. Effectively, his life was owned by his father. Her mind raced through the implications of this. His father obviously wanted to keep a watchful eye on his assets. Most probably, at this very moment, there was a private detective hiding in the back garden.

Realising this was a delicate matter, she sat back down at the chessboard so Richard could see her puzzled expression. "He seems to know rather a lot about us," she said. "I got the impression he expected to find me here."

But Richard did not respond. She decided he was definitely suffering from severe shock. Not wishing to alarm him any more, she decided to make light of the situation by pointing to her knight.

"You need to be looking at that," she said.

But he was looking directly at her. "I love you," he said quietly.

She stared at him. "But you can't," she said. "I'm horrible and diseased."

When he contradicted her, she turned to look into the fire. *Tell him*, she thought. *Tell him that I am now asexual, and have no interest in... becoming a wife.*

"But marriage," said Richard, as if reading her thoughts, "I can never do that, or have a girlfriend, because—"

"Rubbish. Half the girls in my class thought you were a hunk; the other half were brainless morons. You'll get a girlfriend, easy. But I've finished with all of that wife stuff. I've done the most disgusting things with old men, and now I'm full of disease. I never want to endure that torment again."

Richard shook his head and told her she had misunderstood. "I can never get into a long-term relationship," he said, "because I've killed a man and might go to prison at any moment."

"Just the one, I hope?"

"Janet, I'm serious."

"Of course, I know, 'man' singular, but I'm hardly going to let Old Farty-pants bother me. And it was quite a good right hook, if I might say so. I always wondered about that until you told me you did boxing at school. I believe you mentioned those who throw the first punch have a considerable advantage."

He stared at her without comprehension.

Janet detailed how she had seen everything by looking through a little gap in the newspaper curtains. Then she shrugged. "It's fine," she said. "Nobody came out of their house until you were well gone and, even if they caught a glimpse of you running away, there's no way they could identify you now, after eight months."

He then explained about his fingerprints on the satchel. She told him what she had done with it.

"My confession to you," she concluded, "is that I sold the satchel for two shillings. Pretty bad, huh? But it was to buy food, so I plead not guilty on a technicality. Anyway, the satchel no longer has any connection to 'the incident', so perhaps we can now be best friends until you get yourself a proper girlfriend. But when I get my A level results, I want you to be there, because you are my protector and nobody else is going to be interested in my insignificant little life." She knelt before him. "I promise you," she continued quietly, "that I will get all my A levels. And this promise has all the sincerity of the one I made to my mother on her deathbed. It can never be broken."

The night following his father's visit, Richard lay in bed, knowing sleep to be impossible. He had no doubt a private detective would be outside the house, watching. He had always been watched, from the first day he had been driven beyond the estate's boundary walls by his terrifying nanny. Even at university, his father had seemed to know what was happening in his life. And often he had questioned his sanity due to an uneasy but illogical feeling that he was not alone. It had taken Janet saying the words 'private detective' to advance his ideas into a conspiracy theory.

Suddenly, he sat bolt upright in bed. In a single moment he realised that throughout his life he had been the victim of coercive control by his father. When, as a child, he had been told about the cannibalistic working classes, it had simply been a way of keeping him isolated from the wider world. Also, his father had gone to great lengths to prevent him from making friends with women because, once romantic love enters the mind, it takes precedence over financial bribery. That accounted for his refusal to acknowledge Janet's presence in the room: to him, she was a threat. As for offering her a cheque for two thousand pounds, that was to demonstrate his power... no, his father would not have parted with a penny unless he believed there would be some financial return for himself. But however hard Richard thought, he could not see how his father might turn the expenditure into a profit.

Eventually Richard turned his mind to the private detective he was now certain had been employed to keep a frequent surveillance on his life. What he would want was a photograph of Janet with another man. But he would be disappointed, because in the coming weeks she would be attending college as usual. For himself, he would get his doctor to give him a sick note so he could miss school. His first priority was to find a bedsit, a tent being unsuited to late November. Secretly, he wanted something quite small, so he could remain close to Janet.

Suddenly, for the first time in his life, he felt the joy of freedom. He did not want this house! He did not want his father's money! He never wanted to see the evil man again. All he wanted was to hold Janet in his arms. His mind drifted back to the time at Fontainebleau when he had looked outside the tent to see all the magical fireflies dancing in a world that contained no other light. That was the moment he had become free of his childhood fears. And now he was free of his father as well.

Janet also lay awake, trying to make sense of things. She reasoned that, while they were on holiday, a detective could not have followed them without being spotted. Also, she had put a great deal of effort into making a complete break between her schooldays and becoming Richard's pretend niece. Even when he had picked her up at the reservoir, she had lay on the back seat of the car to avoid being seen with the man who was to become her protector. Effectively, she had arrived in his world as an illegal immigrant from a place unknown. Something about the private detective theory did not seem right… but she decided not to tell Richard about her doubts, just in case it upset him more.

The evening following Reginald's visit, a man tapped on the front door with a contract for Janet to sign. As far as Richard could tell, the legal enforcement was largely down to the document's heading 'Janet the prostitute and brothel-keeper'. There was also a statement that the two-thousand-pound payment was conditional on her 'refraining from any further blackmail requests regarding her sexual activity with Richard, while shagging every underage boy in her class'.

Richard was furious. Janet simply glanced at the contract, then tore it in two. Next she turned her attention to the man waiting on the doorstep.

"There is a lot of ambiguity about who is having sex with whom," she said. "There is no way a lawyer prepared this document."

The man took a step backwards. She advanced.

"Are you the private detective who spied on us?" she asked.

"No," said the man, as he quickly walked away into the night.

Janet turned to Richard. "He did not deny a private detective is watching us," she said. "A well-qualified agent would not have fallen for my simple trick. I reckon he's just some minion your father uses when the law is not on his side."

The evening after that, a different man arrived. He seemed slightly more important than the first because he waved a cheque under Janet's nose. But Richard followed her example, took the cheque and tore it in two.

"Oh," said Janet, "let's take it in turns. I bags tearing up the next one."

But Richard could not treat the matter so lightly because he knew his father would do whatever he thought necessary to remove Janet from his life.

So, the following day he drove to a respectable area where he found a bedsit but, as the word implied, it only had one bedroom. However, the landlord said he also owned a larger house that was split into four flats. On being taken to see this, Richard was horrified to discover the so-called 'kitchen' was essentially a gas stove and a sink in a corner of the living room. But it did have two bedrooms, and a private bathroom accessed from the passageway. Reluctantly, he decided it would do as a temporary arrangement, so handed over three months' rent. In return, the landlord gave him two keys: one for the flat, another for the house's front door. As he looked at them, Richard decided they represented a passport to his new life; one in which his father had no significance. All that mattered now was Janet's happiness – but he had no idea how he was going to explain to her that they no longer had a proper kitchen.

The Friday following the confrontation with Reginald, the night-time knock on the front door came as expected.

But this time it was not one of Reginald's staff standing outside; rather, a police sergeant and a constable, both of whom entered without being invited. Once in the living room, the sergeant held up a warrant for Janet's arrest on suspicion of various vice charges, and the murder of a customer outside the brothel she had kept at Number 1 Wellington Place. Richard knew the warrant must have been raised using a great deal of bluff, but his father had a lot of influence with the police, and some of the charges were certain to stick. Instinctively he knew what he must do. He pushed his way between Janet and the policemen.

"I absolutely know Janet did not commit the crime—" he began.

"No!" screamed Janet. "Shut up, Richard."

"Because I did," continued Richard. "Janet knew nothing of the murder until… well, I don't know, because she was not there. I only know that I killed the man known locally as 'Old Farty-pants.'"

Janet pushed in front of him. "He's just telling lies to protect me," she said, "because it was me who killed Old Farty-pants."

The sergeant looked at them, both confessing to the same murder. He thought this situation was not what Mr Edwards Senior had envisaged, when he'd had a quiet word with the chief constable. In fact, the 'quiet word' had come down to from the chief to him as "Just get the prostitute out of Richard's life." How difficult could that be? But now, as the sergeant looked between the two people standing before him, he decided the answer was 'impossible'.

CHAPTER TEN

The chief constable had no interest in anything that happened in Wellington Place, or any of the slums that surrounded it. To him it was a foreign country, where criminals roamed the streets like scavenging pack animals. However, he had never been there himself, so suspected the true conditions to be somewhat worse. As regards the occasional dead body found sprawled across the pavement – well, that was to be expected. Of course, if the deceased was somebody important, like a postman or a rent collector, action needed to be taken. But if the victim was just an ordinary slum resident, his junior workforce dealt with the incident in two stages: first, take the body to the mortuary; second, push the corresponding file to the back of a cabinet, where it could be forgotten.

Then, out of nowhere, Reginald Edwards had expressed a belated interest in one particular case. This confused things, because he made many generous donations to local charities supported by the Lord Mayor. So when, one evening, Reginald had turned up at the chief constable's home, he had greeted him with polite detachment. Once settled on a sofa in the drawing room, Reginald made a request for a prostitute to be kept in the cells for a night. This was a routine procedure, so the chief constable agreed with a silent nod. However, Reginald then expanded upon his idea.

"Just frighten the whore away from my gullible son," he said. "Let the bitch know it would be more profitable if she moved to another part of the kingdom – like the far north of Scotland."

The chief constable wondered how a prostitute would find it more profitable to live in a mountainous region populated mainly by deer. Then he remembered the charitable donations, so repeated the nod of consent – at least to the extent of providing a streetwalker with a night's bed and breakfast.

Reginald then explained that his private detectives had discovered one of the prostitute's customers had been murdered outside the brothel she had kept in Wellington Place.

The chief constable thought Reginald used the word 'prostitute' rather often. He clearly had a keen interest in the subject. However, he merely told Reginald that murder was not something that should be discussed in his drawing room.

Reginald had then pulled a card from his pocket, in the process sending a wad of five-pound notes rolling onto the sofa. "I expect the prostitute to be working outside your area by the end of the week," he said. "All the relevant details are on this card." Then he had walked away, apparently unaware that his pocket was considerably lighter than when he had arrived.

The chief constable had looked at the wad of money on the sofa and decided, if Reginald only wanted the prostitute to take flight, it was not a complicated matter. He had even left the means to pay for her train ticket.

And that should have been the end of the matter. However, at Police HQ a week later, the chief constable was told that, at a local police station, Richard Edwards was occupying one cell and the prostitute another – and both were confessing to the same murder. It was then the chief constable thought it wise to familiarise himself with the case. On removing the file from a cabinet, he panicked – the information it contained could have been written on a postcard. There was not a single witness statement. Then he connected the name Wellington Place to the incident now known colloquially as 'the snog-in-the-bog terror'. That incident, he remembered, had caused much amusement within the local force. The first officers on the scene had been teased mercilessly for running away, possibly exceeding the thirty-mile-an-hour speed limit on foot. However, no one had actually ventured down the entry until the sergeant in charge had arranged for a Territorial Army unit to use it as a training exercise for recovering a body from a battlefield, while under fire.

Considering all of this, the chief constable tried to rationalise the situation into which he had stumbled. He could, of course, make up some witness statements, but this was dangerous territory. Too many people knew the first officers to arrive had fled in terror. In addition, it was obvious the murder charge Reginald had directed at the prostitute was fictitious – the victim had been hit with a fist, not a handbag. The best course of action, he decided, was to return the file to the cabinet and forget about it as quickly as possible.

As the night of the arrests wore on, the duty sergeant at the local station realised they had a serious problem. Richard Edwards knew too much about Wellington Place to not be one of the prostitute's clients, and the murder had happened when the girl was fifteen and still his pupil. There was no way they could transfer the blame to her. Even if she was guilty by association, it would have been her pimp who had done the deed. Girls of her age did not have a right hook sufficiently powerful to break a man's jaw.

The following morning, the duty sergeant explained the difficulties to the chief constable, who understood immediately what needed to be done; namely, to put as much distance between himself and Reginald as possible. His new mission was to keep the girl from being charged, and so keep the case out of court, where difficult questions might be asked. How letting her go would affect Reginald's donations, the chief constable had no idea. But no amount of money was sufficient to protect his son, who had obviously committed the crime.

Meanwhile Janet, sitting in her lonely cell, had guessed how the police would come to view the situation, so was not surprised when, at eleven o'clock in the morning, she was told to leave.

"Not without Richard," she responded.

"Your client made a full written confession within the first hour of his arrest," said the sergeant, "so just accept we have provided you with bed and breakfast, free of charge, and go away – please."

Naturally, she sat on the floor. The sergeant and a constable then carried her outside to the pavement. Here they explained that, unless she wanted to be sent to the magistrates' court on a charge of prostitution, she should go back to her place of work, maybe behind the gasworks. Janet decided a charge of prostitution would not look good on her record, so thanked them politely for their advice, then walked away to find a bus shelter in which to sit and have a good think.

By midday she had concluded her best line of attack was through the local newspaper. First, she needed to kill the story that Richard had been one of her customers. To do this she needed to provide them with a better angle; a story which would sell more newspapers. So she needed to become a terribly wronged heroine, and Richard a good-looking hero protecting her from the evils of the world. However, to achieve this, she needed a better stage than an out-of-the-way bus shelter.

Setting aside her more profound thoughts, she looked outside the shelter at the cold rain splashing onto the pavement. Getting wet would not boost her mood, so she settled into the corner to continue thinking. First, she thought about her promises. The one to her mother had been fulfilled, so this could be filed at the back of her mind. Her new promise to Richard was a work in progress. Somehow she had to stay in college and finish her A levels, and maybe fund them by working at a cafe in the evenings. But in the short term, none of this mattered. Her only real concern was being free, on the outside, and so better placed to get Richard off the murder charge.

Eventually, she remembered Richard telling her that words had a greater impact, if they floated down to the audience from a high stage. *Reckon I can manage that*, she thought. After all, she had once captured the attention of a classroom even as her co-star Priscilla threw a tantrum. And that was before Richard had devoted much of his free time to coaching her on the spoken and written word.

Having promoted herself to the role of actress, she turned her thoughts to Reginald. She decided he would be expecting her to start working the streets again, which would allow the private detectives (who she had seen trailing her from the police station) to get photographs which could be taken to Richard in his cell. In Reginald's warped mind, Richard would then change his story. *In his dreams!* Janet knew that, even from jail, Richard would do whatever it took to keep her safe. If this meant going to the gallows, he would do it. But she would do the same for him – though, having been aged fifteen when the crime was committed, her punishment for murder would be somewhat less.

After taking a moment to compose herself, she hurried across the street to where a man had been pretending to look in a shop window for the past half-hour. She tapped him on the shoulder.

"No point in getting wet," she said. "Please share my bus shelter; you can watch me just as well from there."

"I was just window shopping," he responded.

"Yeah, right – and my dad's Donald Duck," said Janet. "We both know you followed me from the police station. Maybe your friend behind the pillar box could get us all a cup of coffee from the cafe, then we can all sit in the bus shelter together, at least until the rain stops."

The man tried to escape, but Janet stood before him and spoke more firmly.

"I imagine Reginald has locked up the house with everything I own inside," she said. "So I am homeless, and therefore need to sit in a bus shelter. Given that I am unlikely to run off anywhere in a hurry, there is no point in you getting wet while pretending not to watch me. Get yourself in the dry, and I will go and speak to your friend."

It took her a total of half an hour to make the men see the sense of not standing in the rain. Once they were all settled in the bus shelter, with coffee and toasted cheese sandwiches, she began to ask them questions. Then one of the detectives obviously decided to change sides. At first he merely expressed concern that she was wearing flimsy clothes and was likely to die of exposure during her first night of homelessness. Then, most unprofessionally, he said his name was Nick, and gave her his overcoat. Finally he asked how he could assist her.

"Well," she said, "I know how to get Richard out of jail, but I'll need some serious help to do it."

"Or you could just do what Reginald wants," interjected the other detective.

"Your name is…?" asked Janet.

The detective looked nervously around the shelter. "I am a private detective," he said eventually. "I do not have a name."

"Bet you do really."

"Peter," interrupted Nick.

"Well, Peter, my friend," said Janet, "you were saying…?"

"Reginald always gets what he wants in the end," said Peter. "So how about posing for a photograph with a man, just to get Richard to denounce you? I've a cheque for five hundred pounds in the car. Do the photo and, after going down the pub, you'll be free to stay somewhere warm tonight."

"I'm teetotal," said Janet, "like Richard. Now, I am going to tell you what is *actually* going to happen in the real world. You are going to take me to see Reginald. His money stinks, but I need quite a lot of it to keep Richard safe."

The detectives did not seem very impressed with her idea, but eventually Peter went to a telephone box on the corner. He returned to say that Reginald had no interest in hearing anything she had to say.

"Ask him," she responded, "how he would like the newspaper headline 'Girl found dead in bus shelter, after local millionaire locks her out of her house.'"

The detectives looked at each other nervously; then Peter ran back to the telephone box.

Janet turned to Nick. "I know Richard a lot better than his father does," she said. "The photograph Reginald wants would not work. Richard would never abandon me. The only thing that will make him withdraw his confession is if he thinks he can protect me better, if he is free from prison. But this needs fancy lawyers, barristers, and brilliant private detectives such as yourselves, all working together as a team."

When Peter returned from the telephone box he looked rather shaken. He explained Reginald was quite happy to let Janet die of exposure in the bus shelter, because then his son would have nothing to lose by withdrawing his confession. "And once you are dead," added Peter, "the lawyers could reasonably plant the murder on you."

"The weakness in that plan," she said, "is that after Richard is released, the first thing he will do is kill his father. So he'll head straight back to prison anyway – square one."

When the rain stopped, Janet explained to the detectives that a bus shelter made a rubbish stage. She began walking, the detectives remaining a professional distance behind. On coming to a high garden wall, she pulled herself up to look over the top. On the other side a well maintained lawn led to a respectable three-storey house. "Ideal," she said. With the help of the detectives, she ascended the wall to stand on top of it. Next she removed Nick's overcoat and handed it back down to him. "If I die," she said, "and land in the garden, I will have no need of a shroud to hide my lonely corpse. Anyway, now the stage is set, would you please telephone the newspaper? I want Reginald to see my picture on the front page tomorrow morning."

Half an hour later, a journalist arrived to see a small crowd had gathered to watch a girl standing on a garden wall. Two men, who he knew to be private detectives, acted as ushers to prevent the audience spilling into the road. The editor's planned headline of 'Prostitute found dead on wall' faded from the journalist's mind. He scanned the audience to assess their mood – which was difficult, because some looked serious, others confused, and two little boys were rudely poking out their tongues at the girl. All of this was to be expected because the girl was giving the most amazing rendition of Wordsworth's 'Daffodil' poem he had ever witnessed. She was, metaphorically speaking, floating lonely as a cloud on high, while waving her arms about in a way that looked most dangerous, given her narrow stage. Then, after completing her chosen extract from the poem, she manoeuvred herself to sit sideways on the wall, with her legs stretched out, hidden from the boys watching from below. They still had their tongues out, but it was clear she was now addressing them directly, because she was reciting a new poem in a bouncy, childish voice:

I am a mermaid, and half of me
Belongs quite firmly in the sea.
Then again, on the other hand,
The rest of me belongs on land.
I'm even called a little odd;
Quite an insult from a cod.

The boys giggled, and the rest of the audience clapped their hands in delight. The journalist took advantage of the 'intermission' to approach the wall and announce the purpose of his visit. He then gazed at her in admiration.

"How on earth did you learn to recite poetry like that?" he asked. You really brought it to life, and Wordsworth has been dead for two hundred years. I expect you learnt your trade at RADA."

Janet gave a casual shrug. "Back in junior school," she said, "I had the most dotty headmistress ever. She was often to be seen floating around the playground, flapping her arms, while pretending to be a butterfly or something. It was just impossible to ignore her so, following her example, I simply lost myself in cloud-cuckoo land. And, of course, doing the performance on top of a wall gave the impression I might fall off and die at any moment, so it held the additional dramatic tension of a Dylan Thomas poem. Now, may I borrow your shorthand notebook and pencil? If so, I can write you an essay on how an innocent little 'butterfly', such as myself, was made homeless by an overweight, ruthless multi-millionaire."

The journalist handed up the tools of his trade. Of course he would have to rewrite whatever she put down, but it might be a good place to start, given the inquisitive audience seemed to be on her side.

"So," said the girl, "I'm guessing a photograph of me sitting on this wall will take up half the space; will a story in a thousand words be okay for the rest?"

"That's a major feature," he responded.

"A thousand it is, then," she said.

While waiting for her to scribble her notes, the journalist questioned the audience to see what they made of the show. Everyone took the girl's side, so the story Reginald Edwards wanted was obviously not going to happen. Then he spoke to one of the private detectives, who gave him a quote strictly off the record.

"Sod Reginald," said Nick. "The pompous arsehole might pay my wages, but Janet treats me with respect. And the best way to infuriate the daft old fart is to refer to him as a millionaire as opposed to a multi-millionaire. Even with the best lawyers, this gets around the libel laws, I think."

After some more general gossip, the journalist returned to the wall, from where Janet handed down the notepad. As he read the four pages of neatly written text, his mouth began to gape. After he finished reading, he looked up at her, as if in a dream. "This is better than anything I could have written," he said, "but there is nothing about how much you hate Mr Edwards Senior."

"My sole purpose," she announced to the dwindling

audience, "is to keep Richard safe. My hating his father will make no difference to that outcome. The main narrative asks the curious question of why a father would want to keep his son locked up to prevent him from seeing me? For I am merely a poor girl sitting on a garden wall in a bid to win his freedom. Ah! But to know everything, those gathered here today will have to buy your newspaper tomorrow!"

"You need to add the adjective 'angelic' before your name," the journalist said, "but I will attend to that myself. And tomorrow you are sure to occupy the front page. A photographer will be here shortly, so don't go anywhere."

At eight o'clock in the evening, after the fuss had died down, the man who owned the wall on which Janet was sitting stopped being rather cross about it. An hour later, his housekeeper brought her a hot meal. Then the man came out to say that, because Janet was shivering so much, he wanted to invite her to sleep in his spare room.

She thanked him, but said that would mean her two private detective friends would have to wait outside, which they might find an unpleasant experience. Then she looked at Nick. "Perhaps," she said, "you have a sofa? Then we can see what is to be done in the morning, without either of us dying of cold." *And possibly*, she thought, *I have resolved the private detective issue.* Then, without any apparent concern, she swivelled off the wall and looked at Nick. "Guess it's my turn to follow you," she said. "And don't worry, I'll stay a discreet distance behind."

Nick's house proved to be quite small, but cosy, with a nice fire in the hearth. His sister, who also lived there, made a great fuss of Janet, providing her with sandwiches and drinking chocolate. After Janet had been fed and watered, she turned to Nick.

"Those who live in Stink Alley," she said, "don't tell coppers nothing – their expression, not mine. To them, 'grassing' is akin to Devil worship. That is how I know the police have no evidence against Richard – other than his confession, made under duress. We have to make him withdraw it, which will only happen if we reverse what is required to protect me. To do this we need a brilliant private detective, just to see if there is some technicality which might help. Truth is, the fuzz care little about what happens in Stink Alley, so they might have missed something. In the meantime, I need a good night's sleep before I go to live in the bushes as a defenceless heroine. If Richard thinks I might come to harm, he will fight like hell to get himself out of jail in order to protect me."

Reginald sat at the breakfast table, waiting for his butler to arrive with a freshly ironed local newspaper. He knew the story about a prostitute sitting on a wall, flaunting her tits, would fascinate working-class men, or at least the few who could read. But on this occasion only, he might also find it rather amusing.

"My Lord," said his butler, as he placed the newspaper on the table. (Reginald insisted that his household staff used his 'correct' title at all times.)

Reginald nodded to the butler, which gave him permission to leave.

He could not say how much time passed before he managed to refocus his eyes on the newspaper – only that, when he recovered from the shock, the remainder of his breakfast had gone cold. How stupid was it possible for a local newspaper owner to be? He had even been sent all the relevant details. Reginald's own proposed headline, 'Prostitute gets evil claws into gentleman's bank account', was clearly rational. How it had become 'Angelic college girl faces death on wall after local millionaire locks her out of house', he had no idea. Then he exploded with rage. He was an international multi-millionaire, many times over! To miss out the 'multi' was an insult to his manhood. And the article failed to use the word 'prostitute' once – presumably because the editor found it too difficult to spell! Clearly the newspaper owner had baboons for parents, but this was hardly an excuse for allowing such a badly written story to dominate the front page. Within five minutes of throwing the newspaper into the fire, Reginald understood there was only one course of action he could take. He telephoned his stockbroker with instructions to buy the newspaper company.

After spending the night at Nick's house, Janet had walked to the reservoir, where she had made herself a suitable 'home' beneath three broadleaf bushes. A charity had come to her aid with outdoor clothes and a sleeping bag. She had rejected their offer of a tent because it would undermine her vulnerable status. And now she had a good team around her – consisting of two private detectives, a journalist, and a man from social services, who kept coming to the bushes, begging her to take emergency council accommodation – it seemed freeing Richard was just a formality. But what she really needed was for him to become aware of her situation, so he would fight for his freedom. However, in police custody and surrounded by lawyers, access to anyone of 'her kind' was denied.

On her third day in the bushes, a mist was condensing on the leaves above her, causing the odd spot of rain to drip down onto her head. In the hope of seeing an improvement in the weather, she looked out into the main clearing and, to her surprise, saw Freaky Fred peering nervously back at her. Once he had asked her to go tree-climbing, and perhaps now, in this setting, he sensed his moment had come. Still, he looked a bit less weird now, if only because he was wearing long trousers, which made it impossible to know if he was wearing odd socks. *Well*, she thought, *that will never do.* She reached across to lift the turn-ups of his trousers. Fred's face registered panic, followed by a shy, if confused, smile.

"Do not be alarmed," she said. "I've just got a thing about nothing being impossible. As to what socks you might be wearing, it will be our little secret."

A few seconds later, Leonie, the girl who had secretly liked Fred, came to stand by his side. For want of anything better to say, Janet commented it was nice of them to visit. Fred then entered her shelter to squat on the ground.

"Log," said Leonie.

Fred gave the impression he did not understand why she wanted him to sit on a log; only that it was something he needed to do. Leonie then joined them and, after sitting by Fred's side, handed Janet a bag of chips.

Janet responded by putting an old baking tray over her campfire to boil water for coffee. Then, while eating her chips, she put three spoonfuls of coffee powder into empty baked bean tins.

"It was for the press photo," she said, "to reflect the image of destitution they wanted to generate reader sympathy. Also, I only managed to find an old baking tray lying around – saucepans are harder to come by."

After she had eaten, she made the coffee, telling her visitors to be careful of any jagged edges on the cans which might cut their lips. Fred seemed to understand this, while Leonie looked at her drink with some confusion. Then she shrugged and took a careful sip.

"It's okay," she said, surprised.

"It's the ambience," replied Janet, "for the benefit of the newspapers. You don't want to be doing this in posh hotels."

"You – in a posh hotel?" questioned Leonie.

"Well, me and Richard, yes."

"Richard… sir?!" exclaimed Leonie. "So it *is* true: you two really are an item… and staying in hotels too. Wait till I tell the others; they are going to be so jealous."

Janet, feeling quite mischievous, let the misunderstanding pass. "And you two?" she asked. "Are you an item these days?"

"Oh, he's almost normal now," responded Leonie, "but I still have some work to do before I can let him meet my parents. And it's top secret from the girls at school. I mean, how can I officially go out with someone called Freaky Fred? Absolutely everybody would laugh at me."

"He doesn't," said Janet.

"Doesn't what?" asked Leonie.

Janet focused on Fred. "I think you should tell your secret girlfriend your secret name," she said.

He shook his head.

"But you like her lots," said Janet, "so I think the time has come to formally become... well, you can't put 'Fred' on your marriage certificate."

"Hold on!" screamed Leonie. "I haven't even kissed him yet."

"But you will," said Janet. "I can see the desire in your eyes. Now off you go to somewhere private – but, Fred, don't try to teach her to climb trees unless you want a punch on the nose."

Leonie went a little red. "Us being an item," she said, "is not why we are here."

Fred raised his hand, quite forgetting that he was in a den with a low ceiling of greenery. He therefore released a shower of raindrops that had accumulated on the leaves. It was obvious his intention had been to protest about the delay in him and Leonie going somewhere private, but, in the event, he only succeeded in getting a little damp. Leonie used her hands to brush away the water that had collected in her hair. She then did the same for Fred. Janet thought this apparently casual contact was a good sign that Fred would soon get what would presumably be his first kiss.

"We are here," said Leonie, "because we thought you should know Priscilla is telling everyone that Mr Edwards once tried it on with her. Apparently, it was when she was at a posh tennis club and he saw her in the restaurant. Of course, she turned him down, because she was only fourteen at the time."

Janet nodded. This explained why Reginald had employed private detectives to watch the house. Priscilla attending the tennis club also explained his knowledge of Janet's history. She decided to keep this realisation to herself, because it might upset Richard, so she just told Leonie that because Richard would never be able to work in a school again, Priscilla's lies were irrelevant.

"Tell you what," said Leonie enthusiastically, "I'll get a gang of us to parade outside the police station with 'Free Mr Edwards' placards. It will be a hoot – and take Priscilla down a peg or two. Saying my Fred tried to rape her in the stock cupboard, indeed!"

Janet was quite happy with that idea: a load of teenage girls having fun outside the police station was the last thing the authorities needed. The situation was now so messy the police would no longer be asking whether they should drop the case, but how quickly they could do so.

After saying goodbye to Fred and Leonie, Janet sat daydreaming about Richard. Then the bushes parted again, and Nick came to visit. Had she known she would be this popular, she would have provided some proper chairs. But Nick seemed quite happy to sit on a log while he gave her his latest report. He told her the murder had brought Wellington Place to the attention of some very embarrassed council officials. Within a week, all of its residents had been given priority accommodation on a new estate built on an old aerodrome somewhere in the countryside. The entrance to Wellington Place was now boarded up and condemned as unsafe. Demolition would begin in January.

"But," he continued, "we have ways of finding people. To the former residents of Wellington Place, you are something of a heroine. So I got them to talk. Apparently, one of them urinated in the murder victim's mouth as he lay on the ground, dead... or maybe not. Who can say?"

"I don't understand why that is relevant," said Janet.

"Well," said Nick, "consider somebody who dives into the shallow end of a swimming pool and cracks their head open on the bottom. Do they die from concussion or from drowning?"

"Surely that is decided by a post-mortem?"

"Exactly. But all the police wanted was to get out of Stink Alley as quickly as possible. There was no post-mortem. In fact, I believe the urine was not even mentioned in their statements. Who cares about a dead body in such a place? Certainly not polite people who pay their rates."

"So," said Janet, "Farty-pants might have died either by the hand of an unknown assailant, or from choking on his wife's urine?"

"And the coppers at the scene forgot to mention it. Take it from me: they will want this case returned to the filing cabinet as fast as possible. Son of a local multi-millionaire, girl living in the bushes, wife urinating in her husband's mouth – how messy is it possible for a case to be?"

"And thirty teenage girls rampaging outside the police station, chanting, 'Free Mr Edwards,'" interrupted Janet. "That's both messy and noisy."

The chief constable was enjoying a breakfast of toast, while half-reading the local newspaper – something about a swarm of hysterical teenage girls, all screaming and waving their arms. He had seen such a thing at an airport once, when some pop group had arrived from America. It was obviously a hormonal thing, and quite terrifying.

When he realised this dysfunction was happening outside one of his police stations, his smile vanished. Then, feeling quite grumpy, he was distracted by the telephone ringing in the hallway.

"I know," said a dark, menacing voice on the other end of the line. "Wellington Place, your Waterloo…"

Then the line went dead. And, for the first time in many years, the chief constable had to clench his pelvic muscles to avoid wetting himself.

Four days after Nick's visit, Janet looked out of her den to see Richard standing in the clearing.

"I have come to take you home – again," he said. "A little flat this time. My father can keep his dirty money. I don't know what I will do, but whatever it is, so long as I never have to see his ugly face again, I will be quite happy."

CHAPTER ELEVEN

Reginald had no significant understanding of anything that might be happening beyond the high walls of his estate. Was his idiotic son still in jail? Why had the chief constable vanished from the civilised world? How many people had written to the local newspaper to complain about the declining standards of journalism?

For want of anything better to do, he telephoned his stockbroker to enquire why his purchase of the newspaper was taking so long. Unusually for one in such a stuffy profession, the broker told him a joke – though not a very good one – about the owner refusing to sell. Out of politeness, Reginald laughed. He then explained the proprietor had baboons for parents, so could best be tempted with bananas.

Reginald knew himself to be exceptionally clever at calculating how much a company might be worth from just a few scraps of information. In the case of the newspaper this included such things as the circulation, and the receipts from advertising revenue. Using his wisdom, he came up with a value of around half a million. Later, he realised newsagents took some profit from the cover price, so all the money did not all go to the publishers… but he had no intention of messing around with trivial details while such a hideous newspaper was corrupting the minds of the working classes.

"Double the offer," he told his stockbroker. "Just see to it."

Reginald knew himself to be the richest man in the county. He took great care to display this, even remembering to change his Rolls-Royce every two years to keep an up-to-date number plate. The Lord Mayor, in his old, clapped-out model provided by the council, was just a pauper, and a rather stupid one at that. Given all this, Reginald understood his inability to buy a minor newspaper to be a form of impotence – which he found most embarrassing. So, when his offer was declined, he doubled it yet again. How could even the offspring of baboons refuse? Then, impatient with all the haggling, he went to see the owner, to explain that four bananas were better than one. But the proprietor got two burly office staff to escort him from the building. Reginald was furious, but accepted he had no choice but to increase his offer again… and again… and again. When it reached four million, the proprietor gave way to the inevitable. Only after everything had been agreed did Reginald see his situation differently. In a fit of moral outrage, he had just paid eight bananas for something worth only one.

A few days after the deal was completed, Reginald received a photograph from the newspaper's previous owner who, it seemed, had moved to California. The photograph depicted an open-air swimming pool beside a sordid concrete ranch. The Cadillac parked to the side looked very cheap, though Reginald had to admit it was the sort of thing an aspirational middle-aged man might wish to own. On the back of the photograph was a simple message: 'It never rains!'

The first thing Reginald intended to do on acquiring the newspaper was to sack the journalist who had been unable to write a sensible story about the prostitute.

"Whether the story is sensible or not," the journalist replied, "is of no importance. The only question is, does it sell more papers and so increase advertising rates?"

Reginald did not like those who stood up to him but, on this occasion, had to concede the journalist had a point. So, rather than sacking him, he agreed a fifty per cent pay rise – on the understanding any stories concerning himself only went to press if they were positive ones. Also, in future, he was always to be referred to by his correct name of Lord Reginald.

The reporter scratched his chin, then gave a serious nod. "Lord Reginald," he said, with a slight bow, "it will be a pleasure to work for you. All I humbly request is a seventy-five per cent pay rise, to be confirmed in a written contract, and guaranteed to run for a period of three years."

And Reginald knew he had won... for three years, even though it had been rather expensive. He had liked less discovering that the newspaper office building had a leaky roof, so when it rained, machinery competed for floor space with buckets. Also, in order to purchase the newspaper, he had needed to take out a loan against his most profitable shares. But he had been dealing with high finance since his father had given him ten million pounds on his eighteenth birthday – in order to avoid death duties – so he was accustomed to such things. However, his father had then messed everything up by dying two years later. This inconsiderate timing had meant death duties were applied retrospectively. If only he had lived another five years, the inheritance would have been a tax-free gift, and Reginald could have avoided the inconvenience of taking out a loan to pay the duties needed to keep the working classes in their lives of idleness. Compared to this, the loan for buying the newspaper had been a trivial matter, because Reginald knew how to play the stock market. Hence the new Rolls every two years, and no cheap American Cadillacs.

The journalist, meanwhile, did what all journalists are prone to do. He checked things. There was no official record of his new boss ever being made a lord. The journalist shrugged. He was on a much higher salary than any other man doing a similar job, so 'Lord Reginald' was fine by him.

A year after buying the newspaper, Lord Reginald's title was known to all the members of the golf club. This knowledge was reinforced by his six-week-old Rolls-Royce parked prominently outside the VIP lounge. The combination of the car and his title (the latter mentioned frequently in the local newspaper) brought him much attention. Possibly it was this distraction which caused him to walk from the eighteenth hole feeling rather annoyed about a three-over-par round. He headed towards the lounge, thinking only of sitting in an armchair with a waiter delivering a tumbler of fine malt whisky as the need arose. However, before he reached the clubhouse, a stupid female stepped in front of him.

"Oh, Mr Edwards," she squeaked, "how nice to see you again."

"Lord Reginald," he replied crossly, then stepped around the displeasing creature and hurried on his way.

After drowning his sorrows with numerous whiskies, he weaved towards his car and found the same stupid female standing by the driver's door. But this time, she seemed a little out of focus.

"I think it was terrible," she said, "the way that newspaper tried to make the prostitute look like an angel."

"What?"

"The scraggy tramp who destroyed your son."

Reginald could not argue with such a sensible statement. Now, he did not even know where his son was living – nor did he care. When the stupid boy got fed up of living in the gutter, he was certain to come banging on the gates of his mansion. And if he dumped the prostitute, he might even allow him to enter.

"You know," said the girl, "the prostitute was from Stink Alley."

"The journalist did not have the mental capacity to spell 'prostitute,'" Reginald said. "The article was lies, all of it."

"No, Stink Alley was where she lived, until she hooked herself onto your son's wallet."

Reginald realised the girl was actually talking a lot of sense. Perhaps she would even be able to explain what had caused his son's insanity. Obviously, it was something to do with tits, but the photograph of the prostitute sitting on a garden wall depicted her as short, skinny and flat-chested.

How such a trivial creature could have prompted Richard to have a complete nervous breakdown, he had no idea.

To extinguish the painful memory, Reginald looked at the girl standing before him. Though still rather fuzzy, he thought she might pass as attractive. "You were in my son's class?" he asked.

"Yes. He was ever so... such..." Priscilla realised the fumes on Reginald's breath were starting to affect her sensibilities. Not only her ability to use words, but also her plan of getting in the car with him so he might take her to dinner. Now she reconsidered her ambitions – he would surely need both sides of the road to get anywhere. However, being in a car crash in a Rolls-Royce driven by a real lord would look ever so good in the newspapers. Definitely front-page material! She suppressed a scream of indignation. Scraggy Janet had been on the front page for two consecutive days. Herself – not once! And she knew her terrible O level results had all been the fault of Mr Edwards. How could she concentrate on what some guy was doing in 1066, while her mind was permanently stressed by Mr Edwards' bedroom activities with Janet? Her daddy had needed to make a thousand-pound donation to the school's general fund, before they would accept her as an A level student – and now that was going wrong as well. So, she decided if her life was to include an unfair car crash, she wanted it to be in a Rolls-Royce.

Reginald stared at the girl, who seemed to be having deep thoughts; hopefully about how horrible his son's prostitute was. Perhaps if he took her to dinner, he would come to understand how his son had fallen prey to a girl in his class. Of course, the girl now stopping him from getting in his car was only after his money – it was a standard feature of female behaviour. But he was hungry, and the slightly blurred view down her low-cut blouse was rather pleasant. He stared at her cleavage for some time, then told her to get in the car.

Janet thought the flat Richard had found was much nicer than their previous house, with all its unnecessary rooms and gadgets. To one side of their new living area was a small kitchen – at least, if you pulled the only table across to act as a work surface. Ideal for two people! She missed the open fire though, because for heating the flat only had a portable fan heater to plug into an electrical socket.

Initially, Richard had genuinely believed the flat to be a temporary solution to their housing problem. Having a sink and a gas stove in the living room was, for him, clearly too basic for a civilised existence. In the first week he kept apologising to Janet for it. She had responded that, because he was no longer accepting his father's money, it was a great step up in the world. He had tried explaining that he had savings which could improve things—

"And no job," she had interrupted. "Honestly, this is fine, and compared to the bushes, it is a mansion."

Deep down, Richard knew Janet was right. It was just taking him time to adjust to a more basic existence without an allowance, a free house, or a teacher's salary. For their first month in the flat, he became a house husband – or should that be house parent? Anyway, the central purpose of his life was to provide Janet with a secure home so she could concentrate on her college work. In addition, he needed to learn how to live like an ordinary person. He stopped going to the private tennis club, instead taking Janet to the municipal courts which, he discovered, were governed more by a spirit of relaxed fun than a constant need to display wealth and possessions.

What he found the hardest to understand was the different way of shopping for food. Before, he might have visited a grocer, a butcher or a baker where, on request, an assistant would take things down for him from shelves behind the counter. Janet took him to a new sort of place called a supermarket, where you loaded a trolley yourself! During their first visit, she announced that he was unsafe to drive a shopping trolley. She then occupied herself by taking out items to replace them with cheaper brands. When she replaced the butter with margarine, he put his foot down. She was equally firm, pointing out that margarine was what posh people had and, if he was not careful, she would replace it with a block of lard.

"But—" he protested.

She tapped him gently on the head with a half-yard packet of spaghetti. "We no longer have one of your fancy refrigerator machines," she said. "Lard will keep better in warm weather, as will margarine." Then she looked at the spaghetti. "Don't suppose I can put this back on the shelf," she added, "so you'll need to get used to spaghetti on toast for a little while."

Richard was struggling to understand what was happening with their food – that is to say, trying to figure out the difference between margarine and lard, while being attacked with spaghetti. Janet, meanwhile, was staring at her hands, which she knew to be contaminated by the filth of maybe a thousand 'hand-relief jobs'. How she had come to be sharing a flat with such a perfect man, she had no idea, but she must learn to hide her gestures of affection from him.

The next time they went to the supermarket, Janet clipped an L-plate to the front of the trolley. This made everyone laugh, as she told all within earshot that Richard had only just started driving such a thing. Embarrassed, he hurried away to grab a packet of butter from a chiller cabinet. On his return he told her, and anybody else who might be listening, that they needed this.

"No, we don't," she replied. "The correct word is 'want', which is totally different to 'need'. We *need* bread and milk because they keep us alive, but what you keep loading into the trolley is merely something you *want* for frivolous reasons – now put it back immediately."

Then Richard heard a voice – very quiet, and slightly nervous, but definitely female. "If he were single," it said, "I would load him into my trolley and take him home, butter or no butter – oops, do you think he heard?"

Richard suddenly found himself surrounded by a warm glow of magic light. An observer had assumed he and Janet were a married couple! In response, he felt like he had grown six inches in height. Supermarkets, he realised, were wonderful places – butter or no butter!

When they got home, he began a friendly argument with Janet about the want-versus-need issue. To argue his case, he cited a visit to the launderette, which replaced the labour that, for many centuries, had been done in tubs at home.

"So," he said, "I accept we do not *need* the launderette, but neither is it a place I *want* to go. So how do I tell you I am going to the launderette?"

Janet thought for a moment. "You have just answered that question," she said.

At first he did not understand. It took him a few minutes to realise she was an absolute genius when it came to manipulating the English language. The next time the dirty laundry basket was full, he carried it towards the door, shouting, "I am just going to the launderette." This established an intermediate category between 'need' and 'want'. She gave him such a lovely smile that he *wanted* to give her a tremendous hug. But this was an incorrect use of language. He *needed* to hug her and never let her go.

On their fifth visit to the supermarket, Janet announced that he was now safe to be left in charge of the trolley – which made the cashier laugh. (Though probably not the store manager, who preferred customers to think 'need' and 'want' were exactly the same thing.)

Richard knew he had a serious problem: the more he loved Janet, the more he wanted to hold her; yet also to protect her from situations she would find distressing. It was a vicious circle of increasing love and, to use one of her expressions, it was 'doing his head in'. And so, when she was busy taking her A levels, he spent some free time trying to find books about the psychology of sexuality.

There was, he discovered, an almost universal belief that any intimate contact between a man and a woman should only take place in a legal marriage bed. This view, he considered, was unduly influenced by ancient professors who spent their days writing obscure academic papers. Had they been sharing a flat with Janet, they would know such self-control was impossible… except for the fact love inspires overwhelming moral strength. This realisation sent his mind retreating ever further into an isolated world of love and restraint. Of course he and Janet still got together sometimes to play chess or tennis, but mostly she spent her time studying. It seemed they were growing apart, but he pretended otherwise.

After three months of Janet's careful tuition, Richard thought he had got the hang of living in a rented flat which lacked a magic money tree in the garden. So he sat down to consider his cash flow. At his current rate of expenditure, his savings would be gone after two years. The notion of their subsequent deaths from starvation horrified him. So he sold his Jaguar and bought an old Austin 7. Hence, while most men dreamed of owning a car that might do 120 miles per hour along a motorway, Richard's new vehicle was limited to around ten miles per hour up a hill. Even then, he frequently had to stop because the engine was overheating.

Then one day, he and Janet were parked on a hill with steam billowing from beneath the bonnet, when she made an observation. "What we want," she said, "is a picnic basket and a bottle of pop. Then, if it is a particularly high hill, we can sit on the verge to eat."

He thought about this for a few seconds, then realised Janet and the Austin suited his new temperament very well. It made him feel sorry for those who could, theoretically, race up the hill (had his car not been blocking one side of the road). They did not have Janet as a friend – but he did, and this made him feel like a king. His finances had crashed, yet his happiness was beyond anything he had previously believed possible.

While trying to come to terms with these confusing thoughts, he also had to deal with the issue of finding work. He could no longer teach and, until all the recent fuss had died down, it seemed unlikely any high-profile company would employ him, other than in a job no one else wanted. Also, he found it difficult to comprehend that he would have to work two forty-four-hour weeks to earn a fraction of the weekly allowance his father had once provided.

When he expressed his doubts to Janet, her only comment was, "So?" Then, realising he was looking at her strangely, she teased him just a little. "If we ain't got a shilling for the gas meter," she said in a mock-Dickensian manner, "we'll just have to sleep in our woolly jumpers and boots."

What he truly wanted to do then was to rush over and hold her warm and safe in his arms. He realised not having a shilling for the gas meter was completely irrelevant compared to the true meaning of his life. All he wanted was to be close to the woman he loved.

Four months after moving into the flat, Richard was talking with Janet about how hard he was finding it to get work. She replied it was probably because he came across as very posh and not suited to emptying dustbins or whatever.

"I am not posh," he objected.

"Says a man with a degree from Oxford." Then, after a few seconds of thought, she added, "And you know about posh hotels."

"I suppose."

"Of course you do," she said, "we stayed in one, remember? Not so good as a tent holiday, but it does mean you understand how being posh works. So go and work in a hotel."

He thought she might have a point. "By the age of six," he said, "I could recite all my U-words as effortlessly as the twelve times table."

Janet knew U-words were a secret code used by the upper classes to identify themselves to those of similarly good breeding. Some, like 'lavatory' and 'luncheon', were obvious; others, such as 'writing paper', more obscure and coined specifically to weed out pretenders who might use the common term 'notepaper'.

"And," continued Richard, "I remember the day I told my father I had accepted employment in a grammar school. He exploded – or at least leapt into the air while exploding with spluttered words. Firstly, this was because I had used the word 'employment', which to him implied a tradesman. Secondly, because my 'servitude' was to take place in a school accessible to commoners. I did not want him to have a heart attack, so failed to mention I would also be teaching girls—"

"Like me."

"Indeed," said Richard. "Anyway, the school was where I first got to hear non-U words such as 'toilet' and 'notepaper'. Though I do remember being totally confused when I overheard a boy saying he was 'going to the bog'. I thought it meant he was going to marshy ground to play some obscure game."

"And was he wearing wellingtons at the time?" asked Janet. "That would be the giveaway regarding his intentions. However, I strongly suspect he was using the language of Roman soldiers who, long ago, went to the bog to… well, you know. And ironically, they would have been speaking Latin to their nearest squatting neighbour. So, understanding all this allows you to go anywhere you want and fit in, even speaking Latin in posh hotels. QED!"

Richard knew this to be untrue, because what he wanted most was to spend the night in Janet's bed, then wake up in the morning and discover her lying next to him. So her statement that he could go anywhere he wanted was clearly false. But, on the less important issue of earning money, she did have a point. To distract himself from impossible dreams, he returned his thoughts to a world he understood. "'QED'," he said, "is only used by common folk to indicate something has been proved, like in a maths problem. In a hotel foyer, a true aristocrat would say, 'quod erst demonstrator' to demonstrate their superior breeding to the receptionist."

"Ah, but you would know what they were talking about and respond appropriately."

And so it was that, within the week, Richard was working in a four-star hotel as a porter, dishwasher, and occasional receptionist. He was on his way up – at four pounds a week. But the money was honestly earned, so lacked the tainted smell of the ten-pound notes his father had once given him.

Colleges students often complete their A level courses within a single year. Thus, as expected, Janet walked out of her final examination at the age of sixteen. When she returned home, Richard made a fuss of her, then explained on his next day off from work, he was going to take her to a quiet beach. Before she could tell him that phase of her life had passed, he announced it was a place where she could –

unofficially – drive his car. Her actual driving test, he said, was booked for five days after her seventeenth birthday.

"All in all," he concluded, "I think it's lucky I sold the Jag. The Austin has a top speed of forty-five miles an hour downhill, so there is no unexpected rapid acceleration to worry about."

Janet passed her test as anticipated, after which Richard gave her the car to use at will. By the end of July, she had acquired three weeks' driving experience, without even getting a minor 'whoops dent'. Richard finally felt able to relax in the passenger seat as she drove him to Wales for another wonderful – if somewhat shorter – camping holiday.

After the holiday, Richard's frustration finally got the better of him. During his first day off from work he went to the library to study asexuality. But the librarian responded by saying they did not hold any books on the subject. However, Richard would not be deterred.

"Forbidden love," he said, "I believe you keep such works it in the back room under lock and key – for those who wish to do academic research. I am an English teacher, you see."

The librarian gave a sniff, as if to detect any smell he might be emitting, before adding, "I will see what we have on your… academic research." After some delay, this turned out to be one book in pristine condition, except for the cover which had been stamped: *Not to be removed from library.*

Towards the end of August, Richard found himself sitting in an armchair, while Janet sat on the settee reading some book or other.

"We have no secrets from each other," he said.

Such a comment did not need confirmation, so she merely placed the book on her lap to indicate she was listening.

"I've been reading," he said, "hoping to understand about… you know."

"Not really, though if you were reading about collecting matchbox labels, I would prefer you kept that to yourself." Then she saw how serious he looked. "Sorry," she said. "What have you been reading about?"

"Asexuality."

"And what do you want to know?"

"Is it permanent? How long do I have to wait before our lives truly become one?"

"I am diseased—"

"Shut up!" he shouted. "You are insulting the woman I love."

Janet had always held back on the detail of all the gruesome things she had done in her youth. But now she realised Richard needed to know about them, and so understand why she could never have a romantic relationship with anyone. When she explained her mouth was full of germs from all the oral sex she had performed for dirty old men, she saw him grimace. She hated that, so stopped and looked down at her lap. *But he needs to know why I can never kiss anyone*, she thought. "I'm okay living safely untouched within my own clothes," she continued, "but I never want sex again. So, to answer your question, that is forever."

"Okay," he responded, "but I am going to be equally honest: my life belongs to you, and I will never give up hope that one day we might come together in a proper marriage."

She shook her head. "Don't waste your time with me," she said. "Get yourself a proper girlfriend, like you deserve. But just remember: you will always be my best-ever friend, who I love madly in a non-romantic way. I will always be here for you, though perhaps you might warn any future girlfriend that, if she ever hurts you, she can expect me to bop her on the head with a rolling pin."

That will never happen, thought Richard, *because I will always be waiting for you.*

He stood up, walked to his bedroom and closed the door behind him, but she still heard his tears of real grief. But surely he would get over it? Men always did.

In the summer of 1971, Janet received a provisional offer of a place at Oxford University. Richard was happy she was pursuing her dreams, but also traumatised by the idea he would no longer be looking after her. From now on, her living expenses would be funded by a Government maintenance grant. And when, in the autumn, she moved into lodgings, his role in her life would diminish further. To continue, it would need a romantic, sexual bond that would be lifelong – or at least last until they were so old they would be happy just going for country walks and playing chess together.

CHAPTER TWELVE

Reginald had long been aware that his wife, Caroline, was a compulsive liar. When they had first met this was fine because then, aged eighteen, she had a nice pair of tits. Not that he had been allowed to see them at the very beginning, because in the 1940s there were all sorts of daft conventions surrounding such things. However, after he had presented her with a diamond necklace, her dress had accidentally slipped from her shoulders to reveal she was not wearing a bra. She had quickly used her hands as a substitute, but his penis had already taken full control of his brain. The following day he had also bought her a new and expensive dress, which was less prone to accidents. Magically though, it could drop to the floor on his command – at least after he agreed to pay her a weekly allowance, backdated two months.

For the next three years he kept her for occasional sex, which suited them both. Then she announced she was pregnant with his child. (Another convenient accident?) Anyway, given her need to withdraw from public view, he let her stay in the west wing of his mansion, on the understanding that she deal with the accident as soon as possible. This she promised to do, willingly accepting a thousand pounds in cash for the purpose. It was only later that he discovered the accident had not been corrected. Soon after this revelation, Caroline had gone to the hospital to do woman things. Two weeks later, Reginald began to hear the household staff talking about someone called Richard. More importantly, Caroline once again had a flat enough tummy to be good in bed. So they married, which greatly helped Reginald with his tax arrangements. Sadly, Caroline only maintained a reasonable standard of sexual gymnastics for the next five years. After that time, a weaker man might have worried that his occasional inability to get an erection was his own fault.

Of less concern than Caroline's inability to stimulate his manhood, was a report he received from the private detective he employed to keep an eye on his business interests. According to the report, Caroline had been spending a lot of time in the gatekeeper's cottage; a building not visible from the mansion. Reginald had decided to overlook this because, now aged thirty-one, his wife no longer had the body he had once desired. Obviously, he had sacked the gatekeeper, and dubbed his wife a dirty slag, but for appearances' sake, he did not want the world to discover he had temporarily lost control of a simple domestic situation.

By the time Caroline reached the age of forty-two, she had become a wrinkled old prune whose body he only used, if he was drunk, and the light was off.

And then he had met Priscilla. On their first meeting at the golf club, she had usefully told him that a prostitute had targeted his idiotic son. Her second appearance had revealed more of her tits, which led to dinner, and then a hotel bedroom. Here, he explained that refined gentlemen normally gave their manhood a personal name. His was called Hercules, to reflect the fact he was exceptionally well endowed.

"I have to keep him in a special pouch," he said, "to prevent any accidental escapes due to bursting trouser buttons."

Priscilla looked at the ridiculous trouser bulge. *Like the girls at school, stuffing tissue paper into their bras*, she thought. "I don't know anything about rude things," she said shyly.

Lying bitch, thought Reginald. "So I expect you would like me to take control of the situation?" he said.

"But I am a virgin," she whispered. "Still at school."

Then Hercules had responded in a manly fashion. But because Reginald was both drunk and tired, he fell asleep before taking the encounter to its natural conclusion.

In the morning he explained to… whatever her name was… that Hercules wanted to play. She responded in a way he found most pleasing. He then asked for her full name, which was a polite way of saying he had either never known, or had forgotten all of her personal details except for her exaggerated claim of having a forty-two-inch bust.

"Priscilla Parkinson," she said. "You know my father from the golf club."

Reginald was immediately on full alert – a lot of scoundrels wanted to extract money from him, and Mr Parkinson was better at it than most. Keeping Priscilla on his 'payroll' seemed a useful insurance policy. So, in that hotel room, he instructed her to walk around naked for a little while, and decided she did indeed have a nice pair of tits. So the following day he acquired a flat where she might be discreetly installed. But this situation was different to when he had been doing it regularly with Caroline, because he was now more honest about such things. Accordingly, while driving to the flat, he told Priscilla about the private detectives he used to look after his interests—

"Are you really that important?" she squealed excitedly.

Inspired, he exaggerated his status somewhat by telling her he had a worldwide network of secret service agents, the sort normally used by governments. And the silly cow believed him! After such a submission to his grandeur, he simply had to pull the Rolls into a lay-by and shag her on the back seat. Five minutes later, he returned to the subject of his agents, adding that, if she was ever seen alone with another man, he would not give her the benefit of the doubt. In return for keeping the flat in good order and spreading her legs at his command, he offered her a generous allowance. More importantly, he got her talking about her father and discovered the scoundrel had a tape-recording machine in his office! To Mr Parkinson, it seemed, there was no such thing as a secret handshake to secure a gentleman's agreement.

"And have you told your father about us?" Reginald enquired, apparently casually.

She shook her head. "You know what old people are like about romantic things happening outside of marriage," she explained.

"And do you know when he first acquired the tape recorder?" he asked, again seemingly unconcerned.

"When they were first invented."

Bugger, thought Reginald. "I like talking about your old man," he said. "Please tell me more."

Two years after Reginald had installed Priscilla in his flat, his wife annoyed him. One day, when he wanted a quick sexual encounter, she was not there. On reflection, he realised he had not seen her throughout the preceding week – or was it longer? In response, he temporarily transferred the part-time detective he employed to monitor Priscilla to the 'wife situation'. The subsequent report left him horrified. Six days earlier, Caroline had boarded a flight to Switzerland with a man. Immediately, Reginald telephoned his Swiss banker, but it was too late. The account was empty, and there was nothing he could do about it because it was in Caroline's name. The tax advantage in marrying her had suddenly become a loss of three million pounds. Even for him, this was a hard blow.

In addition to losing the Swiss benefits, Reginald knew his business arrangement with Priscilla's father left him exposed to an equally serious financial risk. Accordingly, he redirected the private detective from the wife situation to Mr Parkinson. A week later, the detective whispered his findings in Reginald's ear – and it was not good news. Apparently the scoundrel had recently made two visits to a top law firm, and looked set to take his dealings with Reginald to court. And there the issue of the tape recorder. Reginald knew immediate action was required to destroy Mr Parkinson's reputation – a task which, he remembered, was his main reason for 'employing' Priscilla in the first place.

The first part of Reginald's plan was to transfer Priscilla to the west wing of his mansion which had, until recently, been occupied by Caroline. This would give him better control of the situation. He then sold the flat, which both reduced his overdraft and made it easier for his private detective to keep a casual eye on Priscilla, without charging overtime. All Reginald had to do now was manipulate Priscilla into a becoming a reputation-destroying weapon…

Priscilla, knowing that she had reached the highest level of upper-class society, spent two dreamlike days wandering about her estate, telling the servants what needed to be done. On the third day, one of the household staff told her Reginald wanted to see her in his study.

"*Lord* Reginald," Priscilla corrected.

"As you wish, milady," he replied.

There was something not quite right about the way he said this, but she could not understand why, because she liked the idea of being called Lady Priscilla.

When she entered Lord Reginald's study, he instructed her to sit on a low stool. She found this uncomfortable, particularly because she had to bend her neck to gaze up at the towering, all-important man. She also disliked looking up the dark, hairy voids of his nostrils.

"I dislike the way you are speaking to the servants," he said. "I have been informed you have said the word 'please' – that is akin to begging from those of low breeding."

"Who told you that?"

"Do not concern yourself with such things. All that matters is that you do not repeat this indiscretion. Also, never say the word 'sorry' to the lower orders, because it suggests it was you who made an error, and not them. Likewise, never say 'thank you' because it implies gratitude, when in truth they are merely trying to get their grubby fingers on our money."

Our money, she thought. "I understand," she said.

"You will, of course," he continued, "frequently say 'please', 'sorry' and 'thank you' to me, or any other member of the aristocracy you happen to meet. So repeat after me: 'Thank you for telling me all of this. I am so sorry for my errors; please forgive me.'"

It took Priscilla several attempts to remember all of this, but not saying the demeaning words to the servants came naturally to her. And so it was they all came to hate her... and Reginald knew if they got the slightest hint his property was flirting with another man, they would race to his study with all the gruesome details. *What a terribly clever and cost-effective plan*, he thought.

The second part of Reginald's plan was to drive a permanent wedge between Priscilla and her parents. This would make her totally dependent on him. So, after spreading some basic disinformation against her father, he called Priscilla to his study, this time directing her to sit on a normal chair, as opposed to the little stool once occupied by the six-year-old Richard.

"The time has finally come," he said grandly, "to show your parents everything you have achieved, by which I mean joining the aristocracy and learning how to speak like a lady. I believe they live in a poorer part of the county?"

Priscilla bowed her head in shame. "Sorry," she said.

"But let them be proud of you," continued Reginald. "I assume you now know how to deal with the servants correctly, so consider Maggie to be your chauffeur."

Overwhelmed by this increase in her status, Priscilla nodded. Reginald responded with a disapproving cough.

"Thank you," she said. "Sorry."

"Get Maggie," continued Reginald, "to take you back to your humble home, but do so in style. You may use the new Rolls. Wear your finest clothes and carry that purse I brought back for you from Paris last year. And now you fully understand how to convey your authority over the lower orders, your parents will realise you have become a proper lady."

"Yes, Your Lordship. Thank you."

The following day, Priscilla was driven by her new chauffeur to her parents' house. On her arrival, she instructed Maggie to open the car door. After stepping out, Priscilla walked up the driveway, her four-inch heels announcing her presence by crunching on the gravel. But of course, her impoverished daddy could not afford a doorman to greet her. How embarrassing! Still, overwhelmed with excitement at the prospect of telling her parents everything she had achieved, she rang the plastic doorbell. And this was where her carefully crafted plan started to go wrong. The maid opened the door, but quickly shut it again, leaving Priscilla standing in the porch. Not even a proper reception room! How dare her parents display their poverty to the world?! Then Daddy flung open the door. Before Priscilla could even say hello, he pushed her back out onto the driveway. In the argument which followed, she tried explaining that she was now living in a proper mansion, with a butler and stuff. He shouted that his business dealings with Reginald Edwards went back a long way. According to her stupid daddy, they had ended abruptly when a transaction had gone badly wrong.

"And now," he shouted, "you have become his mistress."

Her mother then came running. "How can I ever show my face to the neighbours again," she yelled, "knowing my daughter is a common tart? I have become a prisoner in my own home."

Priscilla, quite reasonably, kicked her mother hard on the shins, sending her falling back into the hallway. The next thing she knew, Daddy had grabbed her fine Parisian dress and was dragging her backwards along the driveway.

"I no longer have a daughter," he shouted. "Especially one who got such terrible O level results that I had to bribe the school before they would let her stay on. And what do you do in return? Abandon your A levels halfway through to become a harlot."

Priscilla responded with her best-ever tantrum, shouting all the swear words she knew. The final three words she would ever shout at her father all began with an 'F'.

After Daddy had run back into the house to hide, she noticed a few neighbours had gathered to watch. Also that her fine dress had lost much of its delicate stitching, allowing her perfect anatomy to make unpredictable appearances, like that of a proper Hollywood film star. This increased her sense of drama to a new level. Even Maggie stayed in the Rolls with the engine purring. Finally, with one horrendous scream, Priscilla fell to the ground, as if dead from indignation and exhaustion. After a few seconds, she opened one eye to see her audience gazing down in shock and awe, while some guy took her photograph. Accidentally,

Priscilla yanked on her fine Parisian bra strap, which was built for style, not strength. The man clicked his camera again.

"They threw me out," she whispered, to further dramatise her near-death experience, "because I have joined the aristocracy and am living with a real lord." Then she crawled to the Rolls and, after Maggie had opened the rear door, clambered inside. At last, she would be on the front page of the newspaper.

But the following day, the newspaper failed to even mention the great injustice she had suffered. Why? How? It was inexplicable. All Scraggy Janet had done was sit on a stupid garden wall, and she had been headline news for two days. When Priscilla told Lord Reginald about the injustice, he cruelly replied the newspaper's content was an editorial decision over which he had no control. He then added that, in future, the Rolls was only to be used for formal events.

While saying this, Reginald found it hard to resist smiling because, on this occasion only, he had rather enjoyed his Rolls being used to humiliate Priscilla's father. Its presence must have increased their neighbours' gossip immensely. And this proved to be the case, for, a month after Priscilla's "volcanic tantrum" (as Maggie had phrased it), her parents moved house, presumably to something more suited to their reduced social status. Exactly where did not matter. The important thing was that they were no longer in a position to bring up awkward details of their recent business dealings with him.

"Little upstarts," he had muttered to himself after Priscilla had stormed off. He was now by far the wealthiest man in the county, as opposed to merely the richest. And Priscilla belonged to him, as surely as if she were locked in the safe with his other assets.

CHAPTER THIRTEEN

A month after moving Priscilla into the west wing, Reginald received an envelope through the post. He was accustomed to these being stamped with the phrase 'Private and confidential', generally in red ink. Strangely, this one stated, 'To any nosy person who wants to open it'. The postage stamp had been issued in the Bahamas. Opening the envelope, he discovered the enclosed letter was from his wife. It proved to be confused, rambling, and read:

> *I got to thinking that you are a lot like sewage: from a distance, not very interesting, but get closer, with a microscope, and you see all sorts of fascinating bugs and diseases. For instance, how did you become so rich when you have such a small brain? I probably know more about this than your solicitor, the taxman or the police. But do not worry – put a million into my new bank account (number enclosed), and my*

amnesia will become permanent... unless I happen to glance at the tax documents I accidentally copied. And don't forget that Customs and Excise investigation a few years back.

However, if you take a sensible course of action, you may consider yourself divorced and free to shag that Priscilla slag. It is not only you who can employ a private detective – or, more precisely...

You foolish old fart! I cannot believe you failed to notice that Richard looks remarkably like the detective you hired to spy on me. As for sacking the gatekeeper, he was totally loyal to you, but inconvenient for us, given his cottage was by the gates. Your incompetence left us laughing our pants off – quite often, as it happens.

And where is your detective now? I don't know – maybe enjoying an iced cocktail by the pool? But I expect he will be up later to show me what a real penis looks like, as opposed to your floppy inchworm.

Anyway, where shall I send the tax information? To you, or to the authorities? Your choice!

Reginald stared at the letter without comprehension. However, after reading it three times, the truth came into focus. The woman was quite mad! Then came a deeper truth. This was clearly a handwritten blackmail letter, which he believed was all the evidence he needed to prove Caroline was a criminal who should spend the rest of her life in jail. But if he paid her the million, he felt certain she would not pursue the matter further. In any event, it was cheaper than dealing with it through a divorce court, which would cost him half of his wealth, plus legal fees. This method could save him a lot of bother.

Re-reading her deranged ramblings for a fourth time, he realised that, coincidentally, they solved a puzzle that had been bothering him for many years; namely how he had produced such an unintelligent son as Richard. Now he understood there was no biological connection between himself and the boy, the issue of inherited stupidity became irrelevant, except for… Reginald's mind filled with anger. Furiously, he rushed to his office and recovered Richard's file from a cabinet. The cost of raising the bastard child, including the namby-pamby nursemaid, the school fees and his post-university allowance, came to £568,264. That expenditure had given Richard all the skills necessary to marry into a family with a royal coat of arms. Indeed, the boy had even been given lessons in how to meet the Queen: retreating three steps before giving a bow, and the like. But what had the idiot boy done? Hooked up with a prostitute. Then the irony of the situation came to Reginald. Had it not been for the prostitute, he would still be paying for Richard's upkeep. The prostitute – whose name he could no longer remember – had actually saved him quite a lot of money, unlike his crazed ex-wife, who was about to cost him a million pounds.

Thinking of this expenditure, he eventually decided that, rather than demolish his share portfolio, he would take out a thirty per cent mortgage on his estate. This, added to the fifty per cent he had needed to maintain his life-style, did not sit comfortably in his mind. Essentially, his mansion was now owned by a company registered on a Caribbean island. But at least he no longer had a wife or a pretend son scrounging off him, so he would live with it, because he had no choice.

Reginald knew his decision regarding the 'divorce settlement' had shown great wisdom. As promised, his ex-wife returned a note to say she had burned all the relevant papers. Besides this necessary fact, there was a mass of deranged writing. The letter concluded:

I have told all of my new, exciting friends about the inchworm that lives inside your coconut-sized trouser pouch. The idea of it flopping about in so much empty space causes much amusement, especially among the men. Maybe you could send us a photograph?

But you do not know my address, which, given our private yacht takes us all over the world, might change without notice. So my friends will just have to imagine your inchworm as a soft toy designed principally to bring a little laughter into the world.

And so it was that Reginald came to understand Caroline was criminally insane. Then he remembered the four million she had in her bank account, and possibly a yacht. So a better description might be insanely rich – while his own account was now running a significant overdraft.

Anyway, he was glad the ex-wife problem had gone away. What he now owned was Priscilla, who frequently expressed astonishment at the size of his enormous manhood. So, on reflection, he decided to make their arrangement formal. She would not be allowed to leave the grounds without a female escort – generally Maggie.

In return, he would double her allowance. When he told Priscilla what he intended, she squealed with delight and threw her arms around his neck. She then suggested that he visit her bedroom more often – but, aged fifty-six, twice a week was all he could manage.

Having organised his future biological needs, Reginald telephoned his solicitor with the instruction to prepare a document, which would allow him to get rid of Priscilla when her existence became inconvenient. However, with the wisdom of age, he thought a severance fee might be appropriate. After all, kicking the prostitute out of Richard's house had not worked particularly well, and the last thing he wanted was Priscilla sitting on his garden wall. He only controlled the local newspaper, and there was no saying how the wider gutter press might corrupt the story, if she got out her tits. So, he told his solicitor to settle Priscilla's severance at a thousand pounds, on the understanding she sign a media confidentiality agreement. But she had a few years left in her yet, and, if she helped out with some domestic chores, he might even keep her on in the long term. If she became a cleaner and failed to use her feather duster correctly, he could playfully bend her over his knee and spank her bottom.

It only took a few days for the solicitors to settle the legal details with Priscilla. Reginald then began to sort out the remaining household staff. First, he sacked all the males, his intention being to replace them with girls, who would be cheaper and not inclined to complicate things with Priscilla. However, on reflection, he decided not to replace the males. The three existing female staff would just have to work harder – at least until his bank balance recovered.

CHAPTER FOURTEEN

Richard knew his worst fears were starting to come true. After leaving for university, Janet had begun to drift away from him. In fact, he thought that, during the Easter holidays before her finals, she had only returned home to check he was okay. That was not the same as wanting to see him.

As expected, Janet got a double-first in her English degree. A few weeks later, Richard proudly escorted her to the graduation ceremony. The other guests clearly believed him to be her boyfriend – or, at least, that was what he wanted them to believe. And why not? Janet was now nineteen, which made the gap between her age and his seem smaller than it had at the beginning. The important thing for him to do was hold off his thirtieth birthday for as long as possible. After the ceremony, they returned to their flat, she falling back onto the settee, and he into an armchair. This separation had now become instinctive – indeed, her asexuality dominated their body language.

Then, a week after her graduation, Janet left for a job in London, at a publishing house, where she edited book manuscripts and the like. Part of her employment package was a car, which allowed Richard to keep the Austin. He decided he would never part with it, because it reminded him of the time they had been together. Even just sitting in the driving seat, where she had once sat, gave him a sense of well-being. For the same reason, he remained in the flat, sometimes feeling lonely, but mostly remembering when he had shared it with the woman he loved.

As time passed slowly by, Richard felt the emotional distance between them increasing. Partly, this was because Janet's work kept her occupied for around sixty hours a week, while his shifts at the hotel were erratic and often subject to change without warning. Seeing each other for a few days required a great deal of planning, which meant all spontaneity was lost.

When Janet was twenty-three, she realised renting a bedsit in London was silly. When she told Richard of this, he almost took her in his arms to say thank you. But before he could violate her personal space, her second sentence hit him as a cruel blow. She explained that her savings were now sufficient to buy a house in North Wales, so she was moving there to found a literary agency. She would be the sole proprietor, but the operation was to have the grand-sounding name of Sustain Media. If her clients thought this meant she had a dedicated team of editors working on their manuscripts, then fine.

"Just little old me," she added, "though, if you ever want to visit…" She smiled, then handed him a key. "Like you did for me, all those years ago. You never need to open your eyes in the morning to discover you have been sleeping under a bush."

To hide his true emotions, Richard let his mind drift to memories of when, after returning from Ireland, he had woken up with his back against a bale of hay. The important thing about the experience was that he had been close to Janet. On that occasion, he had begun the day by having a good stretch, then having fresh blackberries for breakfast. How he longed for the magic of that first holiday to return.

Two months after Janet had first told him about her agency project, she purchased an old Land Rover from the car auctions – her reason being that, in winter, an ordinary car would find the steep Welsh mountain roads impassable. Also, if she was going to end up in a snowy ditch, it was more sensible to do so in an old vehicle.

When Richard first saw the Land Rover, he was horrified by all its dents and scratches. "It looks like something the army would drive through a battlefield!" he exclaimed.

She confirmed the previous owners had, in fact, been the Ministry of Defence. More importantly, the vehicle's appearance had allowed her to purchase it for fifty pounds. Richard wanted to buy her something better, but she refused.

"I *need* something with four-wheel drive," she responded. "Some people might *want* fancy seats, but not me. Oh, I do hope we are not going to have the margarine-or-butter argument all over again!"

While this light-hearted banter was in progress, Janet was actually thinking of something far more profound. Richard had supported her financially with all the devotion of a father until she had reached the age of twenty. She considered this to be long enough. After leaving university, she had been determined to stand on her own two feet.

Regarding the Land Rover, only after he got down on his knees to beg her to get something safe, did she agree to let him pay a garage to check the brakes – and, because she had already mentioned steep hills, any argument to the contrary seemed rather weak.

And so the day came when Richard stood on the pavement to wave her goodbye, knowing all happiness was leaving his life forever. He then walked back up to their – *his* – lonely flat.

After their parting, he spent most of his free time wandering the countryside, oblivious to what was going on around him. Sometimes he returned to the flat with his clothes soaked with rain, which suited his mood. Other times, he was hobbling because he had tripped over an unexpected obstruction after dark. But all of these walks had the same thing in common: throughout, his thoughts were focused entirely on Janet. Geographically she now lived 150 miles away, but emotionally she was still settled deep within his mind.

Three weeks after Janet moved away, Richard came to understand his life had lost all purpose. Initially he just accepted this as a fact. Then, as he wandered the streets after dark, there came the first true crisis of his unrequited love. It happened while he was walking across a bridge, beneath which a swollen river raged in a succession of swirling whirlpools. Somewhere near the middle of the bridge, he realised that, if he leapt over the parapet, his unbearable suffering would be over within a few minutes. In the next instant, a panic reaction sent him leaping away from the edge to stand in the road. Had a car been passing, his life would have been at an end – *Good!* But fate had decided there was no traffic, so he was spared a premature death. But for what purpose, he could not imagine. Returning to the flat, he threw off his wet clothes and lay in front of the fan heater. For how long he cried, he could not remember; only the strength required to sit up was beyond him.

Richard had always assumed people who had a nervous breakdown remained unaware it was happening. But now he understood the incident on the bridge, where he had wanted to die, could be described in no other way. But at the same time, he had to accept his life without Janet had no value, so bringing it to a premature end made perfect sense.

Presently, he came to consider the fact that he had not slept for the past three nights. This meant he had lost the opportunity to dream, which, he now decided, was the brain's way of doing its 'housework' – generally putting things in good order and tidying away all the messy stuff. Without sleep, his brain had obviously ceased to function correctly, which accounted for the world becoming a strange and confusing place. He looked around the flat he had once shared with Janet to see an emotionally cold room, occupied by an insane individual lying naked on the floor. Then the awful truth came to him. Janet would never return here. To all intents and purposes, his life had come to an end.

Janet thought moving to Wales was the hardest thing she had ever done. She missed Richard constantly, but knew she had no choice in the matter. To keep him hanging on was selfish. He needed to be free to get himself a proper girlfriend, who would provide him with the comfort all men desire.

Richard found it quite easy to keep his breakdown locked inside his head – if only because he never spoke to anyone about emotional matters. And since his midnight walks were solitary affairs, as far as the hotel owner was concerned, he was an efficient employee who had, by default, progressed to become the unofficial assistant manager. However, the owner explained the promotion could not be formally recognised because it was a live-in position, so the holder was on hand for night-time emergencies.

Richard knew this statement to be a slight corruption of the truth. In reality, the present general manager was a late-middle-aged man, who did not want the bother of dealing with guests in the middle of the night... or at any other time, for that matter. According to rumour, this situation was made possible by him and the owner sharing a '*love that dare not speak its name*'. In any event, the owner and the general manager lived together in a grand house, some thirty miles from the hotel.

A further corruption of the truth concerned the term 'live-in'. The accommodation offered was a small room, with a single window overlooking the dustbins behind the building. On the positive side, the room was on the same corridor as the assistant manager's office, so walking to work took about ten seconds. Also, all meals could be taken free of charge in the dining room. The previous incumbent had resigned because, in his three years of service, he had accumulated so much wealth he had been able to retire aged sixty-two.

So Richard knew how to secure a prosperous future... But what use was money without Janet to look after? Nevertheless, when lying on the floor before the fan heater, his thoughts had eventually turned towards the inevitable. Two days later, he had left the flat to begin his new life centred around the hotel.

CHAPTER FIFTEEN

Richard's first task after officially becoming the hotel's assistant manager, was to find replacement cover for his shifts on the reception desk. The newspaper advertisement attracted twelve written responses, which he found most intimidating. His training as a teacher had developed his instinct to say, "Well done" at every opportunity. Now, he was staring into an abyss of negativity; a world in which he would have to tell eleven hopefuls they had failed to get a rather basic job. Anyway, for the time being, he was still stationed at reception, wondering how to professionally conduct a recruitment interview.

Meanwhile, on the other side of the hotel's high boundary wall, a curtain of ivy imperceptibly strengthened its hold on the rough bricks; the stronger tendrils grasping and entombing the nearest tree. This narrow strip of ancient woodland marked the edge of a small nature reserve, where a wide variety of animals went about their daily business, caring nothing for the affairs of men. Some scampered, others burrowed, while a solitary hare stood to contemplate the scene. Dismissively, he took a sideways glance at the rabbits, who he knew to be indistinguishable from each other in both appearance and stupidity. Of course, they had their uses, because their lack of intelligence meant a hungry fox could sneak up on them to devour an easy breakfast. The hare reasoned this was why they had such large families, whereas majestic creatures like himself could remain solitary and aloof.

To enhance his ability to survive, he had tall, pointed ears, which allowed him to hear things from a great distance. And so it was that a crunching noise on a gravel path alerted him to something happening on the far side of the duck pond. Immediately his superior eyesight registered something ginger. Focusing more intently, he realised the distinctive colour could be attributed to hair. Given it was long and curly, he deduced it belonged to one of the animals who moved from one place to another by sliding their two legs forward, one after the other. Watching these creatures always amused him. He considered their comical and inefficient mode of movement made them mostly harmless. However, this particular specimen held a special interest for him because, even if he had been standing on a distant hill, he would have noticed the mass of ginger glowing brightly in the sunshine. In fact, it made him blink, which was something he rarely did. After refocusing his eyes, he realised the creature's hair fell first to its shoulders, then descended to surround a flappy orange cover which came down to float around a pair of knees. Idly, he watched the splash of colour move along the path to a wooden platform. The creature sat on this; a procedure he had observed many times, presumably because some defect in these creatures' legs prevented them from sitting properly without aid.

Tara, a slim lady wearing a floaty orange dress, plonked herself on the bench facing the pond. "Uh..." she said. She had many ways of saying 'uh', and those who knew her well could mostly identify the word's precise meaning in any given context – be it to indicate surprise, annoyance, a question, a euphemism for 'You are completely bonkers'... and so on. This particular 'uh' was due to her stupid ex-boyfriend blocking the part of her brain which dealt with complex and sensible ideas.

The ex-boyfriend, whose name she chose not to remember, was a lecherous laboratory technician in the hospital where she had also worked – until two hours ago. In order to banish him from her mind, she gazed across the pond and saw a lot of ducks heading her way. On reaching the bank, they jumped up to waddle before her, making quacking noises.

"Well," she told them, "you talk a lot more sense than..." Then, not wishing to speak her ex-boyfriend's name, she finished, "Uh..." She realised this would make no sense whatsoever to the ducks, who would assume her ex-boyfriend's name was 'Uh'.

To distract herself from unpleasant thoughts, she began to wonder why the ducks all wanted to be her friend. Ah! They obviously associated people who carried things wrapped in newspaper with food. Unwrapping her sandwiches, she threw them a slice of bread. Only when she looked at the final sandwich did she remember that, because of... Thingy, her nursing career had, two hours earlier, come to an unexpected end; and that, given the nature of her departure, she could never return to collect her wages. Fearing hunger, she ate the sandwich herself, making the ducks rather cross. Then she shook the newspaper to scatter the crumbs, but this failed to impress the ducks, who waddled back to their pond in disgust. However, a robin came to hop around her feet, which helped improve her mood.

Idly, Tara began to read the sheet of newspaper. After a few minutes, she noticed an advertisement for a hotel receptionist. Looking around the nature reserve to get her bearings, she came to believe the hotel in question was somewhere over to her right. In that direction it was mostly woodland, but, through a solitary gap, she could see a curtain of ivy growing up a wall. Then she remembered walking down the lane from the hospital where she had worked until this morning. Just before reaching the nature reserve, she had passed a driveway that was open to the public – that is to say, without gates.

She gave some thought to the work of a hotel receptionist. It might suit her hobby of helping others. Associated with this was her ability to control situations – often in ways those she was trying to help did not expect or appreciate. She looked at the stated wages and realised they were just sufficient to pay the rent on her rather basic bedsit, and to keep her fed without the need to throw herself on the mercy of her parents. Well, at the age of eighteen, a retreat to the family home would be undignified. Also, they would want to know why she had suddenly stopped working as an auxiliary nurse. They would not understand complicated boyfriend issues. Parents were often like that: weighed down by the conventions of old age.

Tara decided the time had come to take control of her life. She left the nature reserve to investigate what she thought might be the hotel mentioned in the advert. At the bottom of the driveway, a board fixed to the wall confirmed the name. Perhaps the time had come to help whoever was doing the job interviews to make the correct decision…

Richard considered there were only two types of woman: Janet, and those who were not Janet. He rarely noticed the physical characteristics of the 'non Janets' because they had no relevance to his life. He was therefore surprised when he looked up from the reception desk to see a woman with a great mass of curly ginger hair wandering around the foyer. The other notable thing about her was that she appeared to be appraising the room for a decorating job. Then she sat on a sofa and bounced up and down a few times, apparently testing it for comfort. Finally she stood up and walked behind his counter to look at the switchboard.

"Err…" he said.

Tara realised the man lacked confidence, which she thought a considerable disadvantage for a hotel receptionist. "I am looking for Mr Edwards," she said.

"That's me," he replied. "And you are…?"

Tara looked over the counter into the foyer. "Your new receptionist," she said. "Out there I reckon there are a lot of people who need my help. Okay, not in a particularly interesting way, but I can start immediately. I know how to operate the switchboard, because we had one like it in the hospital where I used to work as an auxiliary nurse."

Now Richard was really confused. "I am the assistant manager," he said, as much to reassure himself as to make a statement of fact.

"Very pleased to make your acquaintance," said Tara. "I believe my manner is about right for a four-star hotel. Polite, yet not too friendly when dealing with those guests who need help. I am guessing you don't get many aggressive drunks, but I do have basic self-defence skills, if the need arises."

Richard decided to be firm and take control of the situation, so as to reach a rational decision. "I have yet to decide the shortlist," he said.

He would have said more, but two guests walked through the door, and the young woman by his side, whose name he did not know, greeted them with a smile.

"How may I help you?" she asked.

Richard suspected the guests preferred dealing with the woman, and could not think how to protest without appearing rude. But why protest at all? As soon as he found a replacement receptionist, he could relocate to an upstairs office and become a proper assistant manager. So he went along with the woman's desire to become their receptionist – Which suited Tara very well, because it meant she had no need to explain the unfortunate but necessary reason why she had left the hospital in such a hurry.

CHAPTER SIXTEEN

In the early days, Priscilla had liked being the lady of the manor. In particular, she enjoyed listening to Lord Reginald explain how to deal with the lower orders. Most important was maintaining a correct social distance from the servants through simple hand gestures – though, at other times (like when a maid had caught them shagging on the dining-room carpet), a few words might also be necessary.

While thinking about all of this complicated stuff, Priscilla had also set about learning appropriate aristocratic pastimes. But walking down to their lake soon became rather boring. For one thing, she knew herself to be a proper lady, so getting a servant to take her out in a boat just to row around in circles was silly. So she tried other ways to keep herself amused, including playing the piano, watercolour painting, and crochet. The latter had resulted in a great tangle of stuff, and had come to an end when she threw the needles and wool across the room.

As the months passed slowly, the focus of her life

became the delight she found in visiting her bank. Here, she checked the balance to confirm she was getting richer all the time. Indeed, she had heard a rumour that working-class people received a wage packet of about ten pounds a week. How anyone could survive such poverty, she had no idea. But it gave her intense pleasure to realise that, while starvation might be endured by others, she had sufficient funds to avoid scavenging for food in dustbins, or whatever it was the lower orders did to survive.

With the sad passage of time, Priscilla's status became more instinctive. She knew how to treat servants, and how to offer Lord Reginald an aristocratic shag. Every morning she began her day by sitting before her looking glass – only working-class people said 'mirror' – to check for wrinkles, but found none. Then she stood on the bathroom scales and, if she was more than six ounces over her perfect weight, went back to bed until the crisis passed.

But *time* had no room for compassion. Not long after she had endured the nightmare of her twenty-fifth birthday, the cruel looking glass told her she had a wrinkle. Fortunately this crisis happened on a day she was due to visit her bank, which allowed her to divert her mind towards her improving wealth. Naturally, a visit to her bank involved Maggie taking her into town in… a slightly inappropriate car. But, as Lord Reginald had said many times, going to a bank in a Rolls was likely to result in being kidnapped by working-class criminals looking for a ransom which, as a matter of principle, he would never pay.

It was around midday when Priscilla emerged from the bank to stagger dramatically across the pavement towards the car parked on the double yellow lines, perhaps ten feet from the building. Maggie was waiting in the driving seat with the engine running, just in case a traffic warden appeared.

"My allowance has not gone in!" exclaimed Priscilla.

"Not good," said Maggie.

"Oh, I'm sure it's just a mistake made by the bank," said Priscilla. "It was just a bit of a shock, that's all, to discover the balance has not… well, you know what it's like when you are amazingly rich: you expect things to work properly."

Stuck-up cow, thought Maggie. *I'm not going to tell her all of Mr Edwards' staff were paid two weeks late.* Personally, she thought it might be more serious than a clerical error. Her journalist friend had recently told her Reginald had sold his newspaper to a group who prospered by scavenging on failing companies. Due to the paper's plummeting circulation, they had paid only a nominal sum for it. Four days later, the staff had been paid, and the newspaper could print whatever it liked. And Maggie's friend had a lot of stories he wanted to tell, without editorial interference. Hopefully, those stories would increase their circulation, as opposed to primarily boosting Reginald's ego. But Maggie kept quiet, so when Priscilla's allowance was paid, that seemed to be the end of the matter.

In the late summer of 1975, Reginald lay on a soft mattress, his upward gaze trying to focus on something fuzzy. A ceiling, perhaps? But it was not one he recognised. Ah! A hotel ceiling. Having established this, he tried to think what day it might be. Rolling over, he counted the whisky bottles scattered about the carpet. Eight! That suggested four days had passed since he had been outside this room.

Also, the soggy mattress told him that he had not staggered to the bathroom as often as necessary.

Eventually, his brain told him he needed to give Priscilla a shag. But Hercules remained floppy, possibly saving the erection for later, given that returning home would require some sort of journey. So, more sensibly, he climbed out of bed, thinking of breakfast, driving and shagging, in that order. No, alcohol first – he must have whisky to stabilise his thoughts and restore the surrounding world to good order.

On leaving the hotel, he realised he was in London. Ah! He remembered now. He had come down to see his stockbroker, but had been distracted by a tumbler of malt whisky, then the rest of the bottle. Was that really four days ago? Well, yes, because the hotel had charged him for five nights. Then, so as to look important, he purchased a copy of the *Financial Times*, which confirmed it was Tuesday.

When he entered the stockbroker's private office, the broker asked if he was okay.

"Of course," replied Reginald. Sitting down, he placed the newspaper on his lap, then glanced at his stockbroker. The man looked awful, his white face suggesting he was about to keel over at any moment.

"I've been trying to contact you," said the broker, "but I see you already know. I thought you would be furious."

"About what?"

"Page four."

Reginald had no intention of revealing that, after looking to see what day it was, he had simply folded the newspaper under his arm to proclaim his important status. "It's fine," he said. "What was so urgent that you called me to London? Why could you not have told me over the telephone?"

"Because I only got to hear the most confidential whisper," replied the broker. "Last Friday I could have offloaded the Alfrazco shares for two million, but I needed your authority. Sorry, but I did advise against transferring all of your portfolio to one company."

Reginald decided that, before attempting to have any sort of sensible conversation with his broker, he needed to read page four of the newspaper. "I'll be back after lunch," he said. He then headed towards the door, while thinking about the nearest hotel.

After reading page four, he ordered another whisky, which, he reasoned, would help him think better. And it did seem to put things in perspective, because he realised the complete collapse of his Alfrazco shares had left him bankrupt beyond recovery. In fact, a weaker man would have thrown himself from a skyscraper, but not him! He calculated he probably had a week before the bailiffs put a lock and chain around the gates of his estate – and that was plenty of time to organise his affairs.

Sadly, the whisky did nothing to improve his driving skills. Fifty miles from London, his Rolls ended up in a ditch. Nobody else was involved, so there seemed no point in making a fuss about a crumpled lump of metal which was essentially owned by a finance company. By the time a garage sorted it, he intended to be out of the country.

Four days later, Reginald was lying on a Spanish beach, thinking about how skilfully he had outwitted the bailiffs. Everything of value that was not screwed down had been sold, and the funds stored safely across three Spanish bank accounts. Never again would he put all of his assets into the hands of a single company like Alfrazco. A pyramid scheme, they called it; not a term with which he had been familiar. And now, thinking of Priscilla, he smiled. He found it hard to believe she had just accepted all the oil paintings that had hung on their walls had gone away to be renovated. Or perhaps she had been distracted by the way he had power-shagged her senseless three nights in a row? Well, knowing he controlled her mind so completely, his erections had been both spontaneous and spectacular. As for her not knowing what a joint-signatory bank account meant... Of course, he had never intended to use the funds himself, but now he was in Spain, it was no longer of any concern of his, if she sat on the wall of his former estate to display her tits. As for the termination of their contract, well, that was actually watertight in her favour... unless he was sunning himself on a Mediterranean beach, in which case the document had no more value than a used sheet of toilet paper.

Priscilla left the bank in a state of shock. Or, more precisely, her screaming tantrum at the stupid cashier had got her thrown out of the building. No money! Account closed! And what had her chauffeur done? Nothing, beyond saying they needed to hurry back to the estate.

A little later, Priscilla walked up to the front door of the mansion to be met by a man she did not recognise. She thought it odd that Lord Reginald had employed a man, but supposed when hiring a butler it was standard practice. But, to her astonishment, he suggested that he accompany her to the staffroom.

"But that is where the working classes meet," she protested.

"We cannot have you wandering around stealing things," he replied.

"Lord Reginald will be terminating your employment within the hour," she said. "I suggest you pack your bags now."

But the rude man had a dominating presence, so she let him escort her to the place used by the lower orders.

The bailiffs had arrived at the estate an hour earlier. By the time Priscilla entered the staffroom, they were assuring all the domestic staff that their redundancy pay was guaranteed by the Government. Then, on being told Mr Edwards did not give contracts of employment, one of the men said it would be fine, because back-wage slips would be sufficient to give them the benefit of the doubt—

"Lord Reginald," corrected Priscilla.

"And you are…?" asked the man.

"Lady Priscilla," she said, using the special posh voice she always used to introduce herself.

"Ah," said the man. "I have been informed of your existence, and I presume you do not get payslips due to the nature of your work."

"Prostitute," mumbled the cook.

Priscilla had no choice but to give the wrinkled old crow a good slap across the face. She then found herself being carried out of the building and down the driveway by two very strong men. On reaching the lane, they set her down with such casual regard that she might well have been a rubbish sack. It all happened so quickly, she could only blink as they walked back to fix a padlock and chain between the twin gates.

She had been sitting with her back against the wall near the gates for about an hour when she heard footsteps crunching towards her along the gravel.

"You okay?" said a voice from above.

"Fuck, no!" she screamed in frustration.

"You should not use that word," said the voice. "Unless, of course, you are now officially working as a prostitute. Then I suppose it's rather necessary."

Priscilla looked up to see Maggie – or 'chauffeur', as she preferred to classify her.

"Anyway," said Maggie, "I am not here to give you elocution lessons, but to deliver this suitcase. The bailiffs watched while I packed it with things which could reasonably be considered essential for life. Had you not assaulted Cook, they might have let you take two suitcases. Speaking to people nicely helps, you know." She dropped the suitcase on the gravel and hurried away.

Eventually, Priscilla thought back to the men who had escorted her to the gates. They had been talking a lot of gibberish about stuff she did not understand. In response, she had told them that when Lord Reginald found out about this nonsense, he would sack them immediately. And so she spent many hours sitting by the gates, waiting for Lord Reginald's heroic return; hopefully carrying a shotgun. But, other than Maggie, nobody came to talk to her. Finally, when sitting on the gravel became painful, she forced herself to stand. Then, picking up the solitary suitcase, she began walking aimlessly to a place unknown.

Sometime later, she came to a recreational park on

the outskirts of a local town. After walking to the nearest bench, she sat to see what Maggie had packed in her case. Her first reaction was to scream. It contained none of her nice dresses, a whole rack of which Maggie would have found, had she checked the walk-in wardrobe. Instead, it contained a lot of clothes Priscilla did not recognise. No make-up! No perfume! No nothing! Okay, there were bars of soap, toothpaste, a comb, but nothing useful. Oh, and a pair of flat shoes, packed with socks – not her own, obviously, because she always wore stockings. So where had the absurd woolly socks come from? The gardener, probably, because she always wore boots, and dressed as if she lived in a garden shed. That might explain why the clothes included an old coat which had probably once been worn in the trenches of the First World War.

How long Priscilla sat on the bench, trying to muster the enthusiasm to do something, she could not say, beyond a general realisation it was now getting dark, and she was wearing the jumper, the woolly socks and the coat. Then a park keeper told her she would have to move, because he was closing the gates. With no strength to argue, she wandered out of the gates and sat on the pavement with her back against a pillar. A little later she realised staying here overnight would result in her death. Abandoning the suitcase, she got up to begin walking the streets.

And so passed the first night of her new, very temporary life. The following day, she sold her wristwatch and every item of jewellery to a pawnbroker, then headed to a chemist to buy essential make-up. This seemed to help her think better. She hurried back to the park, where she found her suitcase inside the gates, resting against a litter bin. It still contained a few possessions, so she carried it to a shop to buy a shoulder bag, into which she loaded everything she now owned. A suitcase only really worked, if you had a trolley to push it around, so she abandoned it on the pavement.

For the second night of her new life, Priscilla's purse contained four pounds, even though she knew the watch she had sold was gold – or, as the man at the shop had said, gold-plated. Apparently, he knew this because it was not hallmarked. Her earrings, he had told her, were glass, not diamonds.

"Bastard," she had said – not referring to the shop assistant, but to Reginald. The truth, she now realised, was that had the earrings contained real diamonds, he would have taken them from her bedside locker. In fact, she had to accept Reginald's claim to have spent three hundred pounds on her jewellery was completely false... though he had probably spent more than the eight pounds the shop assistant had told her it was worth.

To cope with her new reality, Priscilla went to a pub to get warm, before another long night threatened to turn her limbs to ice. In the bar, she ordered half a shandy and sat on a bench seat to stare at the drink. If this was all she did, it would last all evening. After a lot of staring and a little sipping, the glass was half full. It was then she glanced up to see two men, aged twenty-something, looking at her from the other side of the table. One used his elbow to nudge the other, while nodding towards her. She returned her sad gaze to the half-empty glass, until the men began to speak.

"You working?" said one of them.

"Does it look as if I am working?" she said crossly.

"If you want," said the man. "You could be, if you can do doubles."

Priscilla realised what they were implying. She threw her shandy over them and stomped out of the door.

After a few nights of sleeping in a back entry, Priscilla began to see the world differently. Firstly, four pounds did not last very long, if one's only source of hot food was a chip shop. Secondly, applying her morning make-up in the poor-quality looking glass of a public toilet was really annoying. And thirdly, unless something changed, she had only a few days to live. But thinking about these things did nothing to change the facts – soon she would be found dead in the gutter, with badly applied make-up.

As the day of her death approached, she sat on the pavement in the High Street, waiting for something to happen. Presently, she fell sideways, though whether from starvation or from misery, she knew not – such details are unimportant when lying on cruel paving slabs, awaiting death.

"It's that pro we saw in the pub," said a voice.

"She looked better under dull lighting," said another.

"But…" said the first voice.

Priscilla opened one eye to see four legs, all wearing trousers with turn-ups. Her hunger was unbearable, and she felt certain the approaching night would see her die from hypothermia. Slowly she pushed herself up to a sitting position. Unable to say the exact words, she merely said, "Four pounds", this being the figure that would keep her alive for another week.

The men laughed. "We could get a top-rate pro for

that," said one. "Shagger Lill's good, and fully experienced at doubles."

"But we don't have four pounds," said the other.

"True," responded the first, "but I reckon this one's worth a quid. Fifty pence each. You take the front, while I do the back."

"Okay, then we'll have Shagger Lill when I get my next wages."

Priscilla could only think of the hunger pains in her stomach, and getting off the street and into a warm bedroom. She stood up and, unable to speak, dropped her head submissively in consent.

Twenty minutes later she was in an untidy living room with the men. Until that night she had no idea bisexual men existed; nor the part a woman might be expected to play in a threesome. And it seemed they took great pleasure in telling her what needed to be done. Oh, it was too awful – the taste of her own faeces in her mouth, while the other man did something he called "the thunderbolt position". How could anything that unnatural have a description which did not include the word 'pervert'? As for licking a penis, Reginald had expected her to do that, but he did not do anal sex. Now, in this living room, after it was over, she tried to smooth down her dress while looking at the horrible men, who were now standing to snog, while clasping each other's buttocks. Then they parted a little, and began a perverted sword fight using their soft penises as rather ineffective weapons.

"It was okay," said one, "though not so good as Shagger Lill."

Ignoring his cruel words, Priscilla held out her hand,

her fingers trembling with fear and disgust. "You said a pound," she murmured.

The men laughed. "Professionals get the money before they start," said one. "Now sod off – it'll cost us a quid to get our shirts cleaned."

Priscilla could do nothing but run from the scene of the crime until she came to a dark entry beneath a row of houses. Here she threw herself onto the paving bricks and cried like a child… but she had survived another few hours, and the sweaty heat of the living room would probably delay her death until starvation killed her the following day.

As the first light of morning crept into the entry, two men – who presumably lived in the back houses – stepped over her, pretending not to know she was there. How they could do this was a mystery, not seeing her legs implied they would trip over them. Perhaps, if they came home from the pub in the dark, she would send them crashing to the ground. That would teach them to be cruel.

Slowly, Priscilla raised herself to a sitting position. She had not eaten for thirty-six hours, and sucking water from the tap in the public toilets had not encouraged her to maintain a healthy level of hydration. And recently she had lost a lot of sweat in the living room of the men's house, so now water meant life – however she obtained it. Or perhaps it would be easier to just die in this entry, without making a fuss. But starvation takes a long time to kill. First come the dizzy spells, followed by the legs not working properly due to insufficient calories. Priscilla realised death would come from the cold, because walking through the night to keep warm would lead her to collapse in some forgotten corner of the town.

Early the next morning, she emerged from her resting place, then stole a bottle of milk from a doorstep. That night she climbed a low garden wall to take bread from a bird table. However, with every passing day, her body was entering survival mode, just to keep going like a hunter-gatherer stumbling randomly across food. With every passing second, she felt death draw a little closer. Well, it had always done that, but before, you could ignore an individual second like an old coat at the back of a wardrobe. You knew vaguely it was there, but it was only in the depths of winter it had any meaning. Now she was actually wearing that heavy cloak of death, and knew her fragile existence would soon become nothing more than rotting flesh beneath the earth.

Thinking this tipped her mind into full survival mode, and led her to remember something that had happened two months earlier. Reginald had intended to take her to lunch in a four-star hotel but, on entering the reception area, he had spun around and dragged her towards the exit. Outside, he had become quite angry.

"I no longer have a son!" he had exclaimed. "The bastard in there is nothing to do with me."

"Mr Edwards Junior?" she had asked.

"I believe that is the name of the bastard behind the reception desk," he had said. "I am guessing he's employed to carry people's luggage hither and thither."

At the time, the man had no relevance to her life, so she had not pressed the point – except noting that Reginald's denunciations suggested the hotel worker had probably been disinherited. It implied Reginald had decided she was to inherit his entire estate.

Now Priscilla's mind drifted back further to her schooldays, and the way Reginald's son had helped the Scraggy Prostitute sort herself out. Naturally, he would now want to help herself because, as Reginald had frequently said, she had a nice pair of tits. So why had sir chosen Janet? Well, that was obvious. During her schooldays, her own experience of 'going all the way' had been limited to three occasions in the back of a boy's car. Then she remembered the field course, when she had kept losing knickers to the trophy hunters. But bending over a motorbike saddle did not really count. The significant thing back then was that she had not known how to 'do it' properly in a bedroom, which must be why Mr Edwards had chosen Janet: for her experience. But now she also knew all about sex in bedrooms, so any man would choose her instead. After all, she was much better-looking, with curves in all the right places. Okay, perhaps her tummy was now a little *too* flat, and her rib cage somewhat obvious, but she was still wearing a good bra which made her breasts appear perfect, at least with a little tissue paper shoved inside.

With a new purpose in life, she left the entry and hurried to the public toilets to fix her make-up. As far as Mr Edwards Junior was concerned, Janet was about to become history.

CHAPTER SEVENTEEN

Tara understood two truths about Richard. Firstly, he was adored by the hotel's female staff. Secondly, he had probably been a much better English teacher than… nobody ever mentioned the rest of the idea, because it was obvious, at least to those who had studied management. Besides these truths, there was a vague theory, put forward by his female admirers, that he might prefer '*the love that dare not speak its name*'. Tara knew this euphemism had been used by Oscar Wilde, as he had squatted in a lonely Victorian prison cell for the crime of falling in love with another man. Similarly, Richard seemed to be largely confined to a garret which, according to the housekeeper, consisted of a small domestic room, without a single woman ever coming to visit him. This had led to one of the staff suggesting he had never… you know! She could tell, apparently, because of his mannerisms and the way he stood. However, Tara thought Richard's habit of walking backwards to keep a safe distance between himself and the staff member concerned, was not exactly the same as being like Oscar Wilde. So occasionally she smiled at him, just to see what he might do. But he seemed not to notice. She could only comfort herself by thinking that was how he behaved with all women, however amazing they might be.

Tara liked Richard's undisciplined approach to management, because it meant her role on the reception desk became more important. As for herself, the most frequently used word she overheard relating to her personality was 'bossy'. But that was only because she always knew what needed to be done, and those who held a contrary view were completely wrong.

Her organisational skills had been responsible for her previous job coming to a premature end. She had controlled things better than the grumpy matron, who had not liked being bossed around by a girl then aged eighteen. At least, this was how Tara liked to remember her time at the hospital. The point at which her ex-boyfriend had become relevant, she preferred to overlook. Anyway, his lecherous ways had left her with no choice but to put prescription-strength laxatives in the cup of coffee she had brought him from the hospital vending machine. Making him sit on the loo for a couple of hours to contemplate the error of his ways had been entirely logical. Though, on reflection, perhaps she had got a little carried away with the dose. Him being rushed to the accident and emergency care unit was more of a fortuitous accident. Sadly, the grumpy matron lacked any sense of natural justice, so Tara had found herself grabbing her personal belongings and heading for the exit; eventually to spend some quality time feeding the ducks. Anyway, she now understood her reception desk was similar to the flight deck of an aeroplane: a place where things needed to be done correctly and, when necessary, with ruthless efficiency.

Then one morning, a woman entered the hotel, marched up to Tara's command centre, and said she wanted to speak to Mr Edwards.

What you want, thought Tara, *and what you get are not necessarily the same thing.* "You are?" she asked.

"Priscilla," came the reply. "He'll know who I am."

Priscilla the Gorilla, thought Tara. Whether Priscilla actually looked like a gorilla was irrelevant. It rhymed, so would help her to remember the name of a person she had no particular wish to think about. "Can I ask the nature of your business?" she enquired.

"No, you cannot."

I just have, thought Tara. *Not only does your silly, put-on voice indicate you had a terrible elocution teacher, but your understanding of the English language is clearly that of a child. I have no idea how you can have any connection to Richard.* She gave a little shiver. She often did when thinking about Richard. He was her only weak point. "Maybe," she said, "you could wait outside, while I see if Mr Edwards is available?" *Or at the bottom of the driveway, where the air circulation is better.*

"No," said the woman, "I shall wait on a sofa."

"But that is the waiting area for dining guests."

"So?"

What a horrible, high-pitched squeal, thought Tara. *Guests will think the fire alarm has just gone off.* But, with the woman now sitting on a sofa, the guests did not need a fire alarm to evacuate the building. The smell was quite sufficient. Then Tara recognised it as one which had offended her nostrils when she had worked at the hospital: gonorrhoea, a bacterial infection of the vagina and sometimes the throat and anus. She picked up the internal telephone – physically removing a guest from the premises, using her self-defence lessons, would need Richard's authority.

Richard had learnt to function quite well within the relatively gentle environment of a four-star hotel. It was the sort of place to which he had become accustomed in his youth – even though his father had frequently moaned about the level of service offered in such places. However, former stately homes catering exclusively to the aristocracy were few and far between, and frequently booked months in advance. So, contrary to what his father might pretend, Richard's experience of hospitality had been mostly confined to second-tier hotels, which now gave him a high degree of familiarity with their operation. This was quite useful, because it allowed half of his mind to remain on the subject of Janet, and hotel problems to be resolved by the remaining half.

And so it was that Richard sat at his desk with half of his brain trying to figure out how to resolve a dispute between the chef and the head waiter. Logically, he should view the situation from the chef's perspective, because he had both an explosive French temperament and a rolling pin... Richard's mind drifted back to the time when he and Janet had been in a supermarket, and she had tapped him gently on the head with a packet of spaghetti for choosing an unnecessarily expensive item. Such a wonderful time. Then the 'hotel' part of his brain remembered the way the chef always shouted in French, while the head waiter reverted to his native language of Italian. In consequence, trying to work out what was going on left him completely baffled. Like when Janet had first introduced him to a tent…

Richard was quite accustomed to dealing with such interwoven thoughts, in which Janet, and something less important, competed for his attention. Nevertheless, when the internal telephone rang, he was glad of the interruption. Lifting the receiver, he discovered the caller was Tara. Unusually, she seemed uncertain about a situation which was unfolding in reception. *Strange*, he thought; *she always knows what to do.* However, happy to stretch his legs, he made his way downstairs and looked towards the desk. Then, from the corner of his eye, he saw a young woman approaching.

"Mr Edwards," she said, "how nice to see you again."

He frowned. "I'm sorry," he said, "your name escapes me."

"Priscilla," said the woman. "You were my best-ever teacher in school." Priscilla realised Mr Edwards was looking at her as if he did not remember her. *How dare he?!* "You remember," she said, "all that business with the Scraggy Prostitute, Janet—"

Before she could finish the sentence, a hand flew towards her face. Only at the last moment did it rise to pass over her head.

Okay, thought Tara, *I have a situation which needs to be controlled: Richard has just tried to hit a person.* (For those she decided not like, she never ascribed a gender.)

"You tried to hit me!" screamed the Priscilla person.

Tara ran around the desk to stand between them, directing her gaze towards the Gorilla. "He did not," she said firmly. "He was merely stroking your hair, which, though strange, cannot be classed as aggressive."

Priscilla knew her hair always looked amazing so seductively flicked it to attract sir's gaze to the silky blonde curtain that fell about her shoulders. However, she realised the receptionist had got her head in the way, thereby obstructing his vision with a great tangle of ginger. Quickly, she rehearsed a suitable put-down. "You look like a crazy cartoon character that frightens little children," she said.

But the receptionist did not seem at all concerned about the observation. Instead, she calmly told Mr Edwards to take two steps backwards.

Having told Richard what needed to be done, Tara redirected her attention to the Gorilla. "I have no idea what you really look like," she said quietly. "Your make-up has clearly been applied using a builder's trowel, so it is impossible to see what lurks beneath. Perhaps if you put yourself through a car wash, Mr Edwards might recognise you better."

Then, knowing her observation would cause the Gorilla to lash out, she grabbed the approaching wrist and held it firm, stepping behind the street urchin's back so as to avoid her kicking feet.

"Ow," said Richard as a shoe connected with his shin.

"I did say to take two steps backwards," said Tara, quite cross he had ignored her advice. "However, we now have grounds for an assault charge against the Gorilla, who I suggest leaves the hotel before we call the police."

Priscilla felt the vice-like grip on her wrist loosen. "I hate you!" she shouted. Then she ran for the exit.

Richard also ran – but in the opposite direction: towards the stairs, up which he leapt three at a time.

Tara noticed some astonished spectators. "All sorted," she said to anyone who cared to listen. She then went behind the reception desk to put a little gentle background music on the record player. *Beethoven's 'Moonlight Sonata'*, she thought; *the first movement will reassure the guests that, after the Gorilla incident, everything is now under control.* She then switched on the announcements microphone and moved it towards the record player's speaker. The assistant receptionist, Donna, stared at her while biting her fingers nervously.

"No," said Tara, "like this." She tapped her fingers on the desk in time with the piano music. "And relax," she added. "Now, please take control of reception while I have a meeting with Mr Edwards. We are not to be disturbed."

A few minutes later, Tara walked into Richard's office without knocking. "What happened back there?" she asked. "I know you to be such a gentle person, but it was like watching Dr Jekyll and Mr Hyde… or is it the other way around? I can never quite remember."

Richard, sitting behind his desk, was obviously traumatised. "Sorry," he said.

Tara sat on the chair facing him. "Tell me," she said.

"I can't," said Richard.

"Of course you can," she said. "Perhaps you can begin by explaining about this Janet lady. Your girlfriend, maybe…?"

Then she realised Richard had lowered his head and was crying. She got up, locked the door and, to avoid looking at his tear-stained face, pulled her chair to his side of the desk.

"I bet Janet's really nice," she said.

"You need to be behind the reception desk," replied Richard.

"A horde of guests arriving is merely an inconvenient possibility," said Tara. "But you need someone to talk to, that is for certain. So, where did you meet Janet?"

Richard remained silent, so she edged her chair closer and put her arm around his shoulder. Annoyingly, he did not seem to notice; his mind apparently focused on a distant planet, presumably the one where Janet lived.

"Look," said Tara firmly, "there are three female staff members who are quite potty about you and frequently gossip about your good looks. All think you should be their boyfriend. So we need to know about this Janet lady. Only then can we prepare our plans for a romantic attack and subsequent happiness. Are you still seeing Janet?"

"We write to each other occasionally," responded Richard, "because she now lives in North Wales."

"Telephone?"

"No – her cottage is nearly a mile down a dead-end track. The nearest line is too far away, unless they put up thirty-five telegraph poles."

"To measure love in telegraph poles is silly," said Tara crossly. "In fact, only a man would make such a ridiculous statement. You need to hear her voice, and that is the end of the matter."

"Her voice is in my head all the time," said Richard. "I think I'm still having a nervous breakdown. Everything I do here in the hotel is just an act. Truthfully, I find life without Janet pointless."

"Then it is settled," said Tara. "You need somebody to talk to, and, for the time being, that somebody happens to be me." She looked at Richard, who was now crying into his hands. "And I need to eat," she added. "But not here, because two of your admirers would hate me, if they saw us having lunch together. Am I correct in thinking you have not left the hotel premises in a month?"

"No point in going anywhere without Janet."

"Because while you are here, she knows where to find you, or can maybe go to a telephone box to call you. Not to worry – I'll tell Donna you are having lunch with a friend, and to put any messages Janet might send on the answering machine."

A little later, Richard and Tara walked to the bottom of the driveway, then fifty yards to the left, where staff who drove cars unsuited to the aesthetics of a four-star hotel parked their vehicles.

"I have an old Austin 7," said Richard. "I keep it safe in a rented garage, because it's what I used to take Janet places."

"And it would not feel right to see me sitting in the passenger seat?"

"Sorry."

"It's fine, but you'll have to put up with my driving and, I should warn you, I've only just passed my test. So it's thirty miles an hour max, because I can't get the hang of all this double-declutching nonsense to change gears. For the test itself, I used my dad's car, which has one of those modern synchromesh gearboxes."

Richard smiled. Janet had struggled with double-declutching in the Austin, but her examiner had told her, probably incorrectly, that he could make allowances for vintage cars. As he explained this to Tara, she threw him a quick glance.

"So that's two things me and Janet have in common," she said. "You, and an understanding of the impossibility of double-declutching. I think she and I should meet; then we could have a good gossip, though probably not about cars."

After they had driven a short way, Tara performed an emergency stop.

"You're not taking your driving test now," said Richard, bracing himself against the dashboard.

"No," said Tara. "Back there, lying on the verge. I reckon it was Priscilla the Gorilla."

"Then leave it to rot!"

"Richard, really! I used to be an auxiliary nurse, so not only do I boss people around, but I'm also trained to care for the sick."

She got out of the car and hurried back to the woman, who, after Tara had checked her pulse, told her to "Sod off."

Tara hurried back to Richard. "She'll live," she said, "but she's in a bad way. Help me to get her onto the back seat."

"But I hate her!"

"Because she tried to hurt your Janet, I know. But does hating her make you feel any better? Such a negative emotion. So let's get her into the car."

"Janet always used to say something similar—" began Richard.

"Tell me later," interrupted Tara. "At the moment, we are running an ambulance service."

Fifteen minutes later, Tara and Richard carried Priscilla into the hospital's casualty department and laid her on the floor in front of some seats.

"Found her in the gutter," shouted Richard.

"Well," said Tara, "you can be certain *I'm* never going to say anything bad about your Janet."

Then they instinctively went to the toilets to sterilise their hands. By the time they returned to the reception, Priscilla was on a trolley, being wheeled away down a corridor.

"Who are you?" asked a nurse. "We need—"

"Just two really good friends," Tara called back. "The person on the trolley is called Priscilla the Gorilla. That is all you need to know. Oh, and that stink – I recognised it as gonorrhoea. I used to be an auxiliary here; she needs penicillin, maximum dose."

And with that, they left the building, Richard feeling totally confused by what was happening around him. Tara understood this and approved. It opened up the possibility of an unexpected romantic ambush catching him off guard.

CHAPTER EIGHTEEN

It is a fundamental law of village life that every resident has to know everything there is to know about everybody else who lives within the parish boundary. This leads to much gossip about any stranger who stands out from the crowd, by visiting the corner shop more than once in the same month. More seriously, an unknown woman entering the hardware store to buy a paintbrush is worthy of a mention in the community newsletter.

So, what about a lady in her mid twenties, arriving in a Land Rover from outside the area and moving into an isolated cottage just a mile from the village centre? Well, nothing like it had ever happened before, so the consequences were difficult to predict. Then, after the lady's all-important second visit to the corner shop, she was seen stepping from the pavement to pick up a caterpillar from the road. Excitedly, two older ladies followed the mysterious stranger down the High Street and across the village green. On coming to some bushes, she placed the caterpillar on a leaf.

"There you go, Mr Munchkins," she said. Then Janet heard two female voices speaking Welsh, possibly in a flummoxed tone. She turned to see the women stepping backwards, presumably to a distance where they felt more comfortable. "Sorry to startle you," she said, "but I have come to believe that caterpillars are quite hard of hearing. Otherwise they would not risk death trying to cross a noisy road."

"Oh, you're English, then?" said one of the ladies.

In order to keep things simple, Janet nodded and smiled.

"Ah," said the other lady, "that would explain it. And I believe you bought a paintbrush yesterday?"

"Decorating my cottage," said Janet. "The one on the clifftop."

"Ah, that would explain it," said the second lady. "When we saw you driving a Land Rover towards the next village, we thought you must live down the old dirt track to Mr Owen's barn. But that blew away in the great storm of 1952, so you wouldn't know about that. Sometimes the water can be two feet deep. Mr Elliott had a horse—"

"No," interrupted the first lady, "that was Mr Tomkins. Mr Elliott had a tractor – don't you remember, he always smoked a pipe…"

Then they reverted to speaking Welsh, which Janet assumed meant they were having an argument too involved for them to translate into English. She imagined it to be about tractors, pipes, or other things of which she had no understanding.

Finally they seemed to remember she was there, and smiled. "*Hwyl fawr*," they said as they walked away, no doubt to tell somebody or other about her dramatic rescue of Mr Munchkins.

Janet thought it unwise to run after them to ask why they had mentioned 'the water'. Instead she focused on memorising their last two words, which, she reasoned, meant 'goodbye'.

The issue of 'the water' then faded from her mind until, a week later, when quite a lot of it fell from the sky. This informed Janet any talk of rain in Snowdonia had to include the word 'buckets', or whatever its Welsh equivalent might be. Anyway, when it eased to a light drizzle, she left her cottage to look across the bay. She was genuinely surprised to discover the ocean was the same height as it had been before all the rain, and not halfway up the cliff face, as her recent dream had foretold. Presently, she walked to the Land Rover, her intention being to drive to the village to buy a loaf of bread and a bottle of milk from the corner shop – her third visit! However, before reaching the main road, she had to bring the vehicle to a sudden halt. Ahead, what had been a stream had become a river. *Ah*, she thought, the ladies on the village green had known all about this – the tractor, the horse, and probably a lot of other stuff she had failed to grasp, after they had reverted to their native language.

Looking across the water, Janet realised it had turned her cottage into an isolated, heavenly enclave, well defended from the frenzied gossip of village life. Then, remembering the bag of flour and the packet of yeast in her kitchen cupboard, her thoughts turned to baking bread instead of buying it. Also, the farmer who owned the next field had already said she could fill a jug with goat's milk for a penny. She knew this to be a kindness, so had not liked to take undue advantage of it, but the flood was a good excuse.

After spending the morning attending to her domestic needs, Janet relaxed in the rain-cleansed paradise of her garden. Here, she talked to any animal who cared to listen.

"And the good thing about being friends with you lot," she said to a hare who just happened to be passing, "is you will never judge me for my past sins."

The hare stopped to regard her carefully. Then, presumably deciding she posed no threat, he hopped into the nearby undergrowth where, she suspected, he had a nest.

She squatted on the ground next to his 'entry'. "I used to live down an entry," she said, "so understand how you see the world. Though Stink Alley wasn't half so nice as your rural retreat. I expect you have a cosy bed, and no horrible neighbours. Then, later – though still a long time ago – I also lived under a bush, just like you, so I expect one day we will become really good friends."

The following day, she formed a notion that she should remain in her cottage and garden for… well, however long Noah had stayed on his ark. But she had no idea how long that might be. Forty days rang a bell, which made it most inconvenient when her track became a muddy puddle before the end of the week. But by then she had become accustomed to walking along the narrow clifftop footpath to the village. On one occasion she stopped to watch a pod of dolphins splashing around in the bay. *One day*, she thought, *after I have learnt to swim a mile without difficultly, I will come to visit you lot, just to say hello.* But for now, she gave them a friendly wave, then continued her walk to the village, realising it was much nicer than driving.

As the days turned into weeks, Janet's voice softened to a tone the animals seemed to prefer. Increasingly she felt herself to be among friends, especially after some braver birds thought it safe to perch on her hand to take a piece of fruit. The contact of their tiny feet conveyed a bond of innocent trust, which allowed her to imagine a childhood very different to her own. Perhaps that was why she longed to become proper friends with the hare; to have him hopping about her kitchen while she prepared him a bowl of breakfast cereal. But he remained aloof from her and from the other animals. *So alone,* she thought sadly, *and, as far as I know, without a girlfriend.*

While Janet's domestic life was becoming ever more idyllic, her commercial ambitions were going nowhere. This was because her carefully prepared business plan had overlooked the important detail that her cottage was situated in a Welsh-speaking area. This had not been obvious during holiday visits, because the locals automatically spoke English to an '*estron*'. (This word, she discovered later, meant 'stranger' or 'outsider', and could apply to anyone who lived beyond the parish boundary or even in England; a distant land where some residents had never been, nor had any wish to go. Later still, she realised that '*estron*' could also mean 'strange person', which she found rather curious.) Anyway, aspiring local authors wrote in their native language, while those who were well established, already had a London agent. Not a good combination for Janet, if she wanted to found a literary agency in the area.

And so it was that her first year in Wales required all the survival skills she had learned in Wellington Place – except now her income was mostly scratched together from casual cleaning jobs or helping to bring in the harvest. In addition to this problem, she needed to attend night school regularly in order to learn Welsh. This meant keeping the Land Rover on the road, or ploughing through deep water as the need arose. In order to achieve this, she had to pay a garage to relocate the air intake to the bonnet and extend the exhaust pipe to the roof. As well as this unexpected expense, there was all the other grown-up stuff like buying bottled gas for cooking and heating water, which meant her carefully prepared cash-flow projection led to days without eating.

Janet considered her best idea throughout this period to be taking a tame billy goat (who belonged to a local farmer) for walks along the beach, using a standard dog lead to stop him wandering off. Children ran across to pet the animal and offer him food. This suited the goat very well and, in nearly every case where the children's guardians were having a picnic, they offered her a place on their rug, and a sandwich or a piece of cake.

Initially, Janet's language studies went less well. All the new words left her totally baffled. But why? At school she had learnt basic German within six months. One evening she told the tutor about her concerns. "It's old age," she concluded. "When I was fourteen my brain was like a sponge, but now it has set like concrete."

The tutor enthusiastically explained that Welsh pre-dated the Roman Empire, so was unlike the inferior language spoken by the conquered people of England. He then proudly informed her that Welsh was better suited to conveying complex thoughts and poetry.

"Complex?" questioned Janet. "I don't like the sound of that."

"I have yet to meet an English speaker who could pass O level Welsh in less than two years," he said.

And I want to be a literary agent, thought Janet. *Yet at the moment, I can't even read a children's book with a single line of text on an illustrated page… possibly about a man sitting on a tractor, smoking a pipe.*

As if to emphasise this, on leaving the classroom she stopped to stare at a notice in the passageway which read, *'Dim ysmygu'*. How on earth was she expected to pronounce that?! It seemed to be telling her founding a literary agency in this area would take years. Then the tutor came to stand by her side.

"It means 'No smoking'," he said.

She wondered how something so simple could be spelt in such a way. "And what is the word for despair?" she asked. "Because that is what I feel right now."

"Welsh is the language of Heaven," he said, "so we do not need such a word. Our closest approximation is *'anobeitho'*, which in English means 'hopeless.'"

Janet realised that if Welsh pre-dated all modern European languages, it was obviously what they would speak in Heaven. She asked the tutor how to say, 'Mother, hear my prayer' in Welsh.

"*Mam, clywed fy gweddi,*" he said.

She asked him to write it down for her. From then on, Welsh was to be the special language that her mother would best understand.

Even though Janet's initial inability to understand Welsh held her back professionally, the locals all seemed to like her well enough as a friend. This allowed her to join a chess club and build a fearsome reputation within the local league. And, besides giving her a break from study and work, it had the advantage of being completely free.

Six months after moving to Wales, Janet felt able to attempt her first basic conversation in the village shop – though she found it difficult to ask for certain foods. However, given her financial circumstances, all she really needed to ask for was *tatws* (potatoes) or *bara* (bread). With the motivation of talking to her mother in Welsh, she came to totally astound her tutor with her progress. Within three years she could think in Welsh or English as the need arose. And this became her strength because, just as she had once struggled with Welsh, the locals generally found English weird and back to front. After revising her business plan, her reputation soon grew to a point where she could earn a little money translating manuscripts between the two languages. And so, at the age of twenty-six, Janet was able to take short breaks from work, generally visiting the wilderness in the tent she had once shared with Richard. On one such occasion she found herself standing on a small beach rock with her feet close together. Any slip would likely cause a few scratches, if she landed prostrate on the surrounding seaweed and mud. Having established the rock was unlikely to wobble, she gazed along the Strait towards Stephenson's railway bridge, remembering how wonderful it had been when Richard had led her this way at low tide. Now, part of her wished he had come to her bed during their first night at the hotel. At that time, she had considered herself to be an expert in blanking unpleasant things from her mind, so could have just closed her eyes and waited for it to be over. But as the holiday progressed, Richard had become her trusted best friend, while he had come to fully understand the sordid nature of her earlier life. These facts meant doing anything with him then would have amounted to rape, and he would have lost her respect. Had he tried anything, she would have walked away, hoping never to see him again. No, it was more than that. She had come to regard him as a sort of father figure. The 'sort of' qualification was only because he was too young to be her father. But in her mind, he was what a father should be; at least in a magical, fairy-tale land where everything was perfect. Even now, the idea of having a romantic relationship with him was unimaginable.

So what had it all come to? Here she was, standing near a muddy puddle, gazing towards a bridge, daydreaming about him standing beside her, talking about railway lines. The road on top of the bridge was now carrying vehicles Stephenson could never have imagined. Not even her love for Richard would last that long. On the day she died, the emotion would cease to exist, and all of this nonsense would have no meaning for those who might stand in this very puddle, a hundred years from now...

Standing *in* a puddle? Surely she was standing near it? Leaving her daydream, she looked down to see water washing around her feet. *Help!* The tide was coming in – and rather quickly. She now had the choice of climbing over a barbed-wire fence into a field, from which a rather large bull was watching her with some curiosity, or wading on and hoping she would not be swept away by the current.

A situation like this definitely needed Richard. He would give her a piggyback to freedom… except her body was so disgusting she could not wrap her legs around his thighs. But he would offer and, when she refused, he would guide her to safety.

As it happened, she managed to continue her route with the water only reaching her knees. Then, on arriving at Church Island, she sat among the gravestones and cried like a child. She needed Richard to be her friend; not just someone working in a hotel 150 miles away. How long she sat like this, she could not say, but eventually she heard approaching footsteps.

"Are you okay?" asked a man's voice.

"Fine," she replied. Such a retort was unusual for her, but only because the single word was actually meant to imply, *Please go away*.

"Then why are you sitting in a graveyard, crying?"

How could she deny it? She looked up to see a man in his seventies, but she knew his age did not prevent him from wanting to use her body for half an hour. Then she saw a little girl, aged about eight, trying unsuccessfully to hide behind his legs.

"My granddaughter," continued the man, "came to get me because she thought 'the lady' was unhappy. Is this where someone important lives?" He gestured around the gravestones.

Realising he had modified his speech for the benefit of his granddaughter, Janet leaned sideways to try to get a better view of her. "No," she said. "The man I love lives 150 miles away in a hotel. But he brought me here once, a long time ago, so it is a good place to remember nice things."

"But your sadness is upsetting my granddaughter, so perhaps you would like to come with us for a coffee? There is a cafe in Menai village which also does lemonade, if you would prefer?"

Janet thought quickly. "But that would not be proper, if I don't know your names," she said.

"Alice," said the man, "and my granddaughter's name is Albert. Or is that the wrong way around? I often get confused at my age."

The girl giggled, but shyness still prevented her from speaking.

"So how old are you, Albert?" asked Janet. "I think about twelve?"

"There," said the man, "the lady thinks you are twelve, which means you are old enough to ask her name."

Janet decided such a situation did need a nice sit down in a cafe, with lemonade and cake on the table. If it helped her to remember what it had felt like to be eight years old, when her mother was alive, then so much the better. "I'm Janet," she said. Then she stood up and stepped behind the man. "Come on, Albert," she continued, "let me take you to the cafe for lemonade and cake. Though you will have to show me the way because I am sure your granddad will get confused and lead me in quite the wrong direction."

But the girl merely ran away.

"Sorry," said Janet to the grandfather, "I didn't mean to scare her."

"Don't alarm yourself," he said. "She's just gone to say goodbye to her mother, who lives over there. You understand?"

Rather than say the words, Janet nodded.

While the girl went to 'see' her mother, Janet found herself telling the old man about Richard – albeit a heavily edited version of the story, which avoided talking about her horrible, diseased body. But talking to a stranger helped and, when the girl returned, Janet felt able to pretend a smile. The girl responded by announcing her mother had said it was okay for her to make friends with the nice lady. She then led them proudly along the promenade to the cafe in the village.

Once seated around a table, their light-hearted chit-chat gathered pace. Soon the grandfather asked Janet if she was feeling better, to which she smiled.

"Then," he said, "our work here is done… almost." He went to the counter and returned with a postcard of the bridge. He told her to write a message to Richard – now, because he had paid for another coffee, so she might have a quiet fifteen minutes to consider her wording. "Not too carefully," he added. "Write from the heart. If he loves you, he will come. If he does not…" He shrugged. "But whatever his response, there is to be no more sitting and crying in graveyards."

Then he was gone, leaving Janet to wonder if he and his granddaughter had been angelic visions sent by the church to stop her tears. But no – she had an actual postcard in her hand. The only problem now was what to do with it.

CHAPTER NINETEEN

Following Priscilla's visit to the hotel, Tara spent most of her free time with Richard. Generally her role was to listen to him talking about the magical Janet, but that was okay, because sharing his despair seemed to help his troubled mind. He even started to smile, albeit very occasionally. This had the rather curious side effect of making the other staff believe they were having an affair. The two girls who really liked him sometimes asked Tara what he was like, you know, when… Other times, they claimed to hate her for capturing the best bachelor for miles around. Mischievously, she let the question "What's he like?" pass without comment. It was rather nice if people thought she and Richard were an item.

"Oh," she had once responded casually, "all you need to know is that he is off limits, and you should focus your ambitions elsewhere." Well, that was true, so it needed to be said, just to keep everything in good order. If they had known Janet lived in an isolated cottage 150 miles away, the statement would have carried less weight.

Even though Tara liked being mischievous, it was

obvious any romantic ideas directed towards Richard were pointless. Mostly, she knew this to be true because of her own experience of having a lecherous boyfriend. After their parting, she had worn her bravery like an overcoat, just to let the world know she was okay. But inside, she had believed that her life no longer had any value. Then, after three months, the despair had started to fade, and now it was just an annoying memory on the fringes of her brain. Yet Janet had been living in faraway places for five years, her contact with Richard reduced to occasional letters. Tara realised Janet had effectively become Richard's imaginary friend, or possibly a fantasy which had little connection to the real world. And if that magical kingdom inside his head ever collapsed, there was no saying how he might react. Anyway, Tara was fairly certain that, given time, she could sort him out. So who else could she help in order to keep herself occupied? Should she attempt something really difficult? No, that was too mad!

But something kept gnawing away at her mind. When Priscilla had left the hotel, she had been carrying a shoulder bag. When they had found her lying on the verge, it had been missing. Somewhere along the way, it must have become detached from its crazy owner. Tara thought it must contain everything Priscilla owned, other than the clothes she had been wearing – essentially, a silly summer dress designed principally to display most of her breasts. So, dumping her at the hospital had not been particularly helpful. Saving a person's life was of little use, if they were destined to die at the end of the week anyway. *Okay*, she thought, *better not tell Richard about this, but I'll go to the hospital to see what happens… and it will give me a break from hearing about how perfect Janet is in every possible way.*

Then another thought came to Tara's mind. Richard rarely told her how beautiful Janet was. Well, maybe ten times an hour, but for him that was quite low. No – mostly he talked about her kindness, her personality, how she had bought a tent for their holiday in Wales... so on and so forth. But the truth of the matter was nobody could be that perfect. Tara was certain there were things Richard was not telling her. His tales did not make sense unless there were bits missing. For instance, why had he given up teaching to become a hotel receptionist? What might she discover if she spoke to Priscilla, who would no doubt focus on Janet's bad bits and ignore the good stuff, which Tara already knew about in great detail?

On arriving at the hospital, she first asked around to see if she knew any of the nurses who might be on duty. Having no luck, she went to Matron's office, knocked on the door, and was told to come in.

"Matron," she said.

"Tara," gasped Matron, "the bossy one. What are you doing here?"

"Don't panic. I don't want my old job back."

"Thank Heavens for that!"

Tara advanced and sat in front of the desk, explaining that she was here to help someone... maybe.

Matron softened and even smiled. "If you want the truth," she said, "I actually quite miss you – you can have your old job back any time you want."

"And the ugly lab technician with the big ears?"

"Horrible man. I had to sack him for kissing a patient."

"Excellent news! But that is not why I am here – I'm guessing you have a bed-blocker, name of Priscilla."

"Complete nightmare – take her away, and I'll be your friend for life."

"And the gonorrhoea?"

"You know I can't talk about medical issues."

"It's okay, she's a prostitute; gonorrhoea is just a hazard of the job."

Matron's face contorted in an expression of disgust. "Oral and vaginal," she said. "Oh, stop it! Bossing me around and getting me to say things I shouldn't."

"But you want her gone?"

Matron looked at her for an instant, then went to the filing cabinet. "I'm just going to get us both a coffee," she said. "Oops," she added, as she dropped Priscilla's file on her desk before walking out of the door.

Half an hour later, Tara realised it was possible to have a friendly chat with Matron, even about the old times when she had walked through the hospital doors, clutching her O level certificate in human biology. Her auxiliary nurse position had come with a day release to allow her to attend college. She had enjoyed that part of her life, until stupid… Thingy… had spoiled it. Anyway, now she liked working in the hotel better, because it meant she had a lot more people to organise.

On arriving at Priscilla's bed, Tara looked down to see a pathetic white face. In response to asking how she was, the reply was, "Hungry."

Well, thought Tara, *that is a lot better than starving.*

"I know you," continued Priscilla. "You're something to do with the hotel. A cleaner, possibly?"

"I clean away rubbish from the foyer," responded Tara, "that much is true." She realised Priscilla had missed the comment's hidden meaning. "But," she continued, "I used to be a nurse here, so I know all the procedures. I reckon if you had somewhere to go, you would have been discharged after two nights, once you had been rehydrated and your glucose levels built back up."

"I'm nearly dying!"

"It was me who found you lying on the verge, so I know exactly what you are. I diagnosed the gonorrhoea from the smell."

"How dare you speak to me like that? You're just Mr Edwards' bit of stuff on the side."

"That sounds rather nice, but Richard's not like that. His love for Janet is forever. Trying to offer him your services was just silly—"

"I am not a prostitute!" screamed Priscilla.

"So you announce it to the whole ward? Most curious behaviour. Anyway, I'm going for a meal in the cafe, just to give you a chance to have a good think about your situation. Afterwards, I will come back. If you are still obnoxious, I will walk away forever. If you want my help, I will expect you to behave correctly."

Tara had not thought it possible for anyone to have such a hysterical tantrum while still in bed. She waited for five minutes or so, after which Priscilla's energetic performance caused her to fall back on the mattress, exhausted. Tara gave her an enthusiastic round of applause.

"Bravo," she cried. "Now the whole hospital will know you are fit enough to be discharged this afternoon."

Turning away from the bed, Tara saw a man aged about thirty standing near the exit to the corridor. He was wearing a white coat. Nothing unusual about that in a hospital. The fact his mouth was wide open, as if to display his tonsils was, again, quite routine for a hospital. Tara decided he looked quite friendly, so walked towards him, then put the backs of her fingers beneath his chin to close his jaw. This caused him to blink, which she took to mean he had returned to the real world. She then walked into the corridor to discover Matron hiding behind the door frame, actually laughing. How was such a thing possible? Surely her smiling muscles would have faded away ages ago from lack of use?

"Well," said Matron, "it seems my image as an ogre is ruined. So let us all have lunch together."

Before Tara could agree, she realised the man in the white coat had followed her into the corridor.

"I have been a psychiatrist here for eight years," he said, "yet I have never witnessed anything like that before. There was no way I was going to approach such a hysterical patient without a military escort."

"I've seen it before," said Tara. "She's not that fierce when you get to know her."

Matron turned to the psychiatrist. "This is Tara," she said. "She used to work here as a nurse."

Tara noticed the word 'auxiliary' had been dropped, which represented a significant promotion. And Matron's personality was less domineering than it had been three years earlier.

Then the psychiatrist interrupted her thoughts. "Ah, yes," he said, "I remember now: the bossy one with all the ginger hair. I believe there was some issue with laxatives and a laboratory technician. I am surprised the police were not informed."

"Relegating me to the position of number-two

girlfriend," replied Tara, "is not a police matter, and, even if it had gone to court, he might have escaped justice by claiming insanity."

The psychiatrist took a step backwards. Tara wondered if this was to establish a safety zone, or so he might better examine her from a distance. If it was the latter, was his examination psychological or physical? Before she could reach any conclusion, Matron introduced him as Dr Phillips, then suggested they all go to the canteen, because gossiping in the corridor was unprofessional. Tara gave a friendly smile, and Dr Phillips did not attempt to defend himself from the gesture.

Matron could only take half an hour for lunch, which left Tara and Dr Phillips sitting alone to finish their coffee. Tara sensed he was also struggling to find things to say. Not wishing to let her meeting with a friendly psychiatrist go to waste, she decided to ask him about her problem. She explained that she knew a man named Richard who was suffering from a bad case of unrequited love for an asexual woman. Dr Phillips enquired as to whether the woman had a name. Tara replied it was purely a hypothetical situation. They argued about this for a while, until Tara became rather cross.

"But it's not me who needs advice," she said. "It is my friend."

"Because you like to be in control of things," Dr Phillips responded, "and that's impossible when you are in love?"

"I'm not in love," she retorted. "Look, stop getting me to say things."

"But I'm a psychiatrist; it's my job to investigate the workings of the mind."

Tara felt her wrist being lifted, then enclosed. Looking down, she saw the doctor had sandwiched it between his fingers and thumb. "Uh," she said. It was the sort of 'Uh' that meant her wrist and hand had been taken prisoner.

"Now, tell me about Richard," said Dr Phillips. "Is he the man you love?"

"No, absolutely not. And why are you holding my hand when you are a doctor and I am a nurse – I mean, was? Oh, stop it."

"I am not holding your hand," he said, "but taking your pulse. It responds to Richard's name – when you hear it and, I strongly suspect, when you think about him."

Then, rather disappointingly, he let go of her wrist.

"So tell me everything," he continued. "Maybe over a coffee, after work… so long as you are not my patient, because then I cannot also be your friend."

"I'm seeing Richard tonight," she said.

"Interesting," he said. "Your voice softened when you said his name. So this *is* the man you love, who loves somebody else, who is asexual."

"Shut up – no! Definitely not!"

"A double denial. This generally means a positive. But I am here to listen. Please continue."

Without using Janet's name, Tara told Dr Phillips everything she knew about the girl who claimed to be asexual.

"Until very recently," he responded, "women had little choice but to take a path which led to a marriage bed, so figures are hard to come by – social pressures disguising lesbian and asexual preferences. Perhaps ten per cent of women have no need for a man in their life. But this is not an illness – indeed, some might think it sensible. In any event, I would never attempt to change an individual's sexual preferences. However, from what I have witnessed, nearly every case of asexuality begins with a sexual trauma in childhood."

"I have my suspicions about the latter," said Tara, "but Richard will never say anything bad about her."

"Being a victim is nothing to be ashamed of. And, to answer your question, women often go off sex for a few months for one reason or another. But you mentioned many years of voluntary celibacy. This indicates the damage is permanent. As for Richard, who I gather has never had a romantic relationship with this woman, he may be suffering from de Clérambault syndrome. It is like how some men focus their devotion on a film star or a similar famous person, without any grounding in reality. Possibly she even moved away to avoid him."

"But he's a gorgeous hunk—" Tara clapped a hand over her mouth. "Sorry," she said through spaced fingers.

"Never apologise for being honest," he said. "Those who keep their thoughts bottled up make my life far more difficult."

Tara tried, without much success, to get her thoughts into some sort of rational order. "Richard," she said presently, "says he and Janet share the same mind, irrespective of geographical distance."

"A bit like being 'in love' with a film star. But the question you should ask is, does his de Clérambault syndrome cause him to have suicidal thoughts?"

"No."

"Have you asked? Because obsessive compulsive

disorder is a common side effect. Essentially, the brain is rewired to believe life without the person who is desired is worth nothing. His actions might not be rational."

"No… I mean, I have no idea what he is thinking. I just assumed no sane woman would go to live in another country to put distance between herself and him. But now I come to think about it, Wales is quite a long way to go for no apparent reason."

"Men rarely talk about their feelings," said the doctor. "But what you have described suggests Richard considers his life to be of little value. If so, be careful, because you are dealing with dangerous psychological issues. I suggest you tell him that, if his life is worth nothing to him, it might be of use to others. If he dedicates himself to helping those he knows then, by definition, his existence has some value. Also tell him helping others begins a chain reaction that will survive for all time – or at least until humanity ceases to exist. And by doing this, he will most probably become surrounded by a close circle of friends, which might cure his depressive thoughts."

"I see," said Tara, "and I know just the person he can help. It will keep him occupied for years. Though I have to say, it would be easier for him to climb Mount Everest than to help the person I have in mind."

"There are many ways to die," said Dr Phillips, "so, when dealing with your friend, be aware of this, and tread gently with his emotions. Talking of which, is this still a professional consultation, or am I one of your lucky friends also?"

"Friends, I guess."

In response, he placed his hands over hers. "Maybe I

could take you to dinner sometime?" he said. "And before you answer, be aware that this time I am not taking your pulse for medical reasons. No pressure."

Then he stood up, gave a slight bow, and walked away. To Tara's astonishment, he even left a little card on the table that bore a telephone number!

After her heart rate had settled, she returned to the ward, where she discovered Priscilla had fled – presumably because of the laughter from the other patients. In fact, two of them had been so amused they had felt much better and asked to be discharged. Tara, knowing she had brought some laughter into the world of sick people, was quite pleased – even though it was not the outcome she had been trying to achieve.

Tara's brief encounter with Priscilla the Gorilla had only confirmed that the girl was a complete nightmare, who had probably caused equal disruption in her school lessons with Janet. She was the key to understanding the whole situation – or, at least, would have been, had she not vanished from the hospital.

Ten days after the hospital incident, Tara was sitting at the reception desk, sorting some paperwork, when she was distracted by a very quiet voice.

"Please," it said, "help me. I am waiting outside."

She looked towards the hotel's entrance door. A barely recognisable Priscilla was standing there, wrapped in an old army trench coat and looking close to death. After handing over responsibility to Donna, Tara made her way outside to discover Priscilla sitting on the ground with her back against the wall.

"I can't stand for long," she said. "Not without passing out."

Looks about right, thought Tara. "I'll get a couple of sandwiches from the chef," she said. "Back in a mo. Though I will need to escort you further away from the entrance. In fact, around the back of the building."

Losing four slices of bread and a bit of cheese was of no significance to the hotel. Also, among all the other fun things Tara had been doing, she had resolved the chef's difficulties with the head waiter, so he owed her a few minutes of his time. Though, of course, being a French chef, he believed a basic cheese sandwich to be illegal. The one he prepared for Priscilla came on a plate, with salad and some fancy sauce on the side. This was another reason why Tara could not tell Richard what was happening. Had a diner purchased this, it would have cost them a pound. Using the back door, she returned to Priscilla, dropped the plate onto her lap and placed a glass of water by her side. A moment later Priscilla was pushing the food into her mouth like a squirrel who had just stumbled upon a tray of hazelnuts.

"Well," said Tara, "that solves one problem. I am going to start calling you Squirrel, because it means I can mention you to Richard without him flying off the handle. I mean, squirrels have a reputation for being rather cute, with their bright eyes and their bushy tails."

She was pleased when Squirrel did not argue, though possibly only because her mouth was bulging with food. Squirrels were like this – focused on building up fat reserves for the cold weather. Though it was quite obvious that, without help, this one would not survive the approaching winter.

"I reckon," said Tara, after Squirrel had picked the last crumb from the plate, "you have not eaten for a long time?"

"Three days. I am quite rubbish at earning money, even—"

"Yes," said Tara, holding out a hand to imply more words were necessary to finish the sentence.

"Even as a prostitute," whispered Squirrel. "Yes, I am one of those, like Janet—"

"Stop! Rule number one: never, ever say anything bad about Janet. Richard is very protective of her. I will make up my own mind, when… *if* the time comes for us to meet."

"Sorry."

"It is better for you," continued Tara, "if you consider Janet to be the most perfect thing in the universe. Understand this, and I might see if Richard will help you."

"I was hoping you… well, you always know what to do."

"Of course, but I only have one room in a shared house, and I'm not allowed overnight visitors because there is only one toilet for five tenants. Also, I earn eight pounds a week. I survive, but you need serious help; the sort which requires a kind, generous man like Richard to give. And for that I need you to practise your elocution - like in that film where the actress has to speak correctly for a bet. Something about the rain in Spain falling mainly on the plain - only in your case you have to say that Janet is really nice."

"But she's a scraggy—"

"Stop! I believe it took the actress months to learn her lines properly, so go find somewhere quiet to practise yours. If you walk down the lane, away from the town, you will come to a nature reserve. Go to the pond and tell the ducks what you wish to say. They are unlikely to object. I will come to see you after work, about six o'clock." She went to the food bin and pulled out a handful of crusty bread slices. She wrapped these in a sheet of newspaper from another bin and handed the parcel to Squirrel. "Feed this to the ducks," she said. "It will make them a more appreciative audience for your Janet speech."

As soon as Priscilla was outside the gates, she ate the bread, then pushed the newspaper into her coat pocket. The lack of food meant it had been five days since she had needed the toilet, but now she would have some paper for her next visit to a quiet wood or elsewhere.

Richard walked down to the reception to find everything in good order, as could be expected when Tara was on duty. She gestured to the spare chair, where the assistant receptionist should be sitting. But if the afternoon was quiet, Richard turned a blind eye to staff going for a quiet wander around the grounds. He sat on the chair, and pushed it back on its wheels, just so guests would not think him the receptionist. Not that the title was beneath him, but Tara always greeted visitors with a friendly smile which generally put them into a relaxed mood.

"I've been thinking about the scullery maid," she said. "That is, the scullery maid we do not have since she stormed off last week."

"I've got the advert going into the newspaper tomorrow," he said.

"But we both know whoever you employ will be gone within three months. Some leave the first day."

"Because girls only take such a job if they are really

desperate," said Richard. "They hate it from the moment they are taken to the room in the basement. Within thirty seconds their main aim in life is to leave."

"But what if you got somebody who was really, really, *really* desperate?"

"Well, they would be really, really, *really* terrible."

"But I know a lady who goes by the name of Squirrel. If I started going through all the 'reallies' she deserves, we would be here all day."

"'Reallies' is not a word. And... Squirrel?"

"I expect she had eccentric parents; probably lived in a wigwam or something. Anyway, I'm sure she would do the ten-hour shifts, washing pans and the like."

"I would have to interview her first."

"We pay ten pence an hour; at that rate, it is the candidate who interviews us. Thing is, the few who even know how to drive could not afford to run a car on that. And we're a mile from the nearest bus route. A ten-hour shift which begins at midday ends at midnight. Even in the town, there are no buses at that time. Hence the situation we are in now. Donna is in the scullery now, doing two hours of cover until the cleaner can take over for a bit. The whole situation is a nightmare."

Richard gave a thoughtful nod. "Walking back along the lane after midnight is not exactly safe," he agreed.

"Whereas Squirrel lives in the nature reserve – you know, the birdwatching shelter by the duck pond. It's only a short walk, and she cannot go home until the courting couples have finished using it."

"That does sound a bit desperate," said Richard.

"Yesterday," continued Tara, "I gave her some bread

from the bins to feed the ducks. Then I followed her. As soon as she thought I couldn't see her, she ate the bread herself. Really it was just my way of testing her – had she thrown it to the ducks, she would clearly not be about to die from starvation. But this will surely be the case, unless we help her."

"The bins?" said Richard. "This implies she was in the hotel—"

"Do not concern yourself; I sorted it. You can get into the scullery from the back entrance near the dustbins. And if she's wearing caretaker's overalls, and using our staff showers, nobody needs to know she is homeless."

"Possible… Okay, just so long as it's not Priscilla, the interview will be a formality."

"Maybe I can get the chef to do it; save you the bother?"

"No, it's fine… unless… it *is* Priscilla, isn't it?"

"She'll be in the scullery; you need never see her."

"She's a complete disaster!"

"Like our pots and pans… so they will be a perfect match."

Richard stormed off without comment. When Donna returned, she told Tara that if she ever had to do another shift in "the dungeon", she would resign. Tara replied that she had sorted it.

Donna smiled. "You sort everything," she said. "Thank you."

Tara liked it when people said that – but this time, she thought a case as impossible as Priscilla might lead to her being sacked. But she must prevent the girl from starving to death, and hopefully Richard would come to see it this way too.

At eight o'clock that evening, she went to see him in his office. "The washing-up is in progress," she said, "the cleaner is happy, and Donna has withdrawn her notice. I would be grateful if you do not sack me... but I accept sometimes these inconveniences are necessary to save the life of another human being." Then she knelt by Richard's desk, and bravely reached out to hold his hand.

Richard looked at the delicate fingers surrounding his own. It felt nice. For a moment, he even forgot there was a prostitute working in the scullery.

CHAPTER TWENTY

Since passing her driving test, Tara had saved a pound a week; the general plan being to go somewhere more adventurous than her daily journey to and from work. But where this might be, and for what purpose, she had not the faintest idea. Her initial plan of London had been abandoned after her father had told her there were hundreds of cars everywhere there, all whizzing about without any regard for public safety. Dudley Zoo sounded interesting because she quite liked looking at elephants and giraffes, but, while getting there might involve less traffic, it seemed to lack the necessary pizazz for her first big solo adventure.

While these vague notions were floating around her mind, a postman dropped the mail on the reception desk. It was her job to look after this until the houseboy turned up for work. Anyway, while nosing through the boring assortment of envelopes, she came across a most confusing postcard. On the front was a picture of a bridge. On the back was a simple message:

Richard,

Come to see me whenever you want. Have you got a girlfriend yet? If so, bring her along so I can check her out. If she's horrible, I'll throw her out of my back door – which, you will remember, is only four yards from the sea cliffs. Only the best for you, my dearest.

Massive lots of love,
Janet

Tara thought it a very curious postcard. Then a guest arrived, and she put the matter to the back of her mind.

On the third floor, Richard sat at his desk, staring into space. Near his right elbow, yesterday's post lay unopened, while to his left, the in-tray was overflowing with assorted notes and letters which needed his urgent attention. What was happening to his life? Three weeks earlier it had been really well organised. He woke up, thought about Janet, then a little later, arrived at his desk to begin his duties, while Janet settled into a background of gentle thoughts. This had allowed him to deal with the boredom of real life in ways that were generally effective. Now, he only thought about Janet most of the time. Occasionally, and for no apparent reason, Tara would drift across his mind; perhaps smiling, or trying to be helpful in ways that made no sense whatsoever – like installing Priscilla in the hotel basement. Compared to this, the post waiting unopened on his desk was unlikely to be important.

At eleven o'clock, the houseboy arrived with another

handful of mail. Richard immediately studied the postcard from Janet. It might be important, because recently her letters had reduced to four a year, and this correspondence was a definite bonus. But it was just a normal sort of message inviting him to visit, and some nonsense about him acquiring an alternative girlfriend. He then realised his rule about having no secrets from Janet meant that the next time they met, he would have to tell her about the Priscilla disaster zone in the basement. She would be devastated, and maybe conclude he had developed suicidal tendencies.

Without really thinking what he was doing, he made his way down to the kitchen. It all looked remarkably well organised, at least for breakfast time. The chef's stressed arm-waving had even reduced to a level similar to that of a policeman stationed on an island to direct traffic. This allowed Richard to stand quite close, though he was ready to jump backwards, if the need arose.

"I was wondering," he said, "how the new scullery maid is doing?"

The chef turned his attention from a frying pan of eggs, which, as expected in a four-star hotel, had to be transferred to a plate at exactly the right moment. Though, in truth, Richard knew this time could be three seconds either side, the perfect time being decided by the chef's fluctuating mood.

"Oh," said the chef, "her first morning was a complete disaster. She did not even know the difference between a scouring pad and a scrubbing brush. I had to sack her – or, at least, try to, because she responded by falling across my feet and begging forgiveness. Anyway, Tara sorted it out, then got the housekeeper to give the girl emergency domestic science lessons. She's fine now: everything comes back clean; the potatoes peeled to perfection. I've forgotten all about the scullery – just like everyone else who used to be enlisted for the odd shift. Argh! The eggs – now look what you've made me do."

Richard watched the annoyed chef lift the eggs as if they were going into the bin. But in the event, they were deposited in a clean enamel bucket which already contained two slices of slightly overcooked toast – though only a trained eye would detect this.

"Take these to the scullery," said the chef. "All the waste food goes down there now."

Richard wanted to say he was the assistant manager who should be giving the instructions, but thought it unwise to argue while the chef had a fish slice in his hand. So, picking up the bucket, he went to the narrow doorway and stared down the stone steps beyond. They looked rather like steps that might descend into a castle dungeon... in which Priscilla the Gorilla was now lurking. Why he had started to pick up on Tara's phrases, he had no idea. And anyway, Priscilla's personality was nothing like that of a gorilla – those animals had a reputation for being relatively friendly. He prepared himself for the task ahead by locking his hands behind his back, which was awkward because he was holding a bucket. However, it was also essential, because he knew when anyone said something bad about Janet, a reflex action sent his fists flying. First he had killed the man in Wellington Place, then later, lunged at the prostitute in the brothel, and finally he had gone for Priscilla the Gorilla herself. But now he had some idea of what perverted brothel customers expected for their money, he had no problems with having killed the man who had abused Janet. Deep down, though, he somewhat regretted almost hitting the creature now lurking in the basement.

At the bottom of the steps, he looked around the 'dungeon'. It had whitewashed walls, a slate floor, and no windows, the only light coming from a single bulb hanging on a wire from the low ceiling. Anyone stepping back from their duties could easily bang their head on it, which seemed a little unsafe. Priscilla was standing before a giant sink, furiously scrubbing a pot.

"Hello," he said quietly.

She turned, then quickly bowed her head. He looked at her in surprise – she was wearing overalls, and her face lacked even the slightest trace of make-up. "Sir," she said, "I now think your Janet is really nice."

Whatever was happening in this dungeon, it was nothing like he had been expecting. "I can't believe you mean that," he said.

"Tara has been giving me elocution lessons," she replied. "You know, like in that film where a lady has to learn how to talk about the Spanish weather. At first, I admit they were just words, but now believe my description of Janet to be true because…"

Richard gestured for her to continue.

"Because after I was thrown out, with just the clothes on my back, I had to do certain things to survive. Now I understand how horrible it all is and, if I ever see Janet again, I will beg her forgiveness."

Richard, quite forgetting he was no longer Priscilla's English teacher, said what she was experiencing was called empathy. Then, unable to think of anything better to say, he handed her the bucket. She took it, looked inside, and smiled.

"Why are you smiling at food waste?" he asked.

"Oh, I sort it all out before it goes to the bins," she said. "I feed myself entirely on what would otherwise go to the pig farm."

"But…" Richard could think of no sensible sentence that described this situation. So, rather than stand there looking gormless, he sat down on a three-legged stool used by those who peeled the potatoes.

"It's fine," said Priscilla. "Truth is, quite apart from being rubbish at everything…" She also fell silent, before giving a shrug. "Well, truth is, I was rubbish at being a prostitute. I hadn't eaten for three days when Tara sorted me out with some dry bread from the bins. Sorry, don't shout at her; she could see I was dying of starvation."

Then Richard did something that had no rational explanation. He reached up to touch Priscilla gently on the shoulder. "It is I who should be sorry," he said. "And you have no need to be nice to me, because I know it was my father who did this to you."

"No," interrupted Priscilla, "I did this to myself. Okay, it took Tara to make me see it. Thing is, after I admitted to her that I'm thick and a failure at everything, she asked about my schooldays. She couldn't understand how I became such a failure when you had been my English teacher."

"Half the time you missed lessons," said Richard, "and I can never remember you doing any homework. Apparently your father made a big donation to the gym equipment fund to sort it with the head."

Priscilla nodded. "When Tara told me it's normal to spend three hours a day doing homework, I was astonished. That's like twenty-one hours a week."

"To get top grades, certainly. When Janet was doing her A levels, it was nearer thirty hours of home study, but she had her mind set on Oxford. I suspect some students do less."

"Don't know about that, but Tara's given me her old schoolbooks to point me in the right direction. I keep them under the cupboard there. She only agreed to help me, if I resit my O levels at college next year."

Richard fled the scene – this time not because he might hit Priscilla, but because he was in danger of bursting into tears.

Tara had now saved eight pounds and accumulated three days off work. And so her thoughts returned to a road trip. Then the postcard Janet had sent to Richard came to mind. Why was there a picture of a bridge on the front? Surely, if Janet was going to choose a bridge postcard, she would pick the spectacular Severn Bridge, which also went to Wales? The bridge on the postcard, she remembered, had looked rather short. Also, it had an unusual name: Menai, or something like that. In any event, it sounded foreign, and therefore mysterious.

Tara looked at the road atlas she kept on the reception desk for the benefit of guests who required directions. North Wales, she discovered, looked rather big. Where Janet's cottage might be was uncertain, although she knew it was a long way from the nearest main road. She quite liked the idea of being a detective and finding a missing person by piecing together a few incidental clues. If Janet was not actually in hiding from Richard because of the thingy syndrome Dr Phillips had described, it might be possible to locate her within the space of an exciting three-day trip. Should she invite Richard to go with her? No, that would lose the detective interest. Also, he looked at Janet through rose-coloured spectacles. This would confuse any girly gossip which might allow her to reach sensible conclusions – assuming she could find the cottage. If not, well, it was certain to be a fun holiday, with a vague purpose that might lead her into strange and foreign lands. Richard's contribution to her fact-finding mission would only be to confuse things.

So, a trip to North Wales it would be. With petrol at fifty pence a gallon, everything else would have to be very low-budget. But she had a tent and liked doing outdoor things. As for food, she was happy with a bag of chips. She had never actually been abroad, though, so had no idea if they even had chip shops in Wales. Maybe it was all mountains and sheep – oh, and eating seaweed. As far as her childhood picture books were concerned, that was about it. She imagined herself camped on a hillside, surrounded by sheep, and eating seaweed. On second thoughts, perhaps she should take some cheese sandwiches.

Then she had a eureka moment. Janet would only send a postcard of a boring bridge, if it was near to where she lived. No one, Tara assumed, ever went to Brighton and then sent a postcard depicting Southend.

Then the sensible side of her character took over. *Plonker*, she thought. *Taking a road trip to Wales in October – what am I thinking?* She had only just started using the word 'plonker', having probably picked it up from Richard, who, she suspected, had acquired it from Janet. There was simply no other way for a former English teacher to have heard of such a word. Tara was quite worried about this, because you only copied the words of those you really liked. Was her real reason for going to Wales to see what might happen, if Janet turned out to be a horrible person? If she did, Richard might one day admit to liking herself instead. Her psychiatrist friend had thought this unlikely but, whatever the future held, she needed to know more about Janet. Logic told her the Menai Bridge went across the Menai Strait, so that seemed a good place to start. She could then find a postman and ask if he knew where Janet the literary agent lived. She must get loads of post – heavy manuscripts and the like. Surely he would remember driving a mile down a dirt track to a cottage overlooking a cliff? Ah! Sea cliffs. Janet's cottage was on the coast, so that took away an awful lot of land in the middle. Let the road trip begin… well, starting next Friday, anyway.

CHAPTER TWENTY-ONE

It was just a bridge, and not a very interesting one at that! Twenty feet from where Tara was standing, there was a stone tower. She supposed it might have a grandeur similar to that of the Arc de Triomphe, but because she had never been to Paris, could not say for certain. Anyway, through this tower, twin archways had been created, so traffic might come and go in the manner of a dual carriageway. Then she noticed a bus slowing down and eventually stopping just before an arch. There was no obvious sign to indicate it was a bus stop. She could only conclude it was a secret location where crazy individuals, who liked to live dangerously, could disembark with a degree of risk. Then a hand emerged from the driver's window and pulled in a wing mirror. A moment later, the bus appeared to 'breathe in', so as to squeeze through the archway.

"Uh?" Tara said. The man who designed this bridge must have measured a bus and thought the archways could be the same size. Then she decided he simply liked annoying bus drivers. As if to emphasise this, he had built an identical tower on the far clifftop. Then, after building the bridge, he obviously realised that he had forgotten the footpaths, which had presumably forced pedestrians to walk through the arches, bringing all traffic to a standstill. His afterthought of a solution had been to bolt footpaths onto the outside of the towers – again, for those who liked to live dangerously. That idea rather appealed to Tara's sense of adventure.

Following one of the footpaths, Tara made her way to where the lugs of metal coming down from the towers reached their lowest point. She wondered why the designer had not used suspension cables – perhaps, as a little boy, he had liked making things from Meccano because, essentially, this was how the bridge had been constructed. Okay, the lugs were about three feet long and nearly a foot square, but the principle was the same. Boys with toys!

Deciding the bridge was silly, she leant on the footpath's rail to gaze along what looked like a wide river. It was far below; the designer having used the only available bit of clifftop to play with his grown-up Meccano set. Other than this high ground, the banks on both sides of the river looked rather flat. In any event, there were no cottages to be seen. Crossing the road would have been a suicide mission due to all the ironwork bolted to the lugs. Tara walked back to the tower, crossed the road, then made her way to the middle of the other footpath. Gazing from this, she observed the river opened out to the sea, but neither bank had cliffs nor cottages. After some thought, she reasoned Janet might have sent the postcard from a place to which she could sensibly walk – maybe five miles from her home? Also, a local shop might sell postcards, and have a postbox, indicating it was the nearest place of civilisation to Janet's cottage.

Presently, a gentle breeze drifting across the bridge caused thoughts of Janet to fade from Tara's mind. She closed her eyes and imagined herself on an aircraft, flying through the air, far above the world. This first holiday to the seaside was turning out to be rather fun.

"Don't jump," said a voice.

Tara's reaction was to jump sideways, then turn towards whoever had 'crashed' into her daydream. Two feet away was a most extraordinary man. He was wearing baggy trousers which finished just below the knees, from which point a pair of enormous socks attempted to compensate for the lack of trouser material. Higher up, he wore a waistcoat, to which a gold chain was attached, forming a downward loop before disappearing into a pocket. *Like the Mad Hatter*, she thought, which implied the other end of the chain was attached to a pocket watch. Around his neck was a cravat, neatly tied. Something about him reminded her of a stationmaster from the Victorian era. She reckoned his biological age was mid twenties, but his psychological age considerably less.

"Do I need to hold you back?" said the man. "You are too young to end it all."

"I had no intention of jumping," Tara responded, somewhat crossly, but equally pleased by his concern. Then she resumed her more kindly nature. He looked genuinely worried about her and, on second glance, appeared to be mostly harmless.

"A lot of people jump from bridges," he said, "and this one is pretty effective for... well... what I thought you might be about to do."

Tara understood why a lot of people might jump from this bridge as he approached them. He was not well suited to introducing himself to those of a nervous disposition.

"It had to be this high," said the man, "so tall-masted ships could get underneath."

"Oh," she said, "so it was built a long time ago?"

"1826. People now come from all over the world to look at it. Though I only came from London on the train."

Tara frowned. This information did not fit well with her theory about Janet living within walking distance of the bridge. However, it answered her question about the buses. She told the man about her views on this, which got him very excited.

"It was built for stagecoaches," he said, "which of course, by royal decree, all had a standard wheel spacing of seven feet."

"Of course!" she exclaimed. "How could I have forgotten?"

It worried her that the man missed her sarcastic tone. Instead, he explained the easiest way to remember it was to think about the wide-gauge railway laid down by Brunel. This had been designed so road coaches could have their wheels changed, to become railway carriages. Then, having travelled the greater part of their journey by steam power, with the horses riding on special train wagons, the stage coaches could continue by road.

"Isambard Kingdom Brunel," she said. "I know about him; he dug the Severn Tunnel near the new suspension bridge."

The man looked at her in horror. "Of course he didn't!" he exclaimed. "That was not built until 1886, by John

Hawkshaw. Brunel's railway crossed a bridge in Gloucester, thirty miles upstream. I've walked across it a few times, but it's not so good as this one."

Tara heard this as *I've never had a girlfriend*; a fact pretty much confirmed when he reached out to touch a monstrous nut and bolt to her right.

"This," he said, in a voice which suggested he was in love with the object, "has a loading of 14.6 tons."

"That is not the sort of thing I want to hear when I'm a thousand feet in the air," she said.

"102 feet," said the man crossly, "because it's low tide. Admiralty regulations required the bridge to have a clearance which allowed the tallest sailing ship to pass underneath it in all conditions. Would you like to go and see the famous Stephenson box bridge in Conwy this afternoon?"

She apologised for refusing his kind offer – then realised his knowledge of bridges, and his other great hobby (which, he explained, was trainspotting), might actually come in useful. Well, she reasoned, most places had branch lines. However, this theory went wrong when he pulled a notebook from his top pocket and began to tell her of a recent journey he had undertaken on the Great Northern Line. He had recorded the speed the train had been doing for every incline and summit pass. She tried to interrupt, but his ecstasy seemed to have stopped his ears from working. *Quite big ears*, she thought; *probably evolved for listening to approaching trains.*

"And do you know what?" he said conspiratorially, after his account brought him to a halt at Shieldmuir Junction at 7.05pm.

She looked at him. Did that require an answer? Not wishing to commit herself, she shook her head.

"It was the BR Standard Class 7 4-6-2, number 70002," he said.

"Wow!" she exclaimed. "And did it really do thirty-five miles an hour past Carstairs?"

"I was there, honest," he replied, handing her his notebook, which was neatly written with a load of meaningless facts and figures.

"It's too exciting to take in," she said. On returning the book, she noticed the name on the front. "Thomas?" she added. "*The* Thomas? Really?!"

The man gave her a serious nod. Tara decided that teasing him was completely impossible. Then she frowned. Surely, railway carriages did not have speedometers fixed to the wall? At least, she had never noticed one. When she questioned him on this, he looked equally puzzled. Then he took out his pocket watch.

"Telegraph poles are always fifty yards apart," he said. "All you have to do is count how many you pass in a given time."

"Interesting," said Tara. "I mean, *really* interesting. How far would thirty-five poles cover?"

"Ten feet short of a mile. But unless you have a special watch like mine, the odd ten feet is within the boundary of a timekeeping error. Once, my friend thought we had done an average speed of 41.39 miles per hour up the Lickey Incline, but his watch was wrong. Did we laugh about that!"

"Genius!" exclaimed Tara. "Okay, I need your help."

Learning that Janet lived a mile from the main road gave Tara the confidence to explain her mission to Thomas.

And, yes, his knowledge was very useful. According to him, nowhere north of the Menai Bridge would be considered part of the Snowdonia National Park. The other side of the bridge was Yyns Môn, an island whose fiercely independent residents would always claim this fact with pride. They would rarely claim to live in Wales.

"Until Telford built this bridge, it was very difficult to reach," he continued. "Some island folk still consider the bridge to be a mad English folly – compounded by their rudeness in renaming their kingdom Anglesey."

Thomas then asked if she would care to join him for a cup of coffee. Tara struggled to understand the connection between the warring tribes of North Wales and a cup of coffee. But she felt sorry for him and had not stopped to drink anything since leaving home, so she followed him across the bridge to Menai village.

How this later ended up with her following him to see Stephenson's railway bridge a little way upriver, she could not really say – except that she imagined unusual things were to be expected on holiday. If she had wanted to do normal things, she could simply have stayed at home. After crossing the Menai railway bridge, she heard a train approaching. Then the rails in the nearby cutting began to rattle and shake. This caused Thomas to jump up and down with excitement. When the engine thundered into view, he reached for his notebook to scribble down its number. Next he took out his stopwatch to record the time. Tara wondered if his behaviour on seeing a train should make her cross. She had been by his side for two hours, and not once had he become excited about the way her hair made her look like a mysterious, exciting heroine. Taking second place to a steam train was surely something designed to dent a lady's confidence.

It was quite late in the evening when Tara remembered her mission – or, more precisely, the general direction in which her holiday should be heading. She tried to say goodbye to Thomas, but he seemed glued to her side. However, he did come up with one rather good idea. Apparently, just south of nearby Caernarfon there was an airfield used by amateur enthusiasts.

"Old planes," he explained, "mostly navigate by using landmarks such as railways. The aviators will know every clifftop cottage on the coast that could be classed as being in Snowdonia." Sadly, he did not know about the nearby Llŷn Peninsula which jutted into the Irish Sea, because it lacked a railway beyond Pwllheli, so was not a place he had ever needed to visit. But apparently flying around the coast was the sort of thing the pilots did because it made navigation easier.

Somehow this conversation ended up with Tara driving to the airfield with Thomas in the passenger seat, but he seemed harmless enough. Any man in his mid twenties who had never had a girlfriend, was hardly likely to suddenly grab hold of her knee and ask for a kiss. In order to feel even safer, she decided his full name was Thomas the Tank Engine. Thinking about all of this, she realised that she wanted to know more about him. How did his mind work? Did he have parents who were equally mad? Did all his teacups at home have pictures of the Mad Hatter on them? But in the event, with all the double-declutching she had to think about, she merely mumbled, "Curiouser and curiouser."

On reaching the airfield, Tara was surprised to discover it was just that: essentially, a field. Okay, there were a few strips of tarmac, but they seemed too short to be of any use to a plane wishing to land and – more importantly – to stop. The buildings were more a collection of sheds, or maybe hastily constructed wartime prefabs. It seemed Thomas had been here before because, without asking for directions, he immediately made his way to a canteen. Here, he bought Tara a meal, which meant the four pounds in her purse remained intact. Then, while she ate, he went around asking all and sundry if they knew of any cottage near a clifftop overlooking the sea. Tara realised that though Thomas might be eccentric, at least he understood finding such a cottage worked a lot better, if one was looking from an aeroplane rather than walking.

Eventually, Thomas returned with a man who he introduced as Graham. Also in his mid twenties, Graham had a handsome face blemished with a smudge of oil. His eccentricity, if any, was limited to the fact he was carrying an unusually large spanner. He looked at Tara for a moment, then raised his eyebrows in what might have been a gesture of appreciation. Next he looked at Thomas and frowned. Tara was quite happy to go along with the idea that she and Thomas seemed an odd match, with her being the sensible half of the partnership.

"Well," said Graham, "your cottage – thing is, they are never built close to clifftops because such things tend to erode. So, what we are looking for is an old cottage that has, over the centuries, found itself closer to the edge than the builder intended."

When Tara had first learned the Menai Bridge was

world-famous, so that Janet might have travelled some distance to visit it, her first instinct had been to think, *Oh well, it's a nice place to come for a holiday.* Now, for the first time, she began to think her search might actually succeed.

"So," said Graham, "I'm taking my plane out tomorrow, just to blow away the cobwebs. There's a spare seat behind mine, and it's no problem to fly around the coast. In fact, it will turn the trip into a secret mission."

Tara stared at him. "I've only got four pounds," she said.

"A damsel in distress!" exclaimed Graham. "I like that even better – if your boyfriend here has no objection?"

Thomas gave a shy grin. She thought he might be thinking, *At last, somebody thinks I actually have a real – as opposed to an imaginary – girlfriend.* She thought his innocent look rather cute, though it would have been more suited to a ten-year-old boy. She decided to let the 'boyfriend' falsehood pass. This was, after all, a holiday, when strange things were supposed to happen… though how they could include flying along the coast in a private plane, totally baffled her.

On leaving the airfield, Tara noticed it was starting to get dark. She looked at Thomas, who, she realised, had found himself far away from a railway line, a bridge, or any part of the world he understood. In theory, she could take him back to where she had found him, but with only two gallons of petrol in her car, she did not want to waste any. Then she thought about the excited way in which he had jumped up and down on seeing a train. He was completely safe – it was daft to think he would try anything which involved close contact with a woman.

"I don't reckon you're going to get a bus at this time of

night," she said. "But I saw a patch of ground back there that's okay to pitch my tent. I'll give you a place to stay, but I don't want any funny business. I've got a sleeping bag, and there are some old blankets in the car boot for you."

It worried her that Thomas looked angry. But it transpired this was only because, a few years earlier, Dr Beeching had decommissioned the railway between Caernarfon and Menai. This had, apparently, cut the service between North and Central Wales. Of more relevance to Tara, it meant there was no train service that would return Thomas to his bed and breakfast near the Menai crossing.

That night, Tara lay in her sleeping bag, thinking about her exciting day, though how it had included a bridge, she could not imagine. Thomas was lying by her side but, after half an hour, she had almost forgotten he was there. Then a quiet voice came from the darkness.

"You are so very nice," it said.

She groaned and edged away to lie against the tent canvas. This, it seemed, was all it took to shut him up, because he did not expand the idea into kissing and stuff. A little later, his breathing became a soft snore. *Uh!* she thought, irrationally cross that he had found it so easy to forget about her. Then she thought about the lecherous laboratory technician whose name she refused to acknowledge. Because he was her first and only boyfriend, she had no one sensible with who to compare Thomas. Was it normal for a man to say he liked you, then go to sleep straight afterwards? It almost made her want to 'accidentally' poke him in the ribs with her elbow. It would be nice to feel a hand stroking her hair and… other things as well. Suddenly she realised the lab technician was history

– completely! It was almost as if Thomas's first approach on the bridge had caused the painful memory of her ex to leap from the parapet in terror. Well, presumably even ghosts were frightened of things they couldn't understand. So, with the technician gone, the time had surely come to get herself a new, better boyfriend... But Thomas? Well, not tonight anyway, for he was fast asleep.

Then she remembered her secret mission. First she must find Janet. Obviously Richard viewed her through rose-coloured spectacles. No one could be as perfect as he believed her to be. If Janet turned out to be sort of nice, Tara would leave Richard well alone. If she turned out to be horrible – well, all is fair in love and war.

The following morning Tara awoke and, after a few seconds to realise where she was, wondered why there was no snoring filling the tent. Perhaps Thomas had gone out to do his early-morning ablutions? She sat up and discovered the blankets lying on the groundsheet beside her. On top of them was a sheet of paper, presumably torn from his trainspotting notebook. It took her some time to focus on the actual words. All the note said was:

> *Sorry about what I said last night. It was just because you are so amazingly nice. Too embarrassed to face you this morning, so have gone to catch the bus. But if you ever need a friend, my address is written on the back of this note. There are some really good wooden railway bridges (made of real wood!) on the line to Pwllheli. I can show you.*
>
> *Thomas*

She frowned. How could you make a railway bridge out of wood? Surely it would collapse when a great, thundering train rattled over the top? Also, any burning coal that fell from the firebox would set it alight. Ah! Hence the phrase 'burning one's bridges'. She supposed that, a long time ago, most bridges had been made of wood, but had been unaware of them because only those made of stone had survived, the others having been destroyed by fire—

Why was she thinking like this? She actually had a desire to see what a wooden railway bridge looked like! Thomas had messed with her mind and then left her life forever – if that was what she wished. More importantly, he had left carrying his pocket watch, so she had no idea of the time. To play it safe, she decided not to bother with breakfast or coffee, which seemed sensible because she did not know if Graham's plane had either a loo or a place to be sick. Though, truthfully, the most likely outcome of this morning would be that he failed to turn up, and she would be left to do whatever people did when abandoned at an out-of-the-way airfield.

She arrived at the airfield with half an hour to spare, only to find Graham already there. He was wearing an old-fashioned leather flying helmet with a pair of goggles strapped around it. *Thomas Mark II*, she thought. He then handed her another helmet and set of goggles.

"Ready?" he said. "Or do you need to go to the loo before we set off?"

She shook her head. She liked making the correct decisions, and not having coffee this morning seemed like a good omen. As for what was to follow, well, it was a holiday, when mad things were supposed to happen.

On leaving the building, Graham led her to something that looked more suited to a museum: a biplane, which, he proudly informed her, had been manufactured in 1934. It had a double open cockpit, and wings made of canvas. The single propeller on the front had been carved from wood. It made her think back to her schooldays, when her friends had often debated whether or not they should get on the back of their boyfriend's motorbike. For Tara, it had not been an issue, because the lab technician had only come on the scene when she was eighteen, and was so pathetic he only had a bicycle. But that was history, and now came her 'motorbike decision time', as it had come to her school friends – only multiplied by several thousand levels of danger.

Tara looked critically at the steps which Graham had placed for her ascent. Clearly they were a stairway to Heaven, which, on the positive side, could be viewed as leading to something that would be rather fun. On the negative side, they might be the stairway to Heaven via death. However hard she tried, she could not think of any circumstance in which they were simply neutral. She then realised death in a motorbike accident was pathetic in comparison, because it involved being spread across the road like strawberry jam. In this variation, involving a mad aviator, she would most probably just disappear into the ocean forever.

As she was thinking all these profound thoughts, Graham was fixing her flying helmet, while stroking her hair - accidentally? Or perhaps...? Sadly, he then dropped her goggles to rest on her nose. That completely removed any romantic interpretation from the situation, so she climbed the steps and settled into the rear seat to await her fate.

Graham waved across the field to a man, who came over to say, "Hi!"

Not too high, Tara thought; *I don't want to be hit by a proper aeroplane.*

Then Graham got into the front seat, while the other man pulled down a blade of the propeller. The engined puttered into life and, a moment later, they were moving over the grass. The plane turned to face the wind; then Graham did something with the controls to make the engine roar. It seemed they were still moving quite slowly when they left the ground but, using the wing-and-a-prayer principle, they somehow gained enough height to avoid crashing into any trees.

As the flight progressed, they kept just enough height to clear any electricity wires stretched between pylons. That, in any event, was how it seemed to Tara, as she watched a herd of cattle running away from what they obviously considered to be a monstrous bird. Then the plane turned sharply right to follow the coast, while she looked over the side to search for clifftop cottages. But the peninsula seemed to have few buildings, and nothing perched within a few feet of the occasional cliff edge.

On reaching the tip of the peninsula, they swung around, keeping to the coast, but now heading towards some distant mountains. Tara, counting a line of telegraph poles, reckoned they were doing ninety miles per hour. It made her think about her old school friends – their boyfriends only had little motorbikes with the L-plates removed for legal reasons when carrying a passenger...

Why had she suddenly started thinking about boyfriends? And, in particular, about the man now sitting in front of her? His ability to control two canvas-covered stick-wings as they hurtled through the air, meant her life depended on his actions. Yet, strangely, she was mostly thinking about his hand holding hers.

Suddenly, Graham pointed over the side to an isolated cottage on the edge of a cliff. He swooped up slightly, then circled the building, perhaps fifty feet above its garden. Tara stared in amazement. The garden had all sorts of fancy trees and plants surrounding a small duck pond. It appeared to be a botanical garden, from which hundreds of birds suddenly emerged to flap around in all directions. A second circle of the plane brought a lady running out to look up, smiling. Tara knew immediately this was Janet, because Richard kept her photograph on his desk – plus three more on his office wall. She gave a friendly wave, and Janet returned the gesture.

Graham stopped circling the cottage to buzz above a rough access track. Instinctively, Tara counted the seconds in her head, and they reached the main road as she thought of the number forty-two. Almost a mile in less than a minute – she was still flying through the air at ninety miles per hour! Let her old school friends tease her now for not having a boyfriend! Those who had got on the back of glorified mopeds with immature boys could only dream of such a speed. But why was she thinking about boyfriends again?

After crossing the main road, Graham gained height to head back towards the airfield… or at least, Tara thought that was the plan. What he actually did was pass the field on the left and continue following the channel of water called the Menai Strait. *Too low*, she wanted to scream, *there's a bridge around the next bend!* But she need not have worried, because he lifted the aeroplane to fly over the top, only to lose height suddenly. Before she could shout that there was another bridge ahead, they were passing beneath it, then swerving while rising, to reverse the journey by flying above it. *You are completely bonkers*, she wanted to scream, but only in a happy way. Then they were travelling back to the airfield, which she estimated took less than fifteen minutes. In her car, the same distance had taken an hour. How long would it have taken her to stumble across Janet's cottage by walking – a week, perhaps?

On reaching the airfield, Graham landed on the tarmac runway, diverting to the grass shortly afterwards. Then he cut the engine. Theoretically, thereafter there was silence, but Tara's head was still buzzing.

"Don't tell anyone about the bridge manoeuvre," he said, "because it's not exactly legal. But it amuses any spectators, and it's quite safe in this."

"You buzz about with the agility of a moth," she said. "But why did you not warn me what you were planning?"

"Didn't know if I would have enough petrol, but I located the cottage quickly, and knew the coast had no other cliff-edge cottages. So I reached the Strait with two gallons in the tank. Fun!"

"You bet."

"So, you ready for that coffee now?"

She nodded, smiled, and found herself rather glad that her moment of weakness in the tent with Thomas had not led to anything naughty happening.

After she had made her way unsteadily along the grass to the canteen, Graham bought her a mug of coffee.

"I haven't got you any food," he said, "because I am hoping you will agree to meet my parents and maybe stay for lunch?"

She mostly heard the word 'lunch', so nodded.

"Thing is," he added, "my mother keeps telling me I should sell the plane and get myself a nice girlfriend instead. I know taking you home is only going to be pretend, but meeting someone like you would stop her nagging me about it. She's also quite a good cook."

This time Tara mostly noticed the word 'girlfriend', so her consenting nod was more confused. Her previous thoughts about food had been a lot less complicated.

Tara drank her coffee slowly, while Graham went off to do man things with the plane. For the first time in her life, she did not know what needed to be done in her present situation. Really, the answer was to do nothing before she spoke to Janet. This was now a formality and, after confirming she was a nice person, she could do the required matchmaking. If this ended in Janet and Richard getting together, it would not worry Tara greatly, because having a boyfriend with an aeroplane sounded rather cool.

After Graham returned, she followed him to the car park, hoping that he would drive slowly enough for her to follow in her own car. When he headed towards the gates, she frowned.

"Are you parked in the lane?" she asked.

"Sorry," he said, "we will have to walk. I can't afford both a plane and a car, and I prefer to put petrol in my flying machine. Not to worry – it's only three miles to my parents', and you can catch a bus from my house to Pwllheli—"

"Stop! No more talk about buses; I have a car."

"What?! Really?"

"And why not? Because I am a girl, I suppose?!"

"No, it's just unusual. And anyway, you are not a girl, but a lady."

"And you are a mad aviator buzzing about in a flying machine… but on second thoughts, that works rather well, because together we have both road and air transport."

She was going to apologise for her implied forwardness, but he merely turned and smiled.

"Lead on to your chariot," he said.

Fifteen minutes later, Tara discovered that Graham lived with his parents in a small semi-detached house on the outskirts of Caernarfon. This, he explained, was necessary to support his flying hobby, because his job was that of an ordinary book-keeper earning six pounds a week. She liked the sound of 'ordinary' because it meant if they went out together, she could adopt the ultra-modern principle of paying her share. Had he been rich, with expensive tastes, that would leave her completely skint. At the other end of the scale, there was sharing a bag of chips while sitting on a damp park bench. Graham was neither rich nor poor, which made him just right… *Stop!* Why was she having all these irrational thoughts? Even if he came to visit her in his plane, it would take him an hour and a half. Though the plane landing on the hotel lawn would impress the management, as it would imply the hotel had really classy guests.

As soon as Tara walked into Graham's house, his mother, Deirdre, took one look at her and exclaimed, "At last!" Then she turned to shout down the hallway. "Bill," she cried, "Graham's brought a girl home to meet us."

From that moment on, Tara found herself surrounded by parental affection, the questions coming so quickly, she struggled to keep up. When Deirdre learnt she had been up in the aeroplane, her reaction was one of amazement.

"Whenever Graham leaves for the airfield," she said, "I think I'm never going to see him again. And now he returns with you, a fellow lunatic!"

"He's a good pilot," said Tara quietly. "He can handle that aeroplane like it's a moth fluttering about the sky. The way he flew up the Strait to—"

Graham put his hand over her mouth. "We don't talk about that," he said.

She immediately removed his hand and continued her sentence in a way his mother would find more acceptable – "to fly out across the Irish Sea," she said. "It was so amazing."

She noticed Bill smiling and giving the thumbs up, then down. Graham nodded.

"You've got yourself a cracking girlfriend here," said Bill. "Fearless and beautiful."

"And kind," said Graham.

Tara found it difficult to understand how the afternoon passed so quickly. They sat by an open fire, listening to Beethoven on the radiogram. Then they played a family-friendly game of *Monopoly*, and talked about silly things. She then found herself saying a flying machine controlled by Graham was far safer than getting on the back of a motorbike with a boy. His mother looked doubtful, but his father seemed to approve. And so teatime came and went. Then Tara looked at the clock on the mantel shelf, and explained apologetically that she needed to be going.

"Nonsense," said Bill. "We only have two bedrooms, but Graham can sleep on the sofa tonight. You can stay in his room."

It occurred to Tara that the parents were trying to do some serious matchmaking... helped by Graham, who said, "Of course."

"I can't kick you out of your bedroom," she protested.

"You are not," responded Graham. "I am offering... *insisting*."

And so it was, an hour later, she entered a room with a single bed, the top corner of the blankets and sheet having been folded neatly back. All over the walls were pictures of old aeroplanes, many with three wings, their dates ranging from 1906 to 1915. Graham, she decided, was so passionate about flying machines that she would never let him sell his plane... if they ever, impossibly, became 'an item'.

Tara found getting into a man's bed very odd. All the smells were wrong, but not unpleasant. Why was he sleeping on the sofa? Whoops, there she was again, thinking like a tart. But it was a holiday. And, strangely, though she'd had a completely amazing experience, she still had the same amount of money in her purse as when she had first arrived at the Menai Bridge... oh, ages ago.

She was woken the following morning by Deirdre, who brought her breakfast and a glass of orange juice on a tray. Well, she was not going flying today, so why not? It was eleven o'clock before she finally said goodbye to the kind family, who had provided her with a free bed and breakfast.

As she got into her car, Graham handed her a card with their address.

"Please write," he said. "You will always be welcome here." Gently, he took her hand. "Please," he repeated. "And now, gentle lady, have a safe journey."

And with that, she drove away to begin the second part of her mission to meet Janet and assess the situation. Idly, she thought that Richard had better hurry up in thinking about getting himself a new girlfriend if, as she suspected, his devotion to the woman he had idolised for six years, was starting to fade.

It seemed to Tara that now she had decided to get a boyfriend, she might have three options: Richard, Thomas, or Graham. Oh, and just to confuse things even more, perhaps Dr Phillips!

CHAPTER TWENTY-TWO

Janet's working life was generally conducted in her main living area, using the sort of table Shakespeare would have recognised: handcrafted from thick walnut planks held together with wooden pegs. It had come with the cottage, and the previous owner had told her it was mid seventeenth century. Janet realised this was a little after Shakespeare's time but, given the context, well within the boundaries of poetic licence. Anyway, whenever it had been made, sitting before it helped her to think about words – or, more specifically, what her clients were trying to say when they put them in the wrong order.

One afternoon, she was sitting at the table, with piles of manuscripts and assorted box files rising up from each elbow. Her thoughts were fully occupied by a neat handwritten manuscript. This author was a woman of fifty-something, who lived a wild existence in the mountains on the edge of Snowdonia. Locals believed her home to be an abandoned mine tunnel, though her real claim to fame was her clothes. In summer, she preferred not to wear any. In winter, she always wore military combat overalls with wellingtons. Most of the local children feared her, believing her to be a witch. But now Janet had half-read her manuscript, she knew her to be quite sensible, her mine-shaft residence having been fully converted into practical accommodation. How she had got a settee and a bed so far into the mountains, she did not say. Presumably, to her it was obvious, though the whole set-up would leave any normal person completely baffled.

But the woman's life was far more interesting than her current domestic arrangements. According to her book, between the ages of seventeen and fifty, she had 'bummed' all over the world on freight ships. As for how she had survived such adventure, the text casually mentioned that spit-roasted alligator leg tasted quite nice. But, in books, only men hit such animals over the head with a sledgehammer, and the woman had totally forgotten to explain why she had been carrying a sledgehammer around the swamps of Florida. But by now, Janet knew books which caused the reader to ask questions, were often considered to be the most interesting.

Janet returned her mind to the lady's present accommodation. She realised only someone who had once lived somewhere like Wellington Place, might consider a cave a pleasant abode. No orthodox literary agent would dream of handling this manuscript, even after it had been translated from Welsh to English, then typed up. But Janet believed it had potential – at least with someone like herself promoting it. Looking back at the manuscript, she finally realised what was unusual about it. The work was clearly autobiographical, but totally avoided using the word 'I'.

This obviously left a vacuum into which the reader fell, to become the person facing the alligator or whatever. It went a bit wrong because, when describing the alligator incident, the author forgot to mention the animal's big teeth. She, uniquely, had merely viewed the creature as lunch!

Janet's thoughts about being eaten (or vice versa) were disrupted by a tap on the French windows. She looked up to see a lady standing on her garden path. Glad of the break, she left her desk and slid the window aside.

"Hi, Janet," said the lady.

Janet dealt with many clients, and often found it difficult to remember their faces. She had no idea who this lady might be, so to avoid seeming rude, offered her a coffee, then told her to make herself comfortable, while she ground the beans. Standing in the kitchen, she struggled without success to put a name to her visitor. She thought this odd because the woman had such a mass of curly ginger hair, she could be recognised from a mile along the beach. Returning to the living area, Janet realised the woman appeared to be fascinated by all the manuscripts and sundry papers covering the long table.

"You do all this yourself?" she asked.

"I like to pretend it is otherwise," replied Janet, "but yes, it's just me, burning the midnight oil. Literally, because the electricity board have little interest in running a cable this far from their main network."

"Maybe I know someone who could help," said the woman. "Not with the thirty-five telegraph poles required, but with the writing."

"But this is my home," said Janet, "and it's difficult to find someone I trust. I mean, they would have to put up with me emerging from my bedroom in my jim-jams to get my early-morning cup of coffee."

I still know someone, thought Tara, *but just for now I won't reveal my hand.* "It's a nice cottage," she said. "The surrounding garden is… oh, I don't know; it's difficult to describe."

"'Garden of Eden' is a good description," responded Janet. "Some of the trees are not native to this country, but the birds seem quite happy to use them. Here." She handed Tara a birdwatching book, then pulled a great tarpaulin over all the manuscripts before going to the kitchen, returning with two bowls of food.

What extraordinary behaviour, thought Tara. *Confusing people is* my *hobby.*

Janet placed a large dish of various seeds on the floor, together with a second dish containing sliced fruit. She then slid open the French windows. Within a few seconds, a mass invasion of birds had begun. None seemed worried about their human hosts.

"I have thirty-two species in the garden," said Janet. "See how many you can identify." She held out her palm to offer a piece of fruit cake. A moment later, a bird settled on her wrist and began to peck at it. "This one's easy," she said. "Robin is my second-best friend. Most of the other birds will take food from my hand, but they have to think about it first. And don't be fooled by their dedication to eating – secretly, they are watching us all the time, curious about our strange ways, and perhaps wondering how we manage to cope without wings."

Second-best friend, thought Tara. *This implies there is someone more important to her. It can't be Richard because they hardly see each other now. A local man, perhaps?*

Janet took a pear from her pocket and passed it to Tara. "Eat half of this," she said, "then put some pieces on your lap. But remember, my friends want to get to know you better, so don't panic when they come to say hello."

Tara thought Janet's conversation was getting increasingly weird, but the fruit tasted nice, so went along with it. She found it very hard not to panic when a large bird with black feathers used her leg for a perch. At first it looked between her and the fruit. Then, as if after shrugging its shoulders, it began to peck at the pear.

"So what is it?" asked Janet. "Besides your new best friend, that is."

"Quite big, with claws and a beak," replied Tara. "Er... a crow?"

"*Caw-caw*," said the bird.

"Careful what you say," said Janet, "because he understands some of our words, and gets very cross about being confused with what you just said. He knows his name to be Jack."

The woman is quite bonkers, thought Tara, *though possibly in a nice way.*

"Now," said Janet, "I am going to say a word which gives him permission to perch on your shoulder, because I think he really likes your hair, and wants to take a closer look." She held out a hand towards the bird, and put up a thumb. "Friend," she said.

A moment later the bird took flight, circled behind Tara's head, then settled on her shoulder.

"Wah-haaa," said Tara.

"He will not understand that word," said Janet. "He also struggles with any word containing an 'E'. But it does not seem to trouble him greatly, because his favourite words – 'food', 'feed' and 'friend' – all begin with an 'F' and end with a 'D'. I guess to him, they all sound identical and mean the same thing."

"*Caw-caw-caw*," said the bird.

"Now," said Janet, "read the book, though it is the Corvidae family you want; somewhere around page 260."

Tara found looking at the book, with Jack perched on her shoulder as if he was also reading, rather difficult. "Jackdaw," she said presently.

"Correct," said Janet. "I found him lying on the ground, half starved, when he was a chick. No idea what happened to his parents. Anyway, given his upbringing in my cottage, he now considers himself to be human and me to be his mummy. And he is my best-ever friend, aren't you, Jack?"

"*Cw-ca-aw*," said Jack.

"Notice the different sound?" said Janet. "He likes hearing his name, not what you recently called him."

To Tara, both calls sounded the same, but she decided not to argue the point, given that Jack was now preening her hair, which put his beak rather close to her ear.

"And," continued Janet, "hand-reared jackdaws soon learn to understand our body language. So, for now, concentrate on putting one thumb up while saying, 'Friend.' If something is dangerous, put both thumbs down and say… well, I will have to tell you that later, because he gets in a right flap when he hears it. Anyway, now you have been formally introduced, don't be surprised if he stands on your shoulder without warning. For Jack, such things make a convenient perch."

For the next hour, Tara amused herself by flipping

through the book and occasionally calling out the name of a bird species. Though how she had come to be birdwatching while sitting on an old-fashioned wooden chair and drinking cappuccino was beyond her. Then she watched Janet take the dish of food to the garden, with the swarm of birds following, all wanting to be her friend. Tara gave a more serious frown. She had been in the cottage for less than two hours and had already arrived at 'mission accomplished'. Richard was not looking at Janet through rose-coloured spectacles: because she *was* perfect; though perhaps a little strange for a woman in her late twenties.

"It's nice of you to visit," said Janet as she returned from the garden. "I think it's been a long time since I last saw you."

"Twenty-four hours," said Tara, a mischievous tone betraying her liking for setting up confusing situations.

Janet scratched her head. This was deliberate body language to indicate she had no idea what her visitor was talking about.

"Yesterday," said Tara.

"That certainly sounds like twenty-four hours ago," said Janet, "but...?"

"I was wearing goggles and a flying helmet," said Tara, "so perhaps I looked a little different."

"The biplane buzzing around my cottage!"

"How else was I to find you, without walking for hundreds of miles around the coast? I only knew you had a cottage on a clifftop, and the postcard you sent to Richard suggested you were somewhere near the Menai bridges. I'm Tara, the receptionist at the hotel."

Then the intense gossip sprung into life, dealing with the who, how and the what of the situation. Tara soon realised Janet was telling her story in a way which made Richard sound like the most unrealistically wonderful person in the universe. However, by combining their stories and adjusting for what she had learned from Priscilla, she thought she had a good grasp of the situation. Okay, there was obviously something missing from the middle of the story that neither Janet nor Richard wanted to talk about; but it probably wasn't important because it only related to how Richard had ceased to be an English teacher and instead became a hotel receptionist. Why would anyone leave a job which had so much paid holiday to work in a hotel that had none? When she tried to get Janet to come clean on this issue, she simply replied, "Because he is wonderful."

Eventually, Janet confronted Tara directly. "So," she said, "you have obviously come here to check me out. Can I assume you are Richard's girlfriend, digging into his past?"

"Absolutely not! Recently I witnessed him crying his heart out, saying that his life is worth nothing without you. So yes, I wanted to make sure his rose-coloured glasses were justified, and if not… Well, then I might have expressed some interest. But I have decided he is right: you are the nicest person I have ever met."

"I was a prostitute."

"Rubbish! From what I can gather, you were the victim of child abuse, endured for three years until Richard rescued you."

"I did not have to be a dirty slag."

"You promised your mother that you would get your O levels, and that promise was irreversible. Men took advantage of it, when you probably did not even know about how to make babies, or what exactly was happening."

Janet began to cry, and Tara walked around the table to put her arm around her shoulder. Immediately Janet leapt up and ran into the next room, her loud sobs of anguish coming through the closed door. Something needed to be done! Tara followed Janet into what turned out to be a bedroom, and sat on a high-backed chair, while Janet lay curled up on the bed.

"Here's you," said Tara, "crying over Richard, and somewhere in England, Richard's crying over you. The whole situation is nonsense, and I intend to sort it. I am going to make us another coffee, and wait until you start talking sense. And no more talk about being a prostitute; that description applies only to Priscilla."

Tara knew the apparently casual mention of Priscilla would make Janet think, *What?* Maybe it would reduce her crying and awaken her curiosity. But Janet merely enquired after Priscilla's health, showing not the slightest hatred for the girl who had done her so much damage.

After the conversation petered away to a mutually reflective silence, Tara crept away to give Janet some time to think. On returning to the table, she tried to imagine herself living here and helping Janet expand her agency. Well, she liked reading and, as a hotel receptionist, had to deal with all manner of clerical tasks, including typing quickly and correctly. She picked up a random manuscript and began reading it. The notes Janet had scribbled in the margins clearly improved it, but it still failed to grab Tara's full attention. Then she realised what was wrong with this particular manuscript. Due to its subject matter, it needed an editor who understood 'man' things. Maybe someone who had an English degree, like Richard?

Eventually, Janet emerged from the bedroom. "So," she said, "Priscilla became a prostitute. Poor girl."

"Yes. Initially her views were somewhat Victorian: hook onto a man who would provide for her needs in return for… marital duties."

"Married?!"

"I was being polite. Richard's father had exclusive rights to her body. When he fled the country, he left her destitute, so she became a prostitute."

"Like me."

Tara tried to sound cross. "Stop saying that," she said. "When Priscilla hooked onto Richard's father she was seventeen and knew exactly what she was doing. Or at least, she knew she hated school and it seemed easier just to let a man do it… probably not very often, given his age. I suppose it's a trade-off: once a slob like Reginald is over fifty, the act becomes more grotesque but less frequent. Anyway, all of it was Priscilla's choice."

"I bet Richard would help her."

"Already has. She is now living in the hotel basement as a scullery maid. And if I know Richard, I expect his desire to teach will have got the better of him by now. Anyway, I sorted her out with my old schoolbooks before I left."

Janet listened carefully to Tara's telling of Priscilla's story, from the time she had taken up with Reginald until now. Importantly, Tara forgot she was not supposed to mention that it was Priscilla who had told Reginald his son was sleeping with a pupil.

"We weren't," Janet interrupted. "My Richard would never take advantage of my misfortune."

"*I* didn't say you were," said Tara crossly. "Pay attention.

That is what Priscilla told Richard's father to cause trouble – oh, now look what you've made me go and say! Richard told me it was the one secret he kept from you, to save you getting upset."

"I already worked it out," said Janet. "It's the one secret I've been keeping from him."

Now this shared secret was out in the open, Janet began to retell her story in a more honest way. When she mentioned the word 'asexual', Tara was able to tie it in with what the psychiatrist at the hospital had said. Janet, seeing that Tara did not appear to be shocked, asked if she understood what the word meant.

"You do not need a man," replied Tara, "or a woman, to satisfy your physical needs. Or at least, this is what you believe. When Richard is available, I question the logic of this belief. Half the female staff in the hotel fancy him, but he pretends not to notice because he hopes that one day you will be cured."

"I am full of disease," said Janet. "I would never infect him."

Tara decided this situation was too serious for an armchair psychologist like herself to deal with. Indeed, she thought Janet should be committed to a lunatic asylum for letting Richard slip from her grasp. To distract herself from such serious matters, Tara began telling Janet about Graham, the mad aviator. Then she talked about the polite – if strange – Thomas the Tank Engine. She put forward the view that he was in need of organising, so might suit her better. Then she told Janet about her holiday so far. Janet replied she also liked the circular walk between the Menai bridges, because it reminded her of the time she had trekked it with Richard. Then she lowered her head.

"Had he asked me to do it then," she said, "on our first night in the hotel, I would have let him, because I thought… well, I don't know what I thought, but hopefully I was not thinking too much like Priscilla. But by the time he fell in love with me and wanted… well, by then I had realised how dirty I was, and all my love for him was as a father figure—"

"There's only eight years between you!" interrupted Tara.

"Same age difference as between him and Priscilla."

"No, he never would! Not with her!"

"So," said Janet, "now who is looking at him through rose-coloured spectacles? At the end of the day, he's a man, who has been forced to live like a monk because of me. I hate myself for that. But I would hate myself more if… well, you know."

"He is a perfect man," sighed Tara.

"So *you* take him as a boyfriend," responded Janet, "while I'm living here, so far away, he will eventually forget about me, like I deserve."

"Wait – are you telling me you moved here to get away from him?"

"So he would be free to get a nice girlfriend, partly—"

"Oh my word, it's de-whatsit's syndrome!"

"What?"

"Oh, just something I've heard mentioned. Richard has come to see you as… well, the centre of the universe. And because of this – look, this is serious stuff – you have complete control over his brain—"

"Given time, I am sure you can cure him," interrupted Janet. "Then, if you have no objection, I can return to being his best-ever, non-romantic friend. So now that's sorted, I'll just go and put a hot-water bottle in your bed and give it an airing."

"I have to get back to work tomorrow. My shift starts at two o'clock, and I'm not the fastest driver in the world, especially on narrow country lanes."

"And it will be dark soon, so no more nonsense. I'm making up your bed, and that is final."

"Look, I'm the bossy one!"

Janet shot her hand across the table and grabbed Tara's purse. "You met your match with me," she said, "and unless you want a punch on the nose, this purse is going into hiding. And I can feel your car keys inside it." She ran off and, shortly after, came back smiling. "All sorted," she said. "Now, if you want to get close to Richard, you will need to understand chess. I play in a league and often teach beginners."

While Janet set up the board, Tara's mind worked on a problem. Coming to Wales had involved three projects. First, she had found the Menai Bridge; second, she had located Janet; but what was the third? Of course – the seaweed! She asked Janet if she had any, and was told there was plenty in the bay. Tara modified her request to 'the sort you could eat'.

"Oh," said Janet, "that's called laverbread. It's a great Welsh delicacy."

"What, you eat it like truffles?"

"No – normally it's a breakfast food, fried with bacon. But the very best hotels serve it with cockles... not certain how that works because you have to be a millionaire to eat in those places. I am not, and, as a vegetarian, have no bacon in the kitchen either. So I mix laverbread with oats and pat it into a burger which I fry with onions. It's very healthy – plenty of iodine. But I only serve it to very special guests because it's seriously expensive. So you can have it for breakfast tomorrow morning."

"So you are trying to get me hooked on an expensive iodine habit?"

"This is my evil plan, yes, because then you will have to keep coming back to visit me to get your fix—"

"Of seaweed?"

Janet gave a thinly disguised smile. "You wait until your breakfast arrives tomorrow morning – it will blow your socks off, assuming you wear socks in bed!"

"Okay, you've got yourself a deal. I'll play chess and stay here tonight, but I expect a laverbread breakfast, just like in one of those posh hotels."

"Deal," said Janet.

Later that night, Tara snuggled beneath the blankets, thinking strange thoughts – principally that she had been in this cottage for less than ten hours, yet it already felt like home. Compared to her cheap bedsit in England, it was Heaven. Of course, it was still 'cheep', but only because of the birds waiting to sing her a dawn chorus. How different could two lifestyles be? Perhaps she could stay here and help Janet by typing or whatever. Then the sad truth dawned on her: it was Richard who needed to be here, because he had probably been a much better English teacher than… what he had become. And surely teaching English and correcting manuscripts were pretty much the same thing?

The following morning, Tara had the most wonderful start to her day. In fact, sitting in an armchair before the dying embers of a fire, she let her fantasies about living here take flight. When she mentioned them to Janet, she replied it was a good idea.

"But I can't offer you much work," she added, "though you are certain to get a job in the village, once you learn to speak Welsh."

"No," said Tara. "My job is to make Richard see sense: he needs to be here with you."

"Okay," said Janet. "But if you were his girlfriend, attending to his... err. Well, you could share the spare bedroom; I wouldn't make a fuss about all the marriage stuff you got up to."

"That's completely mad!"

Janet shrugged. "I am not a fortune teller," she said, "but there is quite a good Plan B. The farmer who owns the field on the other side of my hedge has an old gypsy caravan in his yard. The owner, now in his eighties, used to help with the harvest, and left it there after his horse died. He couldn't drive a car and had no wish to get another horse. He only stayed there for a year or so; if you have dodgy legs, you need transport around these parts. He now lives in the village, and the farmer uses the caravan to accommodate a labourer at harvest time. If you can pick potatoes, cut cabbages, that sort of thing, it could be yours all year round. I helped with the harvest last year; fifty hours' work is all the rent he will expect of you. Any extra, and he will slip the odd pound note into your hand. It might be a good way to scratch a living without too much stress. Maybe he would use his tractor to pull the caravan to the other side of my hedge. Home sorted! Do a bit for me, and you can use my kitchen to feed yourself. Food sorted! Then get yourself a little job in the village, and you have money in your purse. Like I said, around these parts, *I'm* the bossy one who organises everything."

"Don't like the sound of that," mumbled Tara.

"But it's a nice caravan, and you can always use the bathroom facilities here."

"No," insisted Tara, "the caravan sounds idyllic. I mean you being the bossy one. But you have been saved by the bell, because I need to be back at work in… oh my God; I need to travel at the speed of light."

"That's settled, then," said Janet. "We'll take a nice walk along the clifftop into the village, where you can telephone work to say you can't get back until tomorrow. Then I'll take you to see the farmer—"

"Whoa, whoa, whoa. Stop organising me."

"I'm not – I'm merely giving you an offer you cannot refuse. But I should warn you: if you ever do anything to hurt Richard – your future boyfriend – you will have me to deal with. And I don't mean a punch on the nose. The caravan is on wheels, and there's a clifftop on the other side of my cottage."

Tara knew any romantic arrangement between herself and Richard would fail. In moments of uncontrolled passion, he was certain to call out Janet's name. But how amazing it would be to have an aviator boyfriend living within twenty minutes of her home – assuming the farmer would allow him to land his aeroplane in one of his fields…

CHAPTER TWENTY-THREE

Donna answered the hotel telephone to hear the operator announce they had a long-distance call coming in.

"Putting you through, caller," she added.

"Hi," said a voice. "Tara. I'll be late starting my shift."

"Sorry, Tara's not here."

"I know – *I'm* Tara, in a phone box in the middle of nowhere. I should be back in about... tomorrow. Can you do a double shift?"

"I'll sort something, but I don't understand why I need to – you're always so organised."

"Oh, holidays, you know what they are like. How's Richard – is he giving Priscilla English lessons yet?"

"He's down there now with his books. And Chef's going to start her cookery lessons tomorrow, but Richard doesn't know about that yet."

"Yeah, I expect Priscilla's first day in the kitchen is going to be a bit traumatic. How's she doing with the housekeeper?"

"She reckons Priscilla's the first person she's met who

has never used a vacuum cleaner – she views her as the ultimate challenge."

"Well, you are obviously doing a good job on the control desk, so thanks."

Then, after a little more gossip, the operator interrupted to say their time was up, and to put more money in the box if they wished to continue. Tara said it was fine, and the line went dead. *Intriguing*, thought Donna. Tara being disorganised was unheard of. She decided not to tell Richard – he always got flummoxed over such things. She would do the double shift herself as a friendly gesture, in return for a reverse arrangement in the future.

Down in the scullery, Richard was back on form as an English teacher, and this time he noted Priscilla was paying close attention to every word he said. He had no doubt she was destined to pass all her O levels, and this would give her a chance in the real world, as opposed to working the backstreets as a prostitute.

When Richard realised his pupil would have to start work in five minutes, he closed his book and glanced around the scullery. The absence of daylight made it look rather small but, in reality, it could lose a space measuring seven feet by four. A hardboard partition, perhaps, then recover an old bed from the stockroom? Well, he reasoned, Priscilla could only sleep in the birdwatching shelter for a few more weeks. Come winter, she would die of cold. It was just far more logical to have her sleeping on the premises. The only argument against this, was a girl living in the basement did not fit well with the image expected of a four-star hotel. But if he kept quiet about it, who would find out? Anyway, if the owners wanted staff to work for a ten pence an hour, some sort of compromise was required. Vaguely, he put the idea to Priscilla.

She smiled, then opened one of the biggest cupboards. Beneath the bottom shelf were three large, square cushions, a pillow, and a pile of old blankets.

"Tara already sorted it," she said, "but she thought it better, if you worked it out for yourself. The time I spent walking to and from the nature reserve each day, I now work down here in the warm, and Chef has promised to give me cookery lessons in return—" She threw a hand across her mouth. "Whoops," she whispered between her fingers, "I wasn't supposed to tell you about that. It's just that I now consider you a friend and trust you completely. Anyway, it's probably better if you stay clear of the kitchen tomorrow morning."

That evening Richard was sitting in his office, idly stroking the framed photograph of Janet which he normally kept on the left-hand side of his desk. Because his work for the day was done, he could not think how to occupy himself until bedtime. Perhaps he could go to his bedroom to stare at another photograph of Janet? In moments like this he wanted everything to be over, for in truth, his was a life without purpose, except for educating Priscilla… Suddenly, his eyes opened wide. Tara had worked that out, and brought Priscilla into the hotel to give him a challenge. And what a challenge! How could anyone above the age of ten spell 'knob' without the silent 'K'? A little later, Priscilla had looked at him in astonishment, when he had said the thing which slides into a desk is spelt a 'drawer'. When she repeated it, pronouncing the '-er', it had made him laugh.

"No," he had said, "the '-er' on the end is silent. It's only a drawer when written down."

Tara felt slightly guilty for telling Donna a fib during her telephone call to the hotel. In truth, she was not in the middle of nowhere, but having a coffee in the village with Janet. Extending her holiday by a full twenty-four hours was, therefore, mostly voluntary – though the deception had been helped by Janet refusing to return her car keys. As they walked back along the clifftop towards the cottage, Janet asked Tara if she could swim.

"I often do twenty lengths in the hotel pool before starting my shift," she replied proudly.

"Good enough," said Janet, "given that I have some armbands in the cottage."

"Absolutely not," said Tara. "I refuse to wear anything which makes me look like a child – what else have you planned for me? A floating rubber duck, perhaps?"

An hour or so later, Tara found herself walking down a flight of steps to the beach. Janet then led her away from the main tourist area along a foreshore strewn with many boulders, which had fallen from the cliffs above. She realised this situation was nothing like a crowded swimming pool, where lifeguards no doubt dreamed of relieving their boredom by having someone to rescue. However, because here she would be swimming in her underwear, the seclusion suited her better. Also, Janet had told her that she often came here to freshen up in the morning, so knew all about the currents and stuff. Tara wondered why she had mentioned 'stuff', because, as they made their way through the waves, it seemed they could both swim perfectly well.

Only when they reached the deep-water swell, did she become a little nervous. Turning, she saw Janet's cottage perched on the edge of the distant cliffs. *So, she thought, while I usually have to make do with the chlorinated water of a hotel swimming pool, Janet simply gets up in the morning and comes here to bob up and down on the swell and breathe the fresh, salty sea air. She lives like a Queen with the ocean as her back garden! And what do I have? A small pool, with one end so shallow I keep banging my toes on the bottom when I swim overarm. Here I have no idea where the bottom might be...* Suddenly, she realised this was serious wild swimming. Quickly, she swam after Janet, who was now treading water.

"Ah, good," said Janet. "Did you just notice that tingling sensation at the base of your spine?"

"A little... ooh, it's rather nice."

"It means we have been spotted on sonar location," Janet said.

"Oh, silly me," replied Tara sarcastically. "When you said, 'currents and stuff', I failed to consider that 'stuff' might mean a submarine passing beneath us."

Janet took an armband, which had been tied to her costume, and blew it up.

"No," said Tara. "To die after being hit by a surfacing submarine would be unfortunate, but to be washed up on some pleasure beach, wearing one of those, would be a disaster. I cannot imagine why you brought them—" Then, without warning, something huge emerged from the water and towered above them. Tara panicked, screamed, and, losing all limb coordination, sank below the surface. After a few seconds, she felt something pushing her back up. "Wah-haaa!" she screamed.

"Well, I did recommend armbands," said Janet crossly. "They would have given you more confidence."

"I'm being attacked," wailed Tara.

Then she noticed Janet was treading water beside a giant fish with a smiley face. A dolphin? Whatever it was, it had a lot of teeth. Then she realised Janet and the creature were nuzzling each other affectionately. Janet threw the inflated armband into the air, and the dolphin flipped it higher with its nose. Janet then tried to catch the band as it came back down. After playing like this for a short while, she dived beneath the surface, and the dolphin followed. Tara panicked again; a sensible reaction to finding herself alone in a situation over which she had no control. Now, she so wanted those armbands.

When Janet resurfaced, she splashed about with her dolphin friend, apparently without a care in the world. "It's okay," she said. "They know we cannot breathe underwater. It's the same for them, except they can hold their breath for fifteen minutes. So we don't have to worry about them. Now play nicely, or I won't bring you here again."

Tara took Janet's advice, saying, "There, there, nice dolphin" in an artificially calm voice. Meanwhile, a pod of dolphins circled around her, sometimes leaping from the water to splash her, as if they were human children jumping into a swimming pool.

After Janet had said goodbye to her 'friends', the pod appeared to fly across the swell, and were soon out of sight. "It's the most efficient way for them to travel," she said. "With a tailwind they can do twenty miles an hour, whereas we need to swim back the hard way, because soon a cross-current will come. Quite safe, but it would take us miles down the coast, meaning you would emerge from the waves in your underwear and need a bus to get home."

On reaching the shore beneath the cottage, Tara felt all tingly clean – and not only on the outside. It was as if the terror had reinvigorated her whole nervous system. She turned to gaze at the water where her new friends lived. She shook her head – why was she having all these mad thoughts? "Was it dangerous out there?" she asked. "I mean, besides the prospect of having to get on a bus in my underwear?"

"Truthfully, the bus service only comes once every two hours, so waiting at the bus stop might have been awkward—"

"Stop! Let's just focus on the fish with big teeth."

"My point exactly," said Janet. "Most people only see the teeth when a big animal approaches; not what they might be having for tea. But truthfully, you should focus on what they might have been thinking. Did you not hear all of their squeaks and clicks? Essentially, they were having a good gossip about us."

In the hope of stabilising her emotions, Tara sat on a large boulder. Meanwhile, Janet dried herself off with a beach towel, which she then offered to Tara.

"When a dolphin gives birth," said Janet, "the mother gets underneath the baby to raise it gently to the surface, so it can take its first breath of air. I expect it's a bit like slapping a human baby on the bottom. So you being lifted up to scream 'Wah-haaa' brought out the maternal instincts of all the lady dolphins."

"Doctor Doolittle!" exclaimed Tara. "You know how to talk to animals... even when they have flippers."

Janet shrugged. "I merely understand how my friends see the world," she said. "Sometimes they share their secrets with me; occasionally by speech, but more often using body language. Maybe if you spend a little time sitting quietly in my garden, by yourself, you too will know what they are saying."

Weird, thought Tara. However when this thought came out of her mouth she said, "I never want to leave this place."

"Then don't," replied Janet simply, putting on her sandals and flip-flopping away.

"Uh…" said Tara. And with that simple utterance, she realised her life was spinning out of control.

CHAPTER TWENTY-FOUR

A few hours after her dolphin experience, Tara found herself sitting in an open-sided Victorian railway carriage with a gentle breeze drifting pleasantly across her face. Idly, she watched the countryside pass slowly by, until they entered a cutting where rock and hanging vegetation were the dominant features. According to Janet, this railway had been opened in 1832 to transport slate from the mountains of Snowdonia to the docks at nearby Porthmadog. At that time carthorses were used, but by the 1870s steam power had taken over. Tara imagined the locomotive now pulling them was only a little faster than the horses which had once plodded between the rails. Leaning out of the carriage to see where they were going, she saw the locomotive pulling them was huffing and puffing like an old man up a steep incline; perspiring and getting all out of breath, like the horses of a bygone age... Tara sat back on the hard wooden bench with a bump. She must have caught something from Thomas! She now believed steam engines to be alive! She confessed this embarrassing fact to Janet.

Janet seemed unconcerned, merely responding that their locomotive had been born in 1863, so was probably troubled by rheumatic joints. "But very brave," she added. "He's pulling twenty-odd carriages and maybe two hundred people. I think I would huff and puff at that."

Tara thought about Thomas… and the fact she had his telephone number. In the hope of dismissing this reckless thought, she again leaned over the side, looking for telegraph poles to count. "Wah-haaa," she wailed. "I've turned into a Thomas."

By the time they arrived at the mining settlement, Tara's panic had subsided to the point where she could ask herself a serious question: why did she not accept Janet's sensible offer of a place to stay? Her bedsit in England suddenly seemed most grotty. "You offered to feed me," she said, "in return for how much work?"

Janet shrugged. "Not much, but I would ask you to be careful with the laverbread because it's so expensive."

Tara laughed; something she had done rather a lot on this holiday. "You are just joking, right?" she said. Then, seeing that Janet was unusually serious, she frowned. "But it's just seaweed."

"You try telling that to the people who produce it. Weight for weight, it's eight times the price of cheese."

"That doesn't make sense; you've got tonnes of the stuff below the cliffs."

"I have often thought the same myself," said Janet, "but I only have it on special occasions, so it's of no great concern to me. And I have no wish to poison you by accident. A special guest dying of seaweed poisoning would not be good publicity for my agency."

"Oh, my word!" exclaimed Tara. "Eight times the price of cheese… and no hotel in England has it on their menu."

"Probably because it's seaweed."

"That's a bit like the French having pigs to snuffle out fungus from beneath tree roots," Tara responded. "Truffles are only served in the best hotels, so men can impress their girlfriends with the thickness of their wallets. But laverbread! If we get the right recipes, we could charge a fortune. Chef will love it – he could be the only laverbread expert in England. Stars of food excellence will be dancing around in his head."

"Which rather sounds like you are thinking about going back to the hotel?"

"For now, maybe… and hopefully carrying a packet of seaweed."

"It comes in cans," said Janet. "And for you, okay, I'll give you a couple to take back. But in return, you must look after Richard for me."

The day after Tara's train ride, Richard was sitting in his office, having gloomy thoughts about Priscilla. Now she had stopped wearing make-up and always wore caretaker's overalls, he had come to see her as a real person who had suffered great hardship. He decided to tell her this to keep her on the right track – and to change the light bulb in the scullery from fifty to one-hundred watts. Priscilla had been hiding down there long enough. Soon, he hoped, she would return to the daylight – a sensible lady reborn, as if from Mother Earth.

Richard was distracted from his thoughts by a brief knock on the door. Without waiting for his reply, Tara entered. "Hi," she said. "Just wondered if you fancied a game of chess later?"

"But when I asked before," he replied, "you said you didn't know how to play."

Then Richard found himself gazing at her lovely smile.

"We'll see," she said. "Tonight about eight okay?"

Richard smiled back. Teaching Tara the moves would be fun. It would be one thing he could do better than her.

That evening, Richard looked across the chessboard at Tara. He was just going to explain the moves when, playing white, she opened with a pawn to king four. He responded likewise, to which she advanced a pawn to king's bishop four. He frowned. That was a dangerous opening; only an experienced player would know how to exploit it. He took the pawn, and she responded with a knight to king's bishop three.

"How did you know about that?" he asked.

"Had I not covered my king's rook four, I would have faced all sorts of problems with your queen attack. I was playing with Janet last night," she added casually. "She said it would impress you."

"What?!"

"Your move," she said.

"No, I mean… how can I be expected to play a sensible game of chess after what you have just said?"

"The thought never crossed my mind," said Tara. "It's still your move."

After Richard's confusion led him to give away his queen in a simple knight fork, his game crumbled, and Tara soon secured a checkmate. She then leant back in her chair.

"All is fair in love and war," she said. "Now I suppose you want to talk about Janet. But not in your office; it's too impersonal."

Without waiting for his response, she stood up and walked into the dimly lit corridor. Previously she had given no thought as to what might exist here, beyond Richard's office. She now realised the low lighting was probably a deliberate attempt to disguise how poorly decorated this part of the hotel was. Indeed, the reception staff had been told not to offer the rooms off this corridor to respectable guests, because it would downgrade the hotel's star rating. However, occasionally it was considered better to offer half-price accommodation to those with limited means, rather than leave them to sleep in their car.

According to the housekeeper, Richard's private bedroom was at the far end of the corridor. Curious, Tara made her way down to the furthest door, which displayed the number 305. This suggested the hotel had many rooms, but, in truth, it was merely the fifth room on the third floor (which had once been better described as the attic). To add insult to injury, Room 304 housed noisy lift machinery, though the conveyance itself only ascended as far as the floor below. On opening the door to Richard's room, Tara found herself looking into a lonely garret. The furniture consisted of a single bed, a coffee table, and a sofa. Richard so needed a girlfriend to bring his emotional isolation to an end. But for now, she settled herself on the sofa and waited for him to join her.

Two minutes later, Richard reached his doorway, from where he looked into his private room. On seeing a woman sitting on his sofa, his brain recorded it as an hallucination;

certainly it was not something he had ever witnessed before.

Tara, sensing Richard was confused, decided to distract him with the sort of light-hearted gossip that normal people might have after a day's work.

"When I was on holiday," she said, "I met a man with an aeroplane. I think he called it a tiger, or a moth, something like that anyway. In any event, he did all sorts of loopy things, while I was in the passenger seat. 'Wah haa,' I screamed, or maybe that was what I said to the dolphin…"

Richard now looked even more confused than before. "Aeroplane?" he questioned vaguely. "And what dolphin?"

"The one in the sea, silly."

Tara realised Richard was completely overwhelmed by her 'bouncy' chatter' She approved. *His expression is that of a little boy looking through a sweet-shop window*, she thought. "Now are you coming in, or do you intend to stand in the passageway all night?" she asked.

Richard, unsure about what was supposed to happen next, entered and sat on the bed, hands nervously fidgeting on his lap. Then, instinctively, he began to talk about the safe, familiar subject of Janet.

Tara, after listening for half an hour, was almost falling asleep. Not because it was boring – though it was, a little – but because yesterday she had been swimming with dolphins. It had made her feel she belonged here… there… oh, her mind was all over the place. Understandable, because that morning she had woken up to a laverbread breakfast, then walked into the village with Jack hitching a lift on her shoulder. An hour later she had returned to the cottage and then, without any obvious break, driven continuously for five hours to reach the hotel to start work. Her mind was struggling to adjust to the shift between the two worlds which, it seemed, had nothing in common. And now here she was, sitting on Richard's sofa! Just as she was about to drop off, she realised he had failed to mention Janet's name for... some time, and now he was looking at her, as if expecting her to take part in a conversation.

"Uh?" she said.

"Precisely," he responded.

"I will need some time to think about it," she bluffed.

"Why? I only want to know if there's some detail you have failed to mention. About Priscilla, perhaps?"

"It depends where you're up to. Have you started giving her English lessons yet?"

"So it seems."

"Because you are a teacher. It's what you've been programmed to do."

"Anything else – like getting me to build a cabin for Priscilla to sleep in, maybe?"

"Her dying from frostbite in the birdwatching hide is not going to get our pots and pans cleaned. Moving her into the hotel was just sensible. Also, I am going to teach her to type. When I leave, somebody will need to take over the reception—"

"Leave?! You can't! It's you who keeps the place running smoothly."

"For me, leaving reception is inevitable. In one scenario, you go to see Janet. If you then stay in Wales, the next time the owner makes an appearance, I will be in your office, sorting things out. He likes an easy life, and I will be quite happy being the new assistant manager... for a short while.

Alternatively, if you cannot work something out with Janet, I will have kept your seat warm and, on your return, I will go to live with her. She's snowed under with work and offered me a live-in job as her assistant. But, quite honestly, you would do the work much better than me. With your English skills you could proofread manuscripts and the like. Then you could be a teacher there and do what you really enjoy – working with words – and not just be an assistant hotel manager because…?"

"I do okay."

"But why? From what you, Janet, and Priscilla have told me, I've got a pretty good idea of things. But you leaving teaching still doesn't make sense. Therefore, there must be something you are hiding from me." Tara held out both hands, as if to say, *Fill these with words.* She gave him an encouraging nod. "Come on, tell your best friend, Auntie Tara. I bet it's not that important really."

Richard stared down at his hands, then looked up with a vacant expression. "I killed a man," he said.

Tara laughed; then, seeing that he wasn't smiling, fell silent. For once, she could not at first come back with a rational response. Then she nodded. "Don't tell me," she said. "The man tried to hurt your Janet."

"He was… one of her clients. A horrible beast of fifty-something," he said. "…no, I can't repeat it."

"And how old was Janet when this happened?"

"Twelve, the first time, I think."

"There you go, then. He was not a client, but a paedophile; part of the gang Janet told me about. But like I told her, she was not a prostitute, but the victim of child abuse. So you did well, and I will never tell anyone. In fact, knowing this means I am finally in a triangle a friendship with you and Janet, and I kind of like that. It gives me a sense of belonging." *And now I am a proper friend to them,* she thought, *I realise I am much too tired to drive home tonight. Nor can I be bothered to argue about trivial details.* She went over to give Richard a gentle push on the shoulder, then snatched the quilt from his bed and returned to the sofa. Pulling the quilt up to her chin, she snuggled down. "Goodnight," she said. "There are some more quilts in the storeroom."

"But—"

"I'm your friend," said Tara. "From now on, the work thing is just a side issue."

Richard knew it was pointless to argue, but also that he must. Then, from beneath the quilt on the sofa, a hand appeared, dropping first a skirt then a jumper onto the floor.

"Checkmate," Tara said from under the quilt. "You can't drag me from the sofa now, so go and get yourself a quilt. I am not yet ready to wake up in the morning and see you lying on your bed in your jim-jams, as Janet likes to call them."

The next morning, Tara peered carefully around the door of Richard's room to see if the coast was clear. This was a pointless exercise, especially since the housekeeper was staring back at her. To emphasise how much of a secret the situation was, Tara put her finger to her lips and tiptoed to the bathroom at the other end of the corridor.

"But I am a housekeeper," said the lady, "and gossip is a perk of the job. Anyway, everybody knows you and Richard are an item… though I strongly suspect two of his admirers will hate you even more now that you are sharing his bed."

A week or so after Tara had spent the night on Richard's sofa, he was sitting in his office when the general manager poked his head around the door.

"Genius," he said. "How you came up with that, I shall never know. A fully booked dining room for breakfast, with night bookings to match."

Richard had no idea why he was a genius, so responded with a bluffed smile.

"Anyway," continued the manager, "me and the owner are going on holiday now – probably for quite a long time. Just keep up the good work."

Richard was quite accustomed to the owner and his 'friend' going away for months on end. Indeed, he gathered it was rather like a recurring honeymoon, which would be illegal in England. In any event, it seemed they had lost all interest in the hotel.

Presently, his mind returned to the mystery of why breakfast time had become so busy. Idly, he wandered down to see the chef. He was in a right flap, which probably meant everything was normal. Richard edged towards a kitchen assistant to make discreet enquiries.

"Your brilliant idea has made us the only place in England to offer such an expensive breakfast," said the assistant. "Any man who wants to flash the cash in front of his girlfriend, has to come here. And Tara tells me she got a fifty per cent discount for a bulk purchase."

Richard nodded, then went to the restaurant to study the menu. Laverbread… how much?! That was certainly the most expensive breakfast in the kingdom. And what was laverbread? Returning to his office, he looked up the word in the dictionary. Seaweed? What was the girl trying to do? Poison all the guests, or just bankrupt them? Panicking, he raced to see Tara, who smiled when he expressed his doubts over the breakfast menu.

"It takes a delicate palate to appreciate the taste," she said. "So sophisticated people have to claim they adore it. And if the working classes cannot afford it, then so much the better."

And finally Richard had to accept a far greater truth. It was obvious he should give up trying to be an assistant manager and instead go to live in Wales with Janet. Tara should have his job and take all the credit for being an organisational genius, just like she deserved.

Tara had a problem with men. With Graham, she could not work out whether she liked him or his aeroplane. Had it not been for her amazing experience of flying through the air, would she still keep thinking about him? Clearly, if it was just the plane that attracted her, it was morally wrong to go with him just for his assets. Also, after half a dozen flights, she might find it rather repetitive – unless he took her to France or something? But separating the aeroplane from Graham was impossible, because it was a fundamental part of his identity. Also, he had one other major disadvantage: he seemed well organised, and she liked solving problems... which took her mind to Thomas. Turning him into a functioning human being would be a major challenge. Also, she liked the way he had not tried to take advantage of her in the tent. He had shown her respect. More worryingly, she was curious as to what a wooden railway bridge might look like.

She now realised both Janet and Richard had a thing about Telford's road bridge, because they had both corrected her when she had mentioned it was made from a giant Meccano set. Apparently it was cast iron, and not to be confused with the later railway bridge, which was made of wrought iron. Was this level of bridge insanity catching? Might she one day be horrified, when she came across an inexperienced person on a wooden bridge, who said it was made of oak, when she knew it to be mahogany or something?

Then there was Richard. He was definitely the prime catch of the three men – at least if she wanted a hunk, who could elbow any Hollywood actor off his pedestal. This led her to think about falling in a more dramatic way – which, of course, applies to all cases of love; but, in this instance, she was thinking about spiralling towards the sea in Graham's aeroplane, after a wing had fallen off. What thoughts might flash through her mind, knowing that her life was about to end? Without doubt, if Richard was in that situation, his brain would be filled with images of Janet, while his vocal cords screamed out her name, so that it might drift across the ocean forever.

But Tara realised that, relative to this, she had no true love in her life. That gave her some flexibility but, sadly, no obvious boyfriend candidate. Eventually, she decided if death was fast approaching, her final word would be 'plonker' – for getting into a 1934 aeroplane with a mad aviator who liked to fly under bridges. And it was thinking about this word that solved her dilemma. It had infiltrated her mind while she had been talking to Richard – which meant she really, really liked him and the sound of his voice. He had clearly copied the word from Janet. That gave the three of them a sort of connection; a meeting of minds regarding how they saw the world. But it also helped Tara to face the truth: Richard belonged to Janet, and she had no wish to become a substitute for his obsessional, unrequited love. She then became rather cross with herself. 'Plonker' – what sort of word was that to say when spiralling towards an ocean in the final moments of your life?

And so it was that Tara had a problem with men.

Richard had first realised he had a problem with his non-existent romantic life, when he had woken to remember Tara was sleeping on his sofa. In order to spare them both the embarrassment of her seeing him changing out of his pyjamas, he had gathered his day clothes, intending to make his way to the bathroom to change. But before reaching the door, he had looked back to see her ginger hair cascading in a mass of colour between the rather dull quilt and the pillow. Then he had looked at her face; her eyes shut tight and a slight curl to her lips, indicating she was fast asleep. She showed not the slightest fear, despite her vulnerable position. How was that possible? Eight hours earlier he had confessed to being a murderer, and a little later her reaction had been to curl up on his sofa and fall asleep. But his response had been even more confusing. Refusing to acknowledge his changing feelings, he had scurried to the bathroom to get changed. And in that moment, he was not thinking about Janet, but a situation he knew to be impossible.

And so it was that Richard had a problem with women.

CHAPTER TWENTY-FIVE

Richard was sitting at his desk when the door opened. Only Tara entered his office without knocking; a practice that he thought lacked the necessary formality during working hours. But when he had pointed this out, she had replied she was his friend twenty-four hours a day. How could he argue with that? Anyway, he liked being her friend all day, so let the door-knocking formalities lapse. However, on this occasion, the person who entered his office was not Tara, but a rather rude man, who gazed around as if pricing up a decorating job – so perhaps a little like Richard's first meeting with Tara, except she was beautiful, while the man standing before him was the wrong side of ugly.

"Can I help?" asked Richard. "Only, I didn't hear you knock."

"You didn't hear me knock," said the man, "because I didn't feel the need to do so."

"Then perhaps you could explain why you are here?"

"Or, more to the point," said the man, "why are *you* here?"

"Because this is where I work."

"I have just purchased the hotel, so know who works here and who does not. You are in the latter category." The man dropped an envelope on the desk. "This is your P45," he said, "and two weeks' pay. You have half an hour to leave the premises. Your bit of crumpet on reception is being dealt with by the new assistant manager. Most unprofessional of you to go around shagging the staff. Oh, don't look so shocked – I've had my loyal employees posing as guests for the past two weeks, so know exactly what has been going on. Did you never wonder why all the rooms have been booked out?"

At that moment, Tara entered the office. "Because of our unique breakfast menu," she answered.

"Ah," said the man, "you mean the seaweed. Well, I intend to upgrade this grotty hole to a five-star establishment. When royalty start arriving, there will be no seaweed on the menu to poison them. Nor will there be any frizzy-haired creatures on the reception desk to terrify them."

"I do not have frizzy hair," said Tara calmly, "and even if I did, it would be better than having a bald patch on top like you. Have you never thought about buying a wig? The top of your head looks like an upside-down pudding bowl."

The man was clearly unaccustomed to meeting women who did not fear him. In fact, Tara's comments temporarily silenced him, while he subconsciously felt the top of his head.

"So is it right," continued Tara, "that you wish to sack me?"

"Your boyfriend's actions have already achieved that,"

said the man. "I presume you two have been using a hotel bedroom in work time—"

Richard leapt from his chair. "No!" he cried.

Tara waved him back down. "It's fine," she said. "That is only what the staff believe, so is not relevant to this situation. The important thing is that Mr Pudding Bowl here is unable to understand basic English. The expression I used was '*wish* to sack me'. That is not the same as actually doing so, except maybe in his wet dreams. That's 'wet' because he will wet himself when he discovers the nuclear weapon we keep in the basement."

The man took a step backwards. "You are completely insane!" he exclaimed.

Tara merely smiled. "And you are a complete plonker," she said. "Back in a mo…" Then she was gone.

The man turned to Richard. "You now have twenty-five minutes to leave," he said. "Your bit of crumpet will also be leaving shortly – in the back of a police car, probably."

Tara hurried down to the lost-property cupboard, from where she grabbed an old camera. It did not have a film inside, but that was not important – those of low intelligence would assume it did. She then continued down to the scullery, where she found Priscilla scrubbing away at a pot, which the sous-chef had forgotten about until smoke had started to rise from what had been a stew with some fancy French name.

"Forget that," said Tara, "you have some really important work to do. Can you still remember how to throw your screaming tantrums?"

"That's all in the past—"

"I know, but if I said a new hotel owner wants to sack the likes of us, what then?"

"Am I to be made homeless?!" cried Priscilla. "No, please; I could never go back to working the streets."

"If you trust me," replied Tara, "I guarantee neither of those things will happen. Nor will you ever have to clean another pot – unless you want to, or it was you who forgot to remove it from the stove."

"This horrible new owner you mentioned," said Priscilla cautiously, "can I pretend he is the bisexual with the smelly dick?"

"His name is Mr Pudding Bowl," replied Tara, "and, yes, I believe he fits that description."

"Then I will give my best acting performance ever. But…"

"But…?" questioned Tara. While waiting for an answer, she went across to Priscilla's sleeping cupboard and put her few possessions into a shopping bag.

"I can't go upstairs," said Priscilla eventually. "People might see me."

"Mr Pudding Bowl," said Tara. "I know."

"Not him," said Priscilla. "But I'm not wearing any make-up, and my hair's a mess. Mr Edwards keeps putting in a bright light bulb, and I keep changing it back because—"

"Genius!" interrupted Tara. Then, without explaining why this might be so, she removed a pillowcase from its pillow.

A little later, in the office, Richard was unscrewing his picture frames from the walls. Mr Pudding Bowl was watching him closely, presumably to make certain he did not steal anything. When the door opened, both men turned around. They gasped in horror, as Tara led something that looked like an Egyptian mummy into the room.

"This," she said, "is Priscilla, the girl you have kept chained in the dungeon. We have to keep a pillowcase over her head because daylight makes her believe she's a werewolf. When this happens, she becomes obsessed with the desire to get her teeth into human flesh."

The man looked at the thing clad in caretaker's overalls, with a pillowcase concealing its face. What ugly sight was waiting beneath? "I have never met this creature before," he gasped.

"The job of a journalist is to tell stories that sell newspapers," continued Tara. "Whether they are true is of no concern to the proprietor. In this story, you owned the hotel, while this poor Cinderella creature was kept chained in your basement, scrubbing pots and pans. Just look at her – she is destined for the front page."

"Front page?" the pillowcase appeared to gasp. "Me?!"

"But she's got a pillowcase over her head," said the man.

"Indeed," said Tara. "But her willingness to display a little of her perfect breasts to a photographer is all we need. I have it on good authority some horrible men, like yourself, find them quite hypnotic."

"She is not like that now," interrupted Richard. "I will not allow it."

"Shut up," said Tara firmly. "You are not helping." She then returned her attention to Mr Pudding Bowl. "Where was I? Oh yes, the newspapers. Not only are Priscilla's breasts to our advantage, but so are your bald head and weaselly face, because they make you look like one of those old perverts, who frequent the viewing area of the public swimming pool."

"I don't go to the swimming pool," interrupted the man.

"Pay attention," said Tara crossly. "I did not say you did; only that you *look like* someone who does. This is purely for photographic purposes. As far as the story is concerned, you are an evil little man who wishes to see his staff destitute and begging for pennies on the street to feed themselves. But that story can be on the inside pages – like the article dealing with the hotel getting downgraded to three stars for using slave labour."

To relieve his frustration, Richard suddenly picked up a glass paperweight and hurled it against the far wall, where it smashed into a thousand pieces. Priscilla's subsequent scream made everyone jump – even Tara, who had been expecting it. The volcanic temper tantrum which followed caused the pillowcase to fly off her head, revealing the ghostly white face of one whose only light came from a fifty-watt bulb. This image of death lent real panic to the situation, which ended with Mr Pudding Bowl backed against the wall, and Priscilla lying in a pretend faint across his feet. Tara casually pointed the camera towards them and clicked the shutter.

"'New hotel owner kicks pleading scullery maid'," she said. "The newspapers will love that."

"I did not... and get the terrifying bitch off me!"

"I saw it," said Tara.

"I was trying to kick her away."

"And whose version do you think will sell more newspapers?" asked Tara. "Quite apart from anything else, the reporter is my most passionate boyfriend ever. We will probably write the story together, after a romantic interlude in bed. Sorry, Richard, but have you never heard of candles when making love, and a foot-washing ceremony with scented soap before you start?"

"You are completely mad," shouted Mr Pudding Bowl.

"We have already established that," said Tara. Idly, she picked up a second paperweight from the desk and began to stroke it with the backs of her fingers, smiling as if in response to secret thoughts of murder.

Mr Pudding Bowl understood only a lunatic would smile in such a situation – a lunatic who was currently holding a lump of glass that could easily crack open his skull. Faced with a situation he did not understand, he called Tara a slag.

"No," shouted Richard, "she's with me!"

"Stop complicating things," said Tara firmly. "This is a simple case. All we want is two months' pay in lieu of notice, then we will walk out of this man's life forever."

Mr Pudding Bowl blinked. His first sign of weakness. Seeing this, Tara went to an anonymous-looking cupboard and opened the door to reveal the safe. "Richard," she said, "would you care to open it for the gentleman?"

"This is armed robbery," cried Mr Pudding Bowl.

"No – we are merely opening the safe for you. What you choose to do next is entirely your decision. For Priscilla, two months' pay comes to twenty pounds. Double that for me, and I'm guessing double again for Richard. So, £140, plus current pay. But because both Richard and Priscilla have accommodation included in their arrangement, let's settle for £210 – then we will be gone forever."

The negotiation continued for five minutes; a period in

which Tara told Richard to keep himself busy by screwing his photographs back onto the wall, because they might not be going anywhere just yet. For a short time, the new owner threatened to call the police, so Tara handed him the telephone. But while he knew that legally he was in the right, practically, did he really want a police car racing up the driveway just as all the well-to-do diners were sitting down to lunch? As for the gutter press, he had to accept they would take the side of the two crazy girls, who still had him trapped against the wall. Admitting defeat, he freed himself from the maniac lying across his shoes, and went to the safe.

Tara took the £210 from him. "And tax-free!" she exclaimed. "Priscilla, everything has now returned to good order."

Priscilla jumped up. "Thank you, Mr Pudding Bowl," she said. Then she turned to Tara. "Did I do well?"

"Very," said Tara. "Come, Richard – our work here is done… forever!"

Out on the driveway, Tara turned to the others. "He should have picked us off one by one," she said, "then he could have saved himself £210. But as a team, we are unstoppable. And because it was a team effort, I think we should divide the money equally – do you agree, Richard?"

After working at the hotel for five years, Richard had no need to worry about the odd seventy pounds. A far more traumatic problem was Tara keeping secrets from him. Why had she not told him about the journalist boyfriend before? What else had she withheld from him?

Priscilla had her hands over her face, at least until Tara stroked the backs of her fingers with the wad of banknotes.

Slowly, Priscilla parted her fingers, then gazed, wide-eyed, at all the money.

"Wow," said Tara. "You are really pretty in sunlight." She elbowed Richard in the ribs.

Richard thought Priscilla's face would have been considered beautiful in the seventeenth century, when deathly-white skin was fashionable. Now it needed daylight, and perhaps a little more time to recover from the starvation she had suffered. But truthfully, all he could think about was how deceitful Tara had been over her boyfriend. Telling lies, it seemed, was in fashion. "Indeed," he said. "Daylight enhances her natural beauty."

"Don't say it to me," said Tara crossly. "Turn to face Priscilla."

Instinctively, Priscilla closed her fingers. Richard, horrified by his basic error, took a firm grip of her hands and took them down to her waist.

"No," he said. "I will not allow it." In truth, he was trying to show he was a man who could control complicated situations. But deep down, his mind was overwhelmed with the need to buy candles to impress Tara – and what on earth was a foot-washing ceremony?

"It's okay to tell a woman she is beautiful," said Tara, "as long as you give her an escape route. So, Richard, let go of her hands. Now, Priscilla, keep your arms by your sides – it's not as if you've just got out of the shower and need to cover your private parts. So go on, Richard, the stage is set. Tell Priscilla the truth."

The truth was that Richard was thinking about Tara emerging from the shower. "You are beautiful," he said.

Priscilla flinched, but resisted the urge to lift her hands.

"Well," said Tara, "I'm glad that's all sorted, because I'm hungry. Let's get some proper cafe food inside us, rather than all this posh nonsense. Oh, wait…" Without explaining what they might be waiting for, she hurried off towards the rear of the hotel, then came back five minutes later carrying something the size of a shoebox. "Laverbread," she said. "If it's coming off the menu, seems a shame to waste it."

Richard was struggling to cope with the way Tara was organising his life – or, more precisely, the disaster it had become. His feeling of helplessness increased further when, instead of taking them to a cafe, she drove a few miles to a patch of wasteland. Many lorries were using it as a parking place, but their massive wheels would cope better with the rough surface of gravel and potholes. In Tara's little car, he could only cling to his seat, as she bounced between the towering vehicles.

After parking, she got out and, without any explanation, walked away. Priscilla followed, which gave Richard no realistic option other than to bring up the rear. On leaving a gloomy space between two lorries, he found himself looking at a dilapidated warehouse, its frontage constructed from rusting corrugated iron, with any gaps stopped with asbestos sheets. Why had Tara brought him to what was obviously a relic of wartime Britain?

For reasons he failed to understand, she insisted that he follow her to the building, where she opened a heavy wooden entrance door, its broken glass pane fixed with tape. Inside, a fog of cigarette smoke made it difficult to see clearly across the large room. However, close by he could make out some tables occupied by oversized men in shabby clothes. In fact Priscilla, in her overalls, seemed to blend in with the fashion of the other customers. Not wishing to bring attention to himself in such a frightening environment, Richard followed her to a table in the darkest corner. Here they sat in a huddle, staring down at the dirty plastic tabletop to hide their faces. Then, slowly, his mind turned to the cafe he had visited with Janet on their first holiday. He now realised that had been a genteel tea room, whose staff practised the etiquette of the Victorian age; a highly respectable place where a naughty governess might secretly bring well-behaved children. This cafe was a new world, where the working classes fed themselves using the dining etiquette of vultures. Their strange customs made him nervous but, at the same time, excited by his brave voyage of discovery.

When Tara arrived at their table, she was carrying a tray with three pint mugs of coffee. She was soon followed by a waitress, who placed three enormous plates of food before them.

"There you go, luv," she said. "Refills for nunk."

Richard frowned. She did not even curtsy. He wondered if the head waiter would bow when he presented them with the bill, for surely he would be keen to increase his gratuity? Then, out of curiosity, he asked Tara what the meal was likely to cost.

Doing her best to imitate the accent of the waitress, she told him this meal was on her, so 'nunk'.

"But I can't let a lady pay," he gasped, the sudden intake of breath taking the smog of cigarette smoke to the back of his throat, which made him cough. Concentrating on breathing through his nose, he then spoke more carefully. "When the bill comes, I must settle it."

Tara laughed, without explaining why she thought it funny.

"Uh?" said Richard. Realising he had used one of Tara's favourite expressions, he said it again, this time in a grumpier way. After all, he was the man, so it was deep within his psychology that, as a strong hunter, he should provide the food.

After they had consumed their ten-thousand-calorie meals, Tara turned to him. "You appear to be homeless," she said, "at least as far as England is concerned. So you are going to live with Janet in Wales. I am too, so that's us sorted."

"Your newspaper friend will not like that," mumbled Richard, trying hard to disguise his jealousy.

"Who?"

"Your secret man," said Richard, "who knows about candles. I don't suppose he treats you very nicely."

"Oh, I made him up," said Tara. She reached out to lay a gentle hand on his shoulder. "You have a lot to learn about the real world. I have absolutely no idea who the local journalist is. I suppose he exists but, to the best of my knowledge, I have never met him. All that matters is that Mr Pudding Bowl believed I had a journalist eating out of my hand – which, at the time, was holding a paperweight. In that situation, there was no way he could think rationally about the facts. And, may I say, the way you threw the other paperweight across the room, in a pretence of uncontrolled jealousy, was equally good acting. Not as amazing as Priscilla, though, who is surely destined for the stage. A great actress indeed."

Tara then withdrew her hand from Richard's shoulder and turned to Priscilla. "It seems you have lost your cupboard in the scullery," she said. "I've paid the rent on my bedsit until the end of the month, so you can sleep there if you wish, but it's a bit grotty. So you will also be coming to Wales with us."

"But Janet hates me!"

"Janet does not understand that word, but it's your choice – unless you decide to stay here. If you do, I will be forced to kidnap you for your own good. And for this reason, I am keeping hold of your seventy pounds."

Richard decided the time had come to take control of things. He took his final gulp of coffee and slammed the mug manfully on the table. Then he folded his arms and said he refused to move until the head waiter arrived with the bill, which he would insist on paying. Tara smiled, which made him feel even more protective of her. Then she leaned across and whispered something in Priscilla's ear. To his astonishment, Priscilla laughed – not something he had seen her do before. He was still struggling to cope with this unexpected development, when Priscilla emptied the table's bowl of sugar cubes into her overall pocket. Next, both girls leapt up and, each taking one of his arms, frogmarched him to the exit.

"We haven't paid," he protested.

"We are outlaws on the run," said Tara. "This morning we robbed a hotel, and now we're fleeing a crime scene without paying for our food. Bonnie and Clyde have nothing on us. So let's hit the road and escape to another country to evade justice."

Dragging Richard to the car, Tara ordered him to jump inside before the police arrived. However, initially their dramatic escape could not exceed two miles per hour because of the wasteland's bumpy surface. Secretly, Richard felt excited by what they had just done, but also uneasy about his changing morals. So, as a gesture, he reprimanded Priscilla for stealing all the sugar.

Immediately, Tara came to her defence. "There was no sign on the table stating how much sugar a customer is allowed to put in their coffee," she said. "Okay, in this instance, the sugar is only going to get mixed with the coffee later, in Priscilla's tummy, but the end result is the same. Let the courts prove otherwise."

Then Priscilla spoke quietly, and possibly with some embarrassment. "When I was... before... you know." After a pause, she lowered her voice to little more than a whisper. "Some days, I would have one cup of coffee in the cheapest cafe I could find, and gradually sneak all the sugar cubes into my pocket. Often it was the only food I had for the whole day. In that transport cafe, well, it was obviously just my habit of feebly attempting to survive, without remembering that sir is now my protector."

Richard felt sick at the very thought of Priscilla's previous hardship. He wanted to reach over to the back seat to hold her hand and tell her everything was okay now, because in the future he would always look after her. Increasingly he felt confused about this, and other emotions that men were conditioned not to talk about.

Tara understood Richard was confused by his new life, so decided not to let him get involved in any decision-making. She alone would organise the military-style operation of getting to Wales. So, without telling him of her intentions, she drove to the lock-up garage where he kept his Austin 7.

"There is only one thing you need to decide," she told him. "That is, are we all escaping the long arm of the law in my car, or is the Austin coming as well? I'll be back here at eighteen hundred hours precisely. Please be waiting and ready to relocate to our new country."

Leaving a bemused Richard standing on the pavement, she then drove to the bank where she had previously opened an account for Priscilla, and paid in her seventy pounds. "I shall be funding the entire expedition," she told Priscilla.

"What expedition?" asked Priscilla.

"Wales, of course," replied Tara. "Do keep up."

Priscilla scratched her head. An hour before, she had been cleaning pots in the scullery, and now Tara was dragging her off to Wales? But before she could ask questions about this unexpected development, she found herself being driven to Tara's bedsit. After loading the back seat of her car with her belongings, Tara then drove to the library to return some books. Next she went to the garage to check the car's oil and tyre pressures, and fill up with petrol.

"Give me time to think about stuff," protested Priscilla eventually.

Thinking is not your strong point, thought Tara. *Best not.* "We need to get to the launderette," she said. "As my clothes come out of the dryer, we will divide them up according to need. I'm guessing you don't want to be waking up in the nude, so you can have my old pyjamas. I now have a very long T-shirt which doubles as a nightdress. So, reality check! You have clothes, and have spent no money, so your understanding of the world is improving. And," babbled

Tara happily, "I have put all of your redundancy pay in your bank account, because carrying that much cash around is just risky. Quite apart from anything else, if the plane crashes into the sea, I don't want to think about you sinking to the depths with seventy quid in your purse."

"Plane?! But we're driving?"

"Graham's plane, silly – do pay attention."

Priscilla was fairly certain Tara had never mentioned anything about a plane before, but realised the girl was on such a power trip, she must be getting muddled between fantasy and reality.

Richard was sitting in his Austin 7, gently stroking the back of the passenger seat that had once been occupied by Janet. He had to acknowledge that taking two cars to Wales was daft. Tara had offered him a lift in hers and, once there, he could... well, the future was a complete mystery to him. He scratched his head; something he had noticed people often did when Tara was taking control of things.

"Whatever comes next?" he said to the imaginary Janet – but she was no longer there, it was just a cold empty seat. He realised the Austin represented a past time in his life. Above all else, it was now a collector's item and worth four times what he had paid for it. Tara's car was just an old banger and destined for the scrapheap within a couple of years. If he got together with her, they could buy something nice. Except, he remembered, she had a boyfriend with an aeroplane. In a gesture of helplessness, he lowered his forehead onto the steering wheel. Oh, why was his life such a mess?

Picking up the starting handle, he got out to bring the

car into life – the last time he would do so. If the man who had once admired it still had £250 to spare, he would do the deal that afternoon, and… and what? He had absolutely no idea.

CHAPTER TWENTY-SIX

Ever since Priscilla had emerged from the hotel scullery with a pillowcase over her head, she had been confused about... well, everything. After some difficult thinking, she came to realise that her life now, on the surface of the planet, was entirely different to anything she had experienced before going to live in the subterranean scullery. This meant she was currently always trying to understand stuff which had happened half an hour earlier. She tried to recall the word which described the feeling of having no control over her life – but the chaotic way in which she kept being moved from one place to another, meant it eluded her. Anyway, by the time she had found herself in the transport cafe, she had been thinking about when they had been standing in the hotel grounds. Mr Edwards had said she looked pretty and this, she knew, was very important. Then he had made a ridiculous statement about make-up, or, rather, the absence of it.

Only while sitting in the launderette had her mind moved forwards to the transport cafe itself. That had been funny because, like Mr Edwards, her upbringing meant that, until her 'difficult' phase, she had only ever gone to restaurants where a waiter presented a bill at the end of the meal. After that part of her life was over, she had gone immediately to the other extreme: where cafe owners had no chance of extracting money from customers once the food was safely inside their tummies. This made her wonder what happened within middle-class establishments. Logically, a waiter there must present the diner with their bill in the middle of the meal, trusting they were sufficiently wealthy to stay put until the pudding arrived.

But by the time this thought came to her, she was in the back of Tara's car – still without any understanding of why she was being moved from one place to another with no say in the matter. When, at the beginning of their journey, she had asked Tara to explain, her reply had simply been, "Go west, my child, go west."

This prompted Priscilla to compare herself to an early pioneer, crossing America in search of something unknown and probably dangerous. However, she was fairly certain their stagecoaches had had springs to smooth the ride, whereas Tara's car obviously did not. In fact, Priscilla's seat had a level of comfort similar to that of a park bench. A few miles into the journey, she mentioned this to Tara.

"Dunno," replied Tara. "I never sit in the back seat when I'm driving… or when I'm parked!"

"Well," responded Priscilla, "if you did, you would know more about the springs which seem to be missing."

"If they were missing," replied Tara, "I would know even less about them. However, I rather suspect they have merely given up trying to support us."

Finding no sympathy for her plight, Priscilla withdrew into her own private world. *I am a famous actress,* she thought, *on a stagecoach going west. My fans on the pavement are gazing at me – but, alas, I cannot wave to them because the collapsing pile of luggage to my left has trapped my arm against the door.* Then, as they took a bend, a cardboard box slid from the top of the suitcases and wedged itself between her left shoulder and the car ceiling. This seemed most unfair, because everything she owned was packed into the shopping bag on her lap. Of course, technically she also owned a cardboard box of Tara's old clothes, but the terror of those was too much for her to comprehend. If she ever wore them, some batty old woman was certain to come flapping across the road to say how much she admired Priscilla's lovely dress, before moaning about her wartime ration card being all used up. Added to her clothing misfortune, Priscilla had to deal with the knowledge that her hair was a mess. But somehow, amid the confusion which had followed their eviction from the hotel, Tara had deprived her of all access to her money. That made her essential visit to a hairdresser impossible! But when she had told Tara about this, emphasising the word 'essential', Tara had merely replied that she looked wonderful. Priscilla's fantasy of being a famous Hollywood actress had now become a dismayed conviction, that she was a seventeenth-century peasant who cut her own hair with a pair of garden shears.

In addition to all of this, she was trying to cope with her increasing terror at the prospect of facing Janet. After all the horrible things she had said and done to her, the only question was, would Janet's assault be verbal, physical, or both? After travelling for two hours, Priscilla decided she could not go through with the meeting. But with sir sitting in the front and Tara driving, she was essentially a prisoner, being taken to face a trial by Janet's anger.

Richard knew his decision to go to Wales had been foolish. He wanted to tell Tara how wonderful she was, and maybe even use the L-word. But with Priscilla sitting in the back, this was impossible. Anyway, everything he owned was now squashed into two suitcases in the boot. If Tara drove away in a panic, he would be both homeless and without possessions.

Tara was thinking about springs. Not the ones in the rear seat, which were only of concern to Priscilla's bottom, but the ones beneath the vehicle. They were clearly carrying far more than their maximum weight, as indicated by the solid clunks vibrating through the chassis. Most probably the springs had been flattened out, so the undercarriage skimmed a fraction above the road. On her first visit, her car had only just managed to navigate the ford which crossed the dirt track leading to Janet's cottage. Now, the lack of an effective suspension system, suggested the water would this time wash over her headlights. Also, there had recently been a lot of rain. If the car stalled in the middle of the ford, everything the three of them owned would have to be abandoned, as they swam to the bank.

"Can both of you swim?" she asked her passengers, partly to break the silence but, more truthfully, to work out a survival strategy.

Richard said, "A little."

Priscilla asked, "Why?"

Tara took Priscilla's response to mean 'no'. "Oh," she said, "no particular reason. But there is a really nice beach near where Janet lives. From now on, swimming is free, as long as you don't mind the odd dolphin popping up to say hello."

Priscilla thought, *Janet will want to take me for a swimming lesson, then feed me to the dolphins, like I deserve.*

Richard thought, *Janet would never do anything so dangerous as swimming with dolphins. Tara is using shock therapy to divert attention from whatever it is I am not supposed to know.*

Tara thought, *So, after the car stalls in the middle of the ford, all three of us will turn up at Janet's door, bedraggled and disorganised.* Then she remembered the telegram she had sent earlier: 'Tara, Richard, Priscilla arriving.' In truth, she had used the minimum number of words to save money, but now she realised the omission of a definite arrival time was quite fortuitous. If the ford was too deep to cross, they could all sleep in the car, and use the narrow clifftop path to reach Janet's cottage in daylight.

As the journey continued, Richard became increasingly concerned about Tara's driving. Not because it was dangerous – in fact, at thirty miles per hour, it was completely safe. However, it did mean they would not reach their destination until nearly midnight. Also, he needed a lavatory but, with two ladies in the car, he found requesting a 'comfort break' far too embarrassing.

After crossing the Welsh border, Tara began looking for a roadside cafe. She stopped at the first one that was open. Immediately, Priscilla ran towards the building. Richard cleared his throat for the love speech that he knew must follow. Then his own urgent need to visit the lavatory took over, causing him to race in the same direction as Priscilla.

After attending to their 'comfort' needs, the three travellers gathered around a table in the cafe. To divert his thoughts from his own longings, Richard turned his attention to Priscilla. "Are you still frightened about meeting Janet?" he asked.

"Terrified."

"Because…?" asked Richard.

Priscilla bowed her head. "Because I am ashamed," she said. "It was me who told your father about… you know… Please don't be angry with me."

"No need to worry," said Tara. "It's like Richard has said many thousands of times: Janet is perfect, so has no understanding of hate. It will be fine."

Richard gazed at the wonderful Tara. He felt ashamed, embarrassed and totally confused. Yes, Janet was wonderful too. Then he frowned. Tara seemed to know what Priscilla had been about to confess, even though the words had been left unspoken.

It was midnight when Tara turned off the main road to begin what, she imagined, might become a nightmare descent into the ford. As it happened, after a few yards she came to a triangular road sign in the middle of the track stating, 'FLOOD'. This brought her to a halt. Attached to the sign was a piece of cardboard with an arrow pointing to a Land Rover parked to one side. Beneath the arrow, in neat handwriting, it said, 'Welcome, Tara, Richard, Priscilla. Keys inside.'

Um, thought Tara, *I have been here for less than one minute, and already I have been out-organised.* She walked across to what she recognised as Janet's battered old Land Rover, and found the keys in the ignition. "This is a crime-free area," she said. "Hardly anybody keeps things locked up around these parts. Well, are you going to help me transfer our luggage across or not?"

"I can't face Janet," wailed Priscilla. "Not after what I've done."

Tara took Priscilla's shopping bag and threw it onto the back seat of the Land Rover, then quickly dumped some boxes on top. "Well, if you want to stand in the middle of nowhere, with just the clothes you are wearing," she said, "don't let me stop you."

"But it's gone midnight," interrupted Richard. "Priscilla is right: we can't just turn up."

"Fine," responded Tara. "I'll leave the tent here. But I believe the nearest grass meadow is on the other side of the ford."

After transferring all of the luggage, Tara found herself sitting in the strange, rather wide vehicle. As expected, Richard and Priscilla were with her.

Right, thought Tara. *Stay in first gear, no more than six miles per hour. We'll be there in ten minutes.* Though, in practice, she actually found driving the Land Rover quite fun. She decided to get one for herself, as soon as she had found a job.

On approaching the cottage, the headlights picked out another sign in the middle of the track. This one had an arrow pointing to a small patch of muddy grass on the left. Beyond that was the five-bar gate which, Tara knew, enclosed the field where the goats lived. They were tame and kept the grass short, making their field an idyllic place to pitch a tent – so avoiding the need to disturb Janet. But Janet had already considered this because, beyond the gate, the headlights illuminated a gypsy caravan. In case Tara had failed to see this, a lit paraffin lamp hung above the doorway, beneath which a ramp effectively extended the living space down to the field. "Uh," Tara said, to indicate she did not like being out-organised – again. Beneath the ramp, a stick fire had been laid between two piles of bricks, and a kettle balanced on top.

Within ten minutes, all three of them were sitting around the flames, holding mugs of drinking chocolate.

"There are so many things I do not understand," said Priscilla. "I mean about this, and everything. It's probably because I got up this morning expecting to work in a scullery, and sixteen hours later I'm… well… in a field, holding a mug of hot chocolate."

"Yes," said Tara, "I am rather pleased with the way I have organised everything. Tomorrow, if you are lucky, you might even stand on a clifftop to watch the dolphins playing far out to sea."

Priscilla almost dropped her mug. That was three ways a murder could be made to look like an accident: drowning, falling, or being eaten by dolphins. How was that lucky? Instinctively, she shuffled across the grass until her shoulder was leaning against Mr Edwards and, in that moment of contact, something changed, deep within her mind. She was not leaning against an all-powerful (if somewhat annoying) man, but a sexy hunk only a few years older than herself. "Sir," she asked, "would you teach me to swim?"

Richard remembered how much he had enjoyed teaching Janet to swim on their first magical holiday. Then, when she could barely manage ten lengths of a heated public pool, she had taken it upon herself to cross a deep lake. That was the only time he had ever told her off, because it was a very dangerous thing to do. He now realised he had been a little bit in love with her back then; as a father protecting a daughter, before it all got confusing. Well, this time, with Priscilla, he would be stricter. "Okay," he said, "but only if you promise not to go swimming with dolphins. I am sure it's much too dangerous."

Priscilla put an arm around his shoulder. "You've got yourself a deal," she said.

Richard felt the gentle pressure resting upon his shoulders. That level of friendship was not something Janet – or, for that matter, any other lady – had ever offered him. Then he remembered his third visit to Priscilla in the scullery. That was when he had started to worry about her, so he had begun to prepare her for a more secure life by helping her to study. Now, he realised, that concern had progressed to caring about her. Of course, his desire to protect her could not possibly lead to anything more complicated; but nevertheless, he liked the way her hand had relocated to the back of his neck, so her delicate fingers could play with his hair.

CHAPTER TWENTY-SEVEN

Waking from a nightmare is fairly straightforward. You sit up in a panic, and wave your arms to defend yourself from whatever was trying to attack you. In Priscilla's case, this was a dolphin that had wanted to eat her – strange, because she could not swim. Then the nightmare mingled with reality when she opened her eyes to see a very low, curved wooden ceiling. She reached up to touch it. Her fingers told her it was real, so not part of the nightmare. For reasons she could not recall, she was in a gypsy caravan which, she did remember, was parked in a field. She had to admit this was totally different to waking up in her scullery cupboard, nervous about the frightening world which existed at the top of the stone steps. Remembering she was on the top bunk, she looked over the side and saw Tara sleeping below. Richard was lying on the floor with an airbed for a mattress. Priscilla now understood he was her special protector, who happened to be very handsome. And here she was, clad in Tara's cast-off, passion-killer pyjamas. Quick action was needed before he awoke.

Wriggling to the bottom of her bunk, she silently swung herself down to the small unoccupied floor space by the caravan door, then hurried down the ramp to the field where the Land Rover was parked. Her overalls were on the front seat and, within a few minutes, she was dressed and ready to begin her day. In the past, this procedure had taken close to an hour. So now what? The answer came from a goat, with big horns, which had stopped munching the grass in the middle of the field to regard her carefully. She had read about goats in childhood picture books, and mostly they liked to butt people on the bottom. Gymnastics had never been her strong point, but she felt certain the speed at which she clambered over the gate, would have impressed her old gym teacher. Standing on the safe side of the fence, she looked back across the field where she had spent the night. Oddly, the scene gave her a sense of well-being. The caravan, too. It was a far better place to wake up than the hotel scullery, knowing there were a lot of pots and pans to be cleaned.

"I thought you would be getting up about now," said an approaching voice. "Did you sleep well?"

Priscilla spun around to defend herself as necessary. "Janet!" she exclaimed.

"Yeah, it's little old me. Guess I've changed a bit since we last met."

"Oh, I'm so sorry."

"For what?"

"How horrible I was."

Janet just shrugged. Then, making no comment, she vaulted over the gate to stand in the field. The goat ambled across and stood before her. "Good morning, Billy," she said. "Did you sleep well?" She then took a biscuit from her pocket and offered it to the goat, while using her other hand to gently stroke its back. The animal seemed to think this quite normal. Janet then vaulted back over the gate and turned to Priscilla. "All his lady friends have gone for their morning milking," she said. "I always feel sorry for Billy, left all alone, so I generally bring him an early-morning treat to remind him that we're friends."

Then she walked away, telling Priscilla to follow. A few seconds later, Priscilla found herself in a magical garden with an ancient stone cottage at its centre. There were birds everywhere, one of which came to perch on Janet's shoulder. She held up a piece of fruit, which the bird took in its rather large beak.

"This is Jack," said Janet. "He often sits on my shoulder when I walk into the village along the clifftop. Though whether it's because he likes the bouncy up-and-down sensation, or because he's simply lazy, I can't quite work out. Anyway, after using me as his personal taxi service, he sometimes flaps up to a lamp post for a spot of people-watching. Though, other times, he stays put, and I've often walked into a shop, quite forgetting he was there. Awkward, because although he's people-trained, if you know what I mean, he's not exactly house-trained. I don't mind because my cottage has slate floors, but, while hopping off my shoulder to stand on a shop's food counter is entirely logical to him, given the limitations of his potty-training, it's not necessarily the view of the sales assistant."

Priscilla could not understand why Janet was not shouting at her. Instead her voice was quiet and her topic of conversation trivial. Then her tone became strict.

"Stop," she said. "Look where you're going."

Priscilla turned her attention from the frightening bird to look where she was going. Five yards ahead, the ground came to a sudden end. Beyond this, a distant ocean shimmered in the early-morning sunshine. She could hear the waves splashing upon the shore below.

Then Janet stepped forwards, nearer the cliff edge, and opened her arms. "I have all this," she said, "so why should I be cross? Had it not been for your intervention, I might have become addicted to Reginald's money, and you know where that ends up. But now I can take an early-morning swim with the dolphins instead."

Priscilla, fearing she was about to faint, stepped forwards to grab Janet's shoulder for support. But Janet stepped quickly away, so Priscilla found herself lying on the ground.

"I don't do touching," said Janet. "You know, because…"

"You hate me, but were pretending otherwise so you could take me swimming and let me drown, like I deserve."

"No. But I need a lot of space. I don't touch anyone."

Priscilla looked confused. "But when you're doing it with sir…?" she asked. "Sorry, I shouldn't have said that – me and my big mouth. It's obvious that you just find me disgusting."

"You should learn to call him Richard," said Janet calmly, "but to answer your question, I've never done it with him."

"What? Never?!"

"It didn't feel right."

"But you lived together in the same house, when you were at school. He must have done it sometimes. For men it's essential."

"If he asked me to do anything I found unpleasant, then he would not love me. So what would be the point? If he just wanted a female body, he could have visited a brothel. Though, if Richard was that sort of man, our friendship would have ended ages ago."

Slowly, Priscilla stood up, then, in order to avoid eye contact, turned to gaze across the ocean. "His father took it whenever he wanted," she said.

"Because he did not love you," said Janet. "Now, enough of our past miseries. Let's get back to my kitchen for coffee and goat's cheese on toast. A little later I will take you to meet the farmer's wife, who makes the cheese. We will let the others sleep in, or..." For a few seconds, Janet looked thoughtful; then she shrugged. "Who can say what will happen with Richard and Tara sharing a caravan? Tonight, perhaps, you might even be sleeping in the spare bedroom of my cottage..."

Tara slowly left her dream world and opened her eyes. Where was her familiar bedroom ceiling? Then a confusing memory of the previous night came to her: something about a goat and a mug of drinking chocolate? She reached up to feel the wooden planks two feet above her head. And so her dream faded to leave her wide awake – England had gone, and she was sleeping in a gypsy caravan in Wales, with no need to get up for work. Oh, and she had abandoned her car to drive a Land Rover across a river. That would account for her dream involving a raft, which kept trying to sink.

Turning onto her side, she looked at dear Richard lying on the floor. Given the limited cushioning of the airbed, he was on his back, mouth slightly open, but not snoring, which she liked. Indeed, the whole situation made him appear vulnerable. Oh yes, that was the other weird thing: Priscilla would be sleeping in the bunk above. And the three of them were rich due to a 'heist' at the hotel – well, rich at least to the extent that they would not need to work for another month.

Tara quickly wriggled out of her sleeping bag, then crawled from the bunk and stood by the ramp down to the field. Looking back at the top bunk, she realised Priscilla was already out and about. *Okay*, she thought, *morning coffee for two*. While she was boiling the water over the open fire, Jack came to perch on her shoulder.

"Hello, Jack," she said. "I expect you would like a biscuit."

Jack understood the words 'hello' and 'biscuit', both of which he liked. He also understood there were two sorts of people: those who fed him, and those who did not. In addition to this, he had developed a theory that there were male and female people. It was difficult to tell them apart because they kept changing their plumage – except for the one who responded to the sound 'Jant'. She was always grey, so when he took a ride on her shoulder, his dark feathers looked particularly handsome. Jack's favourite hobby was people-watching, mostly because he thought they were funny, given the way they bounced along without ever flapping their strange wings. Anyway, this activity had led him to develop many amazing theories. He now believed the people who pushed their offspring around in a nest on wheels, were mostly female. Why they did this, he had no idea. When young, he had nested in a box on a shelf in the place where Jant lived. But recently, he had come up with an even more remarkable theory: those who pushed the movable nests generally had two bumps, so were probably the ones who laid the eggs. So, he reasoned, Jant and her friend, who he had seen earlier, must be females – as must the one with the soft ginger hair, on whose shoulder he was now comfortably settled. Then he turned his attention to the new person lying on the floor. He had no idea how they did this without their legs sticking up in the air. Once, while people-watching on the beach, he had tried to copy their extraordinary sleeping posture. It had got him totally confused because, once on his back, his right eye had been looking at things that should have been on his left, and vice versa. Then, when he had tried to return to the correct way up, he had got himself in a total panic. Looking at what should have been 'down', he saw the sky, and soon a lot of people staring at him, with upside-down unusual expressions on their faces. Finally, one of them had put a hand under his wing and flipped him back over. It was the most embarrassing moment of his life. He had flown away to hide, resolving never to try such foolishness again!

Presently, he was distracted from his memories of a misspent youth by the nice female on whose shoulder he was still perched.

"Friend," she said, raising her thumbs.

Jack understood this, so flapped down to land on its nesting material. Still curious about the other person's ability to sleep on its back, he hopped forwards to take a closer look at the face. Gently, he rested his beak against the person's nose. Without warning, the person sat up, making a horrible noise, and Jack flew back to the safety of the female's shoulder. She was making that funny noise they made when they seemed to be happy.

Richard clutched his nose. "It was trying to eat me!" he yelled.

"Oh, isn't he a silly sausage?" said Tara to the bird. "In our language we call it an Eskimo kiss. Though perhaps I should have introduced you first. Jack, this is Richard. Richard, this is Jack."

Now the new person was half out of his nesting material, Jack could see it did not have bumps, so was probably a male. And not a very nice one at that!

Richard remembered he had been sleeping in nothing but his underpants, so quickly pulled up the bag to cover his tummy. In the next instant, his world focused on Tara sitting outside the entrance to the caravan, her hair catching the sunlight. She was wearing a long T-shirt, or maybe a nightdress. He did not understand ladies' fashion, so could reach only one conclusion: it was the sexiest thing he had ever seen, or would have been, had the Bird of Death not been sitting on her shoulder. Never would he forget the horror of opening his eyes to see a beady black one looking back at him from two inches away. The fact its pupil was surrounded by a gold ring – which, he would only later realise, was the iris – made it look like a medieval messenger of doom. Richard watched Tara make another mug of coffee or, more truthfully, the way her T-shirt dress swirled just above her knees in the morning breeze. Then she came towards him, as if in a beautiful dream. She placed the coffee by his side. He was going to confess his love.

"I…" he began, before stopping himself. He was only wearing his underpants, so any declaration of love could be seen as a threat. Also, the bird on her shoulder was confusing the situation – and that was before he even considered Priscilla in the top bunk. In fact, he was trapped, virtually naked, in a caravan, with the Bird of Death eyeing him suspiciously.

"Well," said Tara, "I think you should say sorry to Jack for being so horrible to him. Here, give him this biscuit, just to let him know you are not really a bad man. For myself, may I say thank you? I am sure your waking was the funniest thing I have ever seen. In fact, I'm off to tell the others about it. Then… well, I don't know; Janet seems to organise everything around these parts. Though maybe I will drive to Caernarfon to see my aviator friend."

Richard wanted to scream out, *No!* But the bird was demanding all his attention, so thought screaming was best avoided. Then, feeling rather pathetic, he simply watched the angelic Tara walk back down the ramp to the field.

"I'm going to get dressed," she called back. "See you later… Maybe."

He still wanted to call her back, but he was in his underpants and alone with Priscilla. No, that did not make sense – his cry of terror on seeing the bird would surely have woken her. He must be alone… except for a goat with big horns, which had just walked up the ramp to look at him, before taking an inquisitive nibble at his sleeping bag. Richard knew these beasts also had some sort of association with the Devil, but the bird attack had left him so terrified, he paid the goat little attention. Then came his second, more serious panic attack: his naked tummy was, he now realised, poking out above the top of the sleeping bag. His belly was too big and floppy – and Tara had seen it and laughed. How had this crisis happened? Presumably it was something to do with working in the hotel, which had mostly involved sitting down. In fact, while on reception duties, his waist measurement had gone up by three inches: though it would be more accurate to say, those three inches of middle-aged spread had been layered upon pre-existing foundations of fat. Until today, this had not worried him because he had never bothered to look at himself in a mirror when naked; and during the day, everything was hidden beneath his shirt. But now Tara had seen the awful truth: that his tummy paid no regard to his trouser belt, simply rising up to overhang the top. Then he realised that she liked him because she thought him funny! However, she liked her other admirer better, because he had an aeroplane.

Before the true horror of realising Tara considered him a figure of fun could sink in, he had an awful flashback to something that had happened with Priscilla the night before. He had agreed to teach her to swim. She too was destined to see him as one of those middle-aged men, who waddled duck-like about the pool with their enormous bellies overhanging their swimming trunks. Would she also laugh at him, or simply consider him hideous? And why was he worried about what Priscilla might think anyway? Then he realised the prospect of sharing a cottage with three women, was making him more aware of his lack of masculinity. And what had Tara meant by calling him a silly sausage? When he had first sat up in his sleeping bag, had she seen his underpants and assumed all men with an overhanging belly had a silly sausage beneath? Immediately, he began to lay plans for a defence. He needed to lose six inches from his tummy before he took Priscilla swimming. The bird had understood this, because it had eaten all of the biscuits, leaving him without breakfast.

After dressing, he tried to do a few exercises in the field, but jumping up and down left him breathless. His body had adapted to the lifestyle of an office worker, without any regard to romantic situations which might arise in the future. But now he was living in wild Wales, where healthy men roamed the mountains... or flew aeroplanes. This situation required urgent action, even if it meant not eating for a day and finding a gymnasium with a lot of weights to lift. Then he remembered Janet saying something about a farmer, who needed help every year when bringing in the harvest. In this new country, he could easily sort out his tummy crisis – especially since he no longer had a car, so would have to walk everywhere.

Thinking of his car made him remember all the cash from its sale, which was still stashed in his wallet. He needed to deposit some of this wealth safely in the bank, which, fortuitously, would involve walking to the village – no, waddling, like a duck. That was how men with fat bellies moved along footpaths. After climbing the gate, he waddled to the cottage and then into its kitchen. The embers were dying in the grate, and the table was clear of anything relating to breakfast. Now there was just a simple note:

We are all away doing girly stuff. Make yourself at home. Help yourself to food. See you whenever.
Love,
    Three adoring females... and Jack (a bird with feathers).

Well, he reasoned, they seemed happy, so he supposed it was okay. Not the bit about the bird (clearly they had all been giggling about his nightmarish awakening); nor the bit about the food (which was obviously incompatible with his project to have a flat tummy). In fact, now he thought about it, he realised it was a completely rubbish note. 'Doing stuff' was probably just a euphemism for what they expected to happen with the aviator.

Filled with the gloom of a premature middle age, Richard left the cottage and went to stand on the cliff in the hope of seeing the dolphins Tara had mentioned. He considered this a great improvement on what had happened before, on the bridge, when he had wanted his life to end. Now he had no interest in throwing himself off the edge to an early death. His new desires were to lose weight and, when the time was right, confess his love for Tara. As he walked along the clifftop, his naturally optimistic outlook returned. After visiting the bank, he could double back to reach the ford and see if Tara's car was still there. Then he closed his eyes. *I am a horrible man*, he thought. *Now I'm checking up on her, at least to the extent of seeing if her car's still there, or if she's gone to see the aviator.* He decided against looking for the car – what Tara did in her own time was not his business. His task was to win her by fair means. Then he remembered he was walking along a clifftop, so opened his eyes – he had no intention of dying today.

Once in the village, he headed for the bank where Janet had her account. She might like a donation for the living expenses of her three guests. After all his years working in the hotel, his finances were sufficiently healthy to keep him alive until he found a job – whatever it might be. In the bank, he pulled out the great wad of cash and, after returning a pound note to his pocket, asked the woman behind the counter, if he could deposit the rest in Janet's account. She replied 'Janet' was too vague a name.

"Sustain Media?" he offered.

"Oh," said the cashier, "*that* Janet – the bird lady. Yes, everyone around these parts knows her. It's because she often walks around with a jackdaw on her shoulder, and, of course, she sometimes walks along the beach with a pet goat. All the children want to feed him their sandwiches. He is just so adorable!"

Not if he tries to eat your sleeping bag at some unearthly hour in the morning, thought Richard. *And why would a bank cashier talk about goats? Back in England, they only ever discuss money. Yet here, it seems, they pass the time of day gossiping with people they've only just met.* Probably without making much sense to the cashier, he said, "Wales is a different country; they do things differently in England."

"*Wn i ddim*," she replied. "*Erioed wedi bod.*"

Whatever she had said, combined with her friendly smile, caused his heart rate to increase to a dangerous level. What was happening to him? All of his romantic sensibilities were descending into complete chaos.

Meanwhile, the cashier realised just how much cash he had given her, and raised her eyebrows. "This Janet a friend of yours?" she asked.

Richard liked this idea, because the tone of the cashier's voice suggested she thought of him as a real man. Though, of course, sitting behind the counter, she could not see his belly, so would think… He realised a single man living with three ladies, was destined to become the centre of village gossip, so strengthened his resolve to deal with his pot belly. Then he could go swimming in the sea without children on the beach laughing at him, thinking he was going to have a baby.

After leaving the bank, he walked to the nearest cafe and ordered a coffee. No food, because he was on a diet. *So, now what?* Then a large map on the wall caught his attention. It was the sort made to look three-dimensional. In the middle was a big pointy thing with the words 'Yr Wyddfa' to its side. Some years before, while standing on a local beach, Janet had mentioned a mountain on the horizon, which was called something similar. She had then told him never to refer to it by its English name of 'Snowdon', unless he wanted the locals to hate him. Now he went to take a closer look at the map. Yr Wyddfa did not look that far away. Maybe the distance would be equal to one inch off his tummy. Somewhat nervously, he approached a lady serving at the counter to ask how hard the mountain was to climb. He totally messed up the Welsh name, but it only made her laugh. She then gave him a lesson in how to pronounce it correctly. She added, more or less as an afterthought, that the greatest challenge in climbing it by the well-known English tourist route, was boredom. Apparently, that route was just one rather long footpath. Locals, she explained, would use… and here she paused.

"Are you fit?" she asked.

He sucked in his tummy. "Yes," he said.

"Not excessively scared of heights? Like, say, when walking across a narrow footbridge without handrails?"

Richard did not think such things existed but, to

question her about details, would make him sound middle-aged. "I like walking across the Menai Bridge?" he said. He knew this was not the same as walking across it with the handrails removed, but they were only there for psychological comfort; he had never needed to grab hold of them to save his life.

"Okay," continued the lady, "then this is where you need to go." She scribbled down a few instructions on her order pad, then tore out the sheet and handed it over. "Do that and you'll be fine."

While finishing his coffee, Richard studied the lady's notes, glancing up to the map occasionally to confirm things. Above all, he needed to lose that first inch from his tummy. He therefore ignored her instruction to catch three local buses, choosing instead to walk their route. So, after leaving the cafe, he took manly strides along a coast road until it became surrounded by flat farmland. Three hours later, he reckoned he had lost half an inch off his tummy. Also, if he had been walking at three miles per hour, he had covered nine miles; a bit further than he had expected for his first mountaineering expedition, but his legs only ached a little. Then the lane entered a gorge, with dramatic cliffs rising beyond a raging river to his right. He decided its waterfalls and rapids made it the sort of thing you might find in the Himalayas. However, more important to his current situation, it meant his lane now went uphill, very steeply. An hour later, he completed the first part of his challenge: reaching the mountain village of Beddgelert. *Let the adventure begin!* At least, that was what his mind thought – his legs had other ideas. He bought a postcard, then sat in another cafe. On the back of the card he wrote,

'Have gone to climb Yr Wyddfa. I might be some time.' By dropping this message, addressed to 'Janet and friends', in a nearby postbox, he was acknowledging two things. Firstly, he would not be back that night; and secondly, his mountaineering expedition was going to be a true epic.

The road from Beddgelert was steep and apparently never-ending. The idea that anything could ascend it faster than thirty miles per hour seemed impossible – a theory disproved when a bus whizzed by and disappeared around the next bend. Much, much later, Richard staggered into the mountain settlement of Rhyd Ddu, knowing that he had now lost the inch from his tummy. According to the lady in the cafe, Rhyd Ddu was the highest he could go by road – in other words, the place where a bus could have dropped him a few hours earlier. He could even feel the cold metal of the bus stop, to which he now clung. He slithered down it to sit on the pavement, with his back resting against the post. So, this was what it was like to be without a car! As for a hotel, in this high mountain settlement there did not appear to be one; or, if there was, he lacked the strength to stagger around searching for it. Anyway, having deposited most of his money in Janet's account, he was essentially destitute. Slowly he walked a few hundred yards to a forest, then lay on the ground, preparing to sleep before tackling whatever challenge awaited him tomorrow. However, he soon discovered lying on a forest floor with rotting leaves for a mattress, had nothing to do with going to sleep. After turning repeatedly from one side to the other, he sat up to reduce his contact with the ground. But this strained his spine, so he crawled to the nearest tree to use its trunk as a backrest. Being a mountaineer, he realised, was a lot more uncomfortable than he had imagined while sitting in a cafe and studying a three-dimensional map.

Graham was sleeping on an airbed in his kitchen, his bedroom being occupied by Tara and Priscilla. Janet was sleeping on the living-room sofa. He found it all very confusing. His mother had spent the evening buzzing with excitement. His father had been more embarrassing, telling the unexpected arrivals that his son had never had a girlfriend and now, rather like buses, three had turned up at the same time. Of course, Graham had blushed, which rather confirmed his father's statement. But despite his innocence, Graham had instantly fallen in love – with Priscilla. In her sensible overalls, just right for flying about in an open aeroplane, she portrayed the perfect image of sensibility. So, for her, he would make his Tiger Moth dance gracefully, swooping down to the ocean and maybe looping the loop – these manoeuvres being unsuited to ladies of a more frivolous nature.

The following day went according to his plan, with him making three trips in his aeroplane with each of the ladies in turn. The last to take to the skies was Priscilla, who returned looking slightly dazed. Tara now acted as the ground crew, moving the descent steps into place. After walking down them, Priscilla fell limply against Graham, as if in a faint.

"What a tart," Janet murmured light-heartedly.

"No," said Tara, "I think she really has passed out."

They watched Graham fold his arms around her, before changing his mind and swooping one under her legs to carry her to the canteen.

"Got it," said Tara.

"What?" said Janet. "A case of insane jealousy, as Priscilla captures your boyfriend?"

"No – why I've been deliberating over what to do about Graham for the past two months. There was no magic between us. I think Graham just wanted a pretend girlfriend to make his mother happy. With Priscilla, he wanted to carry her away. They are certain to be snogging before the month's out."

"So that leaves you with Richard," said Janet.

"I have no intention of hearing him call out your name in moments of passion," protested Tara. "Which, of course, I will never do with him. But I have another secret which I find most embarrassing. I have a fancy to see what a wooden railway bridge looks like. Thomas is rather cute in his own sort of way."

"That statement makes no sense," said Janet, "but this is what normally happens when you are in love. I think you are using Thomas, or wooden railway bridges, to avoid facing the truth: that you are really in love with Richard."

"No," said Tara, "he belongs to you."

"That is not the same as saying you aren't in love with him," replied Janet.

And Tara understood that, deep down, she could not deny Janet's claim with absolute certainty.

CHAPTER TWENTY-EIGHT

Richard's sleepless night in the forest gave him plenty of time to reflect on various memories from his childhood that had, over the years, become buried deep within his subconscious. In particular, he remembered his first-ever birthday party, aged six. Only the chauffeur, his nanny, and his father were there. His mother had no interest in such frivolous things, but she had left him a proper birthday card. This confused things though, because she had got his age wrong.

"I am six," he had grumbled, "not five."

Eventually they all agreed on six. This made Richard feel important, especially when his father mumbled something about him being really grown-up now. Then, immediately after the party, his father placed him on the huge dining table. Richard dangled his legs in space, while Reginald paced the room, acting most peculiarly. Eventually, he gave a serious cough, before telling his son the facts of life – or, at least, the ones relating to buses.

"Buses," he said, "are very nasty things, used only by

working-class vagrants. They, you understand, evolved to live in swamps, so are well adapted to survive harsh conditions. But for our class, buses are metal coffins filled with suffocating cigarette smoke. If you ever accidentally board such a thing, you will hardly be able to see where you are going – so will have no warning when a fat old woman sits on the same seat, squashes you against the side, and then drops a baby with a dirty nappy on your lap, so she can better pick her nose to make a bogey sandwich."

This grown-up talk gradually condensed all of Richard's previously diverse childhood terrors into a single recurring nightmare – from which he often awoke, fearing suffocation, claustrophobia, and faeces running down his legs. By the age of ten, he fully understood some aspect of this bus phobia was going to kill him, as surely as if he stepped in front of one.

Richard's near-religious belief regarding buses had no relevance to his pre-teen years, because he only left the estate in a car driven by the chauffeur or the nanny. However, he did develop a curious habit of always peeping inside any sandwich he was expected to eat, just in case a working-class vagrant had managed to sneak into their kitchen, so as to feed him bogeys. When he was twelve, to highlight the family's social status, the chauffeur delivered him to his public school in the Rolls. Here, he had no reason to challenge the bus belief, because his world worked perfectly well without them.

When Richard reached sixteen, his father had paid for him to have driving lessons around the estate. On his seventeenth birthday, he had passed his test and been presented with a car. He had never needed to walk anywhere since – until now. Yet this, he realised, was why he had not caught a bus to get to his mountaineering base camp. His father had convinced him that boarding such things was akin to Devil worship. And look where that belief had taken him: to spend the night in a forest as a vagrant. Without a car, he was as useless as a baby without a pram. But at least it meant he would soon have a flat tummy.

Wide awake, he began to think about Priscilla – in particular, the way she had laid her arm over his shoulder. It was a level of intimacy he had never before experienced with a woman. He shivered, though whether because of that thought or because of the cold, he could not say. Then his domineering father returned to his mind. It was he who believed 'innocence' could only be lost to a member of the aristocracy, presumably in case a baby accidentally came along – like himself, unwanted and unloved. Next he thought about the lady in the bank, whose friendly smile now made him wonder what a kiss might feel like. Finally the truth dawned upon him. He was having a full-blown, romantically inclined, nervous breakdown.

As the lonely hours passed, he came to understand the chaos in his brain was due to a basic evolutionary force; namely, the need for a physical bond with a woman. Over the years, Janet's wide-ranging comfort zone had become unbearable, so they had drifted apart. Then Tara had come along – a friend, at least until he wanted her for what Janet could never provide. But now he understood his feelings for Tara were not love. They were more a cry for help, in the manner of a drowning man seeking rescue from an emotionally devoid ocean. He hated himself for that, because suddenly Janet returned to completely dominate his thoughts. For the first time, he truly understood what she had endured to get him out of jail: sleeping under a bush while leading a campaign to free him. Compared to this, his unrequited love was a trivial thing. Anyway, his romantic dreams would have to wait until he had dealt with his pot belly, which, given his bus phobia, had probably already lost three inches around its circumference.

By the time dawn filtered into the forest, he was trying to recall Janet's gentle voice, telling him about her nights sleeping under a hedge; something about the morning drizzle and the beauty of first light glimmering through the trees. But now, all he felt was cold, hungry, and exhausted. Slowly he forced himself to stand – or would have done, had his head not hit a low branch. Dropping to his knees, he crawled to a clearing, then stood more cautiously to lean against another tree. When there was enough light to see his wristwatch, he discovered he had forgotten to wind it. But that did not matter – he had twelve hours of daylight to climb the mountain and return to the road, from where he could walk home in the dark. Whatever the rest of the world might be doing, governed by their fancy clocks, no longer had any relevance to him. Having thought about clocks and the nature of time, he then did what any normal man would do: he lifted his shirt to feel his tummy, and decided it was a lot flatter than it had been twenty-four hours before.

When the lady in the cafe had told him about the track from the road, he had imagined it to be Himalayan in nature. Okay, instead of llamas there would be sheep – no goats, because only they could cope with narrow mountain ledges. However, as he began to ascend the path, he discovered it to be a cart track with a steady incline of no great difficulty. Oh, this was going to be so easy!

After walking the track for a mile or so, he was quite warm, which he thought must be due to his aching leg muscles pumping out energy. Then, looking ahead, he realised the cloud had lifted slightly, allowing him to see a col in the ridge which dominated the skyline. To either side of this dip, the ridge rose to disappear into the ceiling of cloud, keeping the summits a mystery. But that did not matter, because the cafe lady had told him that on reaching the col, he should turn left and just follow the ridge. "Keep tending uphill," she had said, "until you can't go any higher." That, apparently, was the summit of Yr Wyddfa. In Richard's mind it had now become a romantic place: where few men had gone before, and, when standing on the highest point, he would think about Janet and maybe scratch her name into the rock using a sharp-edged stone.

When the col was only a little way ahead, he entered an abandoned mining settlement. There were many stone buildings, now without roofs. Looking into one of the quarry cuttings, he noticed it ended in some sort of tunnel. Clearly this was a mine entrance. This high in the mountains, the men who created such a place must have acquired the strength of oxen – just like himself, once his epic deed was done.

As he began his climb of the ridge, the cloud seemed to keep rising and, though not yet clear of the summit, it allowed him to see the ridge for maybe five hundred feet ahead. He doubted that anyone accustomed to city pavements would consider this a footpath and, in a few places, he had to use his hands to get up slabs of rock. But it was okay and safe… at least, that was what he believed until he was halfway across a narrow section of path with a horrendous drop to his right. It needed a handrail! But, so long as he kept both feet planted firmly on the rough scree, and if he clung to a lump of rock to his left, there was no reason to begin a tumble towards death. The only downside of this strategy, was it prevented him from going anywhere. Then he remembered how once, in the depths of depression, he had wanted to die by jumping off a bridge. But now that his Janet was both geographically and emotionally closer, his life had become a precious gift.

Eventually he found the courage to slide his feet forwards a few inches at a time. Then he pulled himself back to the main ridge and sat on the nearest boulder. Here, he realised that, as he had faced death, something profound had happened in his mind. He had thought of the phrase, *his* Janet. Once, he had always thought of her this way, but not recently; because the truth was, Janet did not belong to him… and never had. Then he realised a further truth: Janet belonged to the horrible men who had done terrible things to her body. They still controlled her mind. He thought back to the time when he had taken her to Holland for 'the procedure'. Until then, she had obviously thought her body was diseased. But after they had left the clinic, things had begun to change. Over the years the physical issues had faded, to be replaced by psychological ones. His declaration of love had terrified her; so, before talking about such things again, he must somehow rid her of the bad memories, allowing her to become an independent person once more. Only then would he speak of love. In the meantime, she needed somebody to help out with her literary agency. That would be him.

After all of this sitting down to think, he turned his head to look back along his route. The cloud had lifted from the mountain, which rose from the other side of the col, and he was pleased to discover its dramatic pointy top was now below his present height. Indeed, the entire world seemed far below, and he strongly suspected the summit of Yr Wyddfa was only... Looking in the opposite direction, he let out a gasp. The cloud had finally rolled from the top to reveal the summit was far, far above! His optimism vanished. Once more, he was in a battle to conquer and survive.

Sometime later, he staggered up a rough track, knowing there were only a few painful steps to go. He was now officially a successful mountaineer with a flat tummy. Then he saw a railway station and, beside it, a cafe. There were perhaps a hundred people wandering about, looking at the view or having their photographs taken. He had just endured two days of epic adventure – to reach a railway station and maybe have a cup of coffee in a cafe... except he had spent all his money. Presumably all these other people had come by train, or perhaps walked up "the English footpath", as the cafe lady had called it. Turning his back on the scene, he looked away from the summit to see the ocean shimmering in the sunshine. He then cast his gaze along the coast to where he estimated Janet might be sitting in 'their' cottage. It did not look that far away.

"Oh! The horrible person!" he exclaimed out loud. The cafe lady had been playing a practical joke. She had sent him on a great, circular route which only a fool would follow. Then he closed his eyes to remember her actual words. She had merely told him how to get to 'base camp' using buses. Walking by taking advantage of narrower lanes, where buses might not go, would have halved the distance.

Ignoring the cafe, he walked up to the trig-point marker, which represented the highest place in Wales. Here he took a sharp stone and scratched the name 'Janet' onto a boulder. One day he would bring her to this place, by his route… only bravely using the bus to reach base camp. Then, throughout their ascent, he could protect her and warn her not to trip over a shoelace. He looked down at his own shoes, which had started to come apart at the seams.

An hour later, he had learned another two lessons of basic mountaineering. Firstly, when climbing up, make sure you leave enough muscle power to get back down. Secondly, at high altitude, the weather can change very quickly. Now a wind of impossible strength was trying to blow him off the ridge, while a sudden downpour made him soggy, and the rock slippery. Added to this, after ten paces his leg muscles were screaming with pain, forcing him to sit down. His back hurt and his knees seemed to creak, causing him to curl up like a wounded animal. Stopping for more than a few seconds, made his whole body shiver. Finally, he understood that, on this lonely ridge, he was in serious trouble. Whereas in most sports you could just stop, if the pain got too great, here he had to keep on going and somehow get himself off the exposed ground. If he failed, a night spent out in the open, would bring his life to an end.

As he lay between two boulders, his entire brain focused on Janet. If she were here, she would know what to do. He visualised her. *Oh,* she was saying, referring to the lashing rain, *it's just the wrong side of damp – stop making such a fuss.* With regard to his starvation, she calmly told him that no food was available, so it was pointless to pay any attention to the pains in his tummy – his flat tummy! Thinking of Janet's strength made him realise that he was a totally pathetic man, who did not deserve her love.

Gradually, he came to understand that a human's ability to 'see' an imaginary presence, was a fundamental survival technique, which had developed to give people an evolutionary advantage. In the beginning, he reasoned, those with the ability to visualise a God had additional purpose when going into battle. Those who did not believe would drop their weapons and run, and thereby lose control of the best land. More recently, Janet had passed her O levels because she could see her mother watching her from above. And now Janet herself was watching him undertake his epic battle. This magical insight brought him renewed strength. He could get off this ridge and survive! He pushed himself up and, ignoring the pain in his back and legs, staggered onwards… as Janet would expect.

By the time the col appeared through the storm, he was crawling and his dizzy spells suggested he might faint. He had no strength to plod down the cart track to where he might knock on a cottage door and plead for help. To his horror, he remembered Priscilla lying on a verge, approaching death. "Let it rot in the gutter," he had said to Tara, who, as a trained auxiliary nurse, had nonetheless come to Priscilla's aid. But now he knew how that experience had been for Priscilla and, for the first time in his life, truly understood the meaning of empathy.

"I will not die today," he said to himself. "I will make certain that Priscilla completes her A levels and becomes strong like Janet." How he was going to survive was a more complicated matter. He had not seen anyone since beginning this remote descent. To live, he would need to use all of his wits, as Janet had once done. Then he remembered the tunnel a little to his right, and staggered towards it. There was a foot of water in the entrance. He waded through it, his only desire being to get out of the wind. Then the floor rose to a patch of dry gravel. There was just enough light coming from the entrance to see what he was doing. He sat with his back against the wall. But he was alive and, though in a desperate situation, felt certain he would survive.

Sometime during the night, he realised something drastic like this had needed to happen. It had given him a purpose, a flat tummy, and complete empathy with Priscilla and Janet. But what about the geographical direction he needed to take to get home? All he had was a few notes from the lady in the cafe. He did not have the confidence to devise a more direct route. Tomorrow he would begin the long plod home, to see Janet… and she would see him as both a mountaineer brave and strong, as well as hopefully, a new man.

The night following Richard's epic tunnel survival, the three women in his life were gathered around the cottage table, gazing at a chessboard. Priscilla, with her back to the fire, looked mildly puzzled. Janet, sitting by her side in the role of an instructor, touched Priscilla's king.

"Move that to E6," she said quietly. "It will stop her getting you into a dangerous check."

"Like that?" asked Priscilla, as she performed the move.

Janet nodded and, when the move came back to Priscilla, advised moving the king to F5, so as to tuck it safely away.

One mile from the warm cottage where the game of chess was taking place, Richard staggered through the night; his wasted muscles sometimes causing him to stumble as his legs refused to move. But worse than this, was the agonising pain in his lower back. Then, as his mind floated in and out of consciousness, the Bird of Death began to circle above him. Its *caw-caw* told him his end was near. Sometimes it vanished into the crow-black night, but Richard knew it was still there, watching him from the branches. And sometimes, due to the extra perceptions that exist in nightmares, he knew the evil bird was close behind, its sharp beak ready to peck a hole in his skull.

Only one thought kept him going: that of seeing Janet again. He tried to focus on the image of home; the cottage where she lived. Somehow this gave him the superhuman strength to continue, a few paces at a time, before the need for rest again made him lean against anything that would support him. Without really knowing what he was doing, he left the tarmac road to stumble onto the isolated dirt track which led to the cottage. Beneath the overhanging branches, he became disorientated in the near-total darkness. But the Bird of Death knew he was there, because this was its territory, beyond the world of the living. Then, in his confused mind, Richard came to believe the trees were attacking him, pushing him backwards, or lashing him with their lower branches. As he staggered blindly around what he now believed to be a primeval jungle, his survival instinct forced him to keep heading downhill towards the ford. Eventually he felt water rising up his legs; then a sharp pain in his foot sent him crashing headfirst into the water. After pushing himself up onto all fours, his head broke the surface. Now the water was supporting most of his weight, he slithered like a lizard to the far bank. As gravity reasserted its grasp, he realised the pain in his foot was due to one of his shoes finally losing its sole, the upper leather having been reduced to shreds. On the road, he had imagined leaving a trail of blood, but now, on the stony track, it left him disabled in agony. Half a mile further! How short that distance had once seemed; yet now it would surely be the death of him.

"I am finished," he cried, as he fell flat on his face.

The only reply came from the Bird of Death, who fluttered away crying, "*Caw-caw*", presumably knowing that its work here was done.

In the cottage, the flickering candlelight danced across the long table. Tara gazed at the chessboard. "You horrible people," she said. "Guess I'll just have to advance my pawns to win; you can't stop that."

Janet waited for the advance. "Priscilla doesn't need to stop your pawns," she said. "She has checkmate in four moves, and now there's nothing you can do about it."

"Rubbish," said Tara.

"How?" asked Priscilla.

"That is for you to work out," said Janet. "I'll leave the board set up so you can solve the puzzle tomorrow. In fact, Tara, come to this side of the board. You're looking for mate in four – and don't worry about the pawns; they are going to take at least six moves to get through Priscilla's defence."

Suddenly there came a rapid tapping at the window, followed by a furious *caw-caw*.

"Strange," said Janet, "it's Jack, but he should be in bed by now."

"Not in my bed, I hope," said Priscilla.

Janet looked serious. "That's Jack's way of having a panic attack," she said. "There's something wrong outside."

A minute later, the three women left the cottage, their torches illuminating the bird's chaotic flight. Then, after following him for a few hundred yards, they came across a body slumped on the path. At once Tara found herself transported back to her time at the hospital. She knelt down to feel the man's pulse at his wrist, then ran her torch beam down his body to see how he might have fallen. It looked like a simple stumble; a diagnosis backed up by the shreds of a sock, stained red, barely covering his left foot. Janet and Priscilla stood in a state of shock, trying to convince themselves it was not Richard; merely some drunk who had stolen his clothes. But the faint torch beam could only preserve such an unrealistic hope for a few seconds. Janet, overpowered by the basic human instinct to preserve life, dropped to her knees.

"Richard!" she screamed; then she lay across his body, as if some of her life force would transfer to him, making them a single living entity.

Tara stood up. "He's got a pulse," she said, "but he's very cold. We have to get him inside immediately. I'll carry his shoulders; Priscilla, you support his waist; Janet, keep his legs off the ground."

They then set about carrying Richard to the cottage,

where Tara backed through the door. Here, she promoted herself to the role of matron, telling the others to carry the patient to the chair in the spare bedroom. With this task completed, she turned to Priscilla. "Keep him upright," she said firmly. Then she spoke to Janet. "Go to your room," she instructed. "I want all of your blankets on this bed, then prepare a hot-water bottle. Priscilla, start undressing him; his clothes are soaked through, and we can't have him getting the bed wet. I'm going to grab a towel."

"I can't undress him!" gasped Priscilla. "It's Mr Edwards."

"Shut up," retorted Tara. "He is no longer a man, but a patient."

By the time Tara returned with the towel, the patient was naked above the waist. She put the back of her hand against his chest. "When I was an auxiliary nurse," she said, "I dealt with a couple of tramps who were brought in like this. You can see from his abdomen that he's half-starved and probably severely dehydrated. However, he's only been missing for three days, doing whatever he was doing, so the lack of food may have made him faint, but it won't be fatal." She dried his upper body with the towel, then removed the rest of his clothes, dried him further, then covered him with blankets. "Priscilla," she said, "get in with him and hold him close. Let him take some of your body heat."

"What?!"

"Just do it."

When Janet returned with the hot-water bottle, she saw Priscilla in bed with Richard, while Tara was taking his pulse and looking at the bedside clock. Priscilla was whispering in Richard's ear.

"Please don't die," she said. "If you live, I promise to take my A levels."

At that moment, something changed for Janet. She pushed Tara out of the way and lay on the blankets, her face buried in Richard's hair. "If you live," she sobbed, "I promise we will be together forever and ever."

Tara knew how well the tramps she had once cared for had responded to warmth, and that was without coming around to find a nurse in their arms. However, she still had no idea why Richard's exhaustion had caused him to collapse. She reached under the bedclothes to feel his lower back.

Janet tried to push her away. "No," she shouted hysterically, "he's mine."

But Tara did not move her arm.

Priscilla stared in horror. "You can't feel Mr Edwards' bottom," she said.

"You overestimate the length of my arm," said Tara. "I am merely feeling his lower back."

"It's still near a very rude place," protested Priscilla.

But Tara did not retreat, so Priscilla lay on top of the patient to protect him. A few seconds later, Janet pushed her away with such force that Priscilla landed on the floor.

"It's okay," said Tara, "he has intense muscle spasms in his lower back. He's got sciatica, probably induced by stress and exhaustion. He needs that hot-water bottle on his lower back, and the maximum dose of aspirin for a few days. He should be able to walk again by the end of the week. But the recovery of his sciatic nerve will be very painful, and might leave him partially disabled for a short while. So, Janet, you look after him. Priscilla, follow me."

Priscilla, still startled at finding herself on the floor, slowly stood, then followed Tara to the hallway.

Tara quietly closed the bedroom door. "All Richard needed to do," she whispered, "was lose his godlike status and become a mortal man in need of help. Those two will be fine now."

On reaching the kitchen, Priscilla's attention turned to Jack standing on a worktop, devouring a plate of biscuits. "Are those nice?" she asked. Then she threw a hand over her mouth. She was talking to a bird! What was happening to her? She had only been in Wales for three days, yet her whole way of thinking had changed. Before, she had considered all birds to be stupid, but now she believed they understood what she was saying! Before she could retreat from the insanity, she found herself telling Jack that she wanted to become a nurse like Tara, and help people get better.

Tara was also thinking differently. She smiled, knowing exactly what she must do. Tomorrow, she would find the nearest hospital and present her auxiliary nursing certificate, and so return to her training scheme.

An unexpected development in Tara's plan came the following day, when she set off for the hospital with Priscilla in the passenger seat.

"My Graham," babbled Priscilla excitedly, "would like it, if I became a nurse like you. And first aid might be useful, if his plane crashes. And my Graham told me that he really likes my sensible clothes; and at the airfield I told him how you had confiscated my bank book, so I had no money to buy make-up. He said it would be a crime to paint over such natural beauty, and if I did, he would get me put in jail. Though I'm not certain how that works—"

"Playing *Monopoly*?" suggested Tara. "Maybe by the fireside, together with his happy parents, because their son has found you?"

But Priscilla was not listening. "My Graham," she continued, "would like…"

Tara let her ramble on, while her own mind returned to the problem of double-declutching in order to slow down for the next bend. That was completed without a single crunching noise. Finally, she had done it! As for leaving Janet at home to nurse the now-conscious Richard, that had been a definite success. Tara's new problem would be trying to convince Priscilla that any job interview at the hospital, should not begin with the phrase 'my Graham thinks'. She decided the best thing to do for now was to take Priscilla on a circular walk around the Menai bridges. This would bring her down to earth with a muddy bump; and then, when sitting in the Menai cafe, her first lesson in how to become an auxiliary nurse, could begin. Knowing that her mission to help others had been a complete success, Tara felt herself tingling in a world of happy thoughts. Then she shivered in apprehension. She would be sharing a gypsy caravan with Priscilla, a born-again teenager in love for the very first time.

'Success' seems a strange word to describe the situation in which I now find myself, she thought.

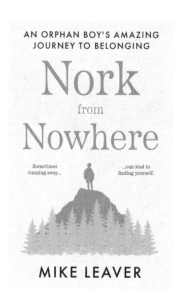

AN ORPHAN BOY'S AMAZING
JOURNEY TO BELONGING

Nork
from
Nowhere

Sometimes
running away...

...can lead to
finding yourself.

MIKE LEAVER

NORK FROM NOWHERE

Upper-class teen Sara flees her parents' middle-England mansion after a disastrous party. She happens upon Nork, a mysterious, young, orphan boy seemingly from nowhere.

Together they go on the run. Evading the authorities and becoming ever more inter-dependent during their long journey, they finally end up in the Scottish wilderness.

They find themselves in a small loch-side town, but will they become the victims of the ruthless, hotel owner McTavish – or can they discover a new life and purpose there?

This is a coming-of-age story with comedy, romance and sexual references, that is both amusing and thought-provoking.

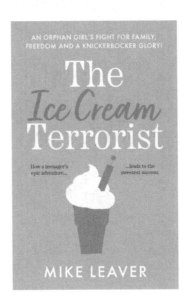

AN ORPHAN GIRL'S FIGHT FOR FAMILY, FREEDOM AND A KNICKERBOCKER GLORY!

The Ice Cream Terrorist

How a teenager's epic adventure... ...leads to the sweetest success.

MIKE LEAVER

THE ICE CREAM TERRORIST

Two forcibly segregated, separate-sex and rurally isolated schools are inhabited by malevolent masters, petrified pupils, more kindly matrons and a handful of true heroes – including The Ice Cream Terrorist.

This titanic tale of redemption shows how pupils and staff – blighted by dysfunctional, post-war, orphanage schools in Britain – escape and reform the brutal system.

Join their journey through school suffering, then on a road trip to a coastal idyll full of kindness, safety and real-life skills, and eventually different lives. Free from oppression with more enlightened care, they create progressive futures.

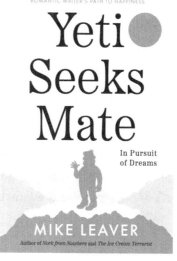

Yeti
Seeks
Mate

In Pursuit
of Dreams

MIKE LEAVER

Author of *Nork from Nowhere* and *The Ice Cream Terrorist*

YETI SEEKS MATE

Yeti (male 28) seeks mate. Can be seen Christmas/Easter roaming Ben Nevis, Snowdon some weekends in between. Migrates to Alps around June. Very friendly, generally harmless, except on ski-slopes. Very safe experienced motorcyclist Britain and abroad – would get sidecar, if nagged. Please write…

(Personal ad published in a national mountaineering magazine.)

From an asthmatic childhood spent on post-war Birmingham bomb sites, Mike Leaver escaped from cruel state boarding schools to careers as a lab technician, accountant, pleasure-boat captain and local builder.

Mike has also been:

A homeless hermit inhabiting a derelict boat surrounded by drug addicts;

An adventurer/mountaineer in the UK, Scandinavia, and North Africa; and

A semi-retired handyman writing books while enjoying an ideal life off-grid in a converted lorry in a pretty coastal town.

Embark on an extraordinary journey of an eccentric pursuing dreams of love, writing and the path to happiness in a memoir that's as charming as it is quirky.

Mike Leaver, 70, lives off-grid in a converted, static truck on a business park in Snowdonia. Like Alan Bennett's the Lady in the Van, Mike has become a well-known eccentric around his adopted home of Gwynedd. He is the author of three saga novels – *Nork from Nowhere*, *The Ice Cream Terrorist*, and *Newspaper Curtains*, and his *Yeti Seeks Mate* autobiography. As well as writing 'Yeti' and his first three modern fictions – almost 500,000 words largely on a battery-powered laptop by candlelight in his lorry – he has just finished penning the second part of his intriguing life story.

Mike is a single, vegetarian, animal-loving pensioner, who writes and plays chess for pleasure. At secondary school, a mischievous gang of girls conscripted Mike – the only boy in their class – to be their nominal male, and renamed him 'Freaky Fred'. So aspects of his own personal experience feature – and are sometimes exaggerated – in the travails and adventures of his fictional characters! His books explore the themes of: power, perversion, and coercion versus loyalty, friendliness and collaboration; adult, teenage and child relationships; destitute homelessness, unrequited love and wider social mores.